O CONTRABANDISTA

THE SMUGGLER

The first book of
three Wye Valley trysts

Ada Ronald Thomas

O CONTRABANDISTA

THE SMUGGLER

Vanguard Press

A CIP catalogue record for this title is
available from the British Library.

ISBN 978 1 784654 20 7

Vanguard Press is an imprint of
Pegasus Elliot MacKenzie Publishers Ltd.
www.pegasuspublishers.com

First Published in 2019

Vanguard Press
Sheraton House Castle Park
Cambridge England

Printed & Bound in Great Britain

Acknowledgments

Thank you to Andie at www.thelittlepixelhouse.co.uk, for the cover design.

And to Jenna Evans, editor at Pegasus Publishers, for her skill and dedication in the production of this book.

Dedication

For Seren and Lloyd

Author's Note

This book is set in times when Chepstow when was a port, and ships were navigating the River Wye as far north as Redbrook. Whilst aiming for historical accuracy, I have used an author's license and permitted myself an occasional lapse where I deemed a little latitude desirable for the purpose of creative interest and intent. By the same token, I would beg your indulgence over my descriptions of some of the places of interest, too.

As for the characters whose stories lie in the telling of this tale – well, they are entirely imaginary, and have no descendants.

CHEPSTOW SMUGGLING SONG

Keep your eyes peeled, boys, set your ears to the ground,
There's run coming off before light.
Don't tell no tales when you're supping your ales
If you drink wi' the petticoats tonight.

Did the parson shift those brandy casks?
Did the clerk steal the letters clear away?
Was the hide made well, so no man can tell
Where there's more coming in by the day?

Did the Factors weigh every bale of wool
From that Flanders ship lade full?
Was the gravity right on the barrels that might
Now have brandy as was hidden in the hull?

For good, brave men are few, are few
Who fear no chain or fetter,
And Monmouth men are true, are true,
But Chepstow men are better.

Will the clouds go thin, letting starlight in
On the lugger that's been hugging our shore?
Will a rattle or a neigh give our presence away
To the Revenue men four-score?

Will the Squire's hounds be let loose tonight?
Or the Sheriff's men waylay us?
Must we run men through with swords pin-new
'Cause a wagging tongue's betrayed us?

For good, brave men are few, are few,
Who will outlive chain and fetter;
'Tis hard to find ten stalwart men,
When dead men fare much better.

Yet each man who is sound, and will stand his ground
Adds the promise of a salvation
From the Judge giving breath to the Rope and Death,
Or Life on a foreign plantation.

We brave th' old Bristol transport hulks,
Have foresworn all bribes and offers;
Though we're roundly cursed we have robbed no purse
Save those in King Charles' coffers.

So, here's a health to outrunning the Revenue men,
And the mort gained on each barrel.
Set a cask aside, let's drink with pride
And make merry with a Christmas Carol!

Chapter One

The hour was early. It was a clear, cold December morning, and in two days more it would be Christmas.

On a muddy road beside the River Wye, with thin shards of ice crushing pleasantly beneath his horse's hooves, a youth in his early teens rode slowly along on horseback, softly singing what bits he could remember of the latest rudely humorous ballad doing the rounds in his favourite ale-houses. He was well wrapped for his journey, but still his exposed fingers stung with cold, his nose was red and running, and his every out-breath between song snippets combined with Timothy's slightly more laboured snorts to create milky vapours in the freezing air.

Tom had arranged to meet his best friend in Brockweir, a small settlement just north of Tintern village, and he was a bit behind his time, but he simply couldn't rush old Timothy. Dawn had broken some time before and the sky was beginning to lighten, but it was still dark along the valley bottom where he was riding. He kept looking across at the Gloucestershire hills flanking the far side of the river on his left, watching for the earliest signs of sunrise. It would be most welcome, once it breasted that old snow-topped ridge, it might start to warm him up a bit. It did put heart into a man, Tom thought, to have a dash of sunshine in winter.

Tom knew his friend must already be hanging about waiting for him, getting colder by the minute. Not that Aaron would complain, he never did; but Tom didn't particularly want to test his friend's patience. He had a very ready, very acerbic wit, and his jokes could be quite penetrating. Tom saw no point in giving him more reasons to chaff him during their onward journey.

The depths of the valley ahead were just beginning to lighten when Tom finally spotted Aaron loitering about, puffing on his clay pipe and leaning up against a tree trunk while he idly kicked at stones. At Tom's shouted greeting, Aaron straightened up and called back cordially.

"Well! About time too. What time of day do you call this, you old toss-pot? I've been freezing my nads off hanging about here."

Tom jumped off his horse, and the two friends embraced closely. Once their greetings were done, they surveyed each other with critical interest. Beneath their rough cloaks, both were dressed simply, in their nicest outdoor clothes.

"You look a wreck," Aaron observed affably. "You'll never out-do me, mate, however hard you try." He flicked at Tom's soft hat. "What's this daft old thing in aid of?"

It was a nice hat, made of velveteen in a colour called gingerline, and it sported a fancy feather. Tom had borrowed it from his father, the Colonel, without his knowledge, because he thought he looked rather grand in it. He was wearing it pulled down stylishly over one ear.

"What, you mean this?" Tom's hand strayed casually upwards. "Oh, I just came across it the other day in one of our old clothes chests. Nice, isn't it?"

Aaron raised a sardonic eyebrow. "Very memorable," he agreed.

"I thought it gave me a certain air."

"Too right it does. If you mean air as in 'airy fairy'. Makes you look a proper dandy. Who are you hoping to bend over for?"

"No-one," Tom said, carelessly. "I just like being well-dressed, that's all. You should try it yourself, instead of wearing that old fustian all the time. Borrow off your father occasionally, the same as me, then you won't have to spend anything to look good. I like a change." He patted at a pair of newish moleskin britches, and tugged at his long leather jerkin rather complacently, settling it down over the tops of his thighs before quickly covering himself back up with his big woollen cloak. "Brrr," he added, briskly. "I don't think it will warm up much today. Come on, you can finish your pipe on the way. Let's get going."

They were on their way to Chepstow market, and their meeting was taking place, as it always did, on the main road a few miles upriver from the town. Tom and Aaron lived on opposite sides of the river, and when they linked up it was from completely different directions, and from two different counties. Aaron had crossed over from his family's comfortable stone house on Hewelsfield Common in Gloucestershire, bringing with him the latest lute his father had made, carefully wrapped in a length of clean flannel. It was his intention to play a few tunes in the market place to demonstrate its merits to a wider public, and hopefully coax someone into buying it, since this was the last market day before Christmas. Tom had simply been allowed a rare day off and wanted to make use of it to see his friends. He lived further away, up in Trellech, a small hamlet set in miles of wild heathland on top of the ridge on the Monmouthshire side of the river, and much closer to Monmouth town than to Chepstow. This was a long trek out for Tom. His journeys of any distance were customarily made on Timothy, an old cob belonging to his father, and it wasn't long before poor old Timothy became, yet again, the subject of a slight argument between the two young men.

Timothy was one of the last remaining horses of what had once been very large and extensive stables, and he was by no means the best of what those stables had comprised. In fact, it was Aaron's half-mocking assertion that, even judged alone and without younger and fitter animals around him, Timothy was by far the worst horse he had ever seen. Colonel Meadows had been in the King's army when the country had been at war, and he had been a wealthy man back then; but now almost all his money was gone, and with it, the greater part of his country estate. Not that Tom remembered those days, he had been far too young; and besides, a general lack of money wasn't something that bothered him, either then or now. Had he owned a better horse, he would have used a better horse; but since he wasn't allowed his father's mount, and since the horse they used for the plough and the farm cart was a brute, he had, with his usual good humour, simply saddled up Timothy well before daybreak, and taken the steep lanes down through Cleddon, and Bargain Wood, so he could link up with Aaron and get the obligatory natter and catch-up begun as early as possible.

Unfortunately, it was already apparent that Tom's plans were not going to roll forward in quite the way he had supposed. A scruffy little rowing boat was tied up against a roughly-assembled wooden jetty driven into the reeds of the river bank beneath them, at a point just below the weir. The boat was a recent acquisition of Aaron's, and this was where the focus of dissent quickly settled once it had moved on from old Timothy. Not only had Aaron crossed the river in it instead of waking the ferry-man as he usually did, he now voiced his intention of rowing on down to Chepstow in it as well, to save time, instead of riding pillion up behind Tom as was customary. Once apprised of this fact, Tom became quite scornful.

"You must be mad," he said scathingly. "You'll get soaked. Or drowned. And what about that lute? The water will ruin it. Whatever makes you think this is the way to get to Chepstow with the least amount of effort? I bet your father doesn't know about this."

"It's the obvious way to travel, mate," Aaron said, putting his arm around Tom's neck with blithe unconcern and ignoring that last contention. "It stands to reason. Look. All I have to do is jump in, make sure I keep the boat balanced, and the current will do the rest. I just sit back and wait to arrive, and then hop out at the other end."

"Yes, I can see you intend to travel in comfort," Tom said irritably. "I noticed the cushions." There were two of them, large and plump, both covered in ancient, fraying, Flemish tapestry cloth, arranged in the thwarts. They looked hugely inviting, and Tom was already feeling saddle-sore. But he had nowhere to leave Timothy, so he couldn't even contemplate joining Aaron in this latest wheeze for saving energy and having some hair-raising fun, as he would privately very much have liked to do. He would have to continue the rest of the journey on horseback, and now it looked as though he was going to have to do it entirely on his own. He felt a keening disappointment. "What are you going to do about coming back?" Maybe they would get the chance of a chat then, instead.

"Horse and cart," Aaron asserted, confidently.

"Horse and...?" Tom was mystified. "Where did that idea spring from? You can't even be sure someone will be coming this far from Chepstow this evening. Can't you just ride with me on Timothy? Who do you know who owns a cart?"

"Nick. He's just been given one, this summer. He's a waggoner now. Didn't anybody tell you?"

"What? No. I haven't seen anybody who would have known. And I haven't seen Nick since last May Day. So how did that come about? He was a drover's boy last time I saw him. How did he manage to get himself a waggon?"

"Some old farmer out Llanishen way died and left him a cart in his will."

"Never! Seriously?" Tom gave a low whistle, impressed. "Lucky dab. I wish someone would die and leave *me* something in his will."

"Yup, that's just what everybody else is saying. Only thing is... now, of course, they're all wondering why. It's the same farm his mother worked on when she was a young girl, so... well, there's been a bit of whispering about it. Anyhow," Aaron shrugged, dismissing idle tittle-tattle. "He's been working on his own with this cart since the September hiring fair, and he reckons he's doing all right. With a bit of luck, I might be able to cadge a few coins off him, if his pockets are jingling enough. But even if he's got nothing he can lend me, he still won't need paying for the lift. I hear he's picking up a load of oranges from the port tonight to take to Squire

Speybury's house, so if that's true, he can drop me off on his way there. The least I'll get is a free ride. I'll still be on a winner!"

"Yes, good idea, Aaron. Great thinking, son," Tom said, sarcastically. "Out at night on the river when they could be doing a run. *Excellent* timing."

"What? Another run? Tonight? Are you sure?"

Tom looked quickly over both shoulders. "Well, maybe not tonight. I don't know. But it *is* market day today, and I *did* overhear one of the Serjeants say something to Mister Noble a few days ago about having men on stand-by because of Christmas, and I *did* think it would be a good time to do a run because the town is busy and there's a lot of other activity to cover it up. But that's my assumption. And that was all I heard. So, assuming a dick like you can avoid blundering straight into something I shudder to even think of, what are you proposing to do with the boat?"

"Coming back, do you mean? Put it in the cart, alongside of me."

"There won't be room, you idiot."

"All right, it can go outside of me. I'll put it in the cart, and sit inside it with the oranges, and offer to take pot-shots at any dangerous marauders who might be out and about. How's that? After that, I can just relax in the cushions till we arrive."

Tom sighed.

"Great, isn't it?" Aaron continued. "Nick does the driving, while I just sit in the back and hop out when I get to this end, too. Man, oh man. What a way to arrange life."

Tom sighed again. "And what are you going to do with this ridiculous boat once you've actually finished with it today? You can't just leave it here, it might get used for something illegal. Don't tell me, let me guess. You've got some poor, thick clodhopper to agree to deposit it somewhere for you and look after it until you want it out again, haven't you?"

"Of course. Can't see the point in having these things if it makes life more difficult, can you?"

"And the utter fool who is doing you this favour is…?"

"Tony Lightfoot."

"Tony? Are you joking? He's never even here."

"Exactly. That's the advantage of asking a pedlar. I can leave my boat anywhere I like, send him word where to find it, and it'll be no inconvenience for him to pick it up whenever he passes by on his travels and put it where I want it."

Tom sighed for the third time, this time resignedly. "You seem to have thought of everything," he remarked.

Aaron gave him a sly wink. "Naturally," he announced. "And now, I must go. I want to speed off and get this lute flogged as fast as possible for as much as possible. All the rich old faggots will be out at crack of sparrow's farts this morning, with full purses and a strong desire to get their business done as fast as possible. With a bit of luck, I'll find out in the first hour whether any of them want to book Dad's music troupe over Christmas for a dance or supper, and after that, the rest of the day will be mine." He gave an elaborate sigh of his own, and added complacently, "Since you say you won't come with me, I shall just have to wait for you in the coffee house. I'll be about half-way through my hot chocolate before you've finished toiling down the last hill, I expect. By the time you join me, I'll have seen Nick and Adela and had all the latest gossip from them, and be putting myself outside of one of Missus Musty's mutton pies. Plus, I wouldn't mind seeing Kitty, if she's around."

"What? You? See Kitty? Aah, come off it. She's too pretty for a lazy tosser like you."

"Here, who are you calling lazy?"

"You. You know I like her."

Aaron gave a withering snort of laughter. "Ha! You? Dream on, mate. I know all is fair in love and war, but let's face it, a man like you will only ever manage to pin Kitty down using low cunning. Like catching her from behind by the knees."

"Ha! Not afraid of the competition, are you, by any chance?"

"Competition? Now, let me see. I'm trying my hardest, but I can't think of anyone who might qualify. After all, what girl wants to ride on a blind old nag when she can glide along in a fine boat like this one?"

"Timothy isn't blind. Or a nag. I'll laugh my head off if you fall out of that stupid boat on the way and get a sousing. You won't dare show yourself to Kitty then."

"And I'll laugh my head off if you fall off that great carcass into the hedge arse-upwards and show up with a face full of prickles."

"You'll never get the chance, mate. Timothy's better than any wormy old boat."

"You wish. Look. Tell you what, let's have a race. To settle the argument. Best man wins."

"Best horse, you mean. We already know who the best man is around here. Right, you're on. Last one into Missus Musty's buys the pies and hot chocolate. *Two* pies to the man who spots any signs of a smuggler's den along the way. Done?"

"Done. Spit on your hand, and we'll shake on it. Got the tuppence on you?"

"I won't need it. Got your groat?"

Aaron stretched languorously. "Ask no questions," he advised, giving another sly wink. Then he became brisk. "All right, no head start for you. My run along the river is a lot longer, even if it's faster; so, you tackle the hills, I take on the bends and the weirs. Agreed?"

"Agreed," Tom said, and he jumped straight onto Timothy's back. "Get into your boat."

Aaron took a light leap into the thwarts and gathered up the oars. "Ready?" he asked.

"Ready," said Tom. "On the count of three: one, two, thr…"

But Aaron had gone, coursing off downriver in a damp, muddy swirl of early morning river-mists and eddying water. Tom quietly clicked his heels and set Timothy off along the miry road at a fast trot, following the same direction Aaron had taken.

It was certain that Aaron would arrive in Chepstow well before Tom, unless the outgoing tide at the other end had left too much mud to negotiate. Despite being tidal, the River Wye had a strong current – any boat would be carried along it fast. But it would take time for Aaron to track round several small weirs along the way, and he would have to find a place to moor on one of the old jetties outreaching the port. After that, there was a long and tiring walk up the hill into the market place. Tom's ride on the pitted road was a shorter route, and he would be on horse-back right into the town. Once there, all he had to do was tie Timothy to a hitching-post at one of the cheaper stables, and he would be in Beaufort Square and Missus Musty's within a couple of minutes. He couldn't wait to see Aaron's face when he should finally come rushing up, puffing and panting, all red-faced from his exertions, clutching his father's lute. As for seeing pretty Kitty Hillenjaar, Tom had already arranged a private meeting with her in the Pig and Parsley tavern later, but there was no need for Aaron to know about that…

Tom's road led through Tintern, and he followed it at a brisk trot. It was still very dark in the village, and much of it would remain so all day. Parts of Tintern never got full sun in winter.

As he passed through, he nodded to a couple of men who were preparing to make the journey to Chepstow themselves, their horses tethered ready at their lighted doors. They each nodded to Tom as he went by, and Tom felt pleased. They would catch up with him before long and make some pleasant company. He went by the Bell and Candle, where no-one was yet astir, and promised himself a drink in there on his way home later. The innkeeper had lit the Yule brand to mark the beginning of the solstice, and the air all the way through the village was redolent with its oak-wood smoke. The Bell and Candle was always a tempting place to make a stop. Tom particularly liked it because it had a little rill that trickled down the wall at the back of the main room inside, emptying into a stone pool that was the tavern's principal feature. He could sit on a bench by that pool and just listen to the sound of the water; he didn't need anybody to talk to. It made a peaceful sojourn on his journeys up and down the valley.

Further on down the road, and just beyond the houses, he passed the Abbey ruins. The old stones gleamed palely in the diffuse gloom, their tumbling profile topped by a single huge Gothic window that traced a skeletal profile over the Devil's Pulpit on the far side of the river and adjacent skyline. Tom liked that view. He thought it was artistic.

His glance trailed across from there to the densely forested slopes rising precipitously above his head on his right. Up there, amongst those creaking, shadowy trees, was the drab little shack to which Tony Lightfoot returned after meandering on foot around the Monmouthshire countryside. Tony was like a man fashioned from sticks and twigs himself: a Jack-o'-the-Green, coming and going a glimpse at a time, with a coat and boots half-rotten from years of exposure to hot sun and freezing mists and rain; and all about him so tattered and loose and shredded, so patched and faded and torn, that everything he wore appeared to hang on him like bushels of autumn leaves scattering about him as he strode along alone. Always alone. People whispered that he was much more than a simple pedlar. They said he was a man who knew the secrets and sources for the ancient woodlands and forests: that he could call up nature spirits, and that he was made the same way the trees were because he belonged to them and was of them: a man of wood and stone. Tom had heard stories about devil-worship up in those woods, too, somewhere up near where Tony lived, yet he couldn't believe that any of the Tintern men he knew would be involved in such practices. He wondered whether Tony took secret powers from the devil, and if Satan was separate from the old pagan gods. It was all a bit confusing. Tom shivered to think of what Tony might see or hear when he was sitting alone at night inside that ruinous old shelter under those stark, overshadowing pines. It might even be that he joined in the rituals. Maybe there would be a witches' coven up there that very night, since it was the end of the winter solstice. The sun would be going down early, and Tom's ride back would be through the same engulfing darkness that continued up under those trees. He would be surrounded by rustling leaves and groaning, shuddering branches all the way from Wyndcliffe to the very edge of the village here. Aargh! Horrible thought! Forget smugglers! And smuggler's hides! Smugglers might be dangerous, and a man might need to avoid them at all costs, but it made Tom far more nervous to think of these other, more sinister matters. He turned and looked behind, to make sure nothing nasty was tip-toeing up behind him, and as he did so, his gaze fell back on the Devil's Pulpit. Its promontory, now showing grey in the first glimmerings of daylight, featured a thick covering of tussocky grass and shrivelled whinberry bushes. Devil's Pulpit. Why *was* it called that, he wondered? Why call it the Devil's Pulpit, when there was an Abbey nearby – or was that why an Abbey had been built there, that the Devil really *had* preached from there, with his forked tail, and goat's feet, and horns? And that was why this bit of forest seemed so fearfully drodsome?

He wished he could go back home on the upper road and take the ridge through Devauden village instead of coming this way, but that route would take him through Itton Woods, and *they* had been haunted since Roman times. There were *things* in Itton Woods. They flapped on one side of you, and knocked on the other, and gurgled right behind you. At night, those woods were more alive, and even more frightening than here. He shuddered and wished Aaron had been willing to come with him. Aaron would have made him laugh and kept his thoughts cheerful.

Of course, he understood why his friend had elected to go by another method of travel. Any method was preferable to poor old Timothy, who was about the least comfortable horse Tom had ever ridden. He had been bred to be a farm horse, and his back was too wide for carrying people. It felt like having your legs slowly prised apart at the hip to sit on him at all: Aaron said it was like trying to mount Bigsweir Bridge. But Tom's pride had been wounded afresh

23

by Aaron's teasing that morning. Blind old nag indeed – he hated it when people criticised old Tim. He was more of a friend than an animal. The old horse was gentle and patient, and he had been with the family since before Tom was born. Tom patted the horse's flank at the thought and the horse turned his head and looked round enquiringly for a second, then continued his steadfast plodding onwards and upwards.

The hill climb ahead was a long one. The road winding out of Tintern village rose further and further into thicketed woods until it reached the cliff-tops of Wyndcliffe, where it followed the ridge along its natural contours above two miles of deep gorge before descending into the lush riverside grasslands that marked its far end.

As he and Timothy made their way round a favourable bend, Tom risked removing his eyes from the treacherous road ahead to peer down through the gaps between the trees to see if he could see any sign of Aaron somewhere along the great ox-bow in the river below, but in reality he knew his friend would be long gone.

Chapter Two

Chepstow was a thriving port town built into a hillside along the western edge of the River Wye, where the river ran deep enough to allow larger boats and smaller ships to pass through, providing a convenient waterway for a wealth of small vessels of all descriptions. Many ships came in to harbour, others took a run upriver to the villages further north, venturing as far as Redbrook in the Forest of Dean, which lay within easy reach of Monmouth.

South of Chepstow, meadows stocked with grazing cattle flattened out within a mile or two of the town to become low-lying wetlands and marshes where, at low tide, broad mud-flats surfaced along the water's edge, exposing a long, grey wilderness that dominated and filled the landscape seawards until the tide came in again. This was a world apart: a world edged with tough marram grass and brittle, matted sedges: a place of sobbing winds and desolate birds and wild, rain-splattered isolation, where river became estuary and joined the Mouth of the Severn before it widened into the Bristol Channel. Here, the clagging mud held rich pickings for gatherers of cockles and mussels, for crab fishermen, and for the eel catchers brave enough to shoulder their creels and venture out across the fertile, but treacherous wastes.

Back in the town and down by the river, Adela Parry and her younger brother Andrew had stopped off to skate on some thick ice that had formed overnight on a big puddle in the Castle Dell. They were supposed to be on their way to the market in the Town Square at the top of the hill, but since it was still early enough to take dog's leave for a while without being noticed, they had decided to stop off and enjoy a bit of fun for now and go up to the town later. They had been given some things to sell by their mother, but it was far too cold to be standing about waiting for customers to chance by. Adela's thinking was that if they waited until the sun was high and the crowds had built up, they should be able to sell the contents of their baskets quickly without getting too chilled, and then have time to spend with their friends in the warmth of Missus Musty's coffee house.

Just a short time earlier, they had sculled across the muddy river on an incoming tide in their grandfather's leather coracle, bringing with them two basketfuls of late apples and a few dozen eggs. Those baskets now lay where they had been put, side-by-side among the sedges, and their coracle was beached at a tiny inlet under the Castle, which was the only place they could climb out when the water was low without getting their clothes ruined.

Chepstow Castle stood directly above them, built on low cliffs right at the very edge of a sweeping bend in the river. Its massive presence made a powerful impression, dominating the entire view everywhere hereabouts, from the Wye Bridge, a few furlongs downriver, to the road from Tidenham on the far side of the water. Adela and Andrew's little home was a simple cottage tucked into the river bank just below that same road, at the point where it began to climb the hill; and from her bedroom window, set level with the long grasses a few feet above the high-water mark, Adela could look out over the broad river banks directly across to the Castle walls.

The surface of the icy puddle was beginning to melt slightly as the sun warmed the gelid air, so it was fast becoming more slippery. This added a good measure more to the morning's entertainment for Andrew, who had been able to make longer and longer slides across the ice into the reedy puddle edges as a consequence. Many of his landings were now ending in slithering great bum-falls of the most pleasing kind. He paid no heed to his sister's pleas to be more careful, and no attention whatsoever to the wetness of his britches. He didn't feel discomfort the way his sister did.

He was taking his umpteenth galloping charge across the puddle when he heard his name being called. He turned mid-slither to see who was hailing him and waved when he saw who it was. Their friend, Nick, was coming downhill from the direction of the town, his long drover's whip held aloft in a gesture of salute. Nick always had his whip with him. It was the one he had carried since his days as a drover's boy, and he would have been lost without it. Despite being the proud and lucky possessor of a farm cart, Nick was still a drover at heart. The whip, his easy walk, and the two rangy sheepdogs lurking habitually at his heels, made Nick an easily identifiable figure, even from a distance.

Andrew picked up the smaller basket and passed Adela the heavier one, which also held the eggs, and together they walked over the sludgy castle green to meet him.

"A Merry Christmas to you," Nick called out, just as soon as they were close enough to speak without shouting. "Cold, isn't it?"

"Wonderful weather. Merry Christmas to you as well, Nick. Where's Aaron? We were expecting him. Haven't you seen him yet?"

"Yup. He's up at the market, waiting for us." Nick turned with them to retrace his steps and took Adela's basket, while his sheepdogs, Trusty and Drift, fell in behind. "We've been there since early, and we've both done really well. Aaron has sold another lute, and he's got an engagement for his father's group at the Butter Market in Ross-on-Wye for New Year's Day, and I've been hired to take some grain barley to a farm the other side of Saint Woolos before then, if we don't get snow; so that's good going, isn't it? We were just on our way to meet you when we bumped into Tom." Nick rolled his eyes and shook his head. "There was a fine old argument when they saw each other, because they couldn't agree who had been in town the longest. It seems they had some bet on, and since they were both insisting they had won, they decided they had better toss for it. Tom called and Aaron won, which Tom decided wasn't fair, so then the argument started all over again. I thought they would finish up settling it with a push-fight, but Aaron decided he didn't want to risk cracking a knuckle because he's got to play at the Squire's tomorrow night, and Tom didn't want a smack on the head for some equally silly reason, so in the end they called it evens. After that, they stayed to watch the tooth-drawer. Old Aubrey Rimmington is having a back tooth pulled, and just about everybody is there, watching. It's taking ages to get it out, he might even still be there when we get back. You should have heard him yelling. He was parting with it awful bad."

They walked on up the hill, flanked by Nick's two dogs, overtaking a flock of geese being led at a slow and gentle pace by a goose-girl from the Forest of Dean. She was almost at her journey's end, the goose pens being only a little further on up, in Middle Street. Half a dozen other pens to hold the bigger farm animals were just around the corner from there, set close to the main market, ready for the eleven o' clock auction. Andrew lingered for a moment, as they passed the pens, to say a few words over the hurdles to some pigs and a sheep and put his hands through the gaps in the wickerwork so they could nuzzle his fingers. Then he ran to catch up with Adela and Nick, who were already disappearing ahead of him into the busy Town Square.

The search for Aaron and Tom began at once. They found the two of them standing together, wedged into a noisy crowd hemming in Mister Winch, whose red plush chair was set up in its usual place at the bottom end of Beaufort Square. The lower part of the market place was always brimming with people. Some were plying their trades at the roadside, others standing about, and yet more were talking with the farmers who had come that way to assess the livestock. But most were vagabonds of different descriptions spilling out of the Broken Drum tavern in various stages of drunkenness. These, together with a few off-duty soldiers, contributed to a turbulent crowd, many of whom had already gathered to watch the tooth-drawer at work. There were plenty of volunteers eager to help hold his clients steady, while a background of roisterers shouted rowdy encouragement to keep everyone hanging on in there for the duration of the desperate treatments. Mister Winch was, as ever, actively and energetically busy. He was a barber-surgeon, the only one in Chepstow, recently retired from the Bristol sailing ships, and he came every month on a market day to pull teeth and do the blood-lettings. On top of that, he was the local horse doctor and leech. Not that he was popular: no-one ever went to him for attention to their toothaches or animals out of choice. First, they tried homemade simples obtained from women like Adela's mother; or if they thought they needed something stronger they went to see one of the hedge-witches in the Forest of Dean for a charm. The better-off among them, and the better educated, paid for more expensive cures and nostrums from the apothecary, Doctor Dranks. Mister Winch was everybody's last resort.

Doctor Dranks was observing the barber-surgeon from a distance, standing in his drab doorway one stop up from Missus Musty's. He and Mister Winch didn't get along too well. Doctor Dranks was an uncommunicative droopy, stoopy, elderly man, rumoured to have been educated at the university in Prague. Irrespective of this – or perhaps because of it – the local community was very much in awe of him. In emphasis of his mysterious doctrinal discipline and doctoral status, he wore a long, sweeping, black gown and a close-fitting hat with strings that tied under his chin, and studied a great many books. It was his earnest contention, whenever he could be persuaded to speak, that apothecaries held the best remedies for every ailment, thus rendering Mister Winch, and the likes of him, useless for any medical condition except possibly battle wounds and gangrene. Doctor Dranks didn't even think people should have their bad teeth taken out. A tiny tussie-mussie of herbs laid alongside the tooth to ease the ague should suffice until the bad humours died away and the jaw healed itself, in his opinion.

Meanwhile, out in the Square, oblivious to Doctor Dranks or his disapproval, old Aubrey had just had his tooth pulled amidst great cheers from the crowd, and was moved to one side with their assistance, where he sat showing weak relief as he took hot-water-and-brandy to wash away the taste and assist his recovery.

Adela left Andrew with the other boys to watch a blood-letting for a horse with windgalls, and went to look for a place in the market where she could stand and sell her apples and eggs. She was enjoying the sight of so many winter festivities round and about the town, they made her feel happy. She was just about old enough to remember when someone called the Lord Protector had overseen the country, when all these Christmas celebrations had been forbidden. Now, all the stalls and shops within the Square were decorated with colourful woodland berries and boughs of evergreen brought in from the Forest of Dean, and there were garlands of gay ribbons woven into the wreaths and corn dollies hanging by the armful from the lintels of shop doorways. People were out for the day, walking arm-in-arm, all cheerful and talkative. Adela threaded her way through the animated groups, looking for an unoccupied space. Before long, she saw a gap about the size she wanted right between two stalls set close together. She stopped, and settled herself in the relative shelter there, putting her two baskets down at her feet. On one side of her was Addiss's Bee Prodductes from Shyrenewtonne, who were a fixture at the market every month, and on the other a simple trestle table, stacked with cooked pork from a pig-killing. Pork-pies and haslets jostled next to slices of brawn, and an ancient brazier was keeping warm two large, open dishes: one cooking up paunch and onions, the other hot chitterlings. The appetising smell rising through the air drew people in for a long look and an appreciative sniff or two. Adela had chosen her spot well. Folk coming up to buy a dish of meat from the pork stall took note of Adela's apples and eggs, and a few of her offerings were added to their baskets as well.

Time passed quickly, especially after a band of mummers struck up a tune on a hornpipe at a corner of the Square at the top end of the town. A dance soon commenced, and Adela listened to the rhythmic clatter of clogs striking the cobblestones with a knowing smile. She was well acquainted with the dance that went with that particular tune. It was a good opener, and she knew what came at the end of it: it was a dropping of britches for a quick flash of bare backsides, and it always made the audience laugh because no matter how well the mummers blacked out their faces someone in the crowd always thought they could recognise a pair of buttocks – sometimes several pairs – from seeing that dance done so often. It was just a question of whose names would get bawled out in identification. Some of the suggestions were so ridiculous, they had people in stitches. Today, the audience was a group of dawdling, mostly approving folk coming in from outlying farms and country places who had just walked in through the Town Gate and hadn't decided yet where they wanted to head for, so they added several names that wouldn't have been mentioned otherwise, including those of an unpopular brewer who they said used piss in his beer, the ferryman at Broadrock who was a bit of a letch, and a notoriously fast dairymaid with a famously wide behind. The Colonel of the troops currently occupying the Castle barracks who was also a landed gentleman had also been confidently called.

Adela heard the gusts of laughter from the crowd, followed by a lot of cat-calling and witticisms from the men, and more laughter from the women, before the music finally stopped altogether. Things went quieter for a while. Then she began to hear parts of 'Saint George and the Dragon.' Oh, nice. Adela liked that play. They had a good dragon in it.

Her baskets soon emptied. So near to Christmas her mother's goods were always in demand: the apples for making sweet mincemeats, and the eggs – a rarity during winter months – for syllabubs and egg-nogs.

Pleased to be finished so quickly, Adela put the baskets one inside the other for ease of carrying and went over to Missus Flagg from Abergavenny, who came twice a year to sell her farm cheeses. She found Missus Flagg sitting closely wrapped in a large shawl with her generous nether regions hanging out over the side of the cart, her nose and cheeks shining with cold, shouting cheerful greetings to people she hadn't seen since summer. Adela looked the cheeses over while Missus Flagg carried on a lively conversation with a muffin man whose head was concealed under his tray, making it look as if she was talking to the muffins, until she made her choice and picked a cheese about as large as a pound-cake, which was the largest she could carry. She added a couple of bundles of fresh thyme and rosemary cut from Missus Flagg's kitchen garden as an afterthought. Missus Flagg had strewn them about in the cart to keep the flies off the cheeses, and such woody herbs didn't grow well in Adela's damp little garden, back home.

By the time Adela had found the others again, everyone was feeling the cold, and they all had aching legs from so much standing. But her friends had had a wonderful time. Mister Winch had just removed a large wem from the side of a young man's chin, and bled a fat man with a gouty toe who had fainted, and he was now preparing to cut down a bunion from the foot of a lady's maid, which also held the promise of much interest; only now the entertainment was bringing increasingly intense jostling under the pressure of a thickening crowd. The town was filling up. Nick suggested it might be a good time to go for a warm-up and a cup of chocolate, to which the others readily agreed. They trooped in single file through the still swelling throngs, past a Punch-and-Judy show and a man on stilts, and headed straight for the sign proclaiming the merits of Missus Musty's Coffye House. There, they peered in through the window for a moment to see if anyone they knew was already inside, but after deciding they didn't recognise anybody, they opened the door and went in.

The interior of Missus Musty's was very clean and simple, with roughly-finished, long oak tables and benches placed randomly about a large room with a scrubbed flagstone floor running wet with muddy ice melt off dozens of tramping, scuffing boots and dirty dogs' paws. A good log fire in a large open fireplace offset the dampness with its cheerful warmth. As usual, the coffee house was hectic. Men from all different walks of life were constantly coming in and out, some to talk boisterously whilst they drank coffee, the rest to sit idly about reading flyers containing the latest news from London and Bristol. Although loud, none of the men were rowdy. Adela preferred the heavy noise of the coffee house to that of the taverns, where there was often brawling with the drunkenness. The men here were all nicer, as well as cleaner. They had had a bit of schooling, and you could tell they were learned in the art of refinement, even if they didn't quite practice it.

The friends fell in behind Nick, who led the way to the longest available bench and two broad-stools, which today just happened to be set close to the door, and Trusty and Drift closed in at the rear. After lingering for a moment to stare hard at a farmer's dog lying under an adjacent table, they tucked themselves quietly beneath Nick's bench and fell asleep.

Missus Musty's daughter, Susan, came over bearing their chocolate drinks, ladled straight out of an iron cauldron kept suspended on a bracket beside the fire. Susan always knew what her friends would order, they had the same thing every time they came. Adela and Andrew would share an open fish pie, called a stargazer on account of the whole little fishes laid out in it with sightless eyes staring upwards; the other boys would fill up on her mother's famous mutton pies, cooked fresh in the kitchen at the back. Her mother's coffee house was known far and wide as the best coffee house outside of Bristol. Susan exchanged a few laughs with the friends, not having seen them in a while, then she went off to see to the other customers. She was a nice girl, quite bright, and the friends all liked her, but her skin was measly from all the pastries she ate, which greatly reduced her overall attractiveness, especially to the boys.

The pies were good, and everyone was hungry, so they all ate in silence for a while. They were still tucking in when the doorbell jangled and someone else they didn't know walked in. Several other customers looked over at the open door as well, their attention caught by the newcomer's appearance. Everything he was wearing, from his oil-jacket down to his blue sea-cloth shirt and galligaskins, indicated the stranger to be from the seafaring community down at the port. But sailors didn't usually come this far up into town, they normally only went as far as the Pig and Parsley tavern at the top end of Roper Street, if they got as far as that – and most just tumbled straight off their ships into the Cocklehouse: a squalid old drinking-place that had sprawled across the larger part of the waterfront for at least a century – so the stares lingered a while longer before everyone gradually resumed what they had been doing.

The sailor was about sixteen years of age, which was slightly older than any of the friends, and they regarded him with considerable interest. He was a good-looking lad, with jet-black hair cascading down his back in rich, glossy ringlets far too thick to be put into a classical sailor's tarred pig-tail. Some of his ringlets were held in loose braids, the rest fell freely down his back almost as far as his waist under a colourful bandanna of red and yellow cotton wound tightly round his head. He was short, of less than average height, and very stocky in build, with a body that spoke a lot more of a love of creature comforts than it did of hard graft. His friendly-looking face was smothered with dark freckles that showed up starkly against a skin unusually fair, given the rest of his colouring. A small blue bird sat quietly on his shoulder.

The sailor was looking about him, evidently searching for somewhere to sit, so he couldn't have come in to meet up with someone, as the friends had at first supposed. Just as his gaze fell on the corner where they were all sitting, Nick looked across and caught his eye. There was a pause – and Nick gestured for him to come over and join them. Since they were the only company of young people in the whole house, and since most of the other tables were full anyway, the young man willingly accepted the wordless invitation. Everyone moved up a bit to allow the stranger to squeeze himself in.

"Feel free to join us, mate," said Nick, companionably, moving aside his battered old felt hat while the young man settled himself down at the table. "Welcome. Share some hot chocolate. Or pie."

"I'm *okey,* th-th-thank you," answered the lad, with a very strong foreign accent. "I'm going to have me a coffee, and an eel pie, and a p-p-piece of plum cake."

"Good plum cake here," Nick said.

"Yeah, so I-I-I heard," the lad returned. "They t-told me back at the ship. We came in with the tide early this morning. Hey, my name is Rigo."

Nick shook Rigo's hand as he introduced himself, before indicating the rest of them.

"We're all friends here," Nick said, his collar-length scraggy dark-blonde hair making a startling contrast to Rigo's marvellous tresses. "Let me tell you who we all are. From left to right, first is Aaron. He's apprenticed to his father, who's a luthier. They make stringed musical instruments and do a lot of the entertaining hereabouts. Very fine they are, too. You should hear Aaron and his dad play sometime, if you ever get the chance – but don't get him talking. He'll wear you out, else."

Aaron took a clay pipe out of his mouth and bowed darkly and silently from where he was relaxing. He wouldn't waste time or energy talking to a stranger unless he had something important to say.

"And to his left is Tom," Nick continued. "His dad has a bit of money, so he's got Tom articled to a notary."

Tom, who had removed his hat in order to eat without messing up the feather, flicked his dark hair out of his large blue eyes, and regarded Rigo with interest. "Don't listen to Nick," he said. "Whatever money my father had was lost in the Civil War. Is this your first time in Chepstow, friend?"

"Yeah. My f-f-first time in Chippistow, and my f-f-first time in England. I'm a cook: a sea cook, as I like food and cooking. I do most of the cooking on my ship – it's easier than being up on deck, mostly. See, I don't really want a sailor's life. What I really want is to be a pirate. That's why I ran aw-aw-awa-a-ay to sea, because I want to be a pirate. I've been on the sea for two years now, looking for Henry Morgan, and when I find him, I'm going to join his crew."

"Henry Morgan? I thought he was dead." Aaron removed his pipe from his mouth and carefully knocked out the ashes on the side of his plate.

"No, not dead; married," said Tom, who could read, and who studied the occasional London or Bristol flyer as part of his job. "But he's still out robbing ships on the Spanish Main, as far as I know. Don't you remember me telling you the rumours?" He turned from Aaron and addressed Rigo. "If you've come here looking for Captain Morgan, you must already know that he hails from these parts. But you won't find him anywhere round here, Rigo. It would be way too dangerous for him to be anywhere near England at present. When our King was returned to the throne, the war with Spain ended. All the plundering was meant to finish with it, our sailors aren't even supposed to carry a letter of marque any more: no more privateering, all raids are off. But if the rumours are right, Captain Morgan has never stopped doing it. I suppose it must be exciting, and it's certainly more profitable, because now it's banned it means everything he captures he can keep for himself and his crew. Nothing gets handed over to the State, not even the prize ships. He must be worth a fortune by now. But if he ever gets caught, they'll hang him. Anyhow, that's his look-out. Our town crier did shout a royal proclamation in the market place a couple of years ago, in case any buccaneers were trying to sneak into Chepstow on the quiet thinking it might be a safer port to put in at being so far away from London, but this lot here seem to have forgotten all about it." He flicked his thumb towards his friends.

But Rigo didn't seem interested in such piffling trifles as what royal proclamations or town criers had to say. He carried on as if he hadn't heard. "He's coming here to visit his-his-his dear old mother for Chr-r-ristmas," he informed Tom and Aaron. "I heard about it one night in a t-t-tavern and took a ship that was bound for England as soon as I could. He's a very famous buccaneer. In my country, people talk about him all the time. He's not dead, he's alive; and he's not married, he's got a girlfriend in every port. All the p-pirates have, I heard it. And I want to join him."

"Where is your country?" Adela asked.

"B-Br-Brazil," he announced. "In-In-In the Americas. My country is a wonderful country, full of beautiful people and big rivers and mountains. Did you ever hear of the mighty Amazon? Or the Plata Basin in the Rio Grande do Sul? These are rivers so wide you can't see the other side when you stand on the banks. I have travelled by canoe into the hottest parts of the Amazon Jungle and nearly been eaten by a crocodile. I have ridden on horseback to the highest and coldest plateaus and got frostbite in my toes. I have been through wide, wet grasslands and over dusty plains, and all these things I have done inside my own country. And the place where I live, R-Rio d-d-de Janeiro, is right beside the ocean. But who are you, Miss? What is your name?"

Rigo had abruptly dispensed with casual conversation to follow his own train of thought, and his black, flashing eyes openly displayed his interest as he gazed at Adela. She felt embarrassed. She was the only girl in the group of friends, apart from Kitty, and she didn't like boys looking her over, unlike Kitty. She wasn't used to it, which was also unlike Kitty. She decided to pretend she hadn't noticed: something Kitty never did.

"Oh, I'm Adela," she answered with calculated composure, adding, to deflect his attention – and possibly his admiration – "this is my little brother, Andrew."

Andrew piped up. "I'm not a little brother, I'm a younger brother. And I'm nine years old, not little at all. Adela is twelve, that's not much older than me. And these others are only a few years older than her. Anyway, what's that bird and what's he doing to your neck?"

"He's a b-b-budgerigar parakeet," Rigo answered, transferring his attention from Adela to Andrew and studying him in turn. "And he's p-p-pecking at my ear-ring. He does that when he's angry or hungry. Hey, Moonlight, stop." Rigo freed his ear-ring – a flashy gold hoop with a tiny pearl suspended inside – and gave the little bird a gentle push away from his neck. It hopped off his shoulder, making small squawks of protest, and went down to his upper arm, where it stopped and began quietly to unpick a seam on his jacket with its beak, instead.

"Moonlight. That's a nice name," Andrew observed. "Does he talk? I heard my grandfather say he's met sailors with birds that can talk."

"Oh, yes," Rigo answered. "I try to g-g-get him to talk all the time, but he's still learning. Hey, Moonlight, say 'Well met'."

"Hilloo," Moonlight chirped, in a fruity little voice. "Chk! Well met, well met." And everyone drew their breath in amazement.

"I w-w-won him off a sailor in a g-game of cards last year," Rigo informed the friends, gratified by their collective admiration. "I'm keeping him until I can aff-ff-afford to buy a real parrot. When I'm a pirate, I'm going to have a proper parrot to go on my shoulder, a grey one from the African forests. I'll call him F-F-Fargo."

At that moment, Missus Musty came bustling up, and surveyed them all with rapid professionalism.

"Now then, my lovelies," she said, "what will you all have now? More of the same? Or do you want to move on, now you've finished eating?"

"Pretty Polly," rasped Moonlight, quietly, from Rigo's shoulder.

"Oh my dear, what a clever bird," said Missus Musty, overhearing. "Most unusual. However, does he know my name, I wonder?" She unconsciously patted the greying curls under her mob cap.

"Give us a kiss," said Moonlight, which raised a guffaw from everyone within earshot. Missus Musty looked rather coy. She was about to hurry off without saying anything more when Rigo arrested her departure by putting his hand on her arm.

"P-P-Please excuse my little bird, Miss M-M-Musty," he said, getting to his feet, and speaking most respectfully. "He-e-e has only mixed with sailors, and they have given him bad habits. You know how it is."

"Not at all, my boy," Missus Musty said, demurely. "No harm done." She was smiling to herself, fiddling with a corner of her apron, quietly pleased at the compliment Rigo was paying her.

Rigo squared his shoulders, and continued proudly, "Ma'am, m-my name is R-Rodrigo de Abílio, and I am from B-Br-Brazil. At your service." He made a low bow. "I have come to your coffee house because I would like to try one of your famous eel pies and a p-piece of plum cake. I have heard how very good your cooking is." He patted his ample stomach. "I know you could almost say I am a little bit fat," he went on, sounding gently regretful, and giving incidental voice to his new friends' unspoken thoughts, "b-but my Mama loves to see me well fed, so I must keep myself filled up to make her happy. I heard this is the best place to do it." He gave Missus Musty a wide and engaging smile that became only slightly deprecatory when he looked down at his gently bulging shirt.

Missus Musty rose to the occasion at once. "Now don't you go worrying about that little bit of puppy fat, my lovely," she declared. "Why, it'll be gone before you know it, bless you, and look at you, still just a boy and all this long way from home. I can't have you going back to your poor mamma looking as if we don't know how to feed you in England, I'd never forgive myself. You shall have your chocolate drink and an eel pie, and two slices from my best cakes right this moment, fresh out of the oven, and no charge to you, so there! Susan!"

She clapped her hands to gain her daughter's attention and hastened away. Rigo sat down again to await his free food and drink, looking slightly smug.

"You've done all this before, haven't you?" Nick said rather sternly, though not without a tinge of envy at the success of Rigo's impertinence. He and the others were perennially short of money. Their limited food and drink had already cost them a penny each, but none of them would be asking for, nor expecting, anything else. Rigo had just wangled himself a whole meal for nothing.

"Yes," Rigo replied simply, looking closely and approvingly at the first part of his order as Susan placed it in front of him. "B-But I do it because I haven't had any pay. We d-don't get our money until the end of the voyage. That won't be for another six months, when we dock back home in Rio; so, unless I can gain some when we call in at a port, I must get by the best way I can. I'm just a p-poo-oor sailor. That's why I want to be with Captain Morgan. I want a share of his spoils, and be rich. Then I'll have my own parrot on one shoulder and a cheeky little m-m-monkey on the other, and live on a *fazenda* in S-S-São Paulo near my father, who is a very great man."

"What's a *fazenda*?"

"Where's Sawo Pawlo?"

"Why is your father a great man?"

"A *f-f-fazenda* is a ranch, I think you call it a f-f-farm, and São Paulo is a town in the south of my country. The grass is very lush there for raising cattle, and there is a lot of free space for people like me to settle in, with good farmland for growing corn. A-And my f-f-father is a great man because he once fought a bull, *um touro,* in *M-M-México* without any weapons, and won. He was not a bullfighter, a *matador de toros.* He was in a crowd, watching a bullfight, and the bull escaped. It was going to charge down a little girl, and m-my father used his coat to distract it, because that was all he had. He w-was gored and nearly d-d-died, but he got the bull secured, and saved the little girl, and everybody was cheering in the

40

arena. He was more famous than the *toreros* in the ring that day. Wh-When he recovered, he was given a big reward for his courage, so from that day on he was a wealthy man. In São Paulo that makes him famous still. The p-p-people still buy him coffee when he goes into the town, and they all want to sit down and talk with him. That is a great man, no?"

"Oh, it's great, all right," Tom said, while the others stared at Rigo, impressed.

"I w-w-want to do something big like him that will make me *my* fortune."

"Well, you won't make anything much round here, mate," Nick commented. "We've all tried to think of ways to bring in some extra cash, and we're all still poor. I'm a waggoner, and I have been a drover. You'd think I could do something to get a bit of gold along the way, fetching and carrying something other than sacks of corn or driving cattle and sheep, but nothing springs to mind. I've never even *seen* a piece of gold, let alone spent any."

"W-What about smuggling?" Rigo asked, with his mouth full of eel. Moonlight was on the table, pecking quietly at a plum in the pudding that was still awaiting Rigo's attention.

"What about *what*?"

"S-S-Smuggling." Rigo had now swallowed his eel pie and spoke distinctly.

"Shh!" and, "Not so loud!" Aaron and Nick whispered fiercely together, while Tom hastily looked all round to make sure that no-one else had heard.

"Don't you know you could get put in the stocks or banged up for even mentioning an interest in something like that?" Tom asked, reprovingly. "You'd be mad to think of doing it. For your information, we've got two horribly incommodious prisons only a short drive away, and you could find yourself getting better acquainted with one of their gaolers if the wrong person hears you talking like this."

"Why?" Rigo wasn't being particularly quiet, although luckily there was so much general noise from the many conversations taking place in the rest of the coffee house that there was no possibility of anyone accidentally overhearing. "Th-Th-The other sailors told me everyone round here is involved with smuggling contraband. We've even brought in some extra cargo ourselves, so the Captain said."

The rest of them received this news in silence. Of course, it was an open secret that things went on in and around the port after dark that were nobody's business. When the sound of muffled cartwheels or hooves were heard rumbling through the streets at dead of night, they were not supposed to look out of their windows to see what was happening. It was understood by the whole community that they were to see nothing, and to say nothing, either. If one of them ever *did* make mention of it to a chosen friend, it was done behind a hand in a tiny whisper. And yet, here was a foreigner calmly eating and drinking, and talking openly about the entire business, as if everything concerning it was completely above board.

"Who is your Captain?" Adela asked at last, speaking quietly as a precaution, and wondering what kind of a captain could possibly be so imprudent as to give freely this kind of sensitive information to someone as indiscreet as Rigo.

"Captain Earl 'Man-of-Wrath' Rothman," Rigo replied, still eating steadily.

"Yes, I thought he might be," Tom interjected, suddenly. "I've heard of him. He doesn't give a damn, does he? In fact, he's as mad as a snake, isn't he? You must have to look out, if he is your Captain. I bet you have a tough time under him. He's a hard man, and never far from trouble, so I've heard. My fa... um, someone I know said Captain Rothman's vessel might be bringing in some items of interest – get that? – some *items of interest* – sometime today."

"Yeah, w-well, I'm going to ask if I can ass-ass-assist with the *items*," Rigo said, laying careful emphasis on the word the same way Tom had, "b-b-because I need some money."

"As do the rest of us. But we won't be there, and neither will you, if you've any sense."

"Why not?"

"Because it's illegal, that's why not."

"Well, wh-what of that?" Rigo demanded, galvanised at last by Tom's words out of his habitual state of comfortable indolence into a kind of sluggish tension. He heaved himself upright, manhandling himself the same way a stevedore might shift a sackful of gravel, and became indignant. "Who cares what the law says? N-N-Nobody's had this stuff stolen from them. Nobody has died in the getting of it. No-one will suffer for it being here, except the p-people taking the risk of running it, and they're only dodging the duty payable on it, anyway. Hey! Who cares if the King doesn't get a bit more money? He has plenty already. And who cares ab-b-bout his revenue officers and men, either? They are just paid henchmen." He finished eating and wiped his mouth on his sleeve. Moonlight did, likewise, cleaning each side of his beak in turn on the seam of Rigo's shoulder.

"Up to you, in the end," Aaron said, laconically, taking his pipe out of his mouth to speak, "but you won't feel so clever if you get caught. Anyway, it's nothing to do with us, so good luck with it." He calmly put his pipe back in again and lapsed back into silence while his friends finished off the bits of food Rigo had left on his plates.

Nick said nothing at all. He was doing some serious thinking about Rigo's last words.

Chapter Three

Everyone had finished eating. Susan Musty brought over a few scraps for Nick's dogs, and after that there didn't seem much else to do but leave, so they all trouped outside in a group to get some fresh air. It had been pleasantly warm inside where the fire had been burning, but the warmth had made the smell of stale bodies more noticeable, so it was nice to be out of doors again. Nick offered Rigo a tour of the market, which he willingly accepted, and they commenced walking uphill together towards the top of the Square.

Doctor Dranks was still standing in his doorway. He grudgingly moved aside to allow them to get past so they could go inside. Adela wanted some dried echinacea flowers from the Americas for her mother, who used them, combined with French garlic and Italian hyssop, for winter colds and sweating sicknesses.

While Doctor Dranks was taking out his wooden steps to reach down the required jar for Adela, the others took a desultory look round. It was very dark in there, despite the shutters being open. So many bundles of dried herbs hung in the window that scarcely any light filtered past. To add to the gloom, almost everything in the room was either dark green or dark brown, from the dried leaves and powders in the tall glass bottles on the ranks of wooden shelves to the smoke-stained walls and floor. All was dark. Dust covered everything, smeared in places where the glass had been handled, with paler glimmerings showing through here and there at the places where labels of varying age and design identified each item, from cupboards to containers, from drawers to drachm bottles. In the background a simple earthenware alembic hung suspended above a copper urn full of bubbling water, puffing wisps of something herby from its long spout into a distilling glass set on a tall stool beside the fire.

Doctor Dranks carefully shook out a pennyweight of dark echinacea petals onto the scales at his table and placed them equally carefully inside a folded paper, which he secured by screwing it into a twist at one end. He then climbed back up the steps to replace the jar on a top shelf, making sure the label faced the front like all its neighbours, before he descended again to his table beneath the shelves.

On the table, underneath the scales and all the papers used for the dispensing of his powders and mixtures, was a large astrological chart pinned down at each corner. This he used, together with a book of ephemera, for all his diagnoses. He would ask a sick or ailing applicant their exact date and time and place of birth, then run his finger over his chart, scribble little notes on the scraps of paper, and finally give such unerringly accurate details about the person in front of him that most people found his assessments quite unnerving. It was even rumoured locally that Doctor Dranks had a secret physick garden hidden away at the back of his house; one that nobody had ever been allowed to see or enter. In there, people said, he grew vast and wonderful exotic plants with different mystical properties, really powerful ones: the ones used for vamping up the decoctions and potions that obtained him his most spectacular, truly amazing cures. A monstrous mandrake root, displayed prominently on a long counter just inside the door, arresting every customer's attention the moment they came in, added considerable weight to these claims. True, it resided alongside an assortment of stone jars holding a much more normal and reassuring variety of creams, lotions, unguents and ointments; but still, it made an impact. A little further along, standing on the same counter, a line of glass-stoppered containers continued the impression of mystical mastery. Some were filled with bitter-smelling oils and unidentifiable unnamed tinctures, whilst yet more were full to the brim with odd-looking mixtures and concoctions whose contents undulated strangely and separated out unless shaken. All these unexplainable aspects of his healing art enforced Doctor Dranks' reputation as a man initiated into impenetrable halls of knowledge.

Doctor Dranks seated himself while Adela joined her friends to continue her look round. It was very small and confined in there. Adela had never been able to decide whether it was meant to be a shop, or whether Doctor Dranks considered the room to be an actual part of his house. Perhaps there was an element of both in his arrangement; perhaps that explained the odd impression of deeply personal brooding in the atmosphere that made it vaguely disquieting to linger. She had a distinct impression that her examinations of his bottles and jars were considered by him to be not only inquisitive, but also intrusive and useless, founded as they were on uninitiated ignorance of their properties; and she wondered if the others felt the same way, since they were all now shuffling together in a tight bunch up and down the length of the counter. She looked back at Doctor Dranks. He seemed harmless enough, writing up a nostrum, absent-mindedly scratching under his hat with his goose-feather quill as he mulled over the combination of herbs and compounds needed for his latest remedy. In front of him was a glass bottle containing a suffering querant's waters, and next to it a chamber pot with a liberal sample of the same querant's dung. He was lost in thought, still considering his patient's case, and seemed to have entirely forgotten there was anybody else in the room. Yes, she was almost sure he was harmless.

She was still deliberating on this when the doorway darkened and a very tall, very lean figure momentarily filled the frame. It was the pedlar, Tony Lightfoot. Unconsciously, Adela took a step backwards and retreated to the shadowy end of the counter, even though her senses told her she must already have been seen by the alert, observant man. She couldn't help it, the pedlar frightened her. The stringy figure walked in, still dark against the open doorway, and swayed across the small room on his long, over-extended legs, his coat tails flapping about his ankles as he walked, bringing with him the redolence of damp leaf mould and churchyards. Without so much as a glance at the young people, he went over to Doctor Dranks, who seemed only to come up as far as the top of his thighs, and stooped low over the table and the old man. The musty odour carried on swirling about the room in the same manner as the coat-tails: not a dirty smell, nor exactly unpleasant, but it wasn't altogether nice, either. Adela turned away and discreetly covered her nose. She didn't want to upset anyone, but that perennial sooty, inky sourness was as off-putting to her as his outlandish appearance. Both made her want to keep her distance.

The pedlar exchanged a few short words with Doctor Dranks and handed over something small inside a knotted handkerchief. Doctor Dranks, who either had no sense of smell or else was used sitting in the middle of peculiar emanations, tucked the handkerchief and its contents into the fold of his robes and continued his inspection of the bowl of dung without saying anything. The pedlar turned, and in three long strides left the room as silently as he had entered. It had probably been no more than a delivery of some collection of quaint or rare herbs requested by Doctor Dranks, located, collected, dried and parcelled up by the pedlar as he had come across them on his travels, and yet the interlude seemed an odd happenstance to Adela. To her, it held an odd air of secretiveness that went beyond what was required for mere discretion – if discretion was necessary for such transactions. But was it so odd? She mentally shrugged at her ideas. She wasn't used to being at close quarters with that strange, itinerant man, that must be it – and when added to Doctor Dranks, a ghoulish atmosphere was bound to be created between the two of them...

During this time, the boys had discovered a fascinating glass container at the far end of the counter, apparently full of dried pithed frogs. A second, similar glass jar proved to be packed with sloughed snake skins, and a fully articulated snake's skeleton, complete with fangs, was coiled up nearby. Viewed collectively, they made a satisfyingly macabre spectacle. While Adela looked over a display of cachets containing a selection of mixed spices for mulling wines and ales, which was the only concession to the Yuletide season Doctor Dranks had made, the boys clustered around the reptilian remains exclaiming quietly to themselves. Within a few minutes, Aaron was pronouncing the snake's fangs to be nearly as long as Tom's, and offering to measure them up to prove it when Tom made objections to the comparison. His next suggestion was a duel, inviting Tom to use a prickly tongue-shaped object as a weapon, and choosing something small and leathery he had just picked up and was waving around for himself. Adela suffered their nonsense just long enough to make her selection, then, giving them both a glare of silent reproof as she went by, she hurried off to pay for everything, making sure she positioned herself so her friends' misdemeanours were hidden from Doctor Dranks as she handed over her silver sixpence. She wasted no time in calling them away from a jar full of bright green beetles labelled *'Cantharis'* which was now claiming their attention, and insisted they take their leave at once, before the boys could cause any real offence by their spirited misuse of the items on display. They parted from Doctor Dranks with a few meek and formal words of thanks, and filed out one by one.

As soon as they gained the street, Tom reached into his pocket and pulled out a stained and partially shredded paper. It was wrapped around a handful of cut barley-sugar sticks, and he prised several of the pieces apart to hand round while they were edging their way to the top end of the Square. As soon as they were out of earshot of Doctor Dranks' doorway, Aaron looked back and breathed a noisy sigh of relief.

"Fancy keeping bits of dead serpent and bats and things in there," he began, dragging a piece of barley-sugar off its paper. "I swear some of those jars had things inside that were ready to start wriggling if you touched them. I bet they would come out after you at night if you slept there. And there was something else big and horrible in one of those jars a bit further down, something with big eyes. I could see them glaring at me."

"Was it ugly?"

"Yes, with these feeler-things, and..."

Tom drew his breath in sharply. "Yes, I saw it, too. Do you mean to say it *wasn't* your reflection?"

"I bet he's got poisonous creatures out the back that he feeds with bits of victim," Aaron went on, warming to his theme and ignoring Tom completely. "I bet that's why nobody knows what's out there. I bet anyone who did stray through that back door would get a poison dart stuck in them from behind and..."

"Victims? What, that old dodderer? Don't be stupid. Even Dame Merrick leaves that shop alive, and she's practically mummified. He'd never be able to subdue a victim."

"Unless it was you."

"Why me?"

"Well, look at you. Muscles like napkins and a bit of duck-weed for a moustache. You've got the physique of a gnat, mate. He could swat you with a butterfly net. You could be disembowelled and hung up to dry with a load of lost wayfarers and vagrants in his cellar by this time tomorrow, and nobody would know a thing about it until they missed you in the New Year. Got any more of that barley-sugar?"

"No. Not unless you take back what you just said about my moustache, I haven't. And he doesn't seem to have strung Tony Lightfoot up yet."

"All right, I take it back. Give me a big piece. Thanks. Plague victims? He could be capturing them when they come in for a remedy."

"Do me a favour. There aren't any plague victims round here."

"Exactly. That's because they're rotting away under his floor-boards."

"Aaron! Don't be so disgusting!" Adela was becoming appalled, but Andrew snickered at the notion.

49

"I bet he goes out at night and digs dead things up," Aaron continued, undismayed. "He's probably got the bodies of men taken down from the gibbet in there somewhere."

Tom pretended to consider the point. "Hanged men?" he said musingly. "Hmm. Nearest place of execution is Monmouth, mate, or the cross-roads outside Bristol. Heck of a long way to drag the bodies."

"Oh, do be quiet, you two," Adela scolded. "You're making me feel ill."

"Thank goodness we made it out alive," Aaron went on undeterred, fully intent on having the last word. "I swear he was watching me, I could feel the hairs on the back of my neck prickling. Another few minutes, and I reckon he'd have turned me into a toad."

"Well, what's wrong with that?" Tom asked, ever cheerful. "It's not that bad an end for someone like you. You'd fit into one of those glass jars a treat if he did. I could have you dried and put on the mantelpiece in our parlour. You'd look lovely."

Aaron took a while to cast off his shudders, but his mood rapidly picked up when they passed Allen Priest standing at the corner by the Town Gate playing a sprightly set of carols on his hurdy-gurdy. Allen had taken over from the mummers, who had moved off to do a tour of the taverns before they departed the town, and he gave the youngsters a friendly wink as they walked by. Aaron pulled out his pipe and waved it in return. He and Allen were well acquainted. Allen was one of the musicians who played with Aaron's father in the musical troupe.

A few yards further on, down the hill and across the Square, they came to the beautifully presented guns in the window display of Lloyd and Fletchers, the Chepstow gunsmiths. The boys pulled up, as they always did, to admire the weapons on their felt-covered mounts. Adela, who wasn't much interested in the attractions of firearms, left them to do their boys' thing together, and wandered on slowly so they would have all the time they needed to enjoy their in-depth perusal and discussions of the display.

She stopped beside Addiss's Bee Prodductes again. The brisk trading from earlier was beginning to slow down, and it was a nice, quiet spot for a wait. The lingering smell of bees-wax and honey hung all about the stall, tantalising, clean, and sweet; full of the forgotten days of summer. A tray of cut honey-cake was laid out at the front of the stall. It was there to be sampled, and Adela picked a piece up and chewed on it idly while she looked over some simple bees-wax candles. Mmm. Addiss's honey samples were always tasty. Behind her, she could hear the boys still avidly comparing the merits of a matchlock arquebus with the latest flintlock rifle. It was a discussion holding a lively level of interest that made it quite clear they wouldn't be moving on just yet.

Her sampling finished, Adela walked slowly up and down the length of half a dozen shop fronts. She noticed a small girl she hadn't seen before standing on a mounting step outside a cheap, run-down hostelry. She was a meagre little thing, wrapped around with a large discoloured shawl, and she was shivering visibly. The child's two large eyes fixed on Adela, who was still chewing the last remnant of her honey- cake, and those eyes contained a wolfish expression that leaked out all over the rest of the drawn, pinched face. Adela knew that look. It prompted her wordlessly to step back a couple of paces and take the largest honey-cake sample she could find from the Addiss's stall and pass it on to the girl, who ate it in one quick swallow and immediately asked for another.

Adela shook her head decisively. "That was a sample. You can only take one, or it's rude."

"It's not for me, it's for my little brother here," the girl said defensively, indicating a boy much smaller than herself sitting huddled at her feet. She eyeballed Adela again, and this time her eyes held a fierce unspoken challenge: one that dared the bigger girl to refuse her request, since she couldn't reach any of the cakes herself, the stall being set so high up.

She had to be older than she looked, this girl, she was so tough and defiant, but she seemed small, diminutive even, because she was a hunchback. A huge, angular hump rose up between her shoulders, lifting the right-hand side of her body until it was as high as her head, taking her right shoulder and upper arm with it until her chest itself was twisted half around. The rest of her was stooped down to accommodate this turn in her bony anatomy, making her unable to stand upright. She was probably about eight or ten years old, although it was difficult to tell with a body so wasted and asymmetric. A few scant locks of fine, silvery-blonde hair were blowing about her face, and these were also thin – thin, and so wispy that the strands barely covered her scalp. Swathes of featureless rags were padding her out against the cold underneath her great shawl, but she wore nothing on her feet except a few strips of curtain material which lapped up to her ankles. Someone had to have done that for her. She could never have reached down far enough to get the job done for herself.

Wordlessly, Adela took a decision. She gave the girl another piece of cake, which the girl passed on to the boy, who ate the morsel as voraciously as his sister had done hers. Watching him, Adela realised that her assumption that both were beggars new to the town must be wrong. A rough wooden box containing some homemade tapers lay on the cobbles at the boy's feet. They were not well made; they had far too much fat on the rush wicks, which would make them smoke copiously and drip all over the floor when they were lit up, but the girl was clearly attempting to sell them nevertheless, while her tiny brother sat with his hands cupped in the hopes of receiving an odd farthing or two in payment. Adela didn't fancy the girl's chances selling anything around Chepstow, where everyone made their own home products; but her mother had always impressed on her the importance of encouraging people who were trying to make an honest penny for themselves, so Adela bought a ha'p'orth of the awful tapers from the little girl's trembling fingers.

"Why, you're chilled to the bone," Adela began when their hands touched, but the girl stopped her at once.

"I'm all right, don't you worry about me," she said stoutly. "I shall stand a bit further out in the sun in a minute, when some more of these people have gone and there's a bit more room. I'll be fine then. I feel quite hot already – inside. And thank you for buying my tapers." Her hand clasped around Adela's halfpenny, and she added, in an aside, "They're good ones. One of the ships' cooks was throwing some fat out. I made them up last night while Anthony and mother were asleep." She looked down fondly at her little brother, whose whole body was shaking with cold under his rags.

By now, the boys had moved off from the gunsmiths and were making their way down the hill, still talking about guns and gun features. As soon as they noticed Adela, they sauntered over to join her. Tom pointed at the girl's tapers the minute he arrived.

"Are you selling those?" he demanded.

"What does it look like?" the girl answered, with a toss of her head.

"You want to watch out, Titchy," Tom said, tartly. "There's a tax on candles, didn't you know? If anybody catches you selling those things, they'll tell you to pay up, and if you can't find the money you'll be fined for a misdemeanour or put in the stocks. Plus you'll have to stay in prison until they hear your case. You'd do better not to sell these on the streets."

"These are tapers, not candles," the girl said, scornfully. "Can't you see?"

"They look more like candles to me."

The girl's confidence deflated slightly at this news. "Well, what am I supposed to do with them, then?" she demanded, looking slightly alarmed. "We've got to have some money, but I can't risk going to prison. My little brother needs me. My mother can't look after him."

Rigo stepped in. "If you'll c-come with me, I'll t-take you to my ship. Maybe some of the men there will buy these off you. We use tapers for lighting our pipes, but we usually make our own."

"I can't come with you," the girl said obstinately, still scared. "Just take the tapers for me while I wait here. You can bring me the money afterwards."

"Wh-Wh-What do you mean, take them and bring you the money afterwards?" Rigo barked, nettled, as Tom had been, by her attitude. "What do you think I am, a sl-l-lave or something? I'm not going to do anything just because you tell me to. I have things to do, the same as you."

The girl's face suddenly crumpled, and her bottom lip trembled. "I can't come," she repeated. "I have to get back to my mother. She's sick." Her voice became tremulous over the last two words.

"Oh. I'm s-sorry to hear that. What's wrong with her? Does she need some medicine or something?" Rigo's anger was readily replaced by sympathy, and he looked back the way he had just come. "There's an apo-po-pothecary just over there, across the Square. I'll go over and get him if you like."

"No! No, don't do that, she'll be all right – I think. All she needs is some good food to eat, and a better blanket." The girl fidgeted impatiently, as if she hated having problems, and wasn't comfortable about owning up to them. "I thought if I could sell these tapers, I could get the things she needs myself. I don't think medicine will help. She had some before, and it didn't make her any better."

Andrew sat down beside Anthony and pulled him under his shawl to share it with him. Anthony leaned gratefully into Andrew's warmth, but his attention was all on his sister, and his bottom lip was quivering, too. The tears were not far off for him, either. His sister looked at him sitting side-by-side with Andrew and seemed to come to a decision.

"I'd better come with you, then," she said at last. "But it must only be for a quick visit. I'm not supposed to. Ma is afraid of the ships, and I promised her I wouldn't ever go on one."

"Listen, don't br-r-reak a promise made to your mother. That would be dishonourable. Just come as far as the quayside by the ship and wait for me there. I'll do the rest. But why-y-y did your mother ask you to make this promise?"

"She's scared I'll never come back if I go on a ship. That's what happened to Dada, when Anthony and me were little."

"Then w-why not just t-tell her you are going to visit a friend and say you'll soon be back? You can leave your brother with her, so she won't worry so much. And I don't mind calling myself your friend, if it will help."

The little girl's head sank down. "I can't," she said. "I can't tell my mother a lie. And if I could, it would only scare her worse to hear something like that. We don't have any friends. Or family. She knows that much, because we're on our own in the world, but she doesn't really understand anything else. She's still waiting for Dada to come home, because he looked after her, and she's frightened she might lose us before he comes. My mother is a natural, you see."

"A n-n-natural what?"

"She means her mother is a simpleton," Tom explained. "She's been born with a weak mind, so it doesn't work well enough for her to think for herself. That's why she's called a natural." He turned his attention to the little girl standing in front of him. "What's your name? And how old are you?"

"Christina. I'm eight. So, what's yours, and how old are you?" It was all couched badly, and made her sound cocky and rude again.

"I'm Tom," he said, breathing out heavily. "And I do wish you wouldn't be so hostile when we are trying to be helpful. Who is your mother?"

"She's called Poppea," Christina said, slackening her defences slightly. "I know it's a funny name to English ears, but she's foreign. Dada brought her back from one of his voyages at sea. She's never learned to speak English. Dada could talk her language, and he knew how to say things in an easy way so she would understand. I know just enough to talk with her a little bit, but she can't make herself understood to other people, so she can't talk to strangers when I'm not there for her. I'd better get back to her now," she added, and hastily gathering up her tapers, ready to depart.

"*Okeh*, well, w-w-we'll come with you then." Rigo took her tiny hand in a spontaneous gesture of friendship. Anthony stood up at the same time, mirroring his sister's every move, and began to shiver again when Andrew's shawl fell off his shoulders. Rigo hoisted the little boy up onto his hip with his free hand so he could carry him, hitching him up as far as he could under his oil-cloth jacket, and then moved Moonlight onto the boy's shoulder to top off the arrangement. Anthony didn't speak, but he looked delighted, smiling broadly as he peeped out from his new vantage point. Christina looked proudly up at him from Rigo's other side.

"This b-b-boy is very young," Rigo commented. "He ought to b-be with his mother."

"He's just one year younger than me," Christina answered. "He's seven, but he hasn't grown properly. We don't know why. His back is straight, not like mine, but he hasn't got any bigger since he was about four, and he still can't talk. I think his mind is like Ma's. At least she doesn't worry about us, if we don't stay away from her for too long. She only worries about things like food and blankets. I hope Anthony will be the same, and not have to worry about bigger things in life."

"Where are you staying? Lodgings?" Tom asked.

"We were, but now we have no money left. We don't beg," she added, in another outburst of defiance. "We never beg. We're all right, I can look after us. Mother is resting in an empty storehouse until I get back. Perhaps we'll be able to find somewhere better to sleep tonight if I can sell the rest of these tapers."

Rigo led the way. They left the bottom end of the market and entered Roper Street, going past Hedley's stable-yard, where Timothy was stabled for the day. Tom spotted him tethered with other horses at the outside wall, calmly eating from a trough, and went over to make sure he was comfortable, adjusting the rug and harness on his back and patting his flank. Timothy turned his head to acknowledge Tom's attention, and nuzzled him before going back to his eating, making an idle clomp of his great equine feet to discourage Nick's two dogs, who were sniffing around in the straw. A few rough woollen horse blankets had been heaped over a trestle at one side of the wall. They were a bit dusty, and some had a few moth-holes in them, but they were all still useable. Tom looked them over and selected the best one and put it over his arm. Then he patted Timothy goodbye and returned to the others, who were now passing the time of day with a man selling rabbits strung from a long pole he carried on his shoulder.

"This is Timothy's," Tom explained, as he re-joined them. "Or if not his, then it's another like it. We keep a blanket here at the stable for him. He has another spare at home, so I can easily bring that for him next time, to use instead. He seems fine with just a rug today. Christina can have this for now, to keep the cold out. It's not great, but it's better than nothing."

Christina and Anthony had been taking it in turns to hold Moonlight while they had been waiting, the little bird submitting to their attentions with little squeaks of protest. Once Tom returned, Moonlight struggled free and hopped back onto Rigo's free shoulder, and they left the rabbit-man and continued walking on slowly, following the long road down to the port.

They passed the Pig and Parsley tavern, where they found themselves under observation from a group of men sitting outside warming themselves in a patch of early afternoon sun. Several empty jugs discarded on the pavement by the men's feet stood testament to the amount of time these men had already spent idling there, drinking beer and watching the comings and goings of the marketplace, trading insults with people they knew and shouting comments after those they didn't. They nodded to Rigo watchfully when he drew abreast of them, then one drew his face down into an ugly scowl.

"Now then, young Rigo," the man grated roughly. "You did ought to watch out for the company ye keep."

"Wh-Wh-What do you mean?" Rigo asked, stopping abruptly to address the man. "What's wr-wr-wrong with my company?"

"Take no notice," Tom said in an undertone, trying surreptitiously to push him on. "He doesn't mean you, he means us. Just carry on walking."

"No," Rigo said, irritably, shrugging Tom off and starting to walk back. "I know th-th-this man, he is from my ship. He's always b-bugging me. What do you mean, Ezra? You know I don't like it when you say these things to me."

"Ha!" Ezra said with bitter contempt, spitting down at the empty ale jugs and missing them by several inches. "Just take another look at that young imp what's a-comin' after ye." He pointed openly at Christina with his pipe. "Devil-made, she be. I seen her afore, up the market, an' here she be again, like a gruesome shadder o' death. I reckon her for a witch, an' a bride o' Satan, that's what her do be; an' a mort o' bad luck it is for any man from our ship to be about her. Get out of her sight, afore she curses ye, an' ye bring a bad spell aboard."

Rigo turned and looked Christina over. "What's wrong with her?" he demanded, baffled, once his inspection was done. "What are you talking about?"

"Ah! She be made all wrong – her an' that great creepin' spider-man what do come and go like a ghoul in the night-time round these parts. I reckon he be a blood-suckin' vampire, a-drainin' the life-blood outa God-fearin' men's veins while they do sleep, an' her won't be long after him." He solemnly pointed at Christina with his pipe again.

"A-A-Are you crazy?" Rigo asked, annoyed. "She's fine. She's just a li- a li- a little girl. So, she has something wrong with her back. So, what?"

"I'm not a witch, you old fool, I'm a hunch-back," Christina interrupted hotly, flaring up in an instant and preparing for an immediate affray. "That doesn't mean I've been cursed. My back is deformed because that's the way I was born, that's all. Happily, the rest of me is in terrific shape and always has been, my mind most of all. *That* is excellent, thank you, and plainly far superior to yours."

Tom quietly caught at Christina, and began forcibly to move her along the street, but Christina was not to be deterred. Her defiance was at the forefront once more.

"I see you were born whole," she called out to Ezra, as she struggled against Tom. "Which presumably means you were also born sound. It's a pity you haven't put God's graces to better use…" By now, Tom was almost lifting her off her feet to carry her off, and she was struggling wildly in his arms. "…You could have done with them, because you haven't turned out too well yourself."

"Why, you little minx," the sailor exclaimed, jumping up and making to go after her, "I'll silence that tongue of yourn by slicing it a few inches shorter, if you don't keep it behind your teeth, where it b'longs!"

"Peace, Ezra, peace," said a young, curly-haired man, whom some called Mark, and others Raddish as they urged him, one after another, to restrain Ezra, which he did easily enough with just one hand. "Take no notice of Ezra," he called over to Christina, who had retreated with Tom to the other side of the street in alarm at Ezra's threat. "He's a Grubb by name, and a grub he is by nature. I'll see he does no harm to ye. But we sailors be a superstitious bundle o' men, an' afeard of such as you, who has the mark of the Devil on 'em. Better ye would have been to be drownded at birth than to live as you do, girl, for ye can't be called one o' the fairer sex wi' a body such as yourn. It will bring bad along wi' ye, wherever ye go, for sure."

"Rubbish," Christina yelled, undeterred. "We are what we are, all of us. Even one of our Kings was deformed, you ignorant man."

"Aye? Overlooked by such as you, was he?"

But Christina had the final word. "Overall, I'd say my body, grotesque though you may think it, is still more winning than any of yours. And my wits are definitely sharper – *and* more pleasing!"

Aaron and Nick had now joined Tom in hustling Christina out of sight before the disagreement could develop into anything more brutal. In the meantime, Rigo strolled along in the rear as though nothing was happening, having no interest in the argument, and absolutely no fear of the seamen involved. He was still carrying Anthony and Moonlight, and he was preoccupied with his own thoughts.

The lower parts of Roper Street were quiet, so after a bit Tom decided it was safe to take the walk more slowly. He set Christina back down on the cobbled road.

"I'm glad you aren't cowed by that kind of stupid hostility," he said to Christina, as he made sure she was balanced properly on her feet, "but I do think you should temper the things you say in return. I know it must be hurtful when people like that remark on nothing but your poor body…"

"They're mean and vile, and I don't care what any of them says!"

"Well you should care. Of course, no-one like me can have any idea of how it is to stand in your shoes and be you, but this much I can say: it's not going to help endear you to anyone, let alone men like those back there, if you fly in people's faces every time they make ignorant remarks to you. Or spiteful ones. Ill-bred folk are everywhere, in every walk of life, and we all have to deal with them, not just you. If we all start dog-fights every time we get upset, life will be just terrible for everyone. Try ignoring the cruelty, Christina. Talk to people nicely, as if they have been kind to you. At least then you'll be showing them a part of yourself they can warm to, which will be much better for you in the end. You don't want to get yourself remembered for the wrong kind of reasons in a town as small as Chepstow. The way you're carrying on, it won't be long before people will walk on by when they see you, knowing you for a sassy little madam they can't stand, rather than a sad little hunchback they would like to help. Pushed aside like that, you'll have to leave, because they won't give you any farthings then, tapers or none."

"Oh, hoity-toity," Christina said, stamping her foot. "What do you know about it? Or me either?"

Tom regarded her. "You're right, I know nothing," he said, starting to walk on after everyone else. "I beg your pardon. Do just as you please."

Christina followed him, and soon began to fall behind. She didn't ask anyone to slow down, nor did she beg for assistance. She lagged along in their wake until Rigo caught up with her. His pace was much slower, and he was still deep in thought, so he had quite missed her passionate exchange with Tom. Unaware of any disagreement, he gave her Moonlight to have on her shoulder while he adjusted Anthony so he could carry him for a while on his other hip.

"Is Moonlight a boy or a girl?" Christina asked, her volcanic fury swept aside by the little feathery creature so much more vulnerable than she was, who had been entrusted to her care by this kind foreign sailor-lad who seemed to understand not only her feelings, but also her condition so well that he didn't even notice them.

"Well, I d-d-don't know. I call him a 'he' because we can't have women on board a ship. It's bad luck, but I don't know if that applies to *animais* as well as people. And the first time M-M-Mark Raddish clapped eyes on Moonlight, he said he would st-st-stand and piss in a gale with a donkey if that bird has ever laid an egg. I guess if he was a girl he would have done by now, but I don't know. Not aboard a ship, I don't…"

The rest of the group suddenly exploded into full-throated laughter as they heard what Rigo was saying. Aaron, Tom and Nick almost collapsed, they were laughing so hard. Christina hesitated momentarily, but eventually joined in the mirth along with the others, although she didn't in the least understand what the laughter was about. But she was happy that her question had furnished a subject for merriment, and she felt that she had gained some sort of acceptance with them, thanks to Rigo's answer. The laughter broke down a lot of barriers, and as they continued their walk, a sense of companionship began to flow between them all that hadn't found an appropriate channel before.

Nick eventually remarked, "You seem to know an awful lot for a young kid, Christina. Fancy you know something about an English king!"

"Yes, I was thinking that," Tom said. "Who taught you about Richard the Third?"

"Who's Richard the Third?" Christina asked, solemnly. "Was he deformed as well, then?"

Tom nodded. "He was a hunchback, the same as you."

"Oh. Well, I only know about Ivarr the Boneless."

"Phtt! We actually had a king called…?"

"Go on! You're making it up!"

"Eva the what? *Boneless?*"

Christina nodded. "It's true. He had no bones in his legs. But he had a very strong body instead which made up for it, and that's what I meant. No matter how badly off a person is when they are born, they can make good use of what they have been given if they choose to — and I *do* choose to. And so did Ivarr. He fought without legs, and he still won all his battles. Only he was a Dane by birth and not an Englishman, so he was more of a Viking really – and he ruled in Ireland more than he did in England – but only because there wasn't a proper England to rule in those days because it was all separate Anglo-Saxon fiefdoms. He *was* a king, and he *did* conquer all those fiefdoms, so he *did* rule England, except it isn't in the history books because it was all in bits and bobs. But I wasn't about to explain all that to that lot back there. I'm not going to empty my head to fill theirs."

She carried on walking, her head held high, while the rest of the group fell in behind her, speechless.

Chapter Four

At the waterfront they threaded their way along the main street, which was the only one that had been cobbled and was relatively clean. All the rest were a network of muddy lanes and alleys spreading out from the waterside that nobody wanted to walk in unless they had to, making the press of bodies in the main street all the greater. The street ran right up to the waterfront, and then followed the wharf along a natural wide curve in the river. It was very busy. The friends worked their way round groups of men in heavy oilskins sitting on upturned fish creels playing games of dice, and through a course of common folk loitering for chin-wags between the stacks of produce from recently off-laded ships. They were headed for the main docks, where the principal business of the port was done. There, on the wharf and in long alleys made up of nothing but warehouses, longshoremen were lifting, carrying, carting, and hauling everything from great barrels of Hereford cider and country ales shipped down in small boats from Gloucester, to pipes and hogsheads of Canary and Madeira wines off a blistered old galleon making an onward journey from Bristol out of La Gomera. Casks of jenever and bales of wool from Holland, destined for the great houses in the Welsh Marches, were standing awaiting collection, as was a stack of good Flemish cloth that would finish up in the wholesalers of inland Welsh towns. Further along, barrels of wine from France had been temporarily pitched against open baskets of fresh laver weed from Pembroke, and piles of sea coal from Swansea spilled perilously close to salt fish in open boxes from Iceland. Waiting to be shipped out was some beautiful old timber logged in Redbrook, and a ship-load of ochre and oak bark tightly packed into hessian sacks brought down from the Forest of Dean.

It was a writhing mass of incessant activity, of shouting, crying, and bellowed warnings, many given just prior to a throwing out or dragging in of thick hawsers and barked heaving lines used for mooring the ships; and in every corner and at every mooring point, where ropes were being coiled or uncoiled beside the huge stanchions driven into the cobbles, a welter of orders were being issued with swearing, hectoring, loud bullying, and an immensity of energetic motion. And it all had to be finished before sundown.

Keeping close together, the friends picked their way carefully around the irritable and intolerant working men, and went on to where the great deepwater vessels were at anchor having their hulls careened. The crowds had thinned out as they left the fish market behind, but people were now replaced by seagulls and guillemots and cormorants. They now found themselves dodging sea-birds instead of people, ducking low under swooping wings as shrieking birds came in to land on abandoned rubbish at every turn of the walkways.

They passed the famous – or infamous – Cocklehouse, filled with sailors as always. Through its open doors and windows the jaunty sounds of a fiddle could be heard, played passably well, blending with a score of shouted conversations and blasts of sudden laughter, carried out on tides of warm air along with a smell of malodorous bodies, stale tobacco, and ale fumes. The cold harbour air outside was charged with a much more refreshing mix of sea-weed, fresh fish and river mud, all underpinning the clean smell of wet canvas and varnished wood.

There was an incoming tide so the water was rising, lapping high enough round the wooden slipways for the last of the fishing luggers bearing the day's catches to come in. The friends stood and watched their seamen take to small boats to pull the vessels in one after another. The skippers had already left, sharing a gig across to the wharf where enough water now swirled around the lowest stone steps for them to disembark and go up the steps without getting their feet wet. The next call for the skippers was obligatory, at the Harbourmaster's office, currently standing empty because the Harbourmaster was out and about directing mooring and docking procedures. Even empty it was a daunting building, carrying an air of somnolent importance, a sanctum into which only the very important could enter. Next to it the Revenue Surveyor's office, where all the goods coming in from abroad had to be registered and assayed, and another imposing place, this one of imperious officiousness: a fussy little neighbour to the mighty Harbourmaster. Inside, wool factors and customs inspectors were making laborious entries into great ledgers of the day's duties and customs payments due; the clerks inside too fully occupied to so much as glance up from their work, particularly at the insignificant trifle of a gaggle of youngsters peering in through the grey window from the street outside.

Down at this part of the river where ships were docked for repairs the air was full of pitch and tar: an intermittent penetrating mix of the sulphurous and sweet, pouring thickly out of bubbling tar cauldrons kept constantly hot over small fires all along the dockside. Afar from the repairs, and beyond the tarring of ropes and caulking of clean hulls, the boat builder's and rope maker's yards marked the extreme outer limits of the port and the docks. The entrances of both yards were open to the river, anyone could go inside, and the work in there would have made interesting viewing; but everyone was feeling the cold again, so instead of going in for a look, they turned and started to walk back.

Rigo pointed out one of the bigger ships moored at one of the slipways, where well-filled hessian sacks were being piled on the wharf one by one. "That's m-m-my ship," he announced. "They're j-just taking off the vanilla pods we brought out f-f-from Rio."

She was certainly impressive, stout and well found, though by no means anywhere near the biggest ship in the dock. Recently built, still reasonably fresh-painted about her decks, and with a hull well varnished, the ship was a two-masted brig of some two hundred and fifty or more tons, called the *Senhora da Luz:* the *Lady of Light.* A stack of barrels and several chests were already standing on the jetty beside the sacks, where more of the *Senhora da Luz*'s cargo had been previously discharged.

"We took that p-part of the cargo on when we put into port at Jamaica," Rigo informed everyone, pointing. "I recognise the chests, I handled them myself."

"Where's Jimayka?" Andrew asked. "It sounds like a racehorse's name."

"It's an island," Rigo said. "N-N-Not far from Brazil. We left Rio carrying vanilla pods and took on molasses and pimentos in Jamaica. But m-most of the cargo must still be on board. They haven't unladed everything yet."

No-one made any comment. It was obvious from the limited amount of cargo standing on the wharf that there must be plenty more still in the hold inside, but they didn't want to say anything. They were afraid that Rigo might start talking aloud about other things that were best kept quiet if they did.

"It still seems a bit strange to see a Spanish ship in dock here," Tom commented, to change the subject. "We don't get that many. Most of the ships in the English ports have been English, since the war."

"Wh-What war?" Rigo asked. "What's w-w-with you Englishmen? You are always fighting somebody."

"Yes, I suppose it does seem a bit like that. Well, there was this war with Spain that we had. It was quite a few years ago, and apparently, they stopped foreign ships coming in until it ended. That's as much as I know, really. I just heard Mister Noble talking about it to a client. I wasn't really listening at the time, it didn't sound all that interesting. Seeing your ship reminded me about it again, that's all."

"But m-my ship *is* English-built. She used to be called *Light o' Love*. Then she had another owner who re-fitted her. That's why her paint still looks fresh. He's the one who called her *Senhora da Luz*. But that was back in B-Br-Brazil, not in Spain." Rigo considered the matter. "She is still owned by an Englishman, I think. S-Somebody told me so, anyway. I don't know what the owner's name is, and I don't know if he is the same man as before. I only saw him once. But whoever he is, it must be *okeh* for him to send her here, because we flew the King's colours when we came into port."

Christina suddenly sprang into the conversation, completely diverting it. "There's all sorts going on, on some of those ships," she announced. "'Specially at night. I wouldn't like to go on them, I don't think. I've seen things."

The others stared at her, taken aback. "What things?" Tom asked at last, incredulous.

"Odd things. Secret things. Mostly it happens after dark. I think it might be something like smuggling. They talk in whispers like this..." She cupped her hand over her mouth. "And go into private huddles like the one over there..." She pointed at a secluded group in a far corner. "And then they all draw off again... And they use dark lanterns. I've heard the revenue men talk about those. You can tell when men are doing something bad, something that shouldn't be going on. When they are doing things they shouldn't be doing, anyway."

The others were following all this, utterly aghast. "Shush! For goodness' sake, keep your voice down, and keep your comments to yourself, Christina!"

"Yes, do!"

"That's right. You should attend your own affairs and stay out of what doesn't concern you."

"And you should attend to yours and stay out of what doesn't concern *you*. I don't need any of you to tell *me* what to do. And I'm not going to listen to your opinions."

"That's a very chancy attitude for a little girl like you to take," Tom warned her, sternly. "You obviously have no idea how much trouble you could wind up in if you carry on strutting about like this in public, talking about such matters at the top of your lungs."

"I don't see why," Christina said, robust as ever. "And I know that what I'm telling you is right, because I overheard Mister Nickerby say so too, and I don't suppose you'd tell *him* to shut up and attend to *his* own affairs. *He* said that people think the brandy smuggling is the biggest thing around here, but it's not. They are wrong. It's not the brandy, it's the wool, and it goes out by the boatload. That's what he said about the local smuggling, and he must know."

"Why must he know?"

"Because he's the parson and he said he knows a good deal more than he would like. He said he gets to hear too much about it, so there."

"I don't believe he said anything of the kind. I know Mister Nickerby very well. And anyway, if you were only listening, you presumably couldn't see, so how could you have possibly known it was him?"

"I know his voice, silly. It wasn't his pulpit voice, it was his ordinary voice, the one he uses when he's talking outside. It was funny. The vestry walls made his voice sound deep and throaty, like a bullock's. Especially when he coughed. And I could hear the noises he made pulling off his cassock and hanging it up."

"What on earth were you doing, listening in on the parson's private conversation?" Tom asked, scandalised. But Christina remained unabashed.

"I was waiting for him to come out so I could ask him to look in the church's charity chest and see if he had a cloak for Mother. It was the end of service. But when I overheard him say that, I thought it sounded interesting, so I listened to hear what he would say next. Only he didn't say anything else. And I didn't find out who he was talking to either, because the curtain was pulled right across so I couldn't see; and when they came out I had to hide in one of the pews, or they'd have known I had been listening. But…"

"Good grief, Christina, is there anything you won't do?" Tom cried, full of horror. "You're a proper little sneak, aren't you? You are obviously overhearing some highly dangerous conversations. You'll find yourself on the receiving end of some dreadful reprisals if you carry on like this and get found out. There are some terrible men involved in these kinds of business, to say nothing of the roughnecks out there on those ships, any of whom could come across you in a couple of footsteps. Haven't you got any sense at all? Use your intelligence, then we won't need to interfere with you."

But Christina was already starting to skip over the cobbles ahead of him, playing an imaginary game of hopscotch. "Look at me," she said proudly. "I may have a bad back, but my legs work all right, don't they?"

She had no real interest in any of it.

They had carried on walking upriver past the Cocklehouse during this altercation, and they continued to walk in silence for a few yards more, each busy with their own thoughts. Then Christina suddenly pulled at Rigo's hand and directed him towards a disused storehouse, saying, "Look, look. This is where we're staying. In there." For her, the recent differences were already forgotten.

Standing at the end of a small, unfrequented alley, not far from where fishwives were calling catches and humping barrels of mussels and whelks, several rotten old wooden buildings were decaying and falling into the ground. The warehouse Christina had indicated was the last one left fully intact, but even it was teetering on its wooden stilts, barely clear of the low-lying, muddy, almost unusable ground. This was the oldest part of the port, containing the most tumble-down buildings. Here, where the walls ran continually wet, and there was rising damp from the boggy ground, it would not be long before this, the last of these buildings, fell apart like its neighbours.

Meanwhile, Christina's warehouse went completely unnoticed. Too tatty to keep out the rain, and therefore useless for storing goods inside, it showed signs of having been once boarded up, but the rotting timbers had given way in several places and Christina was easily able to slide her scrappy little body between the warped planks of wood to squeeze herself inside. She leaned back through the gap and gestured for the others to follow. Anthony went first, handing Moonlight back to Rigo before going inside, and then the others followed one by one.

It was so dark under the saggy, dripping eaves that for several minutes no-one could distinguish anything at all. They could hear only the scampering and scratching of rats frolicking somewhere in the dirt along the far wall. Closer to, a rustling of straw betrayed the presence of a person, and after a short silence, a woman's voice called out softly, "*Quem é esse?* Who is it?"

"*Sua eu, mãe.* It's me, Mother," Christina answered equally softly, approaching a woman who lay curled up in a small heap of straw which had been dragged up onto a small wooden pallet in the middle of the room to keep it dry. "I'm back. I've sold a few tapers, and guess what! I've made some new friends! I've brought them with me! They've been so kind to me and Anthony, I know you'll want to meet them and say *'dia bom'.*" She turned to the silent group still standing uncertainly near the distorted panel that had been their entrance. "She doesn't follow anything I say because she doesn't speak English, but I say it anyway because it makes her feel happy that somebody is interested in her. Just say good day to her like I said you would. Then you can go. Ma won't understand anything else, so it's no good you trying to talk to her, but she'll be pleased you came."

One by one, they all nodded a greeting, and then stepped back. It was all a bit awkward, and no-one quite knew what to do next.

Another few seconds of hesitation followed. Then Rigo stepped up to the woman with Tom's blanket, put it about her shoulders, and began talking to her earnestly and intently for several minutes in a foreign language. Christina listened to him, open-mouthed.

"Look at that! He can understand her," she whispered, amazed. "He can, look, he can speak Mother's language, the same way Dada did. Look at her, see how happy she is."

Her mother had sat forward, and was speaking rapidly to Rigo, clutching at his hands. *"Me chamar Poppea,"* she was saying, at the end. "Call me Poppea."

Rigo answered her, and then turned to the others. "She is f-f-from Portugal," he explained. "Did you know that, Christina?"

Christina shook her head. "I knew she came from somewhere foreign, but I don't know anything about where Porchygull is. All I know about my family is what the people in our village told me. Dada was the only one who really knew about us, and he has been gone for more than five years now. I don't really remember him. Ma doesn't know who she is, or where she's from. She forgets everything as soon as you tell her. That's why I have to be here to look after her."

"Our l-l-language in Brazil is Portuguese, the same as hers," Rigo said. "I can t-t-talk to her quite easily, but she only understands me in any lang-ng-guage if I talk to her like a child. She says her husband went on a big ship, and it lost him in the sea. She th-th-thinks he is coming home soon, and she is waiting for him. I think maybe the Spanish have taken him prisoner or that his ship is delayed."

"His ship is lost," Christina said, sadly. "I asked at the port they sailed from. A kind man at our church paid for us to go to Bristol so we could find out what had happened, and why he hadn't come home. That was a year ago. No-one has heard from his ship, nor seen it, for four whole years now, so everyone who was on it is declared lost, presumed drowned. That was what they told me in the office where his frigate was registered. Since then, we've walked from Bristol to Gloucester, so we could cross the River Severn to get to Chepstow. That was when my shoes wore out. We had no money to pay for the ferry. Or more shoes."

"Why did you come this far?" Adela asked. "Are you from these parts? I haven't seen you before."

"We're from Somerset, near Wells," Christina answered. "When they said in the Bristol office that Dada was lost, we came here to find his family. One of our neighbours in the village said Dada was born here, and that there's a brother who is married and settled here; but we don't know who he is, or where he lives."

"What's your father's name?" Tom asked. "Maybe I can find out for you."

"My father was Hebron Guyles. But your Town Clerk says there are no Guyles living in Chepstow, nor anywhere round these parts. When he said that, I didn't know what to do. Ma is ill. She has a soft cough and spits blood. I've heard that cough before. The milkmaid on one of the farms in our village had it. It's called the tissick, and it means Ma will soon die, the same as Rosie did."

Everyone looked at her, then at each other. They were distressed by her matter-of-factness about her family's awful plight.

"We'll help you," Adela said, after Andrew had wordlessly tugged at her sleeve to urge her to say something. "I don't quite know how, but we'll do what we can. All of us."

"I don't want money," said Christina, stoutly. "Nor pity, nor prayers, unless you believe God can deliver our father back to us. If you think he is dead, like the man in the office, then wish us good luck with finding Dada's family, and let us be. We'll be all right. I can look after us all."

Chapter Five

Adela and Andrew, Nick, Aaron, Tom and finally Rigo, left the old shed the same way they had all gone in, squeezing through the boards one at a time. Once outside, they walked out of ear-shot, and then stopped.

"They should g-get out of that old house," Rigo said, before anyone else could say anything. "Th-That family will all die if they stay there. It is dangerous, and bad people could come by. And P-P-Poppea is sinking fast. I think she has *tuberculose,* the coughing sickness that makes you waste away. I've seen it before, many times. A lot of people in the ports have it, and most of them die. But I think it's better if her children don't find that out."

"Too late, they already know," Tom said. "Or, at least, Christina does."

"What?" Rigo was startled. He hadn't followed the conversation that had taken place in English, because he had been focussed on the sick lady. "Oh, w-well, maybe I should t-t-talk to them about it when I see them again. I don't know. I'll have to think. P-Poppea might still get better yet, if she goes right away from here to live in a warm country."

"Huh. Fat chance of that," Nick said.

"I'm going to call on Kitty's mother, and see if she can put them up," said Adela. "She might have a spare bit of floor in her boarding house, if some of her sailors go home to their families while they are on shore leave for Christmas. Poppea will soon warm up, then. And maybe our own mother can help, too. She makes simples and cures. Maybe she can give Poppea something to take for her lungs. It's just awful for poor Christina to be trying to keep her family together like this. She is so little herself. She needs help, too, although I doubt if she would accept it."

"Not likely," Aaron agreed, speaking for the first time. "We can all see she likes to be independent. But I'll ask my mum to look them out some warmer clothes, in the absence of the prospect of a warmer climate."

"… And I'm going to find out what I can about the Guyles," Tom said. "It should be straightforward. If Christina says there were some around these parts, she'll be right. She's a spry little thing; she won't have made a mistake about something like that. I'll look in the parish registers and ask the priest and the parson. They might know something, if the Town Clerk doesn't."

"And I could ask at the farms as I go around, see if they can do with two children and a woman." Nick frowned and pulled at his lower lip as he deliberated. "There won't be any field-work at this time of year, but the hoeing will start in the spring; and there might be some barn-work they can manage before then, winnowing chaff, or something like that. At least they would be warmer and drier than they are now, and they would be fed, and allowed to sleep in the barn. We'll surely come up with enough useful ideas to be of assistance between us, we're bound to." He noticed Rigo looking thoughtful. "Are you all right, friend?" he asked.

"Sure," Rigo answered. "I was j-j-just thinking I m-m-might see if I can get them a passage on a ship somewhere, but I don't know if that will be possible if they have no way to pay. It makes me even more certain I need to get some money tonight. If I can get a few crowns out of it, that might be enough to get them abroad."

"A few crowns out of what? Are you talking about a run? They are definitely doing one tonight?"

Rigo nodded. "F-F-From the *Senhora.* I'm going to try and get in on it. It's not just about giving away money; it's about s-s-saving a life. It will be my *caridade,* my charity to pay for my penance."

"Penance for what?"

75

"I d-d-don't know yet, I'll find out at m-m-my next confession. I need money, so I intend to help with this contraband to get some. If I break any of God's laws doing it, the p-priest will tell me when I get back to Brazil."

"Are you a Papist, then?" Aaron asked.

"Sure," said Rigo. "W-w-why, what are you?"

"Reformer," Aaron said, simply. "My father was a foot-soldier in Cromwell's army. He fought the Cavaliers in the Civil War: *they* were the Catholics. Sorry," he added.

Rigo shrugged. "He didn't f-fight me, so I am n-not upset. I don't know what this civil war is. Tell me sometime. In the m-m-meantime, with any luck, I'll be too busy keeping out of sight of the customs men to worry about old English causes."

Nobody answered him. They had already given voice enough to their thoughts regarding the danger of what he was proposing.

"Where and when shall we meet up again?" Nick asked. "I have to go now. The *Portabella* will be docking with this tide, and she's bringing my Christmas oranges and lemons from Seville for the Squire. I'm hoping I can get a good, big delivery if I hang around when they unlade her."

"I have something else to do until this evening, as well," Tom said, thinking of Kitty. "I might have to join you later on."

"But what if Rigo lands himself in trouble tonight?" Andrew piped up. "How will we know? I don't want him to be caught."

"I'll leave M-M-Moonlight behind on the ship. Come and ask for me in the morning. If anything has happened to me, he'll be there on his own," Rigo said solemnly. "But I w-won't get caught, I'm used to staying out of trouble. I grew up in Santa Teresa, in Rio de Janeiro. It is very tough to live there. I think it is the worst place I have ever been. When I w-was a little boy, we had to run for our lives when soldiers and sailors came, or any of the other bad men who come to take children away. Here in Chippistow it is l-l-like a little village, very calm and restful. None of your King's men will be able to catch me."

No-one argued. They were sure that Rigo could, indeed, take care of himself. It wasn't his courage they doubted, it was his lack of experience with English authorities that worried them.

"Just watch out for yourself," Tom said, at last. "You could easily walk into a trap, because you have no idea what may be contemplated by English minds. English soldiers don't just chase along the street after you, you know. It's not the fastest runners who evade our customs men."

"What are these things you are talking about?" Rigo demanded, looking puzzled.

"He means the men hide and lie in wait, then jump out at you," Adela explained.

Rigo's face cleared. "Ah! The *e-e-emboscada*! But we have these in my country also. I am above this. I will not get trapped."

"Just as well," Aaron commented under his breath to Nick, who was standing next to him. "I reckon Rigo is too fat to outrun anything faster than a dead weasel."

Chapter Six

Tom and Adela made their way up the hill together, going by way of Steep Street for a change, with Andrew lagging along behind. They split up in Beaufort Square. Tom took Andrew with him to groom and water Timothy, because Andrew thought that was a real treat, and Adela turned off into Bridge Street and headed back down the hill to call on Martha Hillenjaar, Kitty's mother.

The houses in Bridge Street were very tall and narrow, all seemingly squashed up tight together, some standing as many as three storeys high above the street, with two or sometimes three storeys set below, built into the diminishing hillside where the ground fell away to the river. It made them ideal as boarding houses, and most of the occupants let some of their rooms. Kitty and her mother, Martha, lived in the two basement rooms of their house, and Martha rented out the rest, giving rooms mostly to the higher-ranking sea-farers such as mates and skippers, but occasionally to other tidy-looking travellers who came by. It kept her, and her daughter, very comfortably; and compared with many other families in their situation, they lived very well. Kitty's father had been a ship's captain who had died during a battle at sea. He had left Martha the house in his will, but no money. Taking in lodgers had been all she could think of to make a living as a young widow, and it had turned out to be a good decision. Kitty was now an energetic and vivacious girl of fourteen: dark haired and wild-eyed; much admired and sought after by the local boys, of whom Tom was one.

The door was answered by the scruffy little boy they called Jolt, who acted as servant and general factotum to the whole household. Normally, the front door would have been standing ajar whatever the weather, but with winter advancing and temperatures outside now so cold, it had to be kept fully closed to keep the house warm. He gave Adela his usual cheeky salute, and then led her at a clattering speed down the unlit wooden staircase that sank into darkness in a narrow spiral. Adela followed him at a more sedate pace, carrying her full basket held out in front of her. They crossed a narrow, windowless landing on the lower ground floor, and went on down to a basement where an uneven latticed window admitted desolate winter daylight from a bare garden outside.

Martha was bent in front of the fire, fastening two nets of winter kale into a large cooking pot that already contained a huge piece of simmering meat. This, together with the two quartern loaves cooking on a shovel laid at the edge of the fire, was to be the evening meal for her lodgers.

Adela settled on a little stool in the inglenook by the stone fireplace and watched quietly as Martha mixed up some flour and raisins to make griddle cakes, always popular in that part of the country because they were so easy to bake over an open fire. Martha checked the loaves before removing them from the shovel to a little trivet beside the grate, and replaced them with a batch of griddle cakes.

"Keep an eye on these, will you?" she asked of Adela. "Turn them over when they're ready, and don't let them burn."

Idly, Adela wondered why Martha never used the big bread oven built into the wall on the side of the fire where she was sitting. It was very large, well blacked, and was kept bolted shut by the use of two great sliding bars. She put her hand out and felt the oven door. It was warm only; perhaps it never got hot enough to be useful. Two smaller ovens on the other side of the fire were in full use, one for baking and the other for warming and drying. Today, some washed and wrung-out clothes were draped over a wooden clothes horse in front of them, steaming in the steady heat. The Hillenjaars' small back garden was too dark and damp for hanging out washing, it never got the sun.

"I came by to wish you the season's greetings from my mother," said Adela, choosing her moment to introduce the topic of Christina. "… And I wondered as well if you could consider helping me and my friends with assisting a family we have just met. They seem to be in a really sorry state."

She put the first of the cooked griddle cakes onto a clean cloth. It already held half a dozen browned bread loaves, and as she added another batch of griddle cakes to the shovel, Adela told Martha about Christina, and her brother and mother, and of their straitened circumstances. She had been hoping for an offer of some sleeping space on the floor, or perhaps even some room upstairs in the tiny attic where Jolt slept, but Martha listened without comment until she had finished.

"I'll be more than happy to send some food and blankets down to this lady and her children," Martha said at last. "But before I offer anything other than that, I should like to look at the mother, and satisfy myself that she is respectable and wants to get herself back on her feet again. I won't support ne'er-do-wells; such folk are better left alone until they get straightened out and into church. And I can't carry those that won't bother to shift for themselves, either. I have enough burdens of my own."

Despite the lack of warmth in her words, however, she sent Kitty upstairs to look over some old clothes, outgrown and put aside, and to fetch two clean blankets.

"If you will be so kind as to extend an invitation to Poppea to come up tomorrow with her children, she can spend Christmas Day here with Kitty and me," Martha told Adela. "We'll take it from there. If they say they can't come, I'll take it that what I've done for them today is sufficient for their wants."

Meanwhile, Kitty had wrapped up a bundle and put it in Adela's spare basket. As an afterthought, Martha added a few griddle cakes. Adela stopped long enough to take a drink of a sweet nettle wine and make use of the closet out in the back garden, then took her leave with some very sincere thanks. To her surprise, Kitty quietly followed her up the stairs.

"I have to go and see someone," Kitty whispered, as she and Adela wrapped themselves up closely in their shawls on the doorstep, preparing to step out into the rapidly cooling air and diminishing sun.

"Who?" Adela kept her voice low, too, even though they were alone. They had left Martha alone in the kitchen, folding washing.

"Tom!"

"Tom Meadows?"

"Yes! Don't tell anyone about it just yet."

"I won't, you can trust me. But is it a secret?"

"Not secret, but I want to be private about it. I don't want anyone telling my mother. She thinks I'm too wayward and flighty, as it is."

Adela privately thought the same. She wished Kitty was sincere, whilst doubting if this assignation was anything more than a bit of fun for her. She hoped Tom had a heart that would not be too easily touched. Adela knew as well as anyone how many of the boys were vying for Kitty. She could have any one of them she pleased.

They walked side-by-side as far as the Pig and Parsley, where they parted company. The pavement was now empty, the unsociable sailors being long gone. Adela carried on alone, her combined baskets heavy, her mind occupied.

She found Poppea and Anthony on their own, resting weakly on the pallet with Tom's blanket pulled up around them. Adela realised at once that it would be no good extending Martha's kind offer to Poppea, it had to be Christina. Accordingly, she did no more than quietly add the two new blankets to Poppea and Anthony's covering and put the dresses and griddle cakes beside them, while Poppea murmured something inarticulate that might have been thanks. Adela assumed Christina must be out and about, trying to get rid of her tapers again, so, after giving Poppea a few nods and smiles, she left the mother and child and went to see if she could find her. She couldn't spend too long looking; it was time to go home, and she still had to find Andrew. The temperature outside was dropping rapidly, and it was growing very chilly.

Luck was with her. Andrew and Tom had left Timothy enjoying the last few rays of the wintry sun, and they met up with her a short way along the wharf almost as soon as she had stepped out of the warehouse. Tom immediately made his farewells to Adela, apologising for his haste, saying he had to go up into town and meet up with someone. After he had departed, Adela and Andrew carried on walking by the riverside until they arrived at the coracle.

To their surprise, they found Rigo crouched on the river bank waiting to see them off. Christina was tucked in beside him, huddled in to keep warm, protecting herself from a biting wind funnelling along the river with the sinking sun. Moonlight was asleep on Rigo's shoulder between them, with his head tucked under his wing. While Adela passed on Martha's message to Christina, Andrew held out his hands for Moonlight and pointed out the candle glimmering in the window of their cottage across the water, set there to light their way home. Rigo stood for a while and looked over at the welcoming glow himself, as Adela untied the coracle and dragged it the short distance to the wooden jetty at the end of the wharf, ready to get in. When he noticed what she was doing, he picked up the baskets and put them in the bottom of the coracle behind the thwart for her, and then held the painter.

"This is a n-nice little boat," he said, stepping back an arm's length and surveying it. "Like the ones the P-P-Potiguara Indians have in my country. They are great fishermen."

"Thank you," Adela said. "It belongs to our family. My Welsh grandfather gave it to us. He isn't a fisherman, so it was of no use to him. Andrew and I won't be able to fit in it comfortably for much longer, even though it's quite big for a coracle. It's still only meant to hold one man."

Rigo nodded. Then he looked round for Moonlight, who was now with Christina. "Hey! Kid!" he called to her. "We have to go. Br-ring Moonlight over and say 'goodnight', it's time to hit the trail. I've st-still got to sell your tapers, yet."

"Couldn't you do the selling for her and let her go back to her mother?" Adela pleaded, as she gathered Andrew into the coracle in front of her and prepared to cast off. "It *is* winter, and it's dusk, and it's freezing cold. This is no time for a little child with her chest to be out inhaling damp river vapours."

Adela could just discern the dark shape of her grandfather in the gathering gloom on the opposite side of the river, standing at the mooring post set below their house. He had come out to wait for her, obviously thinking along the same lines. She would have to go at once, and trust Rigo to do his bit.

Rigo followed her glance across the river, then nodded. "Sure," he said. "Ch-Christina can only come as far as the quayside w-without breaking her promise, anyway. It makes no difference if she is with me, or not. I think it will be better if I leave her with her mother and brother i-i-in that old warehouse. I don't want to risk her running her mouth off again."

He exchanged a smile with Adela, then stepped back from the jetty as Adela drew away. It was a sweet smile, warm and friendly. Adela gave him and Christina a wave, feeling glad to have made the acquaintance of this unusual and compassionate young man, with his dark, flashing eyes and good looks. Despite his eccentricities, he was growing on her.

"See you tomorrow first thing," she called, and Andrew echoed her words, waving excitedly.

"You bet," Rigo called back.

Christina yelled over him at the same time, "I'll keep an eye on him, don't worry. And on Moonlight, as well!"

"Oh, I do hope so," Adela thought fervently, thinking of the hours of darkness that lay between now and then, and of the frightening activities Rigo was proposing to engage in that night.

"Please God Rigo will be safe, and Christina will stay away from more trouble!"

As she paddled rapidly away into the deeper, tidal portion of the water, Adela looked back over her shoulder and was just able to discern him, hand-in-hand with Christina, walking back to his ship.

Chapter Seven

Adela regularly crossed the river in the family's coracle at the same point just south of the Castle. She and Andrew were so used to rowing over the water that they had no fear of it. Adela's Welsh grandfather lived on top of the mountain ridge north of Chepstow, in the village of Devauden, several long miles from the sea. He was no fisherman and no craftsman either; his claim to the nominal ownership of the coracle was that his son had made it before he had left home. That had been way back. After that, he had skippered his own fishing lugger and married Isla, their mother. Adela remembered her father as a dark, serious man who made great use of his hands and did little talking. He had been drowned during a storm out in the Bristol Channel. Nobody knew how. His ship had just limped back home without him late one afternoon two winters ago, taking in water, both lugsails in tatters, bringing his crewmen bearing the bad news. On winter evenings, Adela and Andrew would still sit at the window in the bedroom and look out over the river and the town as if they were waiting for him to come home. That was how they remembered him, in the river's-edge cottage he had built for them all: the two children, their mother, and her English parents.

Their father had named their house 'Fox-Hole', giving the name from the way he had arranged it, tucked deep into the river bank like a fox's lair. It peeped out from beside a narrow lane, almost closed over by ragged twigs of pale elder and thickly tangled grasses, bordered by rustling leaves and tossing wild flowers, with even the small terraced garden dug into the steeply rising river bank behind having its own fringe. When she was in her bedroom, Adela could peer through the apple tree branches hanging low over the roof above her window and see across the water into Chepstow town, where rows of dainty-looking stone and timber houses lined the streets above the river. The Wye Bridge linking Chepstow to Gloucestershire took tolls from crossing travellers two furlongs downstream of them, and Adela could just about see the comings and goings there too, if she craned her neck when there were no leaves on the apple tree. The family hardly ever used the bridge; they mostly never went down that way, they just used the coracle to get about, instead.

Adela was very proficient at steering using the one paddle, even though she was only just big enough to reach over each side while she was using it. She made a slightly wavy progression, but if she held her course steady she bobbed along in the general direction she wanted, and could bring her boat in to land at the mooring post set just below her house. It was quite hard work, made much easier if she could time her crossing so she caught the tide when the river was nearly full of water, whether it was on the flow or the ebb. Otherwise, if the tide was too far out, she had to scramble up the bank through several feet of smelly mud; and if the tide was too high, she could be carried away by the water currents, especially if the river was in flood or there was a strong neap tide. When that happened, she would as often as not finish up out in the salt marshes and mudflats, which meant either a long wait for the tide to turn in her favour, or else a long and lonely walk home, depending on where she cast up. She wasn't afraid of such events, she had been handling boats almost as long as she had been able to walk, and had sense enough to keep out of real conflicts with the tides; but she did find the curlews mournful company when she occasionally became stranded out at the estuary.

Adela's grandfather was standing waiting for her in the long grass on the bank with his mongrel lurcher, Woody, lying quietly at his feet. Ronald Baker was her mother's father, a Lincolnshire man, who came from a long, long way away. He spoke a different dialect, he dressed slightly differently, and he had a different way of thinking from the men in the Forest of Dean.

"Now then, me ducks," he said, grabbing the painter and helping Andrew, and then Adela as they climbed out. "You took your time gittin' back. We was startin' to worry. Who was that wi' ye on the other bank?" He hitched the coracle to the post, leaving it upturned to dry out.

Andrew immediately took hold of his grandfather's hand and began to chatter excitedly. He started with Moonlight, went on to Rigo's fantastic ear-rings, and even got in a mention of Christina's hump and Anthony who didn't talk before they had crossed the lane, which was quite an achievement, because they were all moving quickly, passing through the garden and into the kitchen as fast as they could to get out of the cold and into the welcoming warmth. Woody, who didn't mind the cold, came trotting after them at his leisure.

Once everybody was safe inside, the door was shut fast with a draught excluder placed along the bottom, the fire was stoked up, and the contents of the baskets examined and approved of by Adela's mother and grandmother, Isla and Julia. Ronald took his usual seat beside the fire, where he sat impassively, alternately chewing on the stem of his pipe and puffing on it, stroking the dog's ears and quietly asking Adela for details about her new acquaintances while the herbs were tied and hung up for drying, along with many others, on the wall nearest the chimney place, and the cheese, still in its cloth, put to store on the cold slab in the pantry. Only then did Julia and Isla feel able to come to join them at the fireside, first moving aside the two cats, Tansy and Queen Elizabeth, to make themselves room on the wooden settle. Tansy and Queen Elizabeth, most unwillingly displaced, yawned widely and stretched themselves out on the hearthrug to claim the fire in front of the dog instead.

Ronald spoke up first. "It don't surprise me they're doin' a run tonight," he began. "Ramsey Horne's doin' the night watch for the lower part o' the town, an' he's as deaf as a post. Has been for years. Got legs as long as a greyhound, owd Ramsey has, he could outrun anybody in his day, you could never have got away from him if he was after you when he was a King's man; but his ears is no good and never has bin. They could run barrels over the cobbles right beside him tonight, and he won't hear 'em. What are they bringin' in, Adela? Did this owd boy tell you?"

"He's Rigo, Grandad. The boy's name is Rigo. And no, he didn't say. I think he would have if he knew, but I don't think he has been told."

"So the top men are keeping it to themselves, then. Hmm. That's unusual. They must have a reason to."

"And are the top men from the ships? Or do they live in the town?"

"Now, that would be tellin'. Ask no questions, you'll be told no lies."

"I quite agree." Julia frowned. She disapproved of this turn in the conversation. "These are not matters for small children to be discussing, Adela. Say no more, please."

"Oh, but I am only asking because I was curious. It made me wonder. Have there been hangings for smuggling in these parts, Grandad?"

"Ah, but not for many years, lass. The last was about seven year ago. Four good men hanged then, and two more was shot in the takin' of them. That was a bad business. I wouldn't like to see it happen again."

"Nor would any of us." Julia seemed more distressed than reproving now, remembering it. "It was dreadful. Good men, as your grandfather says. All gone for nothing. And about eleven transported. It made a terrible impact on the families left behind. I don't think they ever recovered."

"Oh dear. It sounds serious." Adele fell silent while she considered. Then she began again. "I don't think Rigo can realise what danger there is in the risks he will be taking tonight. I wish the other men had told him, at least then he would have some idea, but I think I know why they decided not to. I think it's because he's not very good at keeping secrets. Not because he's careless, or untrustworthy, it's more that he can't see the point in being secretive. And, you see, whether they are right or wrong about not trusting him, keeping him out of the picture is exactly what could create a problem, because right now he doesn't seem to see why he needs to hide what they're doing at all. And I don't just mean the smuggling; he talks quite openly about all sorts of things that the rest of us wouldn't dream of bringing up. He's not careful of what he says, because he doesn't fear the consequences the way the rest of us do. He just ups and speaks his mind and faces people out in a way I find strange and a bit scary. I do believe he really and truly thinks nothing bad can ever happen to him or bring him down. I hope they won't run into any soldiers tonight because if they do, and they ask him what he's doing, he'll probably just go ahead and tell them, and then expect them simply to nod their heads and move on. He wouldn't expect them to act on principle instead of turning a blind eye; and that's the bit that worries me. I know he won't step aside to avoid trouble, if trouble comes. Or a fight. He'll tackle anyone, I've seen him. We ran into some sailors today who were really tough and unpleasant, and there was every threat of a physical fight; but Rigo confronted them without stirring a hair, and that encouraged Christina to see them all off. It's difficult to explain exactly what I mean. I can't quite make him out. Maybe it's because he's Brazilian. Maybe the things I find odd about him are a natural part of his culture."

"Of course, it's because he's Brazilian," Andrew chimed in. "Rigo wouldn't be Rigo if he was from any other country. He's great, Grandad. I wish you could meet him. And Christina. She's so rude to everybody, it's just brilliant. And Moonlight is fabulous. Can you get me a parrot, please? I want a bird that will say, 'go away, I hate you,' like Christina does."

"Did Christina really say that?" Julia glared at him, shocked, but Ronald chortled discreetly behind his pipe.

"Well, no," Andrew admitted. He was lying on the rag rug in front of the fire with the two cats, his feet up on the brass fender to warm them. "But it's the sort of thing she wouldn't mind saying. Christina doesn't care. I like her. She gives as good as she gets the minute people are nasty to her. It doesn't half make them sit up. You should have heard her with those sailors. It was funny. Tom told her off about it afterwards."

"I should just hope he did," Julia said, now pursing her lips. "Two wrongs don't make a right, Andrew – get your feet off the fender, please – and it is foolish to antagonise one's elders and betters. Children depend on the goodwill of the generations senior to them, whether they like it or not."

"Her whole family needs some goodwill, if you ask me." Adela commented. She was sitting on a low footstool beside her mother, resting her head against her mother's knee. "Can you make up a physick for Poppea, Mother?"

Isla considered for a moment before answering, and Adela lifted her head to look up at her. Isla finally smiled and nodded. "Yes, I certainly can do that," she said. "But I am turning the situation over in my mind because I believe cases like Christina's need handling with a degree of caution."

"I agree about that," Ronald said. "It's miserable to have charity pushed at you, however badly off you are. Nobody wants to accept it. They all try and fend it off if they can. All right, it saves folk from the worst of want when there's nowt else for them, but nobody feels better for havin' to take it."

"You've already told us how independent this little girl is and perhaps her mother is *compos mentis* enough to have taught her to be that way. If so, I applaud her for it. This family have already been forced to accept help from a churchman in their parish in Wells in order to get this far, so they may not wish to accept anything more. Remember, everyone has their pride, and everyone has their secrets, and they have the right to preserve them both. Christina and her mother should be the ones to decide what their needs are, and to state them when and where necessary. It should not come from us; nor should we be driving them to be answerable to us by putting them under an obligation. That would ride roughshod over their feelings, however good our intentions. And it may be that other people in the town will be better placed to give this family the right kind of assistance than we are. There is also the possibility that they have actively chosen to be itinerant, in much the same way that Tony Lightfoot has. If so, then that is their concern as well, and not ours."

"But Tony is a pedlar. He has a way of earning his living. Won't they get into trouble if they drift into vagrancy, Mother?"

"They will, if they can't get by with Christina's efforts at scratching a living by selling bits and pieces; yes, they will. That would not be good for any of them, which is why I have said 'yes' to your request. The best way for me to help them is to make the mother well, so I shall make up a bottle of physick which you can take over and give to Poppea in the morning. Hopefully, once she is feeling better, she will be able to find these missing relatives, and then they can take over the care of their own."

"Martha said almost the same thing when I asked her this afternoon," Adela said, thoughtfully. "She sent some food and blankets and said that would be all unless they are prepared to try to help themselves. And yet you said we should support people who are trying to make an honest penny, Mother."

"Indeed, I did," Isla agreed. "But support comes in many forms, Adela, and money isn't always what's most needed. And now," she continued, rising from her chair, "I shall make us all something to eat. Grandad found a few mushrooms this morning in Chapelhouse Wood. They'll go down well, I believe. Do you all agree? Shall I shall fry them up with some peese pudding and a few slivers of our sweet-cured ham?"

Tom, in the meantime, had plodded up the hill to the Pig and Parsley shortly after he had left Adela. It was a popular tavern, set at a conveniently short distance below Beaufort Square, yet well out of the mainstream public's eye, and so busy that two young people on an assignation would not be remarked upon, even if one of them was the attractive and sought-after daughter of a well-known local sea-captain who had met his end in the Spanish wars. Tom was very taken with pretty Kitty Hillenjaar. He had admired her from afar, the same as all the other town boys, for quite some time; but he had never spoken to her until one day when, quite by chance, she had come in to Mister Noble's office with her mother, who was drawing up a legal document. While Martha had been inside with Mister Noble doing the signing, Kitty had waited outside in the clerk's office with Tom, and he had managed to strike up enough of a conversation with her to make her acquaintance. This meeting at the Pig and Parsley was an important one for him. This time, he wanted to establish himself properly with her, and indicate the extent of his interest: to demonstrate that he was a man with good prospects, well above the common herd, and well worth her interest. He also hoped very much to find out more about her, and, if all went well, to accompany her back to her house afterwards so he could ask her mother if she would kindly give him permission to walk out formally with her only daughter.

Kitty was already waiting for him outside the tavern, with her shawl wrapped close about her shoulders. Tom spotted her first, and quickly set his hat more firmly on his head, making sure the feather was at the right angle, before he approached her. When she saw him, she waved and smiled in welcome, and then ran to greet him while he weaved his way around a small crowd of people gathered about a packer's mule which was occupying the whole of the nearby pavement.

The solicitous Tom offered Kitty his arm to lead her inside. Oh, she was pretty. He had chosen well. Demure, but with a hint of mischief, moulded delicately, like her mother, wild, dark hair and pale, translucent skin – and lips that constantly quivered on the verge of some secret, wry amusement. Bright, attractive blue eyes set off so well by those wonderful black eyelashes, which fluttered against her cheeks when she talked, like small provocative butterflies...

His private enumeration of her many merits only ended with their arrival at a rough bench in the dimmest corner of the farthest side of the smoky snug where, over a shared rummer of French brandy, concealed from observation by the dense market day gathering of bull-necked, sinewy farmers all standing in close formation and talking in huge voices, they sat together for an hour by the light of a solitary fuscous candle-gleam, and Tom talked of himself and his plans, and Kitty told him more about herself and her mother, and the candle in the wall niche guttered slowly down into its candlestick. To Tom's great satisfaction, as he shyly took hold of her hand, she agreed to start walking out with him, subject to her mother's approval, after Christmas.

They left the Pig and Parsley just as the main candles were being lighted, and sauntered together up to Beaufort Square, scarcely noticing the people hurrying home through the streets in the fading daylight. Slowly, taking their time, lost in each other, lingering now at Mistress Quarrel's milliner's window for Kitty to admire the bonnets, and then at Bradleys of Hereford, whose sets of fire irons, grates and ornate fenders were being brought in from the flagstones in front prior to closing, they crossed the Square together at the Broken Drum, and finally gained Bridge Street, where they walked ever more tardily, arm-in-arm, down to Kitty's house.

At the door, Tom removed his hat before ushering Kitty inside and following her downstairs. He then sat holding it carefully on his knee while he took a mug of hot ale from Missus Hillenjaar, and told her of his prospects and intentions, and begged leave to walk with her daughter on Sundays after church, once the celebrations for Yule were over and some better weather prevailed.

In response some meaningful looks from Kitty, Martha took the hint and told Tom she had no objections, and that he was welcome to visit over Yule so he could sit with Kitty in the company of her other guests, whenever he liked.

Privately exultant, Tom accepted the invitation, and exchanged some more pleasantries prior to making his *adieus* and excusing himself. Kitty escorted him upstairs to the front door and allowed him to hold her hand again before he left her, which he did with many a backward glance and the feather in his hat now rearranged to point in the other direction, so it swept gracefully over towards his left ear. He gave a final wave before turning to go on down the road to Nick's house at the bottom end of the town. Twilight was well advanced. It would soon be quite dark.

Chapter Eight

Nick's house was a roughly built stone dwelling consisting of one simple room, with an outhouse attached that served as a cow-stall for his ox. The entire place, garden wall, pigsty and all, had been built out of rubble left over from the town wall, and it sat, squat and dumpy, looking like a limpet among a host of similar dwellings, stuck close to the town wall in one of the poorest parts of Chepstow, down almost amongst the dock buildings.

At the sound of Tom's entry into the tiny muddy yard by way of a very squeaky latticed hazel-wood gate, the top half of the house door flew open and Nick looked out with some ready words of welcome for him. Tom stepped round a great pile of rough-hewn logs stacked beside the door for winter firewood, and entered the fire-lit room inside.

He found Aaron sitting with Nick's mother, drinking small-beer in front of the fire where, for his mother's benefit, Nick had hung up two boughs of yew on each side of the fireplace in token of the Yule celebrations. The multitude of tiny specks of red berries glowed richly in the light from the flickering logs, giving an attractive sense of simple festivity to the room and its furnishings, which comprised a wooden box-bed and clothes chest inherited from his mother's family, and a rustic table and bench made by Nick himself. Nick had no real interest in Yule or Christmas; he was hardly ever at home. He slept out at the farms or on the road with his dogs, making one day very much like another to him; but his mother enjoyed seeing the winter evergreens in her house. They reminded her of her days as a milkmaid up at the big farms beyond the ridge.

Nick didn't hang around once Tom was there. Leaving his mother and Aaron to finish their beers, he went outside with his dogs to yoke his ox into the cart, which had both been folded in the yard. Tom looked about him while he waited. It was difficult to tell which part of the house was in a worse state of repair: the part Nick and his mother lived and slept in, or the part next door, where the ox and the dogs lived. The thatch over the entire roof was quietly going rotten, sagging so badly now, under the weight of stones and straw bands holding it down, that it was about to fall in for good. Nick noticed the upward turn of Tom's eyes and nodded.

"Yeh, I know," he said. "Don't tell me. I plan to fix it as soon as I get straw enough. But getting the coin put together, that's the most difficult thing. There always seems to be something slightly more urgent I need to use my savings for. And then, when I do get a bit of straw put by, the ox needs more bedding, so it gets used for that instead." He sighed. "You know, I think there's something to be said for Rigo's attitude to the law. If no-one gets hurt or robbed, except the King, who has a splendid life anyway, why not take what you can to pull yourself up? Look at Christina. She's trying to do things right, and she's never going to escape from all that filth and squalor unless those relatives of hers turn out to be moneyed. How can she, when we have a King does nothing for any of us, and a Church that expects people to present themselves at the door and petition for alms? And we all know what a narrow squeak she has already had from doing that. She won't beg and she doesn't like accepting charity. Quite aside from the things she's likely to overhear by doing so, I can't say I blame her for cringing from asking for help. If I were destitute, I wouldn't want to have to apply to a wealthy establishment and hope they deemed me a worthy cause, either. I would do that she's done, too: stay out in the streets and take my chance. The trouble is, it then falls on the likes of ordinary folk like you and me to try and do something, for her and others like her, and none of us can do much when we have little enough ourselves. There is something wrong, somewhere. I can't work out what it is, but I do know this: I'm going to hang around for a while once I've picked up these oranges and see if I can edge my way into this smuggling business. I don't want much out of it, just enough to put a new thatch up and have a bite of good food over Yule. That will be enough for me."

"Well, you're a lot braver than I am, then," Tom said, as Aaron walked up from behind and joined them. "I'd love to have more money, but I can't take a chance by doing anything like this. I wish I could, though. It would be great to see what goes on."

"Well, come on down to the harbour with me before you go home," Nick suggested. "I know it's cold, but the night is young. It'll be something to do, and there might be some excitement to see, you never know. Do come. You know you'll kick yourself if you don't."

"Shall we?" Tom asked Aaron.

"I'm going to," Aaron said. "I've got to wait for Nick, anyway. I'm hitching a lift with him back to Brockweir. Remember?"

"I certainly do," Tom said, starting to feel smug. He could stay, or go, just as it pleased him.

They both walked alongside Nick, who remained in his cart to guide the ox. Nick kept his dogs close by him as they went. He didn't want them drawing unwanted attention by getting into scraps with other dogs. There were always feral curs scavenging along the waterside after dark, and they were all savage.

The latest ships to come in had all docked earlier, while the tide was still high enough for them to get to the slipways. They now lay quietly at the waterside ready for unlading. The activity in the harbour was steadily diminishing as the hustle and bustle of the daytime wound down. Tom and Aaron looked about them. In the flickering light from the burning flares and rush torches now set along the quayside there didn't seem to be much to see any more, but they were still hopeful of some sort of adventure if Rigo really could manage to get in on some smuggling. They badly wanted to find out for themselves what went on when these runs were done, and to see if Nick could successfully cut himself a slice of the action somehow, too. Any action would do, the very idea spiced up an otherwise predictable, humdrum country existence.

They waited at the quayside with several other carts, lit up by the torches as the last vestiges of daylight drained away and the *Portabella's* oranges were put ashore. Another ship was being relieved of her cargo at the same time, and every hold was emptied, and the harbour front cleared in front of them within the hour, so the longshoremen could finish for the night and go home.

While it was being done, Nick stayed with the cart as Aaron and Tom wandered nonchalantly up and down the harbour front, keeping their eyes skinned for anyone who might be a scout, or even a tout, acting for a smuggling gang. They were also hoping they might see Rigo. As the night closed in, and as they talked things over more, Aaron and Tom gradually talked themselves into seeking their own inclusion into the prospective activities in some way, too. Just in some very safe, very marginal way, something that carried no risk to it – say in a role no-one else wanted because it was too boring, too peripheral, or too trivial to be interesting, like a go-between out of sight of the docks, say; or a look-out somewhere up the road. Neither Tom nor Aaron was averse to a bit tame adventure, and, as Tom pointed out, this 'illicit trading', as he put it, did bring in its participants some very welcome coin. And they *could* do with some themselves. Why not, if the opportunity presented itself? Rigo's philosophy, shocking as it had been to them at its first airing, was now in full accord with their own hitherto untouched daydreams. Tom was already romancing about repairing his family home piece by piece: the house first, then the stables, which would please his father, and before long, say by next year, marrying Kitty and making her the chatelaine of it all. Aaron, meanwhile, was more realistically considering a trip up to London by coach in long stages to see the sights.

One cart had been filled with the *Portabella*'s bushel baskets and had headed off to Saint Woolos, and another had been dispatched to Abergavenny, with a third destined for Hereford where a market was due to take place the next day, before Nick got his consignment of citrus fruits for the Squire's steward, plus a couple of extra baskets which were left over at the end. Not bad, he decided, well worth the wait. He planned to sell the surplus fruit from the roadside in Agincourt Square in Monmouth on his own account after making his delivery, which would hopefully bring in some coppers on top of the one shilling and sixpence he would receive from the steward as payment for his trip.

He was just covering the back of the cart with a tarpaulin to keep the frost off, the orange baskets now being aboard, and the other carts all gone, when a man dressed in sailor's blue came sidling up.

He had overheard Nick tell the longshoremen that he was taking a delivery to Monmouth for the Squire, the man murmured, casually. *Was that right?*

"Yes," Nick answered, wondering if the man wanted a lift somewhere. If he did, there definitely wouldn't be room for Aaron's boat.

Nick's cart seemed to have only a half load, the quiet man observed. *It seemed a shame to leave such a space going a-begging,* the man said.

Nick agreed, without really thinking. This chap was a bit slow getting to the point. Perhaps he had no money. Or some friends who were hoping to come along, too. It wouldn't be the first-time sailors had gone off on expeditions to the Bell and Candle, instead of drinking locally. Nick kept half an eye out for Aaron and Tom as he fastened the last of the tarpaulin ropes. He wanted to get off.

Did a young lad with a half-empty cart want to make some extra cash, the sailor wanted to know, from behind his fingers as he blew on his hands to warm them. *A golden crown,* the man said, *just to add a couple of things to his waggon and ask no questions. There was plenty of room in there,* the sailor said, still blowing, *and he would suffer no inconvenience by considering the offer.*

"Er," said Nick, catching the drift of the man's intent, and hoping he wasn't reading too much into it. He was almost ready to swallow his tongue with excitement.

Just to take the extra things to the Squire's house with the oranges, the man said; *and to leave them there. No need to worry about handing them on, or to say anything to anybody; their onward journey was already taken care of.*

"Um, I think that'll be all right," said Nick, looking up and down the harbour much more earnestly now for some sign of Aaron and Tom. Nick was no decision maker, and now it had come to the point, he needed his friends alongside him to egg him on and get him to fall in with this proposal. He was excited, but he was almost too scared to accept it.

Had he said a crown? asked the sailor, carelessly. *He could even make it two,* said the sailor, equally carelessly.

Two golden crowns! Two! It was the very proposition Nick had been hoping for, though he tried to conceal his thrill of delight behind a casual insouciance, as though such transactions were a normal part of his everyday occupation.

"Yeh," said Nick. "Could do," said Nick. "Don't mind," said Nick. "Oh, sod it, why not?" he said in summary, boldly warming to the idea.

It would be best if the young man went on his way now, the man said, *and came past the Senhora da Luz two hours after midnight.* Then he slipped away.

"Oh! As late as that? I was..." But the man had already gone.

Aaron and Tom came pounding over the cobbles once the man was out of sight, and breathlessly asked what had happened.

"Why didn't you two come sooner? You should have been here to help me out," Nick expostulated. "I nearly said 'no' to him, I was so scared. It's a wonder I haven't wet my britches."

"Well, we thought he might be up to no good, and we wanted to give him chance," Tom said defensively, quietly aggrieved by Nick's reproof.

"Yeh, man. If we'd have come straight over, we would have given the game away," Aaron agreed, backing Tom up. "He would just have dashed off without saying anything, and we would have spoiled everything. So now tell us what's going on. What did he ask you to do?"

Nick told them, his hair still standing on end from his recent thrill of fear and pleasure. His friends were awed, jealous, outraged, wondering, and finally silent for several long minutes as the full implications settled on them. Then they said they wanted to go too: to accompany him in the cart, to watch, and to listen to everything; to lift the contraband and feel it, then put it down again; to help put it in the cart and take it out at the other end. They wanted to engage with Nick's smugglers, find out what smugglers looked like, and see what went on. They wanted to see Rigo again.

"Better not," Nick advised, drifting slowly back down from the seventh heaven he had been catapulted up into at the thought of his first gold coins. "That man said to ask no questions. If I turn up later with a couple of mates, he'll think I can't follow instructions. He might not give me the consignment. He might even think I'm some sort of a cheat."

"Or a tosser," Aaron offered, helpfully. "He hasn't met your mates yet, so he's had no-one to compare you with so far."

Nick made a V-sign and flicked his whip to get the cart going. "Oh well," he said. "I may as well go home and get a few hours kip. The action won't start before two."

"Two!"

"Two!"

"I know," he said. "That's what I thought. I had expected to be in Monmouth by then, getting some shut-eye in one of the Squire's stables." He sighed. "It's a good thing they'll be making this worth my while."

"Why, how much did he say they'd give you?" Tom demanded. "Come on, tell us."

"Two crowns," Nick said, mulling over a mental equation in which nervous tension and inconvenience were weighed against promised financial gain. Gain was winning so far. Just.

"T... *Two!* Just for adding some things to your cart? Wow! I really need to put myself forward for some of this!"

"And me, mate. It beats twanging strings for a living."

"I don't see how you can," said Nick. "Not unless you stay with me now, and then wait for me when I go to collect the goods later."

"You bet we will! Just try stopping us. Will you give us a share of your money?"

"I think I'll have to," Nick said, considering. "One of you will have to get those coins changed into something smaller for me. If I present a coin the size of a crown somewhere – anywhere – they'll start asking how I came by it. Everyone in these parts knows I don't have much to spend. I'll have to bring you in."

"Great!"

"But you'll have to help me do my work tomorrow as well, so you've earned it."

"No problem!"

"Help what with?" It was Aaron doing the asking. "I can't do any heavy stuff, I need to keep all my fingers. I've got to play tomorrow night at the Squire's."

"Well, there's two loads of hay and oats to take to the Drover's Rest from Ellis's farm out at Rockfield. I do that every week, and it usually takes all morning. Then I'm supposed to be calling in somewhere on my way back here. That strange lady, name of Myfanwy, who lives just outside of Trellech, apparently. She wants me to pick up something from her brother's farm in Saint Arvans. I think it might be field beans and some winter cabbages, but I'm not sure till I get there. Whatever it turns out to be, I'm going to be busy all day tomorrow, with no sleep tonight. Do you know, I think I'm looking forward to Christmas this year? Once I get home, I shall stoke up the fire, put my feet up, and sit on my arse all day with a great big tankard of ale in my hand. I don't intend to move, except to go to the privy."

Aaron said, "I shan't come back this way with you. Once we've finished the deliveries to the Drover's, I'll stay in Monmouth and hang round till it is time for me to go on to the Squire's with Dad. I might even bump into him, you never know. If I do, I can cadge a lift there with him."

"I could stay with you as far as Trellech and help you load up," said Tom. "But what about Timothy? I can't pay for an overnight stay where I've stabled him."

Tom and Aaron looked at each other.

"I think I'd better go," Tom said, reluctantly. "I'd better go home."

"No, don't do that. Stick Tim in my yard with the ox," Nick suggested. "I'll be taking the ox out of there when I come back down here again tonight, so he'll have the yard to himself after that. And Aaron was meaning to hitch a ride with me anyway. We won't be leaving till the early hours, and it would be nice if you kept us company in the meanwhile. The only thing is, I don't know whether I'll have room for Aaron's boat now."

"That's all right," Aaron said. "If Tom can't come, I won't. We'd better not, anyway. Dad would have a fit, and so would the Colonel. It was a nice idea, though. Tell you what, we'll stick around until you get the rest of your load, then Tom and me will ride with you part of the way to Monmouth. Tom can turn off at Catbrook after you've dropped me off. We'll leave the boat where it is. I'll get it home some other time. Tony can take it from here just as easily as he can from Brockweir, it's just a pity there's no knowing when he's likely to be around to do it, that's all. To be honest, I'm not sure that the boat was such a good an idea as I first thought."

"Ha!" said Tom, exultant. "Told you!"

Chapter Nine

Rigo had given in to Christina's pleas as they were leaving the Castle jetty, and had allowed her to accompany him to the port quayside while he sold her box of tapers. He just wanted to get the business of selling the wretched things, these *malditas coisas,* over and done with. They were getting smellier by the hour, and he was sick of thinking about them.

The *Senhora* had been moved further upriver, but remained moored at the quay, despite the main bulk of her cargo having been unladed earlier, and as he went aboard Rigo heard someone further along the wharf complaining about that fact. Whoever was on the receiving end of those complaints was answering in an authoritative voice that the *Senhora* was scheduled to be moved over to the buoys at high tide the next morning, and that she couldn't be positioned before then because there were no crew members available to pull her. Someone was inclined to disagree. Rigo stood listening closely after he had crossed the gangplank. He could have sworn it was Leafy's voice he was hearing, though it didn't make sense if it was. As a crewman from the *Senhora* himself, Levi Figley knew perfectly well why his ship couldn't be shifted just yet. The other person was probably the Harbourmaster, or some other official. Rigo climbed up onto the foredeck to gain a better vantage point, but although he peered intently through the darkness from his higher position for several minutes, he couldn't make out the shape of anybody standing on the wharf nearby. Maybe he was mistaken after all, and it was just another ordinary sailor seizing an opportunity to have a beef at somebody he didn't like.

He mentally shrugged the mystery off and went below decks to find a prospective purchaser for Christina's tapers. A few of the

Senhora's crew were gathered at one end of the long table in the smoky ship's galley playing a game of cards, this being a good chance to gain an odd sixpence by betting on the outcome. They were just on the point of starting a new game when they were joined by Levi Figley, who came down the steps accompanied by two sailors from another ship. Rigo sat himself down on a bench at the side, and prepared to wait for a suitable lull in the proceedings. It was no good trying to prise coppers out of his shipmates at this point; their minds were otherwise engaged, and they would just say 'no' or not answer. As he watched, he took stock of the incoming men, and it didn't take long for him to develop an uncharacteristic sense of foreboding. That foreboding increased exponentially the more he looked at them. Things were not looking good, even to him. In an hour, or maybe two, the movement of some sort of contraband was due to start, and in the galley now were two drunken guests of villainous appearance, both of whom had been invited to come aboard. He doubted the wisdom of bringing uninitiated crew members from other ships on board anyway, when there was dirty work to be done, since one of them could easily notice something they might recall later on, should any future enquiries be instituted; but on top of that, he couldn't help wondering how these guests were to be got rid of without arousing suspicion at the end of the gaming, if it turned out they didn't want to go. Even if these two were no more than innocent and unwitting companions-in-transit, every man-Jack in the galley was now steadily getting drunk, and with the gaming thrown in as well there was every chance of a fight starting before the real business of the night was begun. The last thing they needed now was an odd soldier or King's man coming in at the run. Even without these two unwanted additions getting in the way, what price a bunch of drunk and aggressive sailors working contraband at dead of night?

Despite his gloom, Rigo decided that this was another problem that would simply have to be shelved for the moment. He accepted a pint of ale from his companion cook, Matthew Ribtoft, who was also sitting observing the game, and they began talking. On hearing there was a little girl waiting for Rigo out on the wharf, Matthew set down his drink and strode off to find a couple of dainty sweetmeats to send out for her. Christina was still eating them when a latecomer called Maurice Fairweather came staggering in, still searching through his pockets as he came down the steps, because he had noticed her on his way past, and despite his drunkenness, was another soft-hearted fellow who wanted to give her something. At last he found three pennies and sent those out too. Nobody wanted the tapers.

Well pleased with this as an outcome, Rigo sent Christina on her way. He hadn't got her enough for a room, but thruppence would buy her family a breakfast for the next several days. He focussed his intent on his next mission – the important one – which was to speak to his ship's Captain as soon as possible. Rigo knew that the Captain and most of crew of the *Senhora* were involved in this smuggling; but he wasn't sure exactly who was in and who was out, apart from himself. Maybe they were all in. Rigo still intended to find out, and join in, if he could possibly wangle it. Already, fiery images of gold, and gems, and glittering jewellery were floating in glorious imaginary vistas before his eyes. Having never had anything much to spend in the whole of his life, the attraction of riches was a heady one and, unlike Tom, Rigo also fancied the notoriety and fame that went with liberal spending, as well as the grandeur associated with having plentiful amounts of cash. But although he was a dreamer, he was also a practical young man. Treasure chests could wait. In the meantime, a gold coin or two would last a very long time and provide for all his immediate wants, and if that much was not to be had either, why, anything was better than nothing for an impecunious lad like him.

Accordingly, Rigo left Matthew Ribtoft as soon as he had finished his ale and, making his way aft, tapped boldly at the door of the Captain's cabin a few moments later. An ill-tempered voice responded from within, demanding to know who the devil was out there, and what the hell he wanted. Rigo shouted his name through the door and asked for permission to enter, saying there was something he wished to discuss. An equally irritable invitation followed, and Rigo pushed open the door and walked confidently in to Captain Earl 'Man-of-Wrath' Rothman's private quarters.

The Captain was standing behind the chart table with a facial expression indicative of intense anger hovering at the danger mark. This was the habitual facial expression of the tall, strikingly handsome man. It wasn't just the man's perennial and marked bad temper that reminded Rigo of a jaguar from the rainforests of his own country; the Captain's powerful, athletic physique and supple grace of movement were reminiscent of a great cat, as well. Rigo had never heard of panthers. If he had, he would perhaps have compared Captain Rothman to one of those in preference as a larger, darker, and altogether more fearsome beast. The Captain was a man of probably no more than thirty-five years, but already his tightly curled black hair was starting to run into premature silvery rivulets here and there, and despite having great physical prowess and relative youth, he acted like a much older man: one who had seen it all, tried it out, and hated it so much he could hardly bear to think about it.

The Captain's shirt was pulled open, so it lay apart against his chest, revealing skin somewhat darker than Rigo's. The stock he normally wore as part of his dress had been removed altogether with its pin and lay discarded on the table. There was no way of telling if this had been done in a moment exasperation or not, and Rigo had no time to consider taking it into account. Not that the Captain's mood had any effect on him, whatever his level of impatience happened to be Rigo faced it just the same, but he *was* here to ask a favour, so he didn't want to create a diversion or delay that would risk a boiling-over of the Captain's rage.

Captain Rothman was deemed to be an Englishman because of his father, who was a Bristol man, but everyone at sea knew his mother had been a Jamaican, and that at birth Earl had been taken from her to be brought up in his father's house, so he had never known who she was. Rumour had it that he didn't even know her name, because his father would never give it up to him. However, none of this was of even passing interest to Rigo. As far as he was concerned, everyone had their disadvantages to deal with, none were any worse than any others in the long run, so everyone should just get on with his life. He marched straight up to the chart table, touched his brow, and asked for permission to speak.

The Captain waved his assent, and Rigo began his prepared speech, beginning with his steadfast loyalty to the *Senhora* and all who sailed in her, progressing to his great wish that he be considered more than a common seaman, and hinting at a cherished desire to become part of a secret inner circle of brotherhood – but at this point the Captain hotly interrupted him.

"Are you a complete fucking idiot, blast you, or what?" he bellowed ferociously, leaning forward onto his knuckles, which cracked ominously under his weight.

"Wh-Wh-What?" Rigo faltered, not understanding at all why he was being forestalled in such an overbearing and intimidating way.

Fortunately, the Captain took his answer for that of a smart-arse, and he began laughing, his anger evaporating on the spot. When his paroxysm finally subsided, he threw himself back into his chair and poured himself a glass of Madeira from a small wooden tantalus open at his side and took a few mouthfuls of the wine while he studied Rigo reflectively.

"You don't have to go anywhere tonight to be part of a brotherhood, you damned young upstart," he exclaimed when he had finished his deliberations, putting his feet up on the chart table in front of him as he spoke. "The whole damned ship is involved in this contraband every time we go out, blast you. If I don't pull out the entire crew for a job, it's only because the more of you idiots are actively involved, the more likelihood there is that some damn fool will forget himself in his cups and spill the blasted beans to some damned officious revenue officer sitting next to him in some blasted tavern." He took another generous swig of his wine as he considered the point.

"I agree w-w-with you, Captain," Rigo said, and the Captain pulled a wry face but didn't answer. "So, Captain," Rigo continued, encouraged by the silence, "why do you allow men from other ships come aboard on a night when you are doing a run?"

"I don't," the Captain said shortly, between more sips.

"Well, m-m-maybe you should know something, then. There are two men from a ship out of Saint Malo playing cards in the galley right this minute. They came aboard with one of your crew, a-a-and they don't look good to me. Your crew may not be getting drunk in a tavern w-w-with revenue officers, but they are st-till down there getting drunk with strangers. I d-don't think that's much improvement."

"WHAT?" Man-of-Wrath leapt to his feet and cast his glass aside. "Dammit, I'll flog the lot of them! They'll never work for me again! I might even keel-haul them! Cronke! Where is that bastard! Cronke!" He yanked the door open and leaned through it, raising his voice even higher, until the sound ricocheted through the rafters of the entire ship. "Cronke, you fucking bastard, where are you?" A distant acknowledgement followed almost immediately. "Get in here, you goddamned lazy old fool. Now!"

Man-of-Wrath banged the door shut, and returned to his seat, dragging his stock off the table as he passed it by so he could put it back round his neck.

"You know, I-I-I think I ought to tell you as well that I overheard somebody talking on the shore just as I was coming aboard about an hour ago."

"And?" The stock was being pulled into place savagely.

"A-A-And I think he might have been talking to one of the harbour authorities."

"About what? It was probably just ordinary business. We are in a port, after all." The Captain picked up his glass and started drinking again, impatiently.

"Well, he was c-complaining about the *Senhora* still being berthed here, even though her cargo is gone." Rigo hesitated, and then plunged on. "It w-w-was as if he wanted to make sure he drew their attention to it. And I'm not one hundred percent sure, but I *think* it was one of our own crewmen. If I am right, it's the man who b-b-brought the two sailors aboard. I just thought I would m-m-mention it."

"Hmm? Well, I don't think it's anything to worry about, but I'll keep a note of it up here."

The Captain finished re-tying his stock, then tapped his forehead to indicate the place he intended depositing the information, by which time the First Mate had made it into the room, rushing in at full speed, still frantically fastening up the waist of his britches.

"Oh, there you are," Man-of-Wrath said with disfavour, putting his glass down and eyeing the middle-aged man. "Took your blasted time, I must say."

"Apologies, Cap'n," the unfortunate Cronke said, saluting. "I was off-duty, sir, and asleep."

"Were you, by God?" Man-of-Wrath thundered. "You must be damned well past it then, asleep at this time of day. Who gave you permission to go off-duty so close to your outing, I'd like to know, damn you?"

"Er, it was by your own orders, Cap'n, sir – begging your pardon for mentioning it, sir."

"Never!"

"On my life, sir. You told me to get a couple of hours this afternoon, before we make our... er... erm..." Cronke's eyes slid sideways to Rigo, who was still standing beside him at the chart table, and he helplessly made a tiny motion with his finger to indicate he thought Rigo should be removed from the cabin.

"What's that? Oh! Him!" The Captain made a careless gesture and stood up. He began twiddling with his desk charts, then picked up his glass and poured himself some more Madeira. "He's all right, let him stay. He has more nous than that pack of idiots out there, at any rate." He resumed his drinking. "Get those fucking interlopers in the galley chucked out and then get the whole blasted rabble sober before the night watchman calls midnight in the town. Oh, and tell them if they don't comply, I'm sacking the whole fucking lot of them and tipping them into the briny, where they belong. They can sink or swim down there, as they please. I shan't make a move to save any of them."

"Aye, aye, Cap'n. Anything else, Cap'n?"

"No, Goddammit, get out! And take this young *braggadocio* with you. He's going along with you tonight, so make him useful. He has some sense; see you put it to good use."

"Yes, sir."

Cronke signalled for Rigo to leave, and he willingly obeyed, well pleased to have been promoted to inclusion in the night's activities, although he still had no idea from Man-of-Wrath's explosive explanation where he would stand when it came to the final share-out of the takings. Still, at least he would get something. The Captain had his back to them as they shut the door. He was staring out of the cabin porthole into the darkness outside.

"Come with me, my lad, and don't make any noise until you're out of ear-shot of the Captain's quarters," Cronke said, speaking quietly. "It's better not to enrage him when he gets like this. I'll just rouse the Second Mate, and then we'll make sure everybody is properly sobered up and ready for the off."

"With r-r-respect, Mister Cronke," Rigo said, "I think it will be b-b-better if you go straight to the galley. I think you should g-g-get those callers-in out fast. Sobering up the men can wait until the Second Mate gets there. I'll rouse him for you."

"Good thinking, lad," Cronke replied. "Yes, we'll do it your way. Damme, if the Captain isn't right; you *do* have a good head on your shoulders. I never realised that before."

"Thank you, Mister Cronke," Rigo answered, even more pleased. "Sir, w-w-what name am I to call you by when we go out, please? I know you let the other men call you 'Cronky', but I don't feel too comfortable with that. I don't want to be disrespectful."

The First Mate gave a rare smile. "We don't use names of any kind when we're out on a mission, lad. Anyone can give orders, and if they do, we all pay attention to 'em. There's no order of rank when we're operating outside the law, d'you see. As for the rest, just carry on calling me Mister Cronke and you won't go far wrong." He patted Rigo on the shoulder kindly. "I don't mind going as 'Cronky' when we're drinking and off-duty; but only my mother calls me by my first name now. And John Barnes is the man promoted to Second Mate for our next voyage. You'll find him in our cabin. That's Mister Barnes to you, though. Got that?"

Rigo nodded. "Sure, M-M-Mister Cronke," he said. "See you later."

They separated: Rigo to fetch John Barnes from his bed, and Mister Cronke to do a damage limitation in the galley.

It took a little time to prise the visitors from their seats and persuade them that there were no more winnings to be had that night, but eventually both were coaxed out of the galley onto the main deck, and from there, over the gangplank by the light of a binnacle lamp onto the shore. As the departing sailors went off into the night, singing bawdily and shouting absurd jokes to the world in general, the remaining crew of the *Senhora* went below to souse their heads in cold water and clear their thinking ready for the main business of the night.

"Now then," Mister Cronke said to Rigo, drawing him to one side. "The Captain, who, remember, has nothing whatever to do with these nocturnal excursions of ours, has just had another word with me. Final orders, and all that."

"I know, Mister Cronke," Rigo said, "I heard him shouting. I'm very s-s-sorry."

"Ah, don't worry about me, lad," Mister Cronke said. "Broad shoulders, that's what you need if you want to be a First Mate, and nothing more. Then it all goes over your head."

"I understand, s-sir. And what are his orders?"

"You're to be posted as an extra look-out for us. You can't do more than that on a first outing, because you must learn the ropes for a start, and then prove your mettle before we let you further in. But if you carry on like this we'll be counting you as one of us before much longer, so keep it up."

Rigo's face was lighting up by the minute. Praise was rare on the ships, and when it did come, it was very welcome. The main deck was now empty of crew, so there was no danger of Mister Cronke's comments being overheard by any jealous listeners-in; all the crewmen were drying themselves off below. Rigo could hear the sounds from them through the planks of the deck – and he could also hear John Barnes, who was now growling at the men.

"We've lost maybe an hour by your antics, maybe more." The words came up from below, accompanied by the sounds of groans and vigorous rubbing of arms and stamping of feet. The men were apparently making a big effort to warm themselves back up. Many could still be heard shivering from the sousing. "We should have been on our way out now, and the whole night ahead of us," John Barnes' words continued. "As it is, we must wait maybe two more hours, to make sure everybody's abed and asleep and not strolling about surveying the docks and talking to the foot patrols because you lot created all this ruckus. No wonder the Captain's shouting. We'll have to work against the clock to get everything in before the morning watches begin, so you must all buck up, look lively, and keep your wits about you to see we come through safe. With luck on our side, we'll still do it."

Rigo was wandering about on the main deck above their heads, half-listening to the bits of the pep-talk he could hear filtering up through the boards below, half-listening to the muffled imprecations and oaths still issuing at intervals from the Captain's cabin. Then he stopped in his tracks. He was first bemused, and then incredulous of something he thought he had seen. Mister Cronke had gone in to see the Captain, Rigo knew that. He had seen him enter, which was why John Barnes was doing the talking and disciplining instead, and why the Captain was still in full spate; but Rigo had seen someone else make his way into that cabin, just after Mister Cronke had closed the door shut. He was sure of it. Whoever it was, they had glided over the deck rail aft like a slender will-o'-the-wisp at the exact moment that John Barnes had started prowling round down below, hounding and harrying his men. Whoever it was, the deck-rail visitant had been so ghostly that Rigo still wasn't completely sure he had seen what he thought he saw. What he *thought* he saw was an ethereal body come slithering up from the sea over the bulwarks, and then disappear. But it must have been real. Surely. He was still thinking it over a few moments later, when to his increasing consternation he was equally sure he glimpsed, out of the corner of his eye, that same phantom drifting noiselessly around a corner in the shadows close to the quarter deck. Then the Captain's door opened – and closed. Just that. Rigo saw no-one go in or come out. Yet he stood rigid at what he had witnessed, horror-struck, with his hair standing on end. Although the being had been man-like, the eldritch thing had had such a length in its arms and legs it had appeared there was a ghastly giant insect scuttling silently across the deck: a horrible, predatory phantasm.

Rigo had heard the name 'Lightfoot' more than once since he had joined the ship. The name was mentioned in quiet asides when the ship was fog-bound with no sound around them but the waves slapping at the timbers, or in furtive mutterings under faint stars late at night; but, surprisingly, it was never spoken of with genuine fear. 'Lightfoot' was an *ignus fatuus* being, who, the men said, came and went, and the descriptions of him were always the same. All spoke of a strange, gangly creature of no words, who would suddenly appear out of nowhere, swaying fit to topple off his feet when he walked, silently sliding out of the darkness in the dead of night, then skittering in a flash of movement up and down ladders and over walls and bulwarks like some sort of a monstrous spider. Rigo wondered what Lightfoot's role was, and why he came on board a ship at all when sailors were so full of ignorance, intolerance and superstition that they would refuse to have on board anything even slightly out of the ordinary. Yet the man, from what he had just seen, must be a very outlandish character: a frightening human misfit who couldn't be placed anywhere except among the shades of darkness, in dismal hollows among graves in churchyards, or around the phosphorescent excrescences of rotting marshes.

Rigo shivered.

He waited for the night to advance.

Chapter Ten

It was the dead of night. Even the Cocklehouse had fallen silent and been shuttered up. As the stars wheeled their faint course round the moonless sky, half a dozen carts softly rolled up alongside the *Senhora da Luz,* their wheels muffled by loose straw strewn in front of them as they made their progression across the cobblestones. Quietly and efficiently, and with the ease of many years' practice, the crew of the *Senhora* began moving what was left of her cargo, adding more casks from secret stow-holds cut into hidden places beneath and between her decks. They worked as a human chain, passing mostly firkins and small casks containing brandy and fine wine, and then at the end adding several chests of different sizes. These last Rigo had seen when they were taken on, and he knew their contents. The smaller ones held costly lace, thread of gold, and some beautifully worked garments in fine silk; the larger contained a reserve of tobacco, tea leaves and coffee beans. Everything was passed from hand to hand in a line until it was all neatly stacked into each of the carts in turn and carried away. Rigo was standing up on the foredeck patrolling round, eyeing all the dim reaches of the port from every angle, alert for any signs of movement or gathering shapes. The last cart in the gallery of runners, much to Rigo's surprise, held Nick. He didn't know Nick's waggon of course, but he did recognise Nick, even though Nick had abandoned his light-coloured carter's smock in favour of a dark-brown coat and britches. His cart was half-full already when it rolled up, and Rigo briefly wondered if he was carrying more contraband from another ship until he smelt the sweet tang of juicy citrus fruits and remembered. Six casks were swiftly stowed on their ends behind the baskets, and a chest pushed in alongside them. Then everything was deftly covered over with the tarpaulin, Nick quietly flicked his whip, and the ox between the shafts began slowly to depart, taking a different route from the rest of the carts, heading away from the docks to leave the town by a small side gate.

As Nick's waggon moved laboriously and ponderously along, something ghostly fluttered away from it and came flittering up to the ship like a pale, sepulchral moth. It landed on the deck-rail and paused for a moment before taking flight once more, settling this time on Rigo's shoulder. He relaxed as soon as he realised who it was. Having begun a morbid train of thoughts earlier that evening, Rigo had been feeling quite spooked by the spectacle of another unearthly visitant. But it was all right, it was only Moonlight after all.

"Hey! Wh-What are you doing outside, little fella?" Rigo breathed, as he smoothed Moonlight's feathers. "I told Christina you w-w-would be left behind. Stay here with me and be good now."

Rigo kept watching until Nick's waggon disappeared. He saw Nick's two sheepdogs glide silently up to the wheels at the last minute, like two spectral bodyguards, and then the vehicle was gone. With a sigh Rigo descended the ladder from the foredeck to group with the remaining crew.

"Follow the carts along to the other end, lads," Cronke was whispering as Rigo came up, "and give 'em a hand when you get there. Levi, you and Rigo stand on the corners of the last two roads leading up to the town from the end. Keep yourselves out of sight and give us a hoot if you see or hear anyone."

"A-A-A hoot?" Rigo asked, pulling at the sleeve of Levi's shirt as the others began to drift away, "Hey! Leafy! W-W-What's a hoot?"

Levi gave a surreptitious hoot through his fingers to demonstrate. He kept it low and brief, but several of the men close by still turned around and looked back.

"Keep going, shit-heads," Levi hissed at them, his voice mean. "I'm just showing this fuckwit what to do."

There was no time to take Moonlight below and put him to sleep, he was going to have to remain where he was with Rigo, and hope nothing else would startle him and make him take flight when he shouldn't. In step with Levi, Rigo joined the last of the horses being led along the wharf to its end at the jetty, close to the Castle. There, very stealthily, everything was being unloaded from the carts by the light of dark lanterns and moved up the cliff face into two caves, both of which were completely invisible unless anybody knew they were there and actively searched through the scrubby plants to locate them. So well were their entrances concealed by the dense ivy and valerian growing all along the cliff, that although Rigo could see the contraband being lifted and carried, cask by cask, chest by chest, by the light of the lanterns, he could scarcely visualise the caves at all. It looked as though things were disappearing by some sort of magic into thin air once they were hoisted up. Where the contraband was going after that, he had no idea; though he fully intended to ask someone the minute he got the opportunity. He tucked himself into a shadow at the bottom end of Bridge Street and settled down with Moonlight to watch the men and the street alternately, keeping his eyes peeled and his ears honed for sight or sound of passers-by of any description. Levi had disappeared into the shadows enclosing Slushy Lane a little bit further back, and Rigo didn't see him again that night.

Once the barrels and caskets were safely inside the caves, most of the seamen followed them up the cliff, and the last two carts remaining prepared to leave, accompanied by their drivers. The first carts had already gone.

That was the moment when everything suddenly fell apart. A small body came flying up to Rigo out of nowhere, whispering frantically, "Soldiers! Make haste and get out of here!"

Rigo only just had time to recognise her before she was gone, scampering into the shadows of the adjoining street to melt away out of sight and sound. He immediately gave his hoot and followed her direction at a run, as did the other remaining men still present, redoubling their own pace and slapping the horses into a canter, making a desperate effort to get away with the carts before it was too late. But it was no good. There was an abrupt command from somewhere in the darkness, followed closely by a flurry of activity and the sound of swords being drawn, and the runaway carts and their drivers, together with a handful of accompanying sailors including Rigo, were all surrounded by soldiers and revenue men before they could do much more than draw their breath in surprise. Moonlight flew from Rigo's shoulder into the night and disappeared.

"Ha! Got a few of you, anyway," said a voice. "Get 'em in file, men." It was evidently the Serjeant-at-Arms speaking, although it was much too dark to see which one of them he was.

The soldiers, still panting from their short run, and shot through with a blood-frenzy from the struggle to overpower their prisoners, set about vigorously tearing at their captives' clothes to check for hidden weapons, before tying them all together by their wrists with a length of rope and shoving them with rough brutality into the two carts.

"Is this all there is?" said the Serjeant, looking into the carts in turn. "Bit disappointing. Ah well, not to worry. We'll have the rest of 'em locked up before morning." He addressed his next remark to the prisoners before moving on. "Hope you lot enjoy keeping bad company, because you'll be getting plenty of it, from here on. Right, Derrick. Take two men and go with these carts up to the barracks; get some arrest warrants made out for these lumps of shit. And while they're writing them up, send someone to wake the Sheriff so he can sign them straight away. If they can't do that, or if he isn't at home, tell them to wake up whoever's deputising instead. Probably be the nearest Squire. Any problems, keep the prisoners in the carts and take them straight to gaol. The warrants are the most important bit. The rest of you men, head on down to the main harbour, in case there are any more of these bastards hiding in the alleys down there. Some might come back yet and try to get to their ships before daybreak. Now then, who have we got here?" A face peered at Rigo briefly, then at each of the other captured men in turn, illuminating them one by one with a dark lantern. "Hmm. Don't know any of you," the face was muttering. "Anyone any idea who these carts belong to?"

A murmur of negatives was returned, and the Serjeant gave a grunt of dissatisfaction before giving the order for the carts to move. They slowly began to roll, making their way to the Castle and the arrest warrants for the captured sailors.

Three people had secretly watched the taking of the seamen, the carts, and their drivers. Two were Aaron and Tom, who had decided to make a small detour before they collected Timothy and joined Nick on the Saint Arvans road, determined to watch what went on so they could have a good chat about it later. They had hidden in the shadows together and observed the whole debacle with fright and desperation, unable to withdraw without being seen, and powerless to warn anyone of the impending danger from the soldiers they had witnessed arriving. They hadn't dared move or make a sound. Even so, they were themselves discovered, and triumphantly taken into custody during the first sweep of the area immediately after the initial arrests, and were frog-marched off with a soldier on either side of them up to the barracks to join Rigo and the other prisoners. The third person, seen a short time later, was passed over without interest or comment. She was, after all, of no relevance, just a little crippled girl nursing a tiny blue bird, sitting alone on a stanchion beside the water.

Chapter Eleven

Christina observed everything that went on that night, from beginning to end, completely unseen.

She was hiding among some empty fish creels when Nick collected his chest and casks and left town. She already knew he was going to Squire Speybury's house, and that it was near Monmouth, because she had heard him tell the longshoremen so. She hung about for while after he had gone, spending some time with her mother and Anthony, and eating griddle cakes, until the two of them fell asleep. After that, she wandered down to the other end of the harbour for a desultory look-round. She saw the carts having their contents transferred to two caves in the cliff with amazement. Why disguise the entry to those caves so carefully? And who was such a big delivery for? Oh, but perhaps this was what smuggling was, and how it was done. But if it was, where did those caves lead? Christina promised herself that she would uncover the entrances in a day or two, once it was safe to do so, and take a look inside. She wanted to find out as much about Chepstow as she could. And smuggling. She liked it here, it was exciting and interesting, and she wanted to stay. Crouched down and well hidden, she continued to survey the goings-on, observing some of the casks being taken away by rowing boats, rather than being transferred up to the caves. Small boats were taking some of the smaller casks out into the water, and then going upriver, or else across to the other side. One such was a coracle being operated by an elderly man, who carried two casks over to the exact same spot that Adela and Andrew had gone, and who then made a return journey to collect two more.

At last, the bulk of the consignment was dealt with and the operation wound down. The caves were closed and covered again, and all but the last few casks were hidden, and the remaining men were ready to go. Christina saw Moonlight under the starlight as she crept quietly away, and thought how poetic it was to see him sitting on Rigo's shoulder in the shadows at a distance, looking like a tiny little falling star himself. But she couldn't stick around to talk or do any more watching, she had to move about to keep herself from freezing, which was how she came across the soldiers and revenue men as they were forming up, having heard them before Rigo did. One or two stifled curses and rustlings had reached her ears half-way up one of the streets she was crossing, and she silently tracked the noises down. Oh horror! A squad of armed men! How many men, Christina couldn't tell, but it looked an awful lot. She couldn't see who was doing the organising of them either, but she was sure his profile was familiar. Even as she was trying to nail the memory of when and where she might have seen that vague silhouette before, the figure was gone, vanishing into the night as she herself turned and ran in haste to warn Rigo and his friends before it was too late. Oh, so slow, so little time, and the soldiers so quick, coming after her! Never had Christina wished so ardently that she could have been born with a stronger body and longer legs.

The last few seamen left down at the river scattered as soon as she delivered the news, but the soldiers were already behind her. She only just had time to duck into the nearest shadows before there was a sudden rush of feet, and she became a helpless witness as soldiers and customs men closed in and made their arrests after a few minutes of intense scuffling and fighting. It was too dark to see well, but by the light of one of the flickering dark lanterns that had had its horn covers hastily pushed aside, Christina easily recognised Rigo being roped up and pushed into the back of one of the two carts commandeered for the removal of the prisoners. He was with several other men, none of whom she knew. Shortly afterwards, the carts were wheeled away. Moonlight fluttered with a frantic chirp onto Christina's shoulder as they left, and she silently shushed him, smoothing his feathers to calm him while she waited for the coast to clear.

She was just on the point of risking a move herself, when she saw Aaron and Tom being prodded unceremoniously up the road in the same direction the carts had taken. They couldn't have been arrested as part of the smugglers' ring, because they so obviously weren't; but as they had been apprehended in a nearby street at this unseemly hour, she could hear one of the soldiers saying something about aiding and abetting and loitering with intent. She herself was still well hidden. She waited until the soldiers had gone past, then took a chance and made good her own escape, running as fast as she could go, though it was little more than a fast hobbling gait that she could muster because of her breathing.

"Come on, Christina," she thought. "If Ivarr the Boneless could master his difficulties, then so must you. Keep your wits about you, and keep going, that's what you must do. Poor as you are for a messenger, you're all those sailor-men have got."

She headed back down the wharf in a frenzy of anxiety, clutching Moonlight to her with both hands, not knowing where else to run. She was longing to find someone to tell what she had seen, but who was she able to trust? Not any sailors, that was for sure. The trustworthy ones had either escaped or been run in when the customs men had appeared, so who else? She cast her mind over the few other people she knew. Adela! Yes, that was it. She would go to Adela and tell her. She could do it, she knew where Adela lived, but how was she to get over the river?

By this time she had run the length of the main wharf, and had a stitch in her side. Clutching at it, she rested for a few moments by a pile of wine casks left on the quayside. They were empty of wine, but still sweet-smelling and redolent of the grape fermentations they had lately carried, and Christina savoured the winey overtones while she gratefully took the chance to catch her breath and steady her senses. Everywhere about her was quiet, with no sounds of affray or excitement coming from anywhere within earshot. Two soldiers marched by after emerging from one of the alleyways, and she waited until they were out of sight before moving on again. No-one was around to hinder her, so now she must go and get help. If she could only get to Adela. She ran her mind over what she had to do.

A boat. She had to have a boat. She had no money to pay the toll at the bridge, and she wasn't sure she could walk so far, anyway. A boat would be easier, she had seen the men operate them, there wasn't much to it.

Although it was so dark, there was enough starlight reflected in the water for her to see several small vessels moored at the outer reaches of the docks, well away from the deep-water ships, and she remembered seeing more back near the Castle, close to where she had run from. Which should she go for? Near? Or far? Near – the nearest to her crossing-point, obviously. No point in being far away from the place she wanted to reach. She ran back the way she had just come, past the shuttered Cocklehouse, her cloth-bound feet making no noise on the stones, her stitch gone for the moment. The soldiers had all left the area to continue their searching elsewhere and a deep stillness had returned to the whole area.

Hastily, Christina crawled inside her warehouse, where Poppea and Anthony still lay asleep, and quietly put Moonlight down beside them, settling him on a loose plank of wood close by their pallet. Then she tiptoed back outside and carried on running up to the end of the wharf.

She ran her eyes over the smaller boats as she neared the end, and dismissed the first few she saw. They were all too big, with single masts and reefed sails. She needed something much smaller – a small rowing boat. But the rowing boats here were all large as well, of different kinds designed for several men to sit in and throw nets over the side to catch fish in the estuary. Where had the smallest boats come from when she had been watching the smugglers? The ones used for ferrying the casks? She couldn't remember in her panic. She ran on to the end of the wharf, and there, attached to a low wooden outreach beside the tiny jetty Adela had used, were some ordinary little craft belonging to the local men who went out crabbing alone.

Christina ran her eyes over them all and decided to borrow the one nearest her. It was old, it had clearly not been out for some time, and it had a large deposit of sludgy water collected in the bottom; but she knew if she tried to take a better one from the middle of the bunch, it might catch on the others and get stuck. Besides, she was too small and inexperienced to climb over multiple vessels to reach something good, she might end up overbalancing and tumbling headfirst into the icy water. No, she would have to take what was most readily available.

Christina bent down and pulled on the boat's painter the way she had seen Adela do, dragging the boat in towards her six inches at a time. The rope was freezing cold and slimy to the touch from being waterlogged, and it felt hard and thick in her small hands, and very heavy; but the boat itself was not too weighty, and it moved through the water readily enough. Christina continued pulling, constantly looking about to make sure she was not being observed. She was afraid of more soldiers, but everything around her was still and quiet. As soon as the boat was close enough, she hopped down the bank and jumped into it, her small body making scarcely any impact to disturb its equilibrium in the water. A rusty iron pot lay below the thwarts, and she seized it to bail out as much of the water as she could before grabbing the first oar and attempting to put it into its rowlock. To her surprise and dismay she found it incredibly cumbersome to lift, and even harder to manoeuvre into place. Vexation and desperation combined to bring her to the verge of tears as she struggled to get it done. It all looked so simple when she watched the men doing it, why was it proving so difficult for her? Oh, but she had never done anything like this before, that must be it. The thing to do was to keep her head, and hold steady, and persevere. Everybody was depending on her; it would never do to give way at a time like this. Adela wouldn't, she was sure. She carried on, trying her best not to panic at the unexpected delay, but tears of frustration were still brimming in her eyes by the time she eventually managed to get both the oars in place. Feeling exceedingly thankful at her success, she laid them ready on either side of her, reached up and unhooked the painter, and stowed it at her feet.

Her heart was in her mouth as the boat silently slid away from the jetty, slowly at first, then with gathering speed, swirling out into the main stream deep in the middle of the river. Christina didn't know it, but the tide was already on the ebb and its current was rapidly drawing her away from where she wanted to be, over at the other side below Adela's house. She was being swept out towards the river mouth and the desolation of the salt marshes.

She only realised she might be in trouble when she looked up and saw the blackness of the Wye Bridge passing over her head as she was carried under it. However, she still felt confident that she could somehow get across and arrive on the further bank a bit lower down. With difficulty, she got the first oar back out over the gunwale; but her real fright began when she found it was dragging and twisting in the water and felt too heavy to pull back in again. With both hands, she tried desperately to straighten the oar in the water, but she simply couldn't manage it. There was no chance of her getting the other oar operational as well and begin rowing. The boat was now spiralling dizzily round and round in the current, pivoting around the oar she was holding; and with a sinking heart that quickly became a quailing one, Christina realised she couldn't work it. Not at all. There was no way for her to control the boat. She was too small, and the oars were too big. Even a little boat like this was too big. In mounting terror, she looked out over the side and tried desperately to identify the bank and steer towards it using the one oar as a paddle the way Adela had; but seconds later she felt the oar wrested from her grasp by the sucking water surging out with the tide, and she turned and watched helplessly as it twizzled round

126

and round a few times, its light colour marking it out in the darkness, before it was drawn irresistibly away and out of sight.

She looked behind her, still trying to fight the fear engulfing her from the inside, but she couldn't help giving way to it now. This was truly the most terrifying situation she had ever been in. There was nothing she could do, she was in the hands of Fate; and all she could think of was her poor mother's recurring frights about her children going aboard ships, putting to sea, and never coming home again. Had Poppea been having premonitions? Despite Christina's stout heart and inherent bravery, she couldn't prevent a few icy tears from slipping down her cheeks at the thought of her mother and Anthony never seeing her again, and it wasn't long before she began to sob helplessly. Would they ever find out what her end had been?

"I'm not like Ivarr the Boneless at all," she wept. "I thought I was, but I'm not. I had no right to try and compare myself with somebody famous, and be so high and mighty. I'm not even an ordinary girl. I'm just me, Christina. Little, and weak, and frightened. I feel so stupid now. I'm going to die, and I know it serves me right for being too big for my boots, but I only meant to be somebody who mattered for a while, like my new friends. Now look what a quandary it's landed me in. I don't want to leave this world just yet, I want to live. Oh, what am I to do to put this right? Can I try and get over near the mudflats, so I can get out? Or get into a back-water somewhere and wait for the tide to turn, the way the cockle-gatherers do? Oh, please Dada, if you are looking down on me the way they say you do in church, help me to keep my courage up, so I can work something out."

A few lights were twinkling at windows, marking the houses of the now distant town, and dark skeletal hulks and rigs of shipping were still visible against the skyline in the receding harbour. All had gone by unnoticed when Christina's boat had been rushing past; now all were in plain view as signs of hope and life in the bitter, swelling darkness where Christina lay trembling, watching, as her boat washed about in the relentless bubbling water. The last of them disappeared a moment later when she was swept round the final bend in the river and out along the mouth of the Wye into the River Severn. There was nothing but water all around her, and she was alone in the vast reaches of an unfriendly sea.

Chapter Twelve

Adela sat at her bedroom window, wrapped up in a large woollen blanket, with her feet tucked under her to keep them warm. The blanket was rough and scratchy against her skin, but it was the thickest, warmest one she had, and she needed it because the fire was out, and the bedroom had gone cold. A few embers were left in the grate, still glowing faintly grey and red in the dark where the logs had burnt down to a pile of ash earlier in the evening. Adela hadn't wanted to go down for more wood, in case her mother was still up and told her off for not sleeping.

Adela had been awake all night. She had been keeping watch, hoping to see what might be going on over the river in Chepstow harbour, even though she had no idea where the contraband was being taken from, or to, nor at what time they might be moving it. Her thinking had been that she might be able to see enough to work out what was happening and make sure nothing went wrong for her friends. She felt slightly reassured by the fact that, if Christina was right, such operations were rife among the seafaring community, and so things would probably go all right, since there had been no captures or hangings for a good number of years. It was a comforting thought to fall back on. Anyway, if by some mischance there should be any kind of trouble, she could always call out for her Grandad, and get him to help in some way, the way he always did when she had something too big to deal with herself.

Andrew had been keeping Adela company during the midnight hours, but he had gradually nodded off, and now lay asleep under several rugs on top of his bed.

The frozen stars had moved slowly around the heavens, and the night was almost fled away when Adela saw the first signs of commotion at the Castle cliffs and the wharf nearby, clearly indicating some sort of trouble. The lighting was poor and erratic from the lanterns, but she could see the red colour of military uniforms, and large numbers of people. It looked as if there was some fighting going on too, she thought with dismay.

"Oh, my. They've been discovered," she said to herself. "They must have been discovered. I shall have to see what I can do. At least I can find out what has happened, and who has been taken."

Quickly and quietly she put her clothes on and went down the open wooden staircase, taking the steps one at time, and pausing with each step to listen out for her mother. She was using the side of the staircase closest to the wall to avoid treading on the four creaky stairs in the middle, not wanting to disturb anybody else in the partitioned bedroom space above. Nana was a heavy sleeper once she settled into the big feather bed the grandparents occupied, but Mother on her shake-down would wake at any noise, and Grandad was the lightest sleeper of all. Adela was sure he slept with one eye open all the time, the way wolves do. She didn't want to have to stop and explain why she was up at dead of night, there wasn't enough time.

She took the last stair, and then sped across the kitchen. It was still warm in there, where the fire burnt low in the grate. At any other time, Adela would have gladly curled up against it to enjoy the warmth with the cats and Woody, but tonight her mind was on more important matters. She was just getting her shawl from the back of the kitchen door when a low, disembodied voice seemed to creep out of the blackness behind her.

"Now then, me duck, where do you think you're goin'?"

Adela jumped. "Oh, Grandad, you scared me. Sorry, did I wake you? I tried not to. I have to go out."

"Out? Right you are." Ronald didn't waste time asking futile questions, he just picked up his heavy kersey jacket and walking stick, made Woody stay in his basket with a word, and joined Adela on the doorstep as she breathlessly slid back the bolt on the door, being as gentle and quiet as she could. He unlocked the door for her then, his strong fingers turning the key noiselessly where hers would have had to let it go with a click when the tumblers fell into place, his every movement showing how well-practiced he was in stealth.

Together, they glided out of the house and through the garden, and softly undid the gate.

"Where to now, duck?" Ronald enquired under his breath as they stood momentarily in the lane, looking up and down to make sure they were not being watched. He scanned the windows of their house, looking for any signs of movement, but there were none.

"Coracle," Adela breathed, and Ronald made no comment.

It wasn't until they were on the water and paddling across that her grandfather asked any questions.

"Keep your voice down, me duck," he said, quietly. "And tell me why we're out here."

"My friends need help," Adela answered from her place in the bottom of the coracle, where she was crouched under the thwart between his knees, and she quickly sketched out what she had seen.

"Right you are," he said, and skilfully turned the coracle downriver, so they would come in below the main wharf. "Up along there, was they?" He indicated with his paddle as they bobbed past, and Adela nodded. "We need to stay away from the place where they did the arrests," he said, still in a low voice. Sound carried so much further over water, especially at night. "I want to git into town quick, an' keep out of main sight. These sowjers could still be a bit trigger-happy if they've been out chasin' folks and detainin' them. No sense in us getting caught in the aftermath, we won't help nobody if that happens."

Three rhythmic rattling clanks sounded clearly across the harbour from the direction of the river mouth. Three bells. A ship was coming in. It would wait out in the deeper sounds until there was enough tidal water to come in to harbour.

131

"That must be a vessel of the Royal Navy," Adela thought. "We don't see too many of those in Chepstow. I do hope it isn't bringing in more military, but I bet it is. Oh dear. Three bells on the morning watch: that's half past five in the morning." She had assumed the time was later. "It won't be daybreak for a long time yet, then." It was a forlorn thought.

Ronald drew the coracle up to some stone steps cut into the wharf. Two great corvettes were moored, creaking and straining in a light wind, at the place where he was putting in. He had crept in between their huge hulls, so deep in shadow that no-one would be able to spot them, or the craft, even if a search was done right at the waterfront. He listened intently to make sure the coast was clear before attempting to get out, but there had been no sound from anywhere since the sounding of the distant bells on the warship's watch.

"Right, let's go," he whispered, and leapt up the steps. Adela followed him, and together they made their way along the wharf, heading for the nearest street that would take them into town, which at that point along the harbour happened to be Roper Street. What made Adela cast a glance back at the water before leaving the wharf, she never knew; not then, and not afterwards. But she did, and she was glad she did – afterwards. Because what she saw behind her almost stopped her heart.

"Grandad! Grandad stop!" she whispered, frantically pulling at his jacket to arrest his rapid progress. "Stop! Come back, we must go back."

Ronald stepped quickly back into the shadows while he pinpointed the source of her alarm. "What is it, me duck?" he demanded, looking intently where she was pointing.

"There's a boat just gone by in the water. I saw someone in it."

"Sowjers? Or King's men?"

"No, it was someone else, a person crouched down low. But the boat's loose in the water, they weren't using any oars. I think they must be in trouble. We have to go after them," she whispered. "Now. Please, there's no time to lose."

Without another word, Ronald retraced his steps and got into the coracle with Adela, pushing off from the wharf and sculling swiftly out into the middle of the river, where he held it steady while he searched the waters up and down.

"It was going with the current, out to the sea," Adela said, speaking low.

"Sure, about that?"

"Certain."

"Right, we're goin' after 'em," Ronald said decisively, and took the coracle bobbing and weaving past all the ships in the lower docks, over the ripples of the ebbing tide, along the river and out towards the River Severn.

Within minutes, they were in the bitter, spreading reaches of the Mouth of the River Wye, and as he continued to scan the rougher, wider, treacherous watery wastes that made up the confluence around Blackrock, he suddenly gave a loud oath.

"Dang it if I don't see it meself now," he said. "Ted Johnson's owd rowing boat; or I'm a Dutchman." He continued watching for another minute, holding the coracle steady with the paddle. "Bugger me. You're right, there *is* somebody in it. Looks like a little gel to me. She must've took it."

"How can you see so much in this darkness? It's amazing."

"Comes of bein' always out at night. But you've not got bad eyes yourself, lass, spottin' her from where we had got to, back at the wharf. I'd have missed her."

"Is she all right? Can we get to her?"

"I'm just lookin' to see. Ah! You was right, too. Looks like she's lost her oars. That's double trouble, an' no mistake." He began to paddle rapidly through the water, raising his voice to hail the little boat as it washed around, slowly spiralling in helpless circles ahead of them, almost engulfed by the rising waves of the heavier seas. If it stayed afloat long enough, it would soon wash up on the stinking mudflats and deep reed beds marking the banks of the River Severn, where the nauseating smell of mud and dead seaweed was already growing as the waters receded. "Here, me duck," Ronald yelled. "We're coming for you, don't you worry. Just 'owd steady, an' we'll git to you in a minnit."

A tiny voice came over the waves. "Help me! Oh please, please help!"

"That's Christina!" Adela recognised the voice at once, and leaned dangerously far out of the coracle to see better. "Oh, my! Christina. Of all people! What on earth possessed her to try rowing? She's nowhere near strong enough."

With cries of encouragement, Ronald and Adela managed to keep Christina calm in her unsteady little boat, and keep her bailing out the seawater to keep herself afloat, whilst all the time Ronald manoeuvred the coracle close enough to the edge of the tide that he could get both girls safely ashore if either vessel should capsize while he was catching hold of Christina's boat to bring it in alongside. Fortunately, the operation passed without incident under Ronald's fluid management, and the two craft were aligned and lashed nose-to-tail using the two ropes coiled at bottom of each craft. Ronald next edged Adela across so she could get out of the coracle and into the boat with Christina; and once the girls were safely together in the middle of the thwart covered up by Adela's shawl, he moved across himself, freeing up the coracle last of all to make it fast behind the rowing boat. Only then could he begin the long row back to Chepstow, using the one oar and one paddle taken from each craft.

It was some time before Christina could stop crying. Adela held her close and couldn't speak, and even Ronald seemed slightly choked by the emotion of the moment. He studied Christina's starved little face, and then looked at her diminished little shivering form, so thin and wasted, and he seemed sad.

"You'd ha' bin all right, my duck," he assured her, when he did manage to speak, as they slowly made headway back upriver again. "You'd just ha' washed up on them marshes somewhere in the estuary and had to walk back 'ome. It's a good long stride from there, and a mucky one, but you'd ha' bin all right."

Adela looked at him. Her arms were still encircling Christina, who was huddled up tight under the shawl, rigid from fright and cold, utterly exhausted, and wet through. Then they all looked down into the dark, relentless water. Nobody said anything, but they all knew the truth. She would not have been all right. She would never have made it across those mudflats on her own.

Almost two hours later, still in the dark, they arrived back at the house, and Ronald moored both boats together at the pole on the river bank below Fox Hole.

"I'll take Ted's boat back in a bit," he said quietly. "I haven't forgot about your friends, me duck, I still want to find out what's happened to 'em. But fust, we need to git this little chick into the warm an' dry, afore she gits a fever."

Ronald had to help the girls up four feet of steep, filthy river mud before they found secure footing on the rime-covered grass at the top of the bank. Adela was momentarily surprised when she got there to see frost crystals glistening under her wet feet. She had forgotten, in all the drama of recent events, that it had been a frosty night. But it was appropriate, today was Christmas Eve; it might yet be a white Christmas. Ronald took a swift glance up and down the lane, gave her the all-clear, and they crossed together and passed through the garden gate and on into the house.

Everything was still in a state of peaceful repose inside. Woody lay dozing in his basket, Queen Elizabeth and Tansy had taken up the cushions on the two kitchen chairs, and the rest of the family were asleep in their beds upstairs. Ronald went up and woke Isla, while Adela stoked up the kitchen fire and got some water heated. As soon as Isla came downstairs, Christina was stripped, bathed and fed while she told the family of everything she had seen in the harbour during the evening just gone, and what had happened in the streets near the Castle, and how many men, to her knowledge, had been taken. Then, having got the child dressed in a set of Adela's old clothes and into Adela's bed with a warmed stone wrapped in some old flannel set next to her, Isla quietly woke Julia, leaving Andrew still sound asleep. Over a dish of fresh brewed sage tea, they discussed what should be done next. Ronald said he wanted to row back over the river and see what he could find out in the town before dawn. In particular, he wanted to find out where the boys had been taken, if Adela was right in her supposition, and Christina in her assertion, that they had indeed been arrested. It was important to discover their whereabouts as soon as possible, before any sessions might be held.

Isla wanted to talk further with Christina, but that part would have to wait. Christina, exhausted from her harrowing experiences of the long, eventful night, had already fallen asleep.

Chapter Thirteen

Ronald pulled his jacket close about him as he stepped out of the cottage for the second time that night, feeling the pre-dawn chill seep into his bones. He fastened a shawl over his shoulders as well, for good measure, then descended the bank through the mud and got into Ted's rowing boat again. With the coracle still fastened close behind, he rowed across the river to the wharf, freeing the coracle from the boat and tying the two small vessels separately to a nearby stanchion, before taking the road up the hill to the town. Above him, somewhere in the distance, the watchman was calling the last hour before daybreak. It was eight o'clock, and about to get light at last.

Nobody was about. Ronald could hear the first activities of people in their houses as they woke up, and the earliest kitchen servants banging pots and pans in the Broken Drum as he passed by; and he could hear the movements of horses and their ostlers in Hedley's stables, but there was nobody he could approach to pass the time of day with. Even Beaufort Square itself was deserted and silent. Ronald walked all the way up to the Town Gate and called in casually at the toll booth for a bit of a chat with old Jimmy Simpson who was manning it. But despite lingering there, there was nothing to be told. There had been no news when Jimmy had taken over from the last man on duty, and Jimmy seemed immoderately irritated at being asked to provide information of any description.

"'Twas too cold for chattin' when I got here," Jimmy said to Ronald. "I be gettin' too old for this wearisome job. The cold do make my bones ache. An' I don't like to bother wi' Bikk anyway, I don't like his foreign, heathenish ways."

"He ain't a heathen," Ronald corrected him. "He's from Zealand, that's Danish. They're Christians, same as us. An' he speaks good English."

"Well, he ain't the same as me," Jimmy declared, pettishly. "An' Danish is foreign, anyway."

Ronald asked no more. He lingered for a few minutes, talking a bit more of this and that, wanting to ease Jimmy's suspicions and ruffled feelings, and cracked a few jokes to entertain him. Then, feeling sure that Jimmy was happy and had no reasons for mentioning the nature of his unexpected call to anyone, he left.

His next stop was Chepstow Castle, currently garrrisoned by a company of soldiers. A guard was on duty at the gate, leaning half-asleep against his pike, and Ronald exchanged the season's greetings with him from out in the street before sauntering casually over to strike up a conversation. Being a sociable man and easy to talk to, he soon persuaded the bored and weary soldier to invite him into the guardroom for a warm by the fire with a nice brandy and hot water to keep the cold off, and from there they were soon 'chewing the fat', as the soldier cheerfully put it, like old friends.

"Oh, ay. Busy!" the soldier said happily, filling two large pewter tankards with equal measures of first brandy and then water, and sticking a hot poker into each in turn to heat them up, "you wouldn't believe the night we've had. A dozen or more prisoners we've took, some of 'em drunk and disorderly, some vagrants – we'll soon pack them off – an' then afterwards there was a crowd o' men brought to us from the docks, caught red-handed smuggling. Seems somebody snitched 'em out, the way they allus do. No honour among men like that. They'll do anythin' to gain an extra shillin'."

He sniffed, and took his seat by the fireplace, where a generous pile of wood logs lay blazing.

Ronald saluted the soldier with his drink, and asked, "So, where are all these men now, then? I can't hear any noise from 'em. You ain't got drunkards in here, any road."

"No, they all got took away," the soldier said. "I don't exactly know where, but the last lot they brought in was dealt with as soon as the Serjeant got Squire Speybury out of his rooms at the Wig and Mitre. Squire signed the warrants right after he was woken up, then he jumped straight on his horse an' went out o' town."

"Ah. That'll be because the Sheriff's not here till the New Year," Ronald said knowingly. "Squire's deputising. He'll want all those smugglin' charges in apple-pie order ready for when the owd man gits back, I expect. We don't hang about in these parts you know."

"Who is the Sheriff?"

"Ain't he bin in here? I'm surprised you ain't seen 'im. He's Sir Fusby Dikes, an' a tough owd bugger he is, an' all. Squire will want to get them smugglers out o' the way before he gets back. He'll have gone straight back to his house and held a session by now, to get 'em arraigned."

"Ay, o' course. Good work on the Serjeant's part, though, ain't it? Bringin' 'em in like that? So, where are the Assizes held in these parts?"

"Oxford."

"Oh? They'll be on their way there before the day's out, then. Start off this mornin', I shouldn't wonder."

"Nah, they'll hang about till the New Year, see if there's any more, fust," Ronald said. "Take a few cartfuls of 'em together." He hoped, more than he believed it.

He left the Castle with many good wishes from the soldier, and just as many invitations to call in again, with an idea already bubbling away inside his head. Aaron, Tom, and that young sailor-lad would be in those carts, and those carts were now well on their way to one of the local prisons, if they hadn't arrived there already. The lads could be in any of those carts, bound for either Monmouth or Saint Briavels. Or, quite possibly, Monmouth *and* Saint Briavels: they could easily have been split up. Which option was likeliest? This was something Ronald had never had the need to find out before: how prisoners were apportioned to the local gaols. He had had no need to know until now, and for once Ronald was at a loss. There was no way of telling if prisoners were allocated to gaols randomly, or if one gaol was filled up first before the other, or if one gaol was for the more serious charges and the other for lesser. So, where should he head for now, to catch up with them? He had to make a quick decision; they would almost certainly be moved on first thing next morning for the Oxford Assizes if there were enough prisoners, and there very probably would be at this time of year.

He did some rapid thinking. It would be best to go to Monmouth first, he decided, because that was the county gaol. He could check Saint Briavels afterwards. He would call and collect Aaron's and Tom's fathers on the way, to let them know where their sons were and enlist their help in getting them free. It was vain to believe he could do anything much without them.

Ronald went down to the river, untied his coracle, and with aching arms and a painful back, wearily took on the current again, this time paddling up the river as far as Brockweir. There, he left the coracle tied up near the ferry crossing and ran across country to Aaron's family's house. By the time he got there, his legs were about to give way. He had never felt so utterly worn out.

Back in Chepstow, Ted Johnson came past the wooden jetty by the Castle on his way to his daughter's and stopped and scratched his head in puzzlement. His boat was moored right in front of him, more than fifty yards downstream from where he usually left it, and one of the oars appeared to be missing. It was obvious someone had moved it; but how and why it had become damaged and so dirty, and who might have taken it, and where they might have gone, Ted never did find out.

Chapter Fourteen

At the Arundel's house on Hewelsfield Common, Able was pacing up and down in the large kitchen. He was alone. His wife was out paying an early morning visit to a neighbour, and his younger sons were with friends, out on the common, trying to fly a kite. The kitchen curtains were drawn tight shut across the window so no-one could see in. If anyone called, he wanted them to think the entire family was out.

Able had not been to sleep all night. His lute still lay wrapped in its blanket on the kitchen table, where he had put it down and temporarily forgotten about it while he poured himself a stiff drink, followed by several more. He was still wearing his musician's costume of blue and scarlet bays and says because it hadn't occurred to him yet to change out of them. He was still a nervous wreck after what had happened the previous night, and he was trying to work out what to do. His troupe had been playing at the Assembly Rooms in Monmouth, and he had started a brawl there. Another one. Like the one he had set off at that barn dance at the end of November in Lydney. On that night, he had hoofed it home over the fields to avoid apprehension. Last night, he had escaped through a back door and returned to his house by various back roads, galloping through the lanes in his horse and cart, and thus depriving the rest of the troupe of one half of their means of transport home. One part of him felt he was an utter craven to have legged it again, leaving the rest of his troupe stranded with only the one horse, one cart, and a long walk home; but the livelier, more sensible part of him knew it would have been foolhardy just standing around waiting to be arrested by the Sheriff's men once the fight was broken up. The trouble was, he couldn't help wondering now if he had roughed anyone up enough, or caused enough damage, for them to come after him this time. Everybody at the event last night must have known who had set that fight off, and now he bitterly regretted it, but what else could he have done? He was getting far too nervous and jittery to be doing the kind of things he was doing: all this secret, clandestine stuff. His mettle just wasn't as strong any more. No matter where he went, he felt jumpy about careless chatter, excessive drink, and the wrong people being around and hearing too much. Last time it had been a farmer wagging his tongue a bit too freely after he had had a few over the eight. This time, the Colonel had had to be stopped; and a bit of fisticuffs on both occasions had been the only thing Able could think of in a hurry to divert attention away from what was being blurted out. The farmer had learned his lesson, thankfully, and had since piped down completely, but Colonel Meadows was getting steadily worse: deafer, noisier, and less and less circumspect every time he went out and mixed with people. It was getting beyond.

Able almost jumped out of his skin when the knock came at the door.

"They're here for me!" he thought, panicked. "They've come. The game's up." Then his heart steadied, and he realised it was a quiet tap, and not the authoritative banging that arresting officers would have made. Able went and opened the door and Ronald slipped inside, pulling it shut behind him.

Able remained where he was, gaping. He knew who Ronald Baker was, of course, everybody in the Forest did; but he had never had occasion to socialise with him before, and now he was wondering what on earth this man was doing, gaining admittance to his home here in Hewelsfield in such a furtive and mysterious manner so early in the morning. Had he been at the dance, perhaps? Seen the fight? Able wasn't the quickest-witted of men, especially when he was under stress, so he stood spluttering incoherent questions while Ronald made sure the inner doors were all tightly closed before coming over and shushing him.

"Not now, mate," Ronald said, hastily. "We haven't got much time. I'm here to take you with me to Monmouth. I'll explain as we travel. Git your cloak, an' come on. We need to git your cart out."

"Monmouth?" Able asked, struggling to get back inside the cloak he had thrown over a kitchen chair when he had come in, "why Monmouth?" He grabbed his hat and followed Ronald out through the door into the burgeoning daylight.

Ronald led the way out to the stable, where the Arundel's horse was now asleep after its night out. As he briefly disclosed what he knew of the night's events, Able's anxiety levels shot up a thousand-fold.

"Oh, good grief," he moaned. "What a mess. First me, now my son. What are we going to do?"

"We're goin' to go and git 'im out," Ronald declared, leading the horse into the little courtyard and harnessing him into the cart.

"Out? Of prison? How?" Able was uncharacteristically demanding in his distress. "How are we going to spring him? And what'll happen if we don't pull it off? My musical group is supposed to be performing at the Squire's house tonight. If we don't turn up, there's going to be a pretty row. That'll be worth seeing, at any rate," he added, with equally uncharacteristic bitterness. "The Squire cuts quite a figure at a dance. I've no doubt he'll be just as entertaining in a fury. Should be worth seeing, at any rate." He began to fret in real earnest.

"Stop worritin', mate," Ronald said. "You *will* be there, I shall be takin' you meself."

"Ah, but we can't perform without Aaron. We're nowhere near as good without Aaron." Able took off his hat and turned it several times in his hands before starting to pick at the brim.

"Look," said Ronald firmly. "Bring all the equipment, an' all the instruments, an' carry on as if you're just goin' to do the Squire's dance the same as always. Calm down, think normal, and it'll make it easier to pretend to yourself that a call into Monmouth on the way is somethin' ordinary. You've got to do whatever it takes to keep yer wits about you. It's no good fallin' apart, or we'll *all* end up inside. If things go accordin' to plan, Aaron will graft hisself on to the band as soon as we git him out o' prison, an' no-one will be any the wiser. If you think positive, and approach it that way, everythin' should fall into place. Agreed?"

Miserably, Able agreed. He changed into his ordinary clothes, which were warmer, and spent the next half hour putting instruments, changes of clothes and costumes, and stools for the musicians into the cart, his mind dismally engaged with thoughts of all the ways this endeavour could go tits-up. Ronald, ever practical, got the horse harnessed, and put in some oats and a nosebag ready for later.

Together, leaving the rest of the Arundel family to come home at their leisure none the wiser themselves, Ronald and Able set off in the cart along the pretty little country lane, now rigid with frost, which led to the bridge at Bigsweir. Once there, they paid the toll at the turnpike for the crossing, and went up the muddy side-road along the river as far as Whitebrook, where they toiled up the steep hill into the pine forest, and continued on the road to Trellech through gorse-strewn heathland that was the domain of landowners and hunting dogs, snipe, woodcock, rabbits and grouse, where Colonel Meadows' imposing, but decaying country manor house stood in the village itself, close to the Harold Stones, which stood as a stark reminder of the burial customs of the ancients.

The cart turned into the driveway and rolled slowly over the weeds and gravel stones. Tom's father came leaping down a set of crumbling steps to give them a full-throated greeting, accompanied by a chorus of similar baying from his English hunting dogs. He was dressed all in his best and gave the impression he had been on his way out somewhere, but anyone who cared to observe him more closely couldn't fail to realise that he lacked a wife. His colourful embroidered yellow doublet, worn under an unbrushed coat of a shade popularly known as gooseturd green, bore evidence of a number of half-rubbed out food stains, and his black britches needed the attention of a needle and thread. Further – and worse – his dark green hat, a well-preserved relic of finer days, whose huge curled brim swept well below his right eye, was overly ornate for the rest of his dress, as was the ace-of-spades beauty spot inked on his cheek, while his elaborately curled jet-black wig was out of the ark. Had Colonel Meadows been a younger, handsomer man, he might have passed off such an odd collection of finery as injudicious but *avante garde,* and been taken for a lightly mocking rogue. As it was the fancy hat, twirling moustaches and feathery grey dogs' tails waving about in front of him gave him a slightly seedy air, such as an actor from a run-down provincial theatre might exhibit at a risqué performance.

"Aha!" he said, looking into the cart, and drawing his eyebrows together slightly. "Ha. Thought for a moment you'd brought my boy back, but I see now I was mistaken. Annoying! Anyhow, you're very welcome. But I had expected him home by now. No matter, come in, come in. Any idea where the young blighter might be? I was just on my way to see if I could find him."

A servant took the horse and cart round to the stables at the back, and the Colonel led them up the steps into the main hall, calling for some cake and wine as he strode inside. The dogs ran ahead in rumbustious disarray, thinking they were going to be doing something exciting somewhere. When it didn't happen, they flumped down together in a disappointed heap on the huge rug in front of the fire, and gently snored themselves into a bored sleep. Stepping over them, Ronald briefly described the events of the night, as he knew of them, to the Colonel.

Able, who had already heard the main parts of the story, now added wavering questions and comments of his own, accompanied by much hand-wringing. The Colonel listened irritably, and watched the hand gestures with mounting impatience before explosively demanding at the top of his voice to know how the damned young fool could have got himself mixed up in such a business.

Ronald had no answer to give to a question like that, but he was able to tell the Colonel what he knew about Rigo and the *Senhora da Luz* and its contraband, leaving the Colonel furious but immediately sensible of all the implications of the situation, and pragmatic about his available options for dealing with it. He had some money – not as much as he had once had, but enough - and he had good standing with Sir Fusby Dikes and other high-ranking officials in the county. But he needed to hang on to all he had of both if he wanted to continue maintaining his present lifestyle, even though he always lived prudently and kept himself largely to himself, and generally asked no favours of anyone. He knew he couldn't afford to risk his present status, or that of his son, by volunteering to pay a massive fee to get the case dropped. Nor could he do anything else that would look questionable in the light of public scrutiny. The notary would drop Tom, for a start, and Tom would find it very hard to regain his status, or any further livelihood, should that happen. Country people remembered things for generations. They would never live down the disgrace. On the face of it, it was better to let the charges stand, and for Tom to deny them in court: but was that wise?

Dropping his voice somewhat, the Colonel said, rather thickly, "No idea what to do about this. Bad business, bad. My poor, dear wife would turn in her grave if she knew her only son was facing this kind of trouble." He swallowed his wine and stared into the lees at the bottom of the glass, lost for a lingering second in his own private reflections.

"Don't you fret now, Lyndon," Ronald said, patting him on the back. "I reckon I know how we can git Tom out of trouble in double-quick time; an' nobody the wiser for it. The only thing is, you'll have to be prepared to put some money into one o' your most trusted servant's hands, because we've got to have some help. We can't do it all ourselves. We need someone who's reliable come hell or high water. Have you got somebody that would fit the bill?"

"Rowles, my horse-man is the only man I would trust around here, of my own or of anybody else's households. He is impeccable."

"Then we must use him. Call him in. We'll have to bring him in on this."

"Right you are," the Colonel said, and got up to open one of the doors leading to the inner dominions of the great house. He was followed by all his dogs, who had leapt up the minute he moved and were once more milling round in a foment of excitement. "Elsie!" he bawled, into the black abyss beyond. "Send Rowles in here, will you?" He shut the door firmly and returned to his seat, where his dogs promptly collapsed into an inert heap beside him.

Presently, the servant who had taken Able's cart and horse appeared, clutching his cap between his hands. "Sir?" he asked respectfully.

"Ah, Rowles, I've fetched you for a reason. Delicate matter, you understand, delicate! You mustn't breathe word of it beyond these four walls, is that clear?"

Rowles inclined his head and waited. So did the Colonel. The Colonel was looking at Ronald expectantly, and Rowles followed his gaze. Eventually, Able did the same. Ronald returned the gazes, and finally spoke to the servant first.

"Ray, I knew your dad afore you was born. A good man he was, we watched each other's backs for years, till he was finally took fer poachin'."

"I know it," returned Rowles. "And I know you gave him a character reference at his trial before he was transported. You did what you could, and Mother and I were grateful for it. I still am."

"The reason I'm bringin' it up, Ray, is this. I could depend on your dad with me life, and he could depend on me for his. We never split on each other, never would have given each other up, no matter what. Now then. What I want to know is this: are you the same kind of man as yer father, or are you not? Because if not, you're free to walk out of here an' leave us, and there'll never be a word of reproach said from any one of us."

"And if I stay?"

"There's job to be done today that we need your help to bring off. Dangerous, and if any of us git caught, we can't tell on the others. We must go down alone. If you hear me out on it, and decide you won't come, you have to swear you'll never repeat a word of what you've heard."

"Well, I can swear to that, at least."

"What'll you swear on?"

"My mother's grave. She died last year."

"Did she? I'm sorry to hear it. Must've broke her heart when she lost her man that way."

"It did. And I repeat, I swear on her grave never to tell a living soul what I am about to hear."

"Good man. And we swear along with you, though we're already in this up to our necks. Now here's the thing. We have three good lads in gaol somewhere hereabouts, either Monmouth or Saint Briavels; and we have to git them out afore they're moved on. Short of gunpowder to blow the prisons up, the only way I can think of is to put somebody in their place instead, an' then try an' git the substitutes out afterwards by claiming misidentification, or summat like that. I'll work the details out later. But whoever we use, they must be prepared to risk standin' trial, because there's a chance we might not be able to git 'em out before then. One of the lads we're tryin' to free is the Colonel's, another is Able's here. The third is a young sailor-lad we don't know anythin' about, except they was all took together."

"The handy-man might be willing to put himself forward to double as Tom," Rowles said, doubtfully, "but, much as I hate to say it, if any of the warders know Tom, or Able's son, by sight, your strategy will never work."

"It only has to work while we git them out the prison," Ronald urged. "Once the lads are back on the street, they can't take them in again. We'll just swear they was somewhere else at the time the prisoners was arrested, and that they mistook their captives. That's all."

"It could work," the Colonel said loudly, starting to pace up and down. "I agree with Ronald here. We might have to bribe the warder... No, wait, no, no, no. That would never do. Er, what about *tricking* the warder instead? Getting him to hand over the keys because one of the prisoners is sick, or something? And then we all rush in and get the lads out and leave the servants behind in the confusion. Could it be done? ... Hmm? ... If it's dark?" He thought some more and sighed. "It's an awfully long shot," he said to Ronald, the volume of his voice subsiding as he gave in to doubt. "I'm deeply grateful to you old chap, but I fear we really are asking too much of our fellow men. We should not be using our servants as a means of avoiding a spell in prison ourselves. I'll willingly substitute myself for my son if I can get away with it. Let's just do it ourselves. I doubt it will work, since everybody knows me, but I *must* try something."

"And me," said Able.

"I believe I understand your situation better than you think, Colonel," said Rowles, speaking up on his own initiative for the first time. "What you need as the substitute is the kind of person with nothing to lose who needs some ready money in their hand to sort their problems out. I know several of those. Give me half an hour to round three of them up, and we'll make the journey with you. It's worth a try, at any rate, though what will happen if we get found out, I dread to think."

"Never mind the 'what-ifs'," Ronald said. "Leave all that to me. Be back at twelve o' clock wi' these men, an' the Colonel and me will treat you handsome. And many thanks, mate."

Rowles nodded his acknowledgement together with his own thanks, and left.

"Count me in," Able said unexpectedly, from his place by the fireside, speaking up with sudden, fierce desperation. "What's one more fight to me now, the way things are? What the heck. I want Aaron at that dance, or the Squire will have my guts for garters. And if I don't do anything at all, Phyllis'll chop off whatever bits I've got left after the Squire's finished with me, for letting our son get in such a fix in the first place. After the trouble I've already caused, I've not got much to lose."

Ronald sat down with the two men at the fireside with another glass of wine and spent the next half hour sketching out a plan in its entirety, refining it and considering various contingencies, should they crop up, before finally getting them both to agree on it.

"Capable of carrying out orders and acting on your own initiative if things go wrong?" the Colonel suddenly barked at Able.

Able nodded, taken aback, and looked across at Ronald, who had moved away to sit comfortably at a small table beside the great staircase where the wine and cake were laid out, and was freely helping himself to top-ups of both. Colonel Meadows saw the look and followed it until his eyes rested on Ronald.

"Ah!" he bellowed. "Wondering why I'm not asking Ronald the same question, I see. Well." He locked his hands behind his back and began pacing up and down in the hallway. "It just so happens that I know Mister Baker here already. Ha! Steady fellow, good in a tight spot... reliable... trustworthy... and, er... so on! Ha!"

Able couldn't understand how the Colonel would know of such a thing, but it was obvious that somehow, for some reason, Ronald and he went back quite a long way.

Chapter Fifteen

Rowles returned well ahead of his time, bringing with him the two sons of one of the Colonel's former gamekeepers, both of whom had had a few recent skirmishes with the law and needed to keep low profiles for the time being. He was also accompanied by a young ruffian who had been sleeping rough up on the heath since being released from the stocks in Monmouth for having no visible means of support. The three sat with Rowles in the cart while the Colonel rode his horse ahead of them at a fast pace into Monmouth town. Horses and cart were put to stable at the Drover's Rest as soon as they arrived, and there the Colonel left them. He walked over the road to the lane which ran beside the River Monnow, while the young men, under Rowles' supervision, took a swift pint in the Merry Pheasant, an inn they had passed on their way through the town a hundred yards back down the road. There were only a couple of hours left before dusk. They had to be done and finished, and out of Monmouth well before then. After that, the gate-house over the River Monnow closed, and there would be only one road left out of town.

Down beside the river, beyond the reach of even the most penetrating beams of sunshine, and close by the shambles of the slaughterhouses, was the holding-house for the prisoners of Monmouth. Spiritless, comfortless, and chilling, it lay beneath a side street, built into the riverbank, its pollutions, like those of the slaughterhouses, washed clean by the river. Colonel Meadows took off his hat before he went in, not as a mark of respect, but to stop the constantly dripping water coming down off the top of the vault from spoiling its fabric. The door banged shut behind him under its own weight, and he was struck afresh by the cold and damp in there, both of which were deeply penetrating despite good fires being lit in the entrance and in the warder's room to the side. A slatternly woman was cooking something in a pot with her back to him, and Colonel Meadows addressed a request to her that she fetch the warder. She duly waddled off.

"Ha! Wadsworth, my man!" he shouted, when the warder arrived several minutes later, limping with the rheumatics from his long vigils in the damp. "Got your list of the men being held in chokey with you? Like to check it if I may. See who the current lot of inmates are and what they've been up to."

The warder limped out again, and reappeared with a grimy, dog-eared log book. He took up a three-legged stool, placed it before the fire, then sat on it and opened the book, resting it across his knees. He licked his fingers before turning each page to peer at it in the firelight and decipher what was written there.

"Anybody in pertickler you was lookin' fer, Capting?" Wadsworth asked, squinting up at Colonel Meadows.

"Er, not really," the Colonel said. "Just hand the book over and let me look at it myself would you, my man? That's a good fellow. And I'm a Colonel, not a Captain."

The Colonel leafed through the most recent pages, trying to avoid touching the places where Wadsworth's spittle lay smeared across the paper. Rigo's name was on the previous day's list, but not that of Aaron or Tom. Trying not to appear crestfallen, the Colonel handed the book back to Wadsworth.

"Any chance I could speak to this young man named here?" he asked as casually as he could, indicating Rigo on the list before he closed the book. "I'd like to have a word with him, if I may."

Wadsworth nodded and took the book away, returning with a large bracelet-sized metal ring, on which were several weighty keys.

"If you'll foller me, Capting," he said, and led the way down some steps until they were in a wet passageway leading to a tunnel that ran alongside the river, where all the previous day's prisoners were being held in one cavernous cell.

It was hard to make out how many men were in there, it was so gloomy and so many bodies were laid out in the wet straw, but Colonel Meadows spotted a common sailor dressed in blue and called for the man to come over. It was Rigo, still in the clothes he had been wearing the day before, and he came quite willingly to see what they wanted. Wadsworth lit a torch in a bracket on the wall and left the Colonel with the keys and the prisoners, taking his lantern back with him to light his way to the relative comfort of his room upstairs. As soon as he had gone, the Colonel began to talk.

"Listen to me," he said, keeping his voice very low, even though none of the other prisoners were showing any signs of stirring, "I intend to get you and your friends out of here, but I didn't see the other boys' names down on the list. Do you know what became of them?"

"W-Well, Nick's all right, he g-g-got clear before the King's men came," Rigo said. "He left separately."

"Nick the waggoner, do you mean? I didn't even know he was implicated. Thank heaven for small mercies. And the others?"

"Aaron a-a-and Tom have both been taken to somewhere that sounded like Saint Ber-Ber-Bubbles. I heard the order just as we were leaving. The Serjeant said they were to deal w-w-with the ones taken for loitering along with the drunk and disorderly arrests. Only the sm-m-mugglers were brought here."

"Ah, Saint Briavels. Of course. They'll be indicted for loitering, not arraigned. But how did they get off a smuggling charge? I thought you were all in it together."

"N-N-Not really." Rigo turned hastily to check behind him as somebody stirred in the straw, and then lowered his voice even further, so the Colonel had to put one hand behind his best ear in order to hear. "Aa-Aaron and Tom took Nick's dogs to him last night after he got his cart loaded, and then hung around for a while. But they weren't with me. We got taken separately. They were s-s-

153

somewhere in the lanes, back along the wharf, I think. I was still watching the caves."

"Right," the Colonel said, thinking hard. "Right. So, if I understand you aright, they'll now await the next petty sessions for a trial on a misdemeanour charge. That could just mean a fine, or it could carry a gaol sentence. Did you hear anyone say *why* they thought those boys were loitering? What they thought they were doing there?"

"Well, a-at the t-t-time, some of the soldiers s-said they were aiding and abetting, but the others thought they were waiting to steal from the sm-m-mugglers who escaped."

"Escaped, did you say? Do you mean some of them actually got away?"

Rigo nodded. "A lot of them. In f-fact, most of them did, I think. I'm not sure, e-e-everything happened very fast, but a little girl warned us the revenue men were coming, so somebody climbed back up to the caves to warn them. They all got free; the soldiers only caught the last few down at the river leaving with the carts – and me – because we couldn't run anywhere; and even if we could have, w-w-we weren't so f-f-fast. And in the end, they assumed *we* were the ones smuggling, and that Aaron and Tom were just hangers-on, up to no good."

"Ah! They supposed them to be in the vicinity by accident. I see."

"Yes, Sir. I didn't hear wh-what happened to the ones left in the caves under the Castle, but I think there are tunnels up there, and that's why they got away."

"Right," the Colonel said again. "In that case, there's no time to waste. You, Rodrigo, can expect to be taken from here to Oxford, to await the Lent Assizes. After sentencing, you face transportation to one of our colonies as a convicted felon – it'll most probably be Jamaica. We must get you out of here at once."

"Jamaica? D-Did you say Jamaica?" Rigo said, brightening, "Sir, I would like to be sent to Jam-m-maica. I have been there before. I don't m-m-mind waiting to sail from Oxford, if it will get me to Jamaica. I can get to my own country quite easily from there. It isn't far."

"It will be a very long way for you, my lad. As well as a long wait. You can't sail from Oxford, it isn't a port. You'll be kept in prison until the next transport ship goes out of Bristol for Port Royal; and once you get there, you'll be working on a plantation as a slave. You won't be going anywhere as a free man for a very long time, if ever."

Rigo shook his head, and cast down his eyes, looking sorrowful at the Colonel's bad news. It was the first thing to have happened that night that appeared to have upset him.

There came the sound of footsteps, and the gaoler reappeared. "Beggin' yer pardon, Capting," he said, respectfully, speaking at a distance.

"Yes, yes, man. I'll take myself off now. Any idea when this prisoner will be moved? I need to send my manservant back in few minutes with some things for him." The Colonel spoke loudly enough for several of the bundles of desperate humanity lying in the straw to stir and sit up, before slumping, tired and miserable, back into their places again.

"I don't know, sir," the gaoler said. "But I expect it will be tomorrer sometime. They usually waits fer the mornin' delivery, if you understand me, an' goes after that. An' they'll doubtless be givin' thesselves a bit of extra time afore they comes, it bein' Christmas Day. Do church first, an' all that."

"Very good, my man. Well, many thanks for accommodating my request. I'll see myself out."

The Colonel pressed several coins into Wadsworth's hand, which was being held discreetly open palm upwards. Then he handed back the keys, and walked swiftly back the way he had come, along the tunnel with the wet and weeping walls.

After carefully counting the coins by the light of the torch in the wall bracket, the gaoler lifted the flaming brand out of its socket and walked off, leaving the prisoners to the damp and darkness.

Fifteen minutes passed by in deep silence. Then came a furtive rustling, and the sound of some quiet footsteps. Somebody approached the cell by candlelight, making some of the prisoners move fitfully in the cold here and there at the slight noise. Only Rigo remained where he was, standing alone with his hands still on the bars of the cell. The candle went out. Another small noise was just discernible in the penetrating darkness: a slight metallic click and the creak of ironwork, followed by more quiet footsteps, this time fading into the distance.

One of the inmates raised his head out of the straw, blearily. "Who's that?" he asked.

"Shurrup, will you?" another voice said.

Then silence reigned once more, with the only the intermittent scuffling of rats to interrupt it.

Chapter Sixteen

Ronald and Able had made their way in the musician's cart as far as Bigsweir Bridge, there to await the results of the Colonel's foray into Monmouth. It was an anxious wait. It seemed to take forever. Able gnawed at his knuckles and wished more than once that they had gone with him, even though they had all agreed it would render the enterprise far too conspicuous to turn up with two carts, only to depart a short time afterwards with both full of people.

"With a bit o' luck, they should all be out by now," Ronald declared, with cheerful confidence. "The Colonel did say Monmouth was the likeliest place for 'em all to be."

At last, they saw Rowles coming towards them at a smart pace with passengers in the back of his vehicle, and Able sat forward eagerly, full of anticipation, trying to espy his son. Rowles waved his whip as soon as he spotted them, then slowed right up to come over the bridge and pay the toll. He rolled forward from the turnpike until he was well out of earshot of it, before coming to a slow and careful halt a few yards in front of them.

"How did it go?" Able asked, eagerly, scanning the back of Rowles' conveyance. As soon as he realised Aaron wasn't in there, his face fell.

"We got Rigo. That was all," Rowles said. "But it went all right, worked a treat. The Colonel is taking him back to the Manor. You can take Edric's boys here and use them to get Aaron and Tom the same way; they must both be in Saint Briavels. It should be easy enough, once you get there. Say you're there for a visit, take these boys in with you, and just make an excuse to get the cell door unlocked; that's the thing."

The two remaining lads were the gamekeeper's sons, and they each nodded a greeting as they jumped out of Rowles' cart and scrambled in among the musical instruments arranged in the back of Able's, setting one of the lutes twanging gently in the process. Rowles touched his forehead and wished them all luck, then he started off towards Whitebrook and the wooded ridge of the Narth to return to Trellech, while Ronald went through the turnpike and over the bridge and turned Able's cart off the main road into the rough lanes to make the onward journey to Saint Briavels.

It took more time to get to the prison than it did to check with the gatekeeper once they arrived: there were no new prisoners of any description inside. None at all. The ledger held no entries after Saint Thomas Didymus' Day, when six vagrants had been brought in. Prior to that, the last entry made was at Martinmas.

"Now what?" Able wanted to know, trying desperately not to give in to despair, as Ronald took up the reins and flicked them at the horse to make him move off. "What shall we do next?" He inspected his fingernails closely, then chose one and began to bite at it.

"Well, if they're not here, they must've been took somewhere else," Ronald said. "Can't be Saint Woolos or Usk, they're too far away. I don't know what to do now. We can't go wanderin' round lookin' for them, that's for sure. It'll be gittin' dark soon. We'd better make our way back to Trellech an' join the Colonel, see what he can find out for us. We'll only lose a couple of hours that way. They must've bin moved; but where they'd be, I don't know. It don't make sense to me."

"What shall we do if the Colonel's not back?" Able asked, moving on to another fingernail and continuing to chew. "It's a waste of time going to Trellech if nobody's there. We'll lose even more time that way and we can't afford to lose *any*. It could be like here, just deserted. I don't know. I'm worried. Something's gone wrong. I can see I'm going to end up having to do this dance on my own. I should never have let Aaron go and sell that lute yesterday. I knew it was a mistake."

"Now don't start frettin' all over agen, mate. We've still got a bit of daylight left. I reckon they must be in Monmouth, now I think on about it. Mebbe they was asleep, an' the Colonel didn't see 'em."

Feeling somewhat nonplussed and extremely anxious at the absence of the prisoners, though they said nothing more about it to each other, they went back the way they had come, heading for Bigsweir Bridge, hoping against hope that Aaron and Tom might have made their way back to the Colonel's manor by some other way that Rowles had no knowledge of, or that there might at least be news of them to be had there.

Just outside Saint Briavels, at the turning that took them off the main road into the lanes, they caught sight of a cart ahead of them. It was travelling the same way they were, but going extremely slowly, and as they drew closer they could see why. It was being pulled by a most unwilling horse, which ambled along as slowly as it could, munching great mouthfuls of grass from the sides of the lane as it went. The driver, who seemed in no hurry, was soon recognisable as one of the locals, a husky old man with enormous side-whiskers, named Henry Garryll. He did all the ferrying of prisoners to and from Monmouth and Saint Briavels, but today Ronald and Able could see even at a distance that his cart was completely empty. He had no prisoners and no guard with him at all. Coming on top of the empty ledger at the gaol, it seemed most mysterious. It was as if the supply of prisoners had somehow dried up and disappeared.

"Better git yourselves under the covers, lads," Ronald advised the two young men in the back in an undertone. "It's Happy Henry up ahead."

They did as Ronald suggested straight away, and ducked down under the tarpaulin.

"Now then, Henry," Ronald called out, as he caught up with him and drew up alongside. "You started carryin' fresh air to the prisons now, or summat? They're either givin' you lighter duties these days, or else your felons have got fed up an' gone home when you wasn't lookin'."

"Who did thee want?" Henry asked, his face, under his straw hat, a bleary mixture of gingery whiskers, purple veins, and entrenched misery.

"Nobody in particular. Just as well, ain't it? I'd be a long while findin' 'em, the way things are lookin'." Ronald nodded towards the empty cart.

"Oh, that," Henry said. "Bugger me if us wasn't waylaid jus' after dawn in the Forest."

"You wasn't!"

"Us was. Yes." The memory of it seemed to grieve him deeply. "Dree footpads. Took down the guard, them did, an' what prisoners us did have all escaped."

"What was you waylaid for?"

"Thought us might have some strongboxes, I do reckon. Us do carry 'em sometimes, but us didn't have none this mawnin'. All us had were nine prisoners, an' the whole lot of 'em ran off dang-swang into the trees an' disappeared. Lucky I warn't beat up, left on my own wi' desperate men like that."

"What happened to your guard?"

"Found 'un tied up in the Forest past noon, about two hour ago. Him was all right."

"An' yer prisoners?"

"Gone," he said bitterly. "Them was all young sailor-lads what had been arrested for bein' drunk an' such-like."

"Sailors? No-one else?"

"No. Not as I know of."

All three men fell silent and looked about them. Acres of dense woodland stretched away on every side about them, with even denser undergrowth fringing the roadsides and overhanging the lanes. It was certainly a good place to hide out in.

160

"Did this happen anywhere near here?" Able asked, speaking up for the first time.

"Ar. Just the other side of Saint Briavel's." Henry flicked his finger to indicate somewhere behind him. "Come out of Pickethill Woods, them did, right in that dark bit down where the road dips at Aylesmore Brook atween all them tall trees. I just come from her now. Did a bit of a search today wi' a few spare men from Saint Briavels, but they didn't find nothink, so now them'll carry on tomorrer. That's why I aren't in no 'urry. I'll go home now, get a bit o' rest, like. They'm sendin' a load o' soldiers by Tidenham Chase way tomorrer, beatin' the bushes at the roadsides as they d'come through; though I don't think it's worth searchin' so far south, meself. I don't think any o' them prisoners will get so far, all shackled together at the legs, wi' handcuffs on. Them'll be found somewhere hereabouts, I mek no doubt; an' then them'll want my cart so they can git 'em all put back where they b'long. I hope they find 'em all right. Otherwise I might not git paid."

He drew an old blanket closer about him to cover his rough smock, touched the brim of his straw hat, and clicked the horse to move him on. As he turned a final bend in the lane and disappeared ahead of them, Ronald and Able looked at each other.

"Sailor-lads," Able repeated, and groaned softly. "That doesn't sound like my boy. Or Tom."

Ronald was unable to give him any assurances. He didn't think it sounded like them, either. "The arrestin' officers might be wrong," he suggested, after careful thought. "Henry wouldn't know the diff'rence, not unless he spoke to 'em, an' he ain't renowned for his conversational skills. We may as well look round, see if we can find 'em, find out if our boys are among 'em. You'd be kickin' yerself if we got to Trellech and found we'd left 'em behind."

"Oh, stop it. I can't bear to think about it. My nerves are falling apart as it is. You'll have to talk me through this," Able declared, miserably. "Where do we start looking? Where would you hide if it was you?"

161

"Well, not anywhere round Aylesmore Brook, fer a start," said Ronald, who knew the whole of the Forest of Dean like the back of his hand. "It's too boggy in those parts. And not in Pickethill Woods, neither. Nine'll make too much noise movin' about between the trees, an' they'll be hindered by all the boscage round there. No, they need to find somewhere they won't be overlooked, where they can move about quiet, an' they need to be able to light a fire to keep thesselves warm while they git their chains off. Only one place fits the bill, an' it's back the way we've just come."

He turned the horse around, while Able put his head in his hands and groaned with anxiety. "Thank goodness I'm with you," he exclaimed, as Ronald clicked the horse into a gentle trot and made off back towards Saint Briavels. "I'd be going spare if I was on my own. Where are we going? What place are you thinking of?"

Ronald made him no answer.

"Come on, Ron, tell me what you're thinking, man. I can't guess where we're going."

Ronald smiled and said, "If they've got any sense, they'll have waited till the coast was clear, an' then made off up the road to the stone quarry. See if they could find some hammers and chisels left out. It's not that far, an' it's the quickest way to git free."

"Ah! Of course!" Able exclaimed, impressed. "Saint Briavel's quarry! I reckon you could be right, Ron. I think so, anyway. At least it would make sense to go there and look." Relieved, he knocked his pipe out to take a smoke, having chewed all his nails down so far there was nothing left on his fingers now to gnaw at. Once he had filled the bowl with a screw of tobacco, he took a long draw on it. "It's an obvious place, if you think about it. I only hope the military don't think of it as well."

"We're stealin' a march on 'em, even if they do," Ronald said, imperturbably, clicking at the horse again to get him up to a gentle trot. "We'll have time to get your lad an' his mate, an' warn the rest of 'em, don't worry – you can come out agen now, boys," he added, calling into the back of the cart. "Henry's gone, and by the sounds of things, we'll soon have some company for you two to hide out with!"

Once back at Saint Briavels, it wasn't long before they found the missing men. The village was quiet, and they drove straight past the castle and prison as quickly as they could, taking the road that led to Clearwell to get to the quarry, and stopping by the roadside when they reached their destination.

Edric's sons hid inside the cart again while Able and Ronald jumped down and undertook a rapid search of the whole area to make sure it was safe. Once they were certain, they called out for the hidden men to come out join them, and walked together in line, following a faint but perceptible smell of tobacco and wood smoke across several clearings before eventually homing in on a mix of voices coming from a sheltered recess in a rocky outcrop at a distance from the main quarry.

Able's spirits had been rising by the minute once he realised there were people about, especially since there was no work being done, and within the space of fifteen minutes his hopes were fulfilled when they found Aaron and Tom hidden out with the other prisoners in a part of the abandoned end of the workings, doing the best they could with a number of worn-out chisel stumps that had been thrown aside by the quarrymen. Using stones as hammers, and a broken file that had previously been used for sharpening the cutting edges of tools, the escaped men had put the retrieved implements to good use, cutting and filing through their shackles to free themselves one by one. Several had done the business already and made good their escape, while others, who were a bit slower dispersing, hailed Ronald gladly, recognising him as a sympathetic local man and a friend in need. Many of the Wye Valley and Forest of Dean men knew him quite well, and now that they were almost free, they couldn't wait to tell him how the cart had been overcome.

Cut-throats? Robbers? Highwaymen? Bandits? Well, not exactly. More a couple of slices of damn good luck, they said. It had all been accidental and really very simple, they said. Henry the driver had just happened to ask in a friendly way if anyone had something for him to smoke while he was driving, and one of the prisoners had given him a good pinch of tobacco from a pouch he had hidden inside his shirt sleeve, the pouch having been missed when he was frisked at his arrest. The driver had thanked him kindly for sharing it, lit up, and after smoking half the pipe, had quietly passed out. The three 'footpads' were three brothers of one of the men detained, who had been following the cart since Broadrock, trying to persuade the guard to let their brother go free – wasn't that right, they said of the rest, who were still vigorously working at their fetters with the chisels. Oh, yes, that was right, they agreed; the three brothers had overpowered the guard as soon as they realised the driver was unconscious, and had helped all the men in chains make good their escape by leading the way into the deepest and most inaccessible part of the wooded countryside.

"So, the guard didn't tell the Saint Briavels men the truth about what happened, after they found him," Ronald exclaimed, in disbelief. "Now, that's a rum 'un. Who was he? Does anybody know? He must have some good reasons fer keepin' quiet."

"Maybe he was overcome by the tobacco as well," someone suggested. "It sounds as if the driver had a waking dream and imagined he was being attacked."

"Him an' Henry might know who the brothers are," Ronald commented musingly. "They could be frightened of 'em. Do any of you know 'em? There's some rough families come from that neck o' the woods."

There was a general shaking of heads.

"The other thing that's puzzlin' me is what made Henry pass out. He ain't no weakling."

Well, some of the men admitted, now both pleased and rather sly, it turned out it wasn't just tobacco in that pouch, after all. They nudged the man who had provided it, and he stepped forward to elucidate.

"Well, see," he said, coming forward and rubbing the side of his nose, "it's like this, Mester. I made up that pouch o' baccy myself, I did. An' it got made up into a bit of a mix, d'ye see, Mester, after I won some dried herb leaves off one of me old shipmates in a card game in the Cow and Bucket las' night – well, not won, exactly, but more, took. Not that I wanted leaves, but since he hadn't got no money, I made sure he give me *somethin'* as winnings, see, 'cause leaves was all he had on 'im. Then when he made a bit of a fuss about givin' 'em up, I pitched him straight into the briny, arse over tit, back at the docks at the end of the game, which is how I come to end up with these other charmin' companions here this mornin', instead o' bein' back on my old *alma mater,* the *Happenstance,* which has been my place of eddication since I were a nine year old. Now, I had originally supposed them leaves to be some kind o' different-lookin' baccy, Mester. But after seein' what happened to that old driver with his smoke, I'm more of the opinion that they was actually something else, something a mort stronger."

His hand strayed instinctively over his chest as he said this, jealously guarding the rest of those leaves from any further interest.

Aaron and Tom had by this time got their handcuffs off and were handing their chisels over for the next men to use. Soon everybody would be gone, long before anyone in authority got there. The last few men remaining promised to bury the chains and handcuffs where they couldn't be found, somewhere deep in the rubble piled at the edges of the workings, and to return the file and chisels to their places of origin before they left. The two gamekeeper's sons announced their intentions of assisting the last few men to get free and said they would then go off with them. Ronald discreetly put five old sovereigns into each of Edric's son's hands before parting from them. They had acted in good faith when they had offered their services, after all; and he knew he might require their goodwill again one day.

Aaron and Tom, rejoicing in their escape, walked back to the cart with Ronald, and leapt into it once he had checked that the coast was clear. Able, still feeling weak with relief at finding his son alive and well, joined them after emptying his bladder against a nearby tree-trunk, and they drove off, discussing tactics straight away.

Tom was the first to ask where they were all heading.

"No point in going to my house now," he said. "You've found us. You may as well go straight up to the Squire's for this dance. You can always kill a bit of time along the way. Are Aaron and I in much trouble, do you know? We were going to get done for loitering. That was what the Squire said. He dropped the aiding and abetting charges." He smiled complacently. "He said there wasn't enough evidence against us. We told him we were just hanging about after taking Nick's dogs to him. He seemed to accept that Nick would need the dogs on an overnight journey in case of footpads along the way, and he *did* seem to know that the *Portabella* came in yesterday, and what time she was docked. His only suspicion was the time of night we were picked up at."

Aaron gave a dry chuckle. "He nearly dropped *all* the charges. He only decided to do us at all because Tom got lippy and asked him when it became illegal to deliver oranges to the Squire's own steward." He chuckled again. "You should have kept your trap shut, Tom. He must've known what you were talking about. That Squire'll have you ear-marked from now on; to say nothing of wanting to take you down a peg or two for being a smart-arse when you should have been eating humble-pie in front of him. You'd better watch out."

"Talking of loose lips, how did Rigo get on?" Tom asked. "We were split up from the smugglers and got dealt with separately. We saw them being taken off, when we were put in with the drunks."

"They went to Monmouth," Able said. "The Colonel got Rigo out this afternoon. He's back in Trellech now. He'll have to come to the dance, and then one of us will take him to Chepstow. We haven't finalised the details yet, we wanted to be flexible in case of soldiers or Sheriff's men stopping travellers and asking questions. Aaron and I have got a grand ball to do in Chepstow tomorrow night, so he could come with us then. Or he could go with Rowles. Or somebody else we can trust."

"And what about the other smugglers?"

"Good grief, I never gave them a thought!" Able had a crisis of conscience and turned to Ronald. "I was so bound up with Aaron, I forgot about them altogether. That's bad of me. We ought to have tried to get them sprung, as well as Rigo. Don't you think? I don't feel right about leaving them behind."

"Gawd, man. Give me a break," Ronald spluttered. "I've bin up all night, rowin' up an' down the river an' gallopin about across the country just to git these 'ere owd boys back where they belong. Don't start askin' me to go back an' git anybody else, fer pity's sake."

"Up *and down* the river?" Able asked, taken aback. "Why? You know where I live. That's up from your house."

"Ah, but there was a little gel got swept out in a boat just as I was about to leave the river and come up the town after these here boys. I had to go after her fust. A tiny, twisted little pipsqueak of a thing she was. I couldn't have left her, she'd have drownded."

Tom and Aaron both pricked up their ears. "That sounds horribly like Christina," Tom said, with concern. "Is she all right? What was she doing in a boat at all?"

"Comin' to our house to fetch us," Ronald replied. "Tryin' to reach us to git you all some help. Poor little mite, she nearly died. She may not be everything she could have bin in her body, but she's got a wonderful big heart."

"Not half," Tom said. "She tried to give the smugglers a warning that the soldiers were coming, as well. She didn't want anyone to get into trouble."

"Did she now? Well then, she could give many a full-grown man I know of a lesson or two in public-spiritedness an' loyalty."

167

"It wasn't that much of an operation at all, that smuggling run, was it?" Tom said, half-musingly. "What did *you* think, Aaron? It only looked like a few carts to me, and we couldn't really see anything from where we were hiding. Bit disappointing, in the end. I was expecting something bigger."

"Depends what you mean by disappointing," Aaron said. "It was hardly what you'd call a damp squib. More like a firecracker had gone off, once those soldiers pounced on us. I wonder how they knew we were there?"

"Yes, I was wondering that. If that outing had been any bigger, they'd have got everyone. The runners wouldn't have been finished up at those caves, and they'd have been caught like rats in a trap. Once you're at the end of that wharf, there's nowhere you can hide or run to. It was lucky so many had already gone."

"I heard somebody squealed on 'em," Ronald interjected, quietly.

Aaron and Tom received this news in an uncomfortable silence. They were both asking themselves the same thing: had Rigo been indiscreet somewhere where he could have been overheard? Not at Missus Musty's, hopefully; it had been too noisy in there; but maybe somewhere else? Somewhere where his words could have been picked up, and passed on? There was so much danger in English public places that Rigo was blithely unaware of. Was he the unwitting cause of all this?

"Thanks for coming to get us Dad, Mister Baker," Aaron said at last. "We really appreciate it. I thought we'd be walking home from that quarry – via some very circuitous and neglected routes."

Tom echoed his gratitude. They had obviously had more than one reprieve overnight.

The major discussion that followed as they drove slowly along was how to manage the enquiries that would certainly follow on from Aaron and Tom's escape.

"You're going to have to join the group tonight, Aaron, and play your lute in the Squire's house as usual, however rough you feel after last night," Able said. "I can't afford to have you missed, either personally or musically; it'll cause way too much trouble. I'm worried about pulling the evening off, even without my concerns around you two. Tell me, boy: the soldiers who came, the King's men, the customs men, the warders, everybody involved in your arrest: was there anybody among them who you recognised?"

Aaron shook his head. "Only the warders in the Castle were from round these parts," he said. "Oh, and Happy Henry. But I don't think he knows me, and I know for certain the others don't."

"What about you, Tom?"

Tom, who had been studying the floor of the cart, raised his head. "I know the Sheriff and the Squire," he said, "but only through my father, and my work with Mister Noble. They don't talk to me, although it's more than likely they know me by sight. But I doubt if either of them would notice someone like me out of context. I'm just a small-fry in the corner, whether it's our house or the notary's office they come calling at. I don't stand out, and they've never interested themselves in me. Their business, when it comes our way, involves Colonel Meadows who's important, or Mister Noble who's useful, if it involves anyone at all."

Able nodded. "So, as long as we keep you out of main sight, you ought to be safe. For your information, if any questions are raised about you boys' whereabouts over the past day, it's my intention to claim that Aaron has been with me the whole time since yesterday afternoon. I shall say that he left Chepstow after selling his lute and having a dinner, and that whoever was arrested by the excise men and soldiers must have simply assumed Aaron's identity. If no-one arresting and detaining him knows him by sight, they won't be able to say any different."

"In that case, I'll back you up by sayin' I see Aaron with you this mornin' when I called by at your house," Ronald said.

Able thanked him gravely. After some more discussion, it was decided it would be best if Tom went undercover and stuck with the group, since there was a chance he could be recognised, otherwise. He could pretend to be either a singer, or some other musician. Able had a spare costume and an ocarina in his musical baggage that Tom could wave around and pretend he was blowing through; though Tom ardently hoped no-one would be asking him to sing or play in front of them, because he couldn't do either. But it simply wasn't feasible for him to leave the cart and go back to his home just yet, much as he wanted to: his home might be searched, and nobody wanted his father to have to try and tell a lie to cover for him. As things were, the Colonel could truthfully say he had no idea where his son was, or where he might have been when he was supposedly getting arrested; a story that would hopefully prop up Able's claim for Tom, that he had been around with Aaron when Ronald had called by. If Ronald would endorse the claim, no-one could easily prove otherwise; and if Aaron was now to be seen by multiple witnesses giving a performance at the Squire's, that would reinforce the general notion in people's minds that Aaron had been with his father all along, and that Tom, by association, must have been somewhere nearby. That should be enough to get the whole matter dropped, since they hadn't been caught doing anything wrong...

Satisfied at last that they had a reasonably credible story that would mostly hang together, the talk drifted on to other matters, and after a while they stopped to give the horse a rest and walk up and down a bit to stretch their legs. They were now almost clear of the Forest. The quickest way to the Squire's house from Saint Briavels, as well as the most direct, was along the back lanes to Redbrook, and then on to Monmouth by the main road. The Squire's baronial manor house nestled in the hills overlooking Monmouth town, with splendid views of the river. With luck, they should reach it shortly after nightfall. It was only a few miles more to go.

But they lingered for a while before carrying on. No soldiers or peace-keepers were likely to be this far north from the search area, they should be safe, even if they were seen; they were four men together on an obvious journey. Since they had plenty of time in hand, Able brought out three blue and scarlet costumes complete with cloaks and hats, all trimmed with rabbit fur and little bells, that were their regalia for the performance that night, and one by one he and the boys took it in turns to go behind a nearby hedge to get changed. That way they would be ready just to tune up and start playing once they got to the Squire's, which was what would be expected of them anyway. Meanwhile, the late afternoon sun was nice and warm on their backs, and it was pleasing to have time together just to relax after all the tension. They climbed up on top of a field gate and sat like a row of colourful birds, still talking, watching the horse eat grass at the side of the lane, until bit by bit they came around to the mysterious tobacco mix that had so stupefied Happy Henry and enabled the two boys' lucky escape. Able in particular was intrigued by what could have been in it.

"Are you telling me the truth about this, boy?" he asked of Aaron. "Did you have any of it yourself? It's all right if you did, you can tell me. I won't get mad, and I won't tell your mother. I only want to know if it really is strong stuff, or if Henry was just having a bad night."

"Relax, Dad, I didn't have any," Aaron said, idly sucking on a sweet grass stem. "You don't have to worry, you're not going to have to ban it."

"I wasn't asking so I could ban it. Or confiscate it," Able replied, reflectively. "I was thinking more about trying it."

"Well, I wouldn't bother to think too hard, if I was you. I haven't got any put by, none of it was shared out by that bloke," Aaron shrugged his shoulders and waved his grass-blade in a gesture of disinterest. "And if it *had* been handed round, I wouldn't particularly want it. I'd rather stick with what I know and enjoy."

Tom was struck by Aaron's words. "*I* have a bit of something you could smoke," he said, starting to fish about inside his jerkin, which he had laid over the gate beside him. "I had almost forgotten about it. Oh! And that reminds me, I was given this thing when we escaped from that cart. Any idea what I should do with it?" He removed a small package tied up with narrow ribbon, and held it aside almost absently, so he could continue his rummaging for the much more important tobacco.

Ronald rose to the occasion at once. He swiftly wrested the package from Tom's fingers. "I'll pass this on," he said, stowing it away in his jacket. "Forget you had it." Either he was a man who was equal to anything, or he had somehow been expecting to be handed something of this sort at some time from somebody or other.

"Ooh. What was that? Do you know what's in it?" Able's interest in the tobacco was temporarily diverted by the fleeting transaction that was almost a sleight of hand.

"No."

"Letters I would say, by the shape of it," Aaron suggested, his interest piqued, too.

"Any idea who they might be for?"

"No, but I reckon I can find a man who does know. I'll get 'em to him. You attend to your 'baccy, now. Forget all about it."

Able and Aaron barely even registered his words. Their attention was back on Tom, waiting to see what he was still so assiduously searching for. At last, he retrieved what he wanted, and triumphantly held up a tobacco pouch which he presented to Able. Able opened it up and peered inside.

"Where did this come from? Same place as those letters?" Able was both suspicious and curious at the same time.

"No, and it isn't Henry's, either," Tom assured him, feeling the combined penetration of Able's prolonged stare of curiosity and Aaron's indignant one, as the contents were further inspected.

Able took up a pinch and sniffed at the dark brown shreds, then started packing some of it into his pipe while Aaron looked on, dumbfounded.

"You... you're not really going to smoke that, are you?" he asked.

"Well, it's definitely not tobacco, but I am. Purely as a social experiment," Able assured him.

"I'll have some, then," Aaron said at once, getting his own pipe out. "I reckon I should do a social experiment, too."

"Feel free," Tom invited, waving his hand. "It's very good."

"How do you know?" Aaron asked, momentarily diverted.

"Tried it."

Aaron stared at him. "When? How did you get it off that bloke in the cart? I never saw you do it." He started packing his own pipe distractedly.

"That's because I didn't get it off that bloke in the cart," Tom replied smoothly.

Aaron looked from Able to Tom again. "You must have," he said at last. "Nobody else had any tobacco. If they had, I'd have seen them."

"There might not have been any in that prison cart," Tom said smugly, retrieving his pouch from Aaron and tucking it neatly back inside his coat, "but there was certainly a wee bit in Chepstow when I went and saw Kitty."

"What! Phtt! You went and saw Kitty?"

"Yup."

"When?"

"After we left that old shed in the docks."

"Where did you see her?"

"Pig and Parsley."

"And bought some of that stuff off someone on your way?"

"Uh huh."

"Without telling me?"

"Yup."

"And didn't get me any?"

"Nope."

"You crafty bastard."

"You could've come as well."

"I didn't know you were going."

"Could still have come."

"You didn't invite me."

"I would have, if you hadn't gone buggering off to Cheppie in a boat, instead of riding with me on Timothy. I was going to ask you on the way. Serves you right."

"Oh, so *that's* what this was all about was it? Right, well next time I'm…"

A gentle but compelling thud from somewhere just outside of their range of vision brought their argument to an abrupt standstill. Tom and Aaron both turned to see what had happened. Able had toppled backwards off the gate with his pipe still clutched in his hand and fallen into the grassy field behind. All they could see were the soles of his boots sticking out of the long grass. Without another word to each other, they rushed to his aid.

Ronald turned around as well, startled out of his reverie on the gate top, and when he saw what had taken place he started laughing uproariously.

"Daft owd beggar. Look at him, smokin' down there like a bloody owd twitch-heap. I reckon he's passed out from it, an' all," he observed, delighted.

Able was picked up and set back on his feet a few minutes later, dazed but adequately restored. He was unhurt, but he was wet and somewhat muddy from his fall, and his clothes looked dishevelled, especially when viewed from the back. Aaron and Tom surveyed him critically.

"We need to tidy him up," Tom said. "It's no good letting the Squire see him looking like this."

"In that case, we'd better git goin' agen," Ronald said. "Or you two'll git yourselves slathered up an' all. Come on, we'll git Able cleaned up in the river at Redbrook."

They arrived at the Redbrook turning, part-way down the ridge, about a half hour later just as the sun was sliding down behind the high tops of the trees panning the ridge at Penallt, leaving the valley in between to sink into a somnolent, frigid dusk. They stopped off at the Lugger Inn when they got to the village, leaving the horse and cart beside the road while they walked in single file over the narrow wooden footbridge that spanned the river to the inn. There, Able was cleaned up at a little freshet that came tumbling down the hillside from Penallt, before they went inside for a brandy and hot water to keep the cold out for the last leg of their journey. Able's clothes were, unfortunately, well wetted by the time they had got the mud off his back, because under the influence of his recent smoke he was convinced that they were soldiers trying to sprinkle him with fairy dust, and he kept trying to fight them off with a large stick. In consequence, he did a lot of complaining about the cold during the last couple of miles, and by the time they got to the Squire's house, where they arrived safely about one hour after sundown, he was chilled to the bone. He couldn't stop his teeth rattling long enough to respond to the formal welcome given by Squire Speybury and his wife, which was probably a good thing after all, Ronald decided.

It wasn't Able's evaporating spirits that were bothering Ronald so much, it was the fact that Able was still disordered and incoherent from his experimental smoke. It was extremely fortunate that Aaron, who had packed a pipeful of the mix, had not had chance to smoke it, due to his argument with Tom. Ronald hoped there weren't going to be too many repercussions from their little unexpected escapade *en route*: complications were already starting to pile up thick and fast. With one part of Ronald's gaol-breaker's consortium attending this dance deaf, and another part now plain daft, there were just too many things that could go wrong from here on. As he looked at Tom and Aaron, Ronald's doubts deepened. Those two lads lived in a world of their own, he thought. They carried on as if nothing out of the ordinary ever happened, as though everything around them was always as usual – which for them, he supposed resignedly, everything very probably was. When you treated life and everything in it as one great big joke, what could possibly fall out of alignment? Some unexpected goings-on, maybe, a few surprising turns of events even; but no happenings could ever extend beyond the normal bounds of likelihood with such an outlook. He decided he had better stick around, instead of leaving, as he had originally intended. He had a feeling he was going to be needed.

Chapter Seventeen

Once he was safely brought to Trellech, Rigo was swiftly ushered into the Colonel's house. It was a welcome relief to reach journey's end after the precarious ride on horseback from Monmouth. The cart, with the Colonel's men in it, had gone on to Bigsweir in quest of Aaron and Tom; and he had spent the entire ride bouncing about in front of the Colonel instead, crouched under a great oilskin cape so he wouldn't be seen on the road.

Inside the Manor, the Colonel led Rigo into a comfortless parlour, and there he sat restlessly with his young guest for the next hour, sitting before a very small fire set in a very large grate. No Yule log was evident anywhere in the house, not even in the huge fireplace of the great hall. Whenever the Colonel got up to pace about the room, or look out of the French windows, which he did quite often to see if Rowles was back yet, Rigo grabbed the poker and tried to surreptitiously stir some life into the smouldering logs; but the flames were most unwilling, and the pile of wood very slow to catch; and before long he grew really cold. Also agonisingly hungry. He applied the bellows in a futile effort to get the blackening wood to flare up, and stared dispiritedly at the feeble glows trickling over the mildewed bark on the logs, and wondered if perhaps the wood was too green to burn, or if it was just damp.

The Colonel, in the meantime, was staring out of the window across the draggled lawn and wintry-looking garden, talking loudly. He had been talking loudly ever since they had got in. Rigo was clearly expected to listen with inexhaustible interest as the Colonel delivered repeated lengthy encomiums to his foreign guest on The Way Things Are Done in England. It made no difference whether Rigo answered, or whether he didn't. The Colonel couldn't hear most of his replies, and the ones he did hear didn't interest him. Every remark from Rigo led the Colonel into another monologue on England; and although most of his speeches were boring, Rigo was as happy to encourage him to drone endlessly on about England as he was to hear him talking about anything else, since the Colonel's voice had far too much volume to be secretive. Every servant in the house must know what was going on at every level in the Colonel's life. Rigo fervently hoped they were all loyal. And discreet. It was his own experience that none of them were. Ever.

"Expect you miss the sun," the Colonel barked, returning to his chair by the fire and stroking one of the hounds absently as he passed.

"I am a little bit cold, Sir," Rigo admitted, "and a l-l-little bit hungry. If there is…"

"In England," the Colonel said, taking command of the conversation, "the summers are warm, but the winters are not. English winters can be very cold indeed. And wet. They can be both very cold and very wet. Take today, for instance. It started off cold and dry, but now there are clouds forming, indicating the certainty of rain, or snow, to come. By morning, it will be cold and wet. Or snowy. And possibly icy. Most inconvenient, but we Englishmen do not complain. We take the good times with the bad. Therefore, we will take the oilskins to cover us again when we go to the Squire's house tonight. Once there, I intend to convene quietly with Able Arundel *et al* in order to get my boy back, and then decide how to move you on safely to Chepstow. You must re-join your ship and be back under your Captain's command before it sails in two days' time, in the early morning. That is rather a short space of time in which to accomplish our various tasks and complete the mission ahead of us, but we English do not repine. We always rise to the occasion, and never quail at a challenge."

He slapped his knee a couple of times, then looked round as the housemaid knocked at the door.

"Eh? Ah! Elsie! Tea is it?" he enquired.

"Yes, sir. Shall I light the candles, sir?"

The Colonel couldn't hear what she was saying and wasn't listening anyway. He waved at her impatiently as she set down a tray laden with cold mutton and bread on the table.

"Light the candles, would you, my good girl," he ordered. "We need to be able to see in here. And if Rowles is back, get him to pick up that chest of clothes he dug out for me. I need it bringing in. And draw the curtains, if you please. Oh, and ask him to see if he can get this fire burning, as well. Damn thing is almost out."

The maid did all he requested, and quietly withdrew, to be replaced by Rowles, who had only just come in after stabling the horse. He was still damp and muddy from his journey, and he staggered under the weight of a cumbersome old wooden chest bound up with leather straps. At the Colonel's indication, he set it on the thin turkey carpet in the middle of the room, and next directed his attention to the fire, which he got going within the space of a few minutes. Meanwhile, the Colonel was opening the chest and inspecting the contents. He beckoned Rigo to come over, his whole attention on what was in front of him. Rigo complied, casting looks of longing at the laden tray on the table as he passed. The maid returned with a second tray bearing two tankards of ale and a whole cheese, and set the table with a pickle jar and some honey. Then she withdrew once more.

"We must disguise you somehow, my boy," Colonel Meadows informed Rigo, disregarding Elsie's recent contributions entirely. "It is imperative that no-one should find you. How though? That's the thing." He fell into subdued, but audible musing, as one by one the dogs woke up and joined Rigo in a wistful contemplation of the tea-table that no amount of oratory from the Colonel could deflect. At last, the Colonel noticed; but it was the dogs his eye fell on, not Rigo.

"Ah, hungry are you, old boy?" he asked, with bluff geniality, addressing one of the dogs.

"Oh, y-y-yes, I am, very," Rigo started to answer, relieved, but he was drowned out as the Colonel commanded his hounds to come with him to the kitchen for their din-dins. By the time he returned, Rigo had given in to desperation and decided to just help himself to the food, and deal with the consequences afterwards. He was sitting at the table with his plate piled high, chewing at a frantic pace in case he was stopped when the Colonel walked back in. But the Colonel didn't even notice, occupied as he was with the details of his scheming; and the Colonel's own chair at the head of the table remained empty as he sank back down on the cold floor in front of the chest and resumed his ruminating. Rigo continued to eat, thankful that he hadn't offended his host, and even more thankful that he had taken the liberty of falling to, without waiting to be invited. With the Colonel's mind focussed only on the evening's plans, Rigo would have had very short commons if he'd been too polite to try it.

"I think it would be best if we disguised you as a girl," the Colonel said, at last. "I'll get Rowles back in here to assist us in a minute."

Rigo's answer was incomprehensible. His mouth was full of food.

The Colonel searched through the contents of the chest and laid several items of clothing out on the floor one by one, shaking them out to remove some of the dust and creases first. They smelled powerfully of damp.

When Elsie came back in to remove the trays half an hour later, Rowles came in with her, and remained, at Colonel Meadow's request, to lend a hand with getting Rigo into some clothes that fitted. Elsie came back with a needle and thread, and between them all, they got Rigo into a colourful bodice and skirt that didn't look too bad on him, all things considered. Given Rigo's colouring and hair, the outfit rendered him rather gypsyish in appearance, but then, as Rowles pointed out, Rigo would never pass for anything else in female guise whatever he wore, and if they tried to dress him up as a proper lady he would be much more noticeable, because he would look much more startling. Better to pass him off as a group follower attached to the musicians, and let his roughness be attributed to that. That way, Rowles said, people would tend to avert their eyes rather than stare at him, especially the women, because, Rowles added, glancing at the maid, everyone knew what women are like for bitching on about each other, once they get started.

The maid left with her face flaming as Rowles and Colonel Meadows regarded their handiwork. "Not bad," Rowles conceded. "But he needs something down the front." He nodded at Rigo meaningfully and eyeballed the Colonel, but the Colonel hadn't heard and didn't understand the significance of the look by itself, so Rowles had to raise his voice and shout it out all over again, this time making an appropriate gesture with both his hands.

"Ah! I get you!" the Colonel said, with zest. "Yes! Let's try apples!"

There was a dish containing some wizened fruit on the sideboard, and the Colonel went and looked them over, seizing two moribund apples of comparable size.

"Here you are!" he said with gallantry, handing them to Rigo. "Now then. Tactics." And he went into a huddle with Rowles again for several minutes.

Rigo was bored. And tired. He went and sat down on a sofa and looked at the pictures up on the walls. All were of hunting scenes, with horses and dogs. Absently, he took a bite out of one of the apples. It was reasonably tasty, though its texture was a bit floury. Still... He chewed his mouthful thoughtfully, swallowed it, then took another bite. Several bites later he had almost finished it, when the Colonel returned his attention to him.

"Now then. I only have Rowles on the premises, there are no other menservants I can use, so you'll be —" he broke off. "Good God, man, what's that you're eating? Not one of those apples I just gave you, surely?"

Rigo stared down at it, astonished. He hadn't really registered what he was doing. "S-S-Sorry," he said, after a pause. "I didn't realise you still wanted them. Have this one." Contrite, he offered the remaining apple back to the Colonel.

"*I* don't want it, you young fool," the Colonel thundered. "I didn't give them to you to eat, you're supposed to put them down your…" he flapped his hand vaguely towards Rigo's bodice.

Rigo looked down his front, and realisation dawned. "Oh. S-Sorry," he said, again. "I d-d-didn't think. But you know, I d-d-don't think it would make that much difference whether I have something there or not, because I eat a little bit too much, so there's not much room. In fact, you could almost say I am a little bit fat." He offered up his deprecating smile, but the Colonel had no time for such tomfoolery.

"Yes, yes, whatever you say," he agreed, waspishly. "Just push what's left of that apple down there, will you? And put the other one the other side; and we'll see what it looks like."

Rigo did as he was told, but Rowles quickly shook his head as the Colonel stood back to get a better look.

"Won't do, sir," Rowles said emphatically, speaking into the Colonel's ear. "It's not just that he's lop-sided; he looks too round, even on his good side, with whole apples in there. Looks more like a couple of door-knobs than knockers, if you take my meaning. I think he'd be better off chopping that good apple in half and using the two halves instead." He indicated the sound apple, still inside Rigo's bodice. "Oh, and get him to cut off the stalk, sir. I can see it from here."

A few moments later, the apple had been split using the Colonel's pen-knife, and the two halves were in place, supplemented by a few fronds of dead bracken stuffed into the spaces for extra shaping, pulled by Rowles from the fringes of the open heath-land just beyond the garden fence. Rowles and the Colonel finally seemed satisfied with the result.

"It's a bit wet and scratchy inside with these things down there," Rigo said uncertainly, pulling at the bones in his bodice to try and shift things around a bit. He wasn't really expecting much sympathy, based on his last couple of hours with the Colonel, which was just as well.

"Yes, yes, well brace up, my man," Colonel Meadows said, growing brisk now that things were almost done. "A little discomfort is nothing! We English never complain about inconveniences; we're all made of sterner stuff. Now then, I've borrowed my neighbour's horse, and I've borrowed my neighbour's servant, so you'll be going on their horse, with Rowles up behind you, while I'll have my own mount. Got it?"

Rigo nodded, wondering how he would get by on horseback in such voluminous skirts with a second person up close behind; but there was no time to voice such concerns.

"Bit of a squash for us all," the Colonel conceded, "but we English understand the necessity for compromise in situations like this. I will have to come along to make sure my boy has been recovered without incident. If anything has happened to him..." he turned away momentarily. "However, that may be, I must think of his poor mother, who would turn in her grave over this matter, if she knew of it. I simply must get everything sorted out, so she can continue to rest in peace; and if that means coming with you, then so be it. Now. We only have today in which to get those boys back; and as you don't sail for two more, you must understand the necessity of falling in and accompanying us while we undertake our own, more urgent mission. We intend to get you back to your ship as soon as we can, but we want you at this dance in the meanwhile, so we know where you are and can thus keep in touch with you. It is the only safe option. We cannot leave you here alone, and it is far too cold to place you anywhere outside."

Rowles had gone to saddle up the horses and bring them round from the stables.

"Oh, and one last thing," the Colonel said, as they were making their way to the steps outside. "You must hide at back of troupe and stay out of sight while you are at the Squire's. Don't go anywhere, don't talk to anyone. Got that? Good," he said, over-riding what Rigo was trying to ask him. "The neighbour's servant will be driving my old cart to Monmouth behind us, while we go ahead. If all goes to plan, you'll be going off to Chepstow in it afterwards, once we have my dear boy back in the comfort of his own home."

Chapter Eighteen

Inside the Squire's house the Christmas celebrations were just getting started. Ronald took the horse and cart round to the back and handed them over to a stable lad, then took himself off to the kitchens to find someone to talk to, and to pick up a drink before he continued with his other business. He had been to the house many times before and knew his way around the whole building.

It was a beautiful new house, finished with mullioned windows and a gabled roof, and accessed via an archway through a stone gatehouse, with a long, winding driveway leading up to its wide entrance. Virginia creeper was establishing itself from a corner of the *plat* before the main doors, and was already covering a substantial part of the front wall. On a sunny day, the image of the splendid leafy manor was truly spectacular; particularly when viewed from the road below.

Within, high decorated ceilings and ornate woodwork panelling finished the *décor* of the rooms throughout. Everything had been done in the latest English style. That night, hundreds of beeswax candles were alight in the chandeliers, and torches flamed in sconces on the walls, combining to illuminate all the rooms with dazzling brilliance. With all the fires aglow as well, the added warmth made good cheer for the guests now coming inside in droves, filling the entrance hall with their chattering, restless hubbub. New arrivals stood about, looking slightly uncertain after having their coats and cloaks removed, before being formally conducted into the adjacent salon, where they were announced by the footman, given their drinks by the steward, and then welcomed by the Squire, who had assumed his usual position beside the great fireplace.

Able's troupe had provided entertainment for the house before, and they all knew their way to the ballroom, minstrel galleries and closets, but not to any other part of the house. They had no idea where Ronald had disappeared to. There were eight musicians in all, including Able and Aaron, and between them they covered the full repertoire of dance and incidental music required to fill any house on any public occasion. Sam Chantry was already playing a Basque Christmas carol on his pipes and recorders, creating some background music in the so-far empty ballroom, as an encouragement for people to drift in his direction and make a start with the dancing. In due course, Allen Priest would be joining him with his bagpipes and hurdy-gurdy. Meanwhile, a stately galliard was issuing from the drawing room, where Phil Good's Celtic harp was supporting the early evening's first tentative conversations. Within the hour, the musicians would all be convening to commence with the music for the ball proper. Able and Aaron, on lutes of different sizes, would cover everything from sedate dance music and troubadour songs to plaintive medieval lute solos calculated to set the listeners' heart strings a-quivering; Paul Heath's fiddle would provide some sprightly jigs, slip-jigs and reels in medleys for the livelier dance tunes, with Alan Fielding's bodhran, cymbals and tambourine to beef up the volume and set the tempo for the dancers. Carl Santos, the most recent member to join the troupe, was not available that night. Whenever he was, he brought his dulcimer. He was a Spanish immigrant, an ex-prisoner-of-war the government hadn't been able to ransom, and new to the Forest since the war with Spain had ended, and he had to slot in his musical interests with his work as a tin miner.

The music they provided between them was a delightful eclectic mix of the elegant, the traditional, and the spirited, all organised and chosen carefully by Able to cater for everyone's wishes. From the old to the very young, for the married, courting, past caring and not thinking-about-it-yet, from those wishing to display courtly gracious formality to the injudicious ranks of young rowdies, from the well-dressed and comely to fun-loving, assorted carefree country swains and their lasses: at some point during the course of the evening, everyone there was going to hear a tune or medley that tickled their fancy, and pull up a partner from their chair, saying delightedly, 'Come on, my old beauty, up you get. Let's see if we can shake a leg to this.'

The troupe arranged themselves on a low dais covered with turkey carpet at one end of the large and splendid ballroom, with all their spare instruments concealed at the back behind a tapestried curtain which also covered a small recess in the wall. Within a very short space of time they were all set up and ready to go, and commenced by playing the Sir Roger de Coverly, which was always a good signature tune to mark the start-up of a ball. More guests came trickling in, joining those who had been idly listening to Sam and Allen, and the room filled rapidly. Several sets were made up for the dancing, people took to the floor with much laughter and jesting, and conversations began to swell the room. Small children came capering in around the legs of the adults and, in step with the activity, the mood in the ballroom drifted from a gentle bonhomie to a spirited exuberance and the evening took off.

Colonel Meadows had been sitting in the gun room with the Squire for the last half hour, taking several large brandies as he engaged in a good long talk about the shooting season and quality of the game being bagged that year. When he heard of the arrival of the Forest of Dean musicians, he hastily took his leave of the Squire, who himself went off to resume his greeting of the most important among the remainder of his guests. There was one in particular the Squire was waiting for, and he didn't want to miss her. Her name was Flora Delaney. Flora was an unmarried rumbustious bit of upper-class crumpet he had met at one of the Monmouthshire fox hunts during the previous hunting season, and he liked her enormously. She laughed boisterously at all his jokes, made him feel hugely amusing, and she didn't mind cutting a caper or two with him at the county balls, which made him feel vigorous and manly. He hoped very much to persuade her to partner him when the country dances were struck up later. The Squire liked to let his hair down and join in with the jovial parts of the celebrations, being a countryman and a simple fellow at heart. He was pleased to have found a local lady who liked sharing his simple pleasures. He happily left the airs and graces to his wife, who would have been ready, had Sir Fusby Dikes been present, to stand up with the County Sheriff for every formal dance.

The Colonel, meanwhile, had moved into the ballroom and was actively seeking the other members of his gaol-springing contingent, wanting to meet up with them before they became too immersed in the entertainment to talk. He hardly registered any of the actual music; he couldn't hear it well, and was tone deaf anyway. He was now making his way stormily through the ranks of assembled people in search of Able, weary of socialising already, and desperate for a sight of his beloved son.

"Excuse me, madam, could I... oh! It's Missus Podmore isn't it? Charmed, madam... Excuse me, I must just... Last year? I don't think I... Oh, good God, yes, I remember. Oh, come now, madam. I really can't. No, no, I don't think there's any mistletoe. Can't stay, must dash now... Ah! Mister Links, thank heavens. Come and be introduced to Missus Podmore. That's it, that's it. Off you go, now... My pleasure... Good evening, Mister Leveridge, so glad to see you. How are you sir? How's the gout these days? Oh dear, is it really? Oh well, never mind, bear up. After all, it can't get much worse, can it? ...Oh, dear me, is it? Tut, tut. Oh well, old age, and all that, what? ...Are you really? Well, I never. *Will* you excuse me for just one moment? Someone I must see... If I may, please... Please... Would you please... Oh get out of the way, man! I want to come by. Excuse me, sir... whoops, *madam,* sorry! *So* sorry, I *do* beg your pardon! Couldn't see what you were from behind..."

He eventually linked up with Ronald.

"Aha!" he shouted, delighted. "Just the fellow I was looking for. Or one of 'em, anyway. Ronald, my good fellow, how is everything? And where is that errant son of mine?"

Ronald took him by the elbow and ushered him to one side of the room.

"Not so loud, Lyndon, old friend," he said, his tones subdued. "You know I can't tell you anything now."

"What?" Colonel Meadows said, and drew back, testily. "But I want to know where my son is, and more importantly, *how* he is. I must satisfy myself that he is well and sound, for his dear mother's sake, if not my own."

"Shhh!" Ronald said, warningly. "Little pigs have big ears!" He had observed several children leaping about at the fringes of the dance sets nearby.

Unfortunately, the Colonel was not to be fobbed off. "Now look," he said, sternly. "I'm not about to be told to wait until the end of the evening to gain the information I want. Do you, or do you not, have my boy Tom with you?"

"Run along, kids," Ronald said sharply to the children; and they scampered away into the midst of the dancers, hopefully to forget that Ronald Baker, retired gamekeeper and general nobody, was hob-nobbing with Colonel Sir Lyndon Meadows, retired high-ranking military officer and Knight of the Realm. Ronald watched them until they were clear out of sight, then he took a couple of swift steps up to the performers on the dais.

"Get the boys to play something loud," Ronald whispered to Able, who was twirling round on the dais with his lute, on the side closest to him. "I've got to deal with the Colonel."

It was impossible to tell if Able had heard or not. He made no acknowledgement and carried on playing with the other musicians, facing the wrong way until the tune finished; at which point Sam, who had observed Ronald with the Colonel and had mercifully worked out what was needed, laid down his recorder and picked up a cornet to start another melody, blasting out all the other instruments and bringing every conversation in the room to a full stop.

Ronald took a deep breath and began shouting into the Colonel's ear. The Colonel bent his head and nodded several times, then allowed Ronald to take him round the back of the dais behind the curtain, to where Tom was sitting quietly with Rigo, safely hidden. The Colonel's relief when he saw his son was touching to see. He even embraced him: a most unusual demonstration of affection from a man of his status and character. The next moment, his great relief was extending to a loud *résumé* of the day's events, just to bring his son up-to-date with the current state of affairs. His opinion on the present situation was included, as were his predictions regarding the best possible outcome, followed by the totally unnecessary bidding of his son to remain hidden at back of the ballroom as instructed and to stay out of sight until he could safely be removed, and the equally superfluous statement that his mother would turn in her grave if she could see him like this.

None of this was what Tom had wanted to hear from his father at all. He had been hoping to join in with the main assembly and participate in a few of the dances once his father was around again to protect him and vouch for him. After all, the plan was to brazen the whole thing out as a case of mistaken identity. He returned to Rigo feeling rather sulky. It was going to be a very long evening, at this rate.

Ronald, who had made a quick foray into the kitchen for food, brought out several platters at intervals during the next hour or so, together with a pitcher of spiced wine, which kept Rigo happy; but Tom baulked miserably at being presented early on with a plate of some nameless fish.

"What is this?" he asked, staring at the grey-coloured flesh and sightless eyes with undisguised distaste.

"Perch," Ronald informed him, sitting down on the bench the two boys were sharing behind the great tapestry curtain. "What's the matter? Don't you like it?"

"I don't know," Tom said, scrutinising it. "I don't think I do. I've never had perch before. Where has it come from?"

"Cannop Ponds, I expect," Ronald said. "That's where most of 'em are caught. Never mind. If you don't want it, I'll take it back." He got up and left.

"Any chance of bringing me some chicken instead?" Tom called after him.

"And me," Rigo said, scooping up several handfuls of Scotch egg to clear his plate, so it could be refilled.

Ronald took the plates and disappeared, reappearing shortly afterwards with a whole chicken, some forcemeat balls, several quails, and a loaf of bread. Rigo and Tom tucked in again with gusto, while the band started up a cornetless medley of assorted jigs and reels for the heaving, puffing elite of Monmouth, all of whom were decorously hopping and skipping up and down in the centre of the ballroom.

"Have you still got those letters?" Tom asked of Ronald, after an interval. "Did you find out who they were for?"

"Wh-What letters?" Rigo asked. "Who's got letters?"

"Mister Baker has," Tom said, chewing on his chicken leg. "A whole pile of them. But I don't know who they were for. They were wrapped up under a cover, so I couldn't read the addresses."

"Ah, an' you never will know about 'em, either," Ronald said smartly. "You ask to know too much, my lad. What you was give could cost a few men their lives if anyone got to hear about it; so, don't ask, an' don't mention 'em again to anybody. You would never normally have so much as *seen* 'em."

"Oh, I get it," Tom said, clarity dawning. "I did wonder when that chap threw them at me before we all made off. We had been talking, and I had been saying I was local. He just said, 'For the love of God, take these.' I see now. They were smuggled in as well. Are they all for you…?"

"Shhh! No more, you young fool. None of 'em's for me. Howd yer peace, now. Say no more."

"I-I-I won't say anything, M-Mister Baker," Rigo assured him, earnestly. "I won't ask questions, either. You c-c-can count on me."

"And me," said Tom, though he spoke the words much more reluctantly. He was secretly burning with curiosity, and wished he had had the temerity to open the letters while he had had the chance, back when they had been sitting idle in the quarry. But those letters hadn't seemed anything like so important back then, when thoughts of how to retain their newly-won freedom had been uppermost in their minds.

"Good lads," Ronald said with a smile, and quaffed his wine before standing up abruptly. "Right. I'm off now."

"Where are you going?"

"Got to see a man about a dog."

"A d-d-dog?"

"A dog," he repeated gravely. Then he gave them a wink and left.

As they were quietly watching the proceedings, partially covered by the sides of the curtain, still drinking their spiced wine and occasionally laughing, Tom and Rigo were observed some time later by Lady Speybury, who fixed her eye on them through her lorgnettes and came across with the intention of exchanging some pleasantries. She made it her duty to address everybody present at her balls at some point during the course of the evening, considering it to be a sign of good breeding that she took the time to do so; and she had decided that she would kill two birds with one stone here, and along with a demonstration of her proverbial good manners, find out what these two knockabouts were doing, hanging about half-obscured on the side-lines.

"Good evening," she began unctuously, when she had edged her way through enough backstage paraphernalia that she could make herself heard over the music without raising her voice to an undignified level. "Can I help you?"

Rigo stared at her with open curiosity, his head poking out of the curtain. "I don't know," he said, guilelessly. "Who are you?"

"I am Lady Speybury," she uttered, shocked that anyone attending one of her balls could fail to recognise her. "Come out of there, dear, and let me see you."

Tom cringed, but said nothing, hoping he could disassociate himself from what was likely to follow. Rigo might be all right if he spoke out, but it was imperative that Tom himself should not be recognised or acknowledged. He hoped Rigo would have the sense just to say a few polite words and withdraw. But it was a vain hope.

"Good evening, L-Lady Spr-Spr-Spray Berry," Rigo said, sweeping the curtain aside, and making a low bow that revealed the tip of a curling strand of bracken. "Please allow me to i-i-introduce myself. My name is Rodrigo de – ouch! Oof!"

"*So* sorry," Tom murmured delicately, following him out. "Definitely lost my balance there for a second. Please may I present Miss er - Rita de Glorio, ma'am, who is just back from – er – foreign climes as you can see, and of foreign parentage – Italian, or something – er – possibly – living in a village near Gloucester you won't have heard of, called – er – er —"

Tom was spared the effort of any more desperate ad libbing by Lady Speybury's indignant response.

"You don't even know my name!" she declared, outraged. "This is monstrous! My name is Speybury, gairl, not Spray Berry! Who are your people, and how do you come to be here at this gathering? Did you receive an invitation to it? Speak up!"

"Please accept my apologies, Lady Speybury," Tom said, turning his charm up to maximum and nudging Rigo aside. "She came with us. As you can see from my attire, I am one of the musicians. I do apologise for my cousin's foreign manners, and her strange pronunciation of English. Her accent takes some getting used to, and she has a bit of a lisp. She was..."

"It's s st-st-stammer, not a - *ooof!*"

"Yes. As I was saying. She was trying to say Speybury, madam, I do assure you. Oh yes, really. After all, there's nothing in your name for anyone to get wrong, is there? It's such a clear name. And distinguished. She makes worse mistakes, sometimes, oh yes. Much, much worse. Always making them. Why only the other day, when she was introduced to Lady Walton-Walls-Burton, she addressed her as... oh, you'll hardly believe it, but she actually called her... er – Lady Washerwoman."

"No! Did she really? Oh, goodness me, what a *faux pas!*"

Lady Speybury gave Tom a playful slap on the back of his hand with her fan, then opened it up and held it in front of her face to conceal a delighted smile. So, she knew Lady Walton-Walls-Burton did she, this Rita De Lorio, or whatever her name was? Mmm. She must have some standing, then, however strange her appearance. Probably had government connections. She must remember to ask Colonel Meadows when she saw him. He had been in Westminster; and he was here, somewhere... Well! ...Well, well, well! Lady Washerwoman indeed! Lady Speybury didn't like Lady Walton-Walls-Burton. She would certainly remember *that* for a soubriquet the next time the old faggot needed taking down a peg or two...

"Do forgive my error," she said to Rigo, graciously. "As well as my little outburst. No offence, taken I am sure; and none given, I trust. The heat in here is rather trying when I am moving around. Please enjoy the rest of the evening. Would you care for some mince pies? Or brandy-snaps, perhaps? Or I do believe we have some fish left," she added, as a servant bearing unappetising plates of it came wandering listlessly by.

"Er, thank you," Tom said, concealing a shudder, "but my cousin and I are – er – vegetarians."

Rigo nodded. Even he didn't fancy the fish.

"Really? Vegetarians? That's odd." She reflected for a minute. "I could have sworn I saw you with some of the chicken and quails earlier. Oh well," she shrugged. "No matter."

"That's r-r-right, ma'am," Rigo said, as Tom repressed an urge to jump on him and throttle him. "We are v-v-vegetarians who eat meat. It was very delicious chicken."

"I am so glad you enjoyed it," Lady Speybury said, bowing. Then she remembered something. "Oh, my dear Miss De Labia," she said, "I hope you won't mind my mentioning it, but um, you seem to be having a bit of a problem with - er - *your stays are coming adrift,*" she whispered, putting her fan up close to her mouth, and holding it strategically so no-one else could see or hear what she was saying, as she pointed discreetly at the tiny tuft of bracken still visible amongst the topmost strands of Rigo's chest hair. "*You can get good corsets from Mrs. Stalls of Monmouth.* Mention my name there, and you will be well looked after," she added, in her normal voice. Then, looking around her to make sure she had not been overheard, she continued, in an aside to Tom, "Is this gairl married?"

Tom shook his head vigorously.

"Parents still living?"

Tom shook his head again, rather more faintly this time. He was wondering where these questions were tending.

"No, I thought not. She needs taking in hand, poor thing. A mother's touch needed, I fancy. So much body hair, and in some most unfortunate places. I've been told it's a common feature among some of these foreign gairls, but she really ought to try and remove at least *some* of it. Perhaps if I...?"

Tom simpered and tried to keep his wits about him. "I don't think Rita sees it as a problem," he said, desperately trying to keep track of this wild improvising, and hoping he wouldn't forget any of it later.

"Doesn't she? How extraordinary. Thank heavens I don't have that problem. Neither does my own daughter." She inspected Rigo thoughtfully for another minute before making several pretty adieus and leaving them.

The band was now breaking up into its component parts to allow the musicians to take some staggered breaks for rest and refreshment. Phil, after retuning his harp, was to continue with some Baroque music so that the higher echelons of Monmouth society, the ones who regularly went up to Saint James's Palace, and to fashionable London, could engage in some elegant court dancing while the rest of the assembly looked on and admired such superior accomplishments. The rest of the musicians had a half hour's break. Able went to the back of the stage to deposit his lute, wiping at his forehead, which was shiny with effort. He was still slightly spaced out from his earlier pipe smoke, and he shook his head when Aaron offered him a refill. Aaron insouciantly trailed along in his wake, his own pipe already alight.

"One of us needs to go and find the cart for Rigo while we've got a few minutes," Tom muttered to Aaron, while Able and his colleagues laid down their instruments and took a drink from the pitcher, which had been renewed and was now standing at the back of the stage. "I don't know how soon they can take him away, but it can't come soon enough as far as I am concerned. That bloke is a menace."

"Aren't you two going to get away together?"

Tom shook his head.

"Not even as far as Trellech?"

"Too risky. The Forest will be crawling with soldiers looking for nine escaped men, he can't go that way. They'll remember him from his arrest for sure; he stands out a mile among English people. And we don't know if his substitution in Monmouth gaol has been discovered yet. If it has, soldiers or the Sheriff's men will be stopping carts and travellers outside of the Forest as well, and two of us together will attract a lot more attention. Better for me to go singly and send Rigo with Rowles or somebody. He can be passed

196

off as another servant, then. I'll travel back as myself, with my father. After all, I've got nothing to hide. I was with you all day today, that's no lie."

"I'll go and see if I can find out what's being fixed up, then. But if I'm not back before we get called back on stage, you'll have to cover for me."

"Me?" Tom asked, aghast. "You know I can't do that. Rigo will have to do it."

"He can't," Aaron said. "He's dressed as a girl. And what's that he's doing now?"

They both turned to watch in disbelief as Rigo absently stuck a finger down the inside of his bodice to scratch at a couple of itches the fern was giving him. Then he gave the bodice a hitch to get it back into place, stood with one foot on the dais, and took his turn with a bombard, hand on hip, swigging great mouthfuls of wine at a time. There was nothing remotely feminine about the way he was behaving. He was oblivious to the faces Aaron and Tom were pulling at him, and to the stares he was beginning to attract from the musicians, and from other onlookers as well. It was obvious he had forgotten he was supposed to be a woman. Several people had drawn up to congratulate the band on their performance, and several were looking Rigo over with fascinated interest.

"Oh well, I'd better get going," Aaron whispered. "Keep an eye on Dad, he's still high."

"Will do," Tom whispered back. "Wait a minute though. What is it you've got in that pipe you're smoking? It smells like…"

But Aaron was gone.

"I say." Someone spoke softly from Tom's side. "Interesting girl, that. Haven't seen her before. What's her name?"

"Eh?" Tom said, still staring after Aaron, distracted. "If you mean the person at the back with the dark hair, it's – er – oh, it's Rita." Tom remembered just in time.

"Who's she with?"

"Um, you could say she's a sort of relative." Tom was trying hard to concentrate and be intelligent, but he was wondering for a second time how much more fabricating he dare undertake before he would start forgetting what he had already said. Rita. He mustn't forget that. Rita. What had he said her family name was?

"A relative of yours?"

"Sort of."

"Would you introduce me?"

"What?" Tom turned and faced his interlocutor for the first time, his full attention gained at last by the person's insistence. "Oh! I mean, naturally, I'd be honoured... er, sir." He corrected himself hastily, seeing it was the Squire's teenage son Miles who was doing the asking. "But may I ask the nature of your interest in her? She's an, an – er – honourable lady and all that."

"Oh no, she's not." The Squire's son spoke with affable certainty. "But she looks interesting." And he pointed.

Rigo was sitting on the edge of the stage with his legs slightly apart, absently drinking some more wine, which somebody had brought to replenish the refreshments. Musicians and their followers filled the space around the dais, and since he was unobserved, Rigo had hitched his skirt up slightly to free his legs and cool himself down. Parts of his shins were now visible, mossy with thick black hair. His bodice, which was hanging slightly awry, was still displaying a tiny residue of fern, and more strands of hair. The Squire's son watched, enthralled. Tom also watched, but he was horrified. He hastily moved in front of Miles to block his view, before asking him to follow so that he, Tom, could make the requested introduction.

As soon as they joined him, Tom bent and quickly pulled the skirt back down, so all Rigo was showing was a demure amount of ankle.

"Rita, Rita," he said, jocularly. "My dear cousin. Remember where you are. You're not in Italy any more, are you? Heh, heh."

"Eh?" Rigo said, turning his head and peering up at Tom, "I-I-Italy? What's in Italy? I never went there. Hey! Leave my skirt alone. I'm t-t-too hot in here in all these clothes." He hitched the skirt back up and replaced his arms on his legs resolutely, then took another long drink and picked up his pipe. "I want some tobacco f-f-for this. Can you give me some from your pouch?"

"Rita, my dear cousin, ladies in this country don't smoke." Tom gave another tittering laugh. "I think you are playing one of your tricks on me again." He had moved nonchalantly back in front of Rigo in another effort to conceal him, but the Squire's son quickly moved aside so he had another clear view.

"Miss," the young man said, rather breathlessly. "I'm charmed to make your acquaintance. I am Miles, Miles Speybury, the Squire's son; and I asked your – er – cousin, did you say?" he asked, turning to Tom, "I see, yes, cousin, if he would kindly introduce me…" His voice trailed away as Rigo took Tom's tobacco pouch and started packing his pipe. "…Er, goodness me, you must have strong lungs. Are you really going to smoke that thing?"

"Yes, I am," Rigo asserted with a touch of asperity. "I'm hot, and I'm t-t-tired, and I'm bored with this house and this noise and this music and this ballroom and this stage and all these people. I w-w-want to go home but I can't, so I'm g-g-going to have a smoke instead." He finished packing his pipe and lit it up.

Miles eyes grew rounder as wreaths of smoke began to curl around Rigo, and some of the nearest people returned their attention to him, too.

Miles exchanged a look with Tom, delighted. "What a girl," he breathed. "I've never met anyone like her before. Are all Italian girls like this?"

Tom grew stern. "No, they are not," he said, casting a proprietorial eye over his supposed cousin. "And you shouldn't be asking. Are you sure you're old enough to be showing this kind of interest in a young woman? Er, sir?"

199

"I don't know. How old do I have to be?" Miles asked, his eyes still fixed on Rigo. "How old are *you,* Miss?"

"S-S-Sixteen," Rigo answered carelessly, puffing on his pipe.

"Really! Well then I am, yes," Miles spluttered, excitedly. "I'm sixteen, too."

Tom started to rampage. "What's this I'm hearing?" he exploded, setting his arms akimbo. "Neither of you is old enough and that's all there is to say about it. Miles, you can't pursue this – er – person because she is too young, and she's my cousin, so I'm in charge of her, and Rig – Rita, you can't accept any attentions, because you're not old enough, and it's most important that you stay away from young men, do you hear? At least for tonight. I hope you are listening to me," he added, because it didn't appear that either of them was.

"I'm listening," Rigo said, putting his pipe away. "Where are the closets? I need to go outside." He got up, re-setting his bodice, and tucked his pipe inside it.

"I'll take you," Miles said, eagerly. "Come with me."

"Oh, no you won't," Tom said. "I'll do it. Er, sir."

Miles was nudged away like the rest of the interested onlookers, and Tom escorted Rigo firmly out of the house by the front door, which still stood open, and took him round the side to a large cobbled yard at the back where the kitchen gardens were laid out in neat terraces. From there he went on to the outdoor privies for the servants, sited well beyond the gardens behind a tall yew hedge, where there was a large group of servants hanging about, some standing, some sitting. All were men, the maidservants being given the use of latrines inside the house on big occasions like this, since they could not be spared for long.

Rigo, forgetting he was in women's attire, made use of a privy at the end with a loose door, taking another pipeful of tobacco off Tom and disappearing inside, banging the door shut and keeping it in place by jamming an old broom up against it. After a few moments, smoke began to curl out of the holes under the roof.

"D'you know, I reckon that girls got the right idea," one of the stable hands said to his friend, indicating the tobacco smoke. "Save me my place, I'm going to go back and fetch my pipe."

"And mine, fetch mine as well, will you?" his friend asked him.

"And mine."

"And mine."

Several more voices added their requests and the man nodded and sped off. Tom just stood and waited, wondering how Rigo could keep his head and not be affected by that tobacco. It didn't appear to have touched him so far, not unless a total disregard for consequences counted as an effect. He hoped Rigo would get a move on. It was too cold outside to linger and smoke, in his opinion. The winter night sky was jewelled with a thousand tiny stars, each one of them glinting like a tiny splinter in the frozen sky. All the clouds that had formed earlier in the evening had gone. There was going to be a cruel frost before morning. He pitied anyone left out in the open on such a night as this.

To pass the time, and to keep warm, Tom took a walk up and down the kitchen garden. The smoke had stopped coming out of the privy door holes, but there was no Rigo. More time went by. He took another walk. When he came back, more smoke was wafting out again. Tom spoke to one of the menservants.

"Do you know who is using that privy, friend?" He pointed to the one Rigo had gone into.

The servant looked at him curiously for just a split second before he became aggressive. "What do you want to know for?" he demanded. "What's your game here?" Several men standing nearby murmured their concurrence over the question.

Tom returned the look, cast his eye over the other men, and finally gave an exasperated sigh. "Listen," he said, "I'm not getting fruity, I just want to know where my friend has got to. He went into that privy there a while ago for a smoke, and as far as I know, he hasn't come out yet. I think I must have missed him, unless he's on his second pipeful. But if he is, God alone knows what it is he's smoking, because there's no tobacco anywhere within reach of where he's sitting."

There was another murmur of voices from the men, and eventually one of them said, "I reckon he might have gone off while you were away, pal. A few people did. They went together. What does he look like?"

Tom opened his mouth to reply, and then realised he couldn't possibly tell them. He had brought Rigo out to the wrong lavatories. He should have taken him to the ones inside the house.

"Um, it doesn't matter," he muttered, wondering if he should be making yet another effort to be light-hearted and inventive. The trouble was he felt several hitches short of the amount of play he needed to begin even trying, so instead he said, "Thank you, I'll just go and see if I can find him."

He shuffled away feeling rather shame-faced until he got out of sight of the men, then he bolted back to the ballroom at top speed. Surely Rigo would already be there, settling into his place of refuge at the back of the stage?

But he wasn't. The crowd had dispersed, and reformed as dance sets, and the band were centre-stage again, playing a medley of jigs and reels from Ireland, which happened to be Tom's mother's place of birth. Colonel Meadows was standing at the front, getting in everybody's way, listening to the tunes with mournful sentimentality. Of Rigo, there was no sign.

He felt a tug at his elbow, and Miles accosted him.

"Seen anything of Rita lately?" Miles asked.

Tom shook his head.

"Well, if you do, tell her I want a word with her."

"I will. And if you see her, tell her the same from me, will you?"

"All right. Anything important?"

"Well, yes. Quite urgent. And you?"

"Same." Miles scanned the room before he gave up, temporarily defeated. "She's a bit elusive, isn't she, this cousin of yours? Tell me a bit about her."

"Not now. Another time, maybe. I'm not in the mood right now. Er – sir."

Miles moved off, and Tom was left standing alone, feeling nonplussed. Then his face cleared. Of course! Rigo must have been put in the cart when he came back in. It was high time he was removed from sight and sent on his way to Chepstow, perhaps he had already started out on his night-journey. Tom decided to go to the stables and see for himself. He threaded his way through the throngs of people now massing in the main entrance hall, and went back out into the chilly night air. He went the other way around the house this time, and reached the stable yard, which was set round a courtyard featuring an ornate clock tower with its own weathercock. The courtyard was teeming with conveyances, horses, and people. As he reached it, the clock in the clock tower struck the hour. It was eleven o' clock.

The middle of the courtyard was full of parked carriages and chaises. All the carts, being inferior vehicles, were crammed together at the edges beside the stable doors, and Tom made his way round them looking for one he could recognise. The first one he saw was Nick's. Hello! Nick, the waggoner! Here! Here tonight, at the Squire's ball! Now what in the wide, wide world was Nick doing…? Aah, he must have brought Timothy up from Chepstow for his father and been invited to stay on. That must be it. Tom's eye then fell on the cart standing next to Nick's, which was the one belonging to his father, and with a great jolt of surprise he had his second shock of the night when he realised he didn't know which cart he was supposed to be looking for. Whose cart had been assigned the task of getting Rigo to Chepstow? Was it the Colonel's? Or was it perhaps the one that he and Aaron had come in earlier that afternoon with Able and Ron Baker – and come to that, where had *he* got to, all evening? That was an interesting question, as well, and one that could bear some scrutiny. Or could it be Nick the waggoner's, who was around here somewhere, and was presumably going back to Chepstow sometime before morning? There was only one thing for it, he would have to search all three carts, and see which one Rigo was hidden in. But a short while later, after an increasingly frantic search, Tom was as puzzled as he had ever been in his life. All three carts were present, but all three were empty of everything except straw and a few bits and bobs rolling around in the bottom. He would stake his life on it, Rigo must still be somewhere inside the great house.

Fighting a feeling of desperation, Tom ran back into the ballroom, scanning the hall as he passed through it. But there was no sign of him. He had gone.

Chapter Nineteen

Rigo pulled the privy door shut behind him as he came out and joined three valets sitting on a low wall beside some winter kale growing in the kitchen garden. He looked around, but he couldn't see Tom. He must be in one of the other privies, Rigo supposed. He took a place beside the valets and held up his pipe.

"Hey! Guys! Do a-a-any of you have some tobacco I can bum, please?"

One handed a pouch over wordlessly, while the other two stared.

"Th-Th-Thanks." Rigo filled his pipe, oblivious to the stares.

He handed the pouch back, and lit up and ruminated for a while on his situation. When his pipe went out shortly afterwards, it began to dawn on him that the valets' looks were still lingering, and that those looks were not altogether friendly. The intermittent glares clearly indicated he had no business being there, but it was only when he saw the way one of them was looking him up and down that he remembered he was dressed as a woman. No wonder they had thought he was sitting too close. He got up and moved a distance away, then sat down again. He still had a dottle of unburnt tobacco in the bowl of his pipe, and he struck his flint and lit it back up.

He was there for some time, waiting for Tom. He was fed up of waiting. He was fed up of quite a lot of things, by now. Someone came up quietly and sat beside him. He didn't look up. He didn't want to see who it was, because he didn't care. He didn't want to encourage anybody to talk to him. He was starting not to like this country, with its cold, and its damp, and its filthy prisons and smelly carts and bullying military men and foul-mouthed peacekeepers.

The food was good, though. At the reminder, Rigo made a mental note to have a top-up of something delicious once he got back inside the ballroom, as a reward for getting through so much inconvenience, and as a means of keeping himself from deprivation. It might be a long time before he ate again on the journey back to Chepstow. He wasn't looking forward to it. It was almost certainly going to involve another cart. Or another horse. Rigo heartily wished his ship was close enough that he could just walk.

"Penny for them," the person sitting next to him remarked. It was a young girl's voice.

"W-W-What's that? You need a p-p-penny for something?" He looked up, but scarcely attended to her. "I'm s-sorry, I don't have any money, Miss."

"No, stupid. I said, 'penny for your thoughts.'"

"No, you d-d-didn't," Rigo retorted, nettled. "You said s-s-something else. I don't know what it was, I didn't understand it. But you surely don't look as if you need money to me. You look as if you're doing all right."

"Huh. That's all you know, smart-arse. Money isn't everything, you know."

"It is when you don't have any," Rigo said, abruptly. "And I d-don't. Now just go away, will you? I don't want to talk."

"No-one ever wants to talk. Not to me, not ever. I hate everybody. Why won't you talk to me?"

"B-Because you're a g-g-girl, and a girl can't help me."

"Why, what's so special about being a boy? I hate being a girl. It wouldn't matter so much if I was a boy."

"W-What wouldn't matter?"

"Anything. Everything. That I'm ugly, for a start. I've just overheard some people in there talking about me. Again." She pointed back at the house. "I hate being ugly. It's all anybody ever says about me. I'm not going back in there."

Rigo made no answer and the girl lapsed into momentary silence. He was dwelling over the difficulties ahead of him. And his lack of money. That was his biggest problem; and the way things were turning out, it would be another six months before he would be given some.

The girl's voice intruded again. "You don't look very happy."

"S-S-So what?" Rigo asked, irritably, annoyed at his thoughts being jumped on and grabbed by a passer-by once more.

"No need to get arsy," the girl rejoined. "I was only saying."

Rigo made no answer.

She tried again. "What have you got that pipe in your mouth for? You look stupid. Only men smoke."

"Shaddap," Rigo replied, finally turning to her properly. "What do you know about anything?"

She was older than he had first taken her to be. In fact, she was more a young woman than a girl. She was eighteen or thereabouts, with a heavy body shaped like a wheat-sack collapsing under the weight of its own contents, and brown, flyaway hair elaborately tied up in a fine orange ribbon. Her ball gown, a robust, well-made, rose-coloured damask with *moiré* trimmings, was designed for a woman of forty, and a large beauty spot also aged her significantly. Underlying all the powder, rouge, and finery was a flattened, featureless face, a pronounced squint in one eye, and a mien of intractable ill-humour. She dressed in a manner calculated to display all the best qualities of a fine young lady, but it had been done without style or taste. Even her feather fan seemed absurd and out of place. Next to the equally squashy Rigo in his garish regalia, she looked rather like an abandoned relic off an old Aunt Sally stall, a most unfortunate happenstance for the already discontented young woman. The expense of her evening dress was never going to compensate for her patent lack of good looks, even when disguised and ornamented: they were given too heavy an emphasis by her ungracious behaviour and lack of good manners.

Not that Rigo cared. Nor did he notice any of this. To him, she was uninteresting merely because she could have introduced herself with a kindly enquiry about the nature of his predicament, and she hadn't, she had scoffed at him instead, and then expected him to listen while she talked about her own dilemmas. He decided to tell her so. He spoke quietly and rationally. Far from wanting to give offence, he wanted her to understand only what an imposition it was to impress her nosy enquiries and personal quandaries on a stranger far from home. She listened in acquiescent silence.

From there, he went on to point out that, despite being a woman herself, she didn't seem to understand the discomfort of wearing restraining clothes that didn't belong to a person and didn't fit; nor did she seem to realise how miserable it was to be in a cold, foreign, inhospitable country that had already tried to incarcerate him. And, thanks to her interruptions, he still hadn't got as far as dealing with the problems relating to his lack of money yet.

Her face gradually turned down as she listened, and by the end she looked as if she wanted to cry.

"All right, all right," she said grudgingly, after he came to a stop. "I'll say I'm sorry. There now. Happier? I do feel sorry for you, honestly, I do. I had no idea at all how sad you were feeling when I sat down beside you. You really are in a lot of trouble, aren't you? Phfff." She heaved a lugubrious sigh. "Will you tell me your name? Mine's Fanny. Horrible, isn't it? I hate my name. You don't know what it's like to have a name as ugly as your face, do you?"

"No," Rigo agreed, candidly.

"Huh. Lucky you. Well, go on then, tell me. What's *your* name?"

"Rigo."

"Ree-goh," she repeated, thoughtfully, pronouncing it the same way he did. "Hmm. Unusual name for a girl. Is it short for something? I don't think I've heard that name before."

"That's because it's a boy's name," Rigo said, putting his pipe in his mouth.

"Oh no!" Fanny gave a disgusted curl of her lip. "Urgh, you poor thing! It's worse for you than it is for me, then. At least mine's a girl's name... not that it helps." She threw a sulky look in the direction of the house. "They don't understand," she said, indicating.

"Who don't?"

"My family, of course." A thought struck Fanny, and she turned and looked at him, her mind working. "You don't you know who I am, do you?"

"No," he said, without much interest.

"I'm Fanny Speybury."

Rigo inspected his boot, adjusted his skirts, and made no comment.

"The Squire's daughter," Fanny expounded, impatiently. "There. Now you know. I don't expect you want to talk to me any more now, do you?"

"Why shouldn't I?" asked Rigo, still not particularly interested.

"Because everybody's heard of me, that's why," she exclaimed. "They all laugh about me, and everyone feels sorry for me, and I expect you will too, now won't you?" She gave Rigo a challenging stare from her one good eye.

"W-Why would people laugh at you?" Rigo sucked at his empty pipe as he temporarily diverted his attention to consider the matter. "I don't understand that. That's n-not nice of them."

"I know it isn't," Fanny said, moodily, kicking at a stone. "But they do it all the same. My looks are famous far and wide." She gave a bitter laugh. "If I was just ugly, that would be bad enough, but as it is, everything is stacked against me. Everybody knows Papa is desperate to get me hitched, but he's such an old skinflint, nobody wants to take me on. Oh, they'd put up with a changeling like me for a wife, at a price. Or they'd put up with Papa for a father-in-law. But both, they will not have. Not for love, and certainly not for the kind of money Papa thinks is adequate. Mamma is ready to give up. All I ever hear her saying about me these days is, 'Oh la! Whatever shall we do about Fanny?' And Papa says, 'Don't worry,

someone will come along, dear. Even the old mares get mated.'
What can I say to a father and mother like that?"

Rigo continued sucking at his empty pipe for a while. "You c-
c-can't help the way you look," he said, at last. "They shouldn't
blame you for it. In m-m-my country, a woman's worth is weighed
by what's inside her head and her heart. Your head seems fine to
me. I don't know about your heart," he added. "I w-would need to
be with you for longer to find out about that."

"And where is your country?"

"F-F-Far away from here," Rigo said, sadly, putting his pipe
back down his front. "I come from B-B-Brazil. In my country, we
like our women to be *sympática e gentil*. Friendship and kindness
make the men happy. Then, when we are happy, we make our wives
happy, and give them many children. You have a-a n-n-nice smile.
In my country, that is enough for any man. Why don't people notice
your smile here as well?"

"I don't know why. But thank you anyway," Fanny said.
"That's the first compliment I've ever had in the whole of my life.
It feels a bit funny. Do you think I would like it in your country?"

"Sure," Rigo said off-handed, getting up and rubbing at his
chilled behind. "E-E-Everybody likes Brazil."

He scanned the garden around him for Tom, then offered
Fanny his hand. She took it and heaved herself up off the wall. They
both stood for a moment, smoothing their skirts.

"If you don't mind me asking, why are you dressed in those
clothes?" Fanny asked, presently.

"It's a d-d-disguise," Rigo answered.

"I know, I realised that; it looks a bit odd," she said. "But
why?"

"I'm on-n-n the run from your father."

"Ah. So *that's* why you were talking of being imprisoned! I
did wonder what a girl like you could have done to get herself put
in chokey. I could only think of one thing... So, are you by any

210

chance one of those escaped prisoners Papa came in ranting about this afternoon?"

"Yes. Two of the o-o-others are in the band. The rest we don't know about, they were n-n-nothing to do with us."

"Ah! So, you're really a boy! That explains the oddness about you. Well, Boy. You *do* know that you will be re-arrested if anyone recognises you tonight, don't you?"

"Yes. I'm being taken b-back to my ship tonight. I'll be leaving here soon, hiding in the back of a cart. My ship sails i-in t-t-two days with the tide."

"From Gloucester?"

"From Chippistow."

"Ah. And the other two who escaped with you? The musicians? What will they do to lie low?"

"I d-don't know."

"You ought to make it your business to find out. They need to leave with you. They'll be transported as escapees, if they are caught. Papa was furious. Even if they are all retaken, Papa will still get a roasting from Sir Fusby when he comes back in the New Year. And Sir Fusby is bound to hand them over so they can be given a maximum sentence, for giving everyone so much trouble. He won't be lenient, he never is."

"S-S-Seriously?"

"Seriously."

"I'd better f-f-find them and t-t-tell them. Thanks for your help, Fanny."

"Thank you for yours."

"I have to go now," Rigo said. "*Okeh?* I m-m-must find my friends."

"Okey. I would try and help you, but I'm afraid I don't know what any of them look like. Good luck with everything."

"And w-w-with you. Goodbye, I hope you will find the happiness you d-deserve in your life." He shook her hand.

"And you in yours," Fanny said. "Goodbye, Rigo. You've already made me happy. Thank you."

They parted, Rigo for the house, Fanny for the stables. She had a plan already half formed, and it was rapidly gaining strength in the making.

In the ballroom, Rigo had no time to search for Tom. Before he could even sit down, Able came rushing up to him in a panic.

"Where have you been?" he demanded, his face red and flustered from a recent noggin of wine. "Why has everything gone pink? What are those spirals in your eyes? I don't like them, they're making me dizzy. Listen, where's Aaron? And Tom? We must go back on in a minute. I don't feel well."

Rigo was trying to answer, but Able seemed to be having difficulty focussing. He thrust Aaron's lute into Rigo's hands.

"You'll have to play this," he cried. "You've got to join us. I think we're going to get arrested." And he disappeared into the crowd.

Rigo took no notice whatsoever of Able's paranoia. But he was pleased with the lute. He inspected it. He had never played one before, but he had played a gittern back in Brazil, which was a very similar instrument. He adjusted the tuning, took a few experimental strums, and decided he liked the sound. There was no time for him to do anything else, because he was grabbed by the sleeve of his blouse and hustled up onto the stage by Sam Chantry in the same minute.

"Come up and stand behind me, lad," Sam said quietly, as they assembled and arranged themselves. "We need to keep you and Able out of sight."

Rigo nodded and took a corner well behind Sam's broad back. "What are we playing?" he asked, in a whisper.

"Same as the first half," Sam hissed through his teeth, over his shoulder. "We don't have any more tunes. Just stand there, and pretend you're playing."

"Don't w-worry," Rigo said. "I c-can play this, no problem, and I think I r-r-remember how most of the tunes went."

Able was placed gently and tactfully beside Rigo. It was a strange arrangement to have the lutes out of sight, but at least it gave the other members of the troupe a rare chance at gaining some prominence when the full outfit of musicians were performing. Had they been younger and better-looking men, they could have started quite a following.

The session went very well. Rigo was a natural musician. His playing was extremely good, and his memory almost faultless. Sitting with Tom behind the scenes earlier he had absorbed most of what he had heard the first time around; and when the musicians finished their playing, there was a round of enthusiastic applause from the assembly.

"I th-th-think I could get quite used to this," Rigo said, gratified, as they all took another short break, this time leaving Allen Priest to play his pipes and hurdy-gurdy alone, creating a little interlude for the guests to sit and have a listen while everyone rested.

"Aye, lad, I think you could an' all. You're not at all bad," Sam Chantry assured him. "If you ever decide to give up the life of a roving sailor and settle in these parts, you could do worse than come and join us. We'd be glad to have you along."

"Thank you, S-S-Sam," Rigo said, secretly delighted.

"You're finished for the night now," Sam said, after they had both had a cup of wine together. "The rest of our pieces are trios, so none of us will have to be out there all at one time. Able will do all the lute from now on, if Aaron doesn't come back. He'll manage, even if he *is* off his face. The music is a part of him; he doesn't have to think about it. You can go off now, although if you should happen to see Aaron along the way, I would appreciate it if you could pick him up and send him back to us. I don't know where he's got to. Probably chatting up some little piece with a pretty face. I haven't seen him recently though, have you?"

Rigo shook his head. He hadn't seen Aaron, and he hadn't seen Tom yet, either.

It was, in fact, quite some time before Rigo found Aaron, and he never did find Tom again that night. Aaron was sitting in the kitchen with Nick the waggoner, quaffing pints of beer with Rowles, who would normally have already gone home well before now, but who couldn't leave ahead of the Colonel. Rigo quietly slid onto the end of a bench at the table and joined them.

"Have a beer, mate," Nick invited, but Rigo shook his head.

"No thank you," he said. "I d-d-don't need any more to drink."

He looked about him, hoping to find some food, but it had all been put away. Undeterred, he hailed a passing kitchen maid.

"Hey! Miss! Is there a-a-anything I can eat around here?"

The kitchen maid tossed her head. "I should think not!" she answered, tartly. "We've got more than enough to do, thank you, clearing up what's been brought back, without getting out more!"

She disappeared into the pantry. Rigo waited until she came back out and tried again.

"I know I am a little bit fat," he said, detaining her by her arm and trying to give her an alluring look, "but I am a long way from…"

"Can't stop," she said, dragging her arm free and marching out.

"Leave it," Aaron said wearily, just before he rolled off his bench and onto the floor. "She thinks you're a girl."

Rigo was indignant. "Hey!" he said. "I-I-Isn't there any service around here? I'm hungry, and I'm eating for my mama…" He tried to arrest the kitchen maid's attention again as she passed with a pile of dirty plates, but she side-stepped around him and carried on into the scullery to do the washing up, and Rigo gave up. Disappointed, he began to droop. He was tired, he had been up all night the night before, and he had had enough excitement to last him for a very long time. If there was no food to be had, what he really wanted was some sleep. He put his head in his arms on the table.

"Tired?" Nick asked, sympathetically.

Rigo raised his head momentarily and nodded.

"Why don't you go outside and wait for us?" Nick asked, pouring himself some more beer.

"Right," Rigo said, "I th-th-think I'll do that. Will there be a blanket I can put round me? It's p-p-pretty cold out there."

"Unlikely," Aaron said, rousing himself temporarily, and propping himself up on one elbow on the floor. "You know the Colonel." He gave a groan and lolled his head, so it hung down between his arms. Then he prostrated himself on the floor again and began quietly snoring.

Rigo most certainly did know the Colonel. He wasn't likely to forget him in a hurry. He watched Aaron quietly collapse and decided against trying to steer him back to the music troupe.

"We won't be here much longer," Nick continued, cheerfully. "Once we get the Colonel away from the Squire, we'll all be off. Aaron is just about spent. I don't think he's very well. No need for you to lose any more sleep though. You can get in the Colonel's cart, that's the one with the orange wheels, and I'll be out in a bit. I'm the one who's going to drive you back to Chepstow in it."

"Are you?" Rigo asked. "I thought I was going with the Colonel's driver."

"Are you? Oh. Well, I don't know, then. I thought we were all leaving together and going our separate ways once we got past Monmouth, but maybe not. Anyway, it's the Colonel's cart you're to go in, because it's the one least likely to be searched by soldiers, if there are any around."

Rigo got up and made his way outside to the stables, which were still crowded with carriages, the gentry's horses, and many and various stable hands. A good many people were now departing. He pulled a fine woollen blanket out of an open chaise that was standing unattended and went to find the cart with the orange wheels. He had almost done an entire circuit of the courtyard before he spotted it, pushed back into one of the far corners. It was much smarter than he had expected it to be, but then, as the Colonel had fallen on hard times and had no carriage, it had probably been spruced up and put to some extra usage. It had been quite hard to distinguish the different colours by torchlight as he walked around, but mercifully the colour of this one was accentuated by their flare, and he could see it was the one he wanted. It wasn't just the wheels that were orange, the whole body was painted the colour of pot marigolds as well, with a nice red trim along the top edge and the inside of the wheel rims. It really was quite gay. Rigo threw the blanket into the back and climbed wearily in after it. It looked to be quite full inside. There was some straw in there, some empty burlap sacks over a chest, and two casks smelling strongly of brandy. Underneath the straw and sacks, lying between the casks and the chest was a pile of sheep's wool fleeces: a score or more all bundled up together. Rigo pushed the barrels up to the end nearest the shafts to make himself some room and brushed the straw aside. Then he man-handled the fleeces so he could burrow into the middle of them, made a pillow out of the sacks, and put the blanket over the top. The wooden floor of the cart was hard, even through the sheep's wool, and cold air came seeping up through the cracks between the planks around him, but he was too tired to care. He was at least well covered. Last of all, he distributed the straw over himself and the fleeces, and then he lay back, slightly inebriated from all the wine he had drunk, exhausted from lack of rest, and fell asleep.

He didn't wake when the driver arrived half an hour later. He remained asleep as the horse was harnessed into the shafts, and it did it not disturb him when the driver stepped up and seated himself at the front. He didn't even stir when the cart began to move off over the stone paving flags, weaving through the other vehicles to make its departure.

Many of the carriages had now driven off, leaving the stable courtyard more than half empty. What few carts remained were all easy to see, lit up by the flaming torches on the stable walls. Just beyond the empty space left by Rigo's departing cart, one farm waggon remained. It had been pushed part-way under an archway leading to a storeroom, and then left. There was little to distinguish it from any of the others in most respects, and it looked almost forgotten. It was large and cumbersome, evidently well worked, and much of its paint was flaking and worn. Apart from the spokes of the wheels, that is. On them, the paint was chipped, but still substantially intact. And it was bright orange.

Chapter Twenty

Tom went back to his lonely retreat behind the curtain at the back of the dais and sat for some time in quiet deliberation, calming himself down and working out what to do. Eventually, he came to a decision. Leaving his hiding place, he went off to find his father to see what he knew about Rigo's disappearance. Perhaps Rigo had simply been removed at an opportune moment using another mode of transport. It was always a possibility. The problem was, Tom hadn't seen his father since he had been listening to the Irish music more than an hour earlier. He had no idea where to even begin looking for him now. But time was pressing. He went out into the great hall and arrested the Squire's steward who was just passing through and asked him if he knew where the Colonel might be found. The steward, who, together with the housekeeper and several maids, was carrying great armfuls of wraps and cloaks for departing guests, looked Tom up and down impatiently before telling him with stern emphasis that the Colonel was an important man and was not to be bothered by a young jackanapes like him. The steward then hurried on after the women servants bearing a collection of surtouts and ulsters for the gentlemen, leaving Tom standing. On his way back a couple of minutes later, the steward added that anyway, the Colonel was in conference with somebody, and the Squire had left specific instructions that they were not to be disturbed, and would the young man *please* oblige the household management by returning to the musicians, and not try to mingle with the house guests. Tom made a rapid resolution. It would be much the best if he were to remove himself from the house at once and follow in Rigo's wake: first, to be sure that Rigo had got off safely, and second, to head for home before one of the Squire's servants rumbled him. If he was quick, he should overtake Rigo somewhere on the other side of Monmouth, and they could travel together. He wouldn't have got all that far, he hadn't been gone long enough. It ought to be possible to catch up with him before he got to the turnpike for the Trellech road.

Tom walked swiftly outside to the stables, where he pulled up a spare groom and asked him to get the Colonel's horse saddled up as quickly as possible. But to his surprise and dismay, the groom returned a few minutes later and informed him that the Colonel had left on his horse with someone about a half hour earlier. Despite Tom's entreaties, the man was unable to give any further information. And so, another decision was required: the farm cart. He would go home in his father's farm cart instead. After all, it might still be needed for Rigo, even yet. There was no time to go and look for Rowles; Rowles would have to shift for himself. Tom harnessed the horse into the shafts on his own, so as not to waste time waiting about for another groom, then he clopped off as fast as the unfamiliar beast could carry him, the orange wheel spokes spinning dizzily in the last of the torchlights as he left.

It was just after three o' clock in the morning when Nick went out, got on the front of his waggon and drove off, whistling up his dogs as he went. They came sloping out from somewhere inside the stables, silently licking their lips. Nick had already been out and yoked up his ox ten minutes earlier. He had done it as soon as he saw the Colonel's cart had already been taken and realised there had been a change of plan.

His animal had rested that evening in the Squire's barnyard. There was never any chance of Nick exchanging his own ox for someone else's to make his return journeys, because so few people ran their waggons with one. They all used cart-horses. His beast was stronger, and had more stamina than a horse, but it still needed some respite between runs, so wherever he went Nick had to hang around to give his ox a breather, and then yoke it back into the waggon once he thought it had recovered enough to get him home. However, it was hardly an inconvenience. Speed didn't matter to Nick, who would arrive when he was ready, no matter what the commission.

He was enjoying himself hugely on this one. It was great to be included in all this smuggling stuff, real fun – better by far than boring old farm work. Nick had hardly been able to contain his swagger after the Squire's steward had surreptitiously pushed two gold coins into his one hand, while at the same time counting out one shilling and sixpence payment, plus six silver shillings to cover the cost of the oranges into the other. Those two pieces of gold now lay under the leather insole of Nick's boot, almost burning into his skin, and he had a hundred plans for them. Additionally, he had sold his two extra baskets from the *Portabella* earlier that day, making two extra shillings for himself out of his operative side-line, and *that* was gratifying as well. He felt he was becoming quite enterprising. Now, he was to take Rigo and a load of straw to Chepstow via the Trellech road, and that was the icing on the cake. It marked the culmination of a wonderful evening's sojourn with the Squire's stable hands and kitchen staff. It was turning into a marvellous Christmas.

Since the Colonel's cart had apparently been moved on sometime during the evening, Nick supposed he was now meant to be going to the Manor at Trellech, to meet and exchange carts there before dawn. Or something. He hoped he might be permitted to call in at the great house and say Merry Christmas to Tom, whom he hadn't seen all evening – hadn't seen since two nights ago at the port, actually – but even if that should not prove possible, he would at least get to carry on to Chepstow with Rigo – it should be safe for Rigo to come out by then – and he would have a good old chin-wag along the way, find out more about this sea-faring business, and then maybe get Rigo to help him stack the straw once they got to his house. He wanted to look after that straw. It was the first part of his payment for going back to the Squire's and helping, and it was good stuff. Once he got the promised second part – which he would collect at the earliest opportunity, which would be soon – it was most *definitely* going to be used for new thatch. Nothing else, definitely not bedding. Unless it should transpire that some other arrangement was necessary in the meantime, of course. But it would have to be an emergency, if so.

A few miles along the road, he quietly said, addressing no-one in particular, "Hilloo back there. I think you'll be all right to come out now, if you want. There's nobody about."

There was a considerable amount of rustling from the straw in the back, and then a head protruded, shaking the straw out of its hair. But it didn't look much like Rigo. In fact, it didn't look *anything* like Rigo. After glancing back, Nick gaped, retook the glance, and gaped again. What the...? What was going on?

"Where are we?" the head asked, looking around. "And who are you?"

"Save me!" Nick said, going pale, and pulling the ox up. "Miss Speybury! What are you doing in there?"

"I should have thought that was obvious," Fanny said airily, checking her cleavage for straw. "I'm absconding."

"You can't do that!" Nick cried. "Please, Miss, think of me. You can't stay with me. I'll get pilloried if I don't take you back!"

"Hmph. I know. That's why I'm here."

"What? Not for...? You don't mean...?"

"I don't mean I'm here for *you*, dolt," she retorted, witheringly. "I'm here for Rigo, wherever he is. I thought he was going to be in this cart," she continued, rather wonderingly. "But he seems to have gone another way. Drat. I was looking forward to getting better acquainted with him."

As she spoke there was some further rustling, this time from the straw beside her, and another head broke through the surface.

"Rigo!" Fanny exclaimed, delighted. Nick waited with bated breath.

"No, Fan, hard luck. Try Miles," the other person said, spitting straw out of his teeth. "And I heard what you just said. I'm jolly well going to tell father when we get back."

"Oh, no you won't," Fanny said, plunging him back down with one hand and holding him firmly submerged. "You're not coming back up again until you promise me faithfully you'll keep your mouth shut."

"Aargh!" Miles was gurgling from deep under the straw. "Gerroff! Ow!"

"Miss." Nick began pleading again, "Miss, please. Let this boy go, if he is Miles. He's your brother, isn't he?"

"*Yes – He - Is*." Fanny hissed, separating out each word. "And I wish he wasn't. I hate him."

"And *I* wish you'd let him go," Nick said, wretchedly pursuing his own thoughts. "You're only going to make things worse for me if you hurt him. I don't think you'd be doing this if Rigo was here, would you?"

Fanny let her brother go at once and tossed her head. She began smoothing out her hair, which had become very tousled from being under piles of straw.

"It really wouldn't matter two str… two hoots if he *was* here," Fanny declared, haughtily. "I'm going to run away to sea, with or without him. So there!"

Nick sat, dumbfounded.

"Well – start the cart up, idiot!" Fanny cried. "Don't sit there gaping!"

Nick did as he was bidden without another word. He was overwhelmed by this turn of events.

Miles reappeared and began brushing himself down. "Who is it you're after this time?" he demanded disparagingly. "I know you, Fan. Hoping to get wed before you have another birthday, that's you. Is it this Rigo you're after?"

"Never you mind," Fanny said, imperiously. "It's none of your business. Anyway, what about you? Why are you here?"

Miles looked sheepish. "To be honest, Fan, I had the same idea. You know how it is at home. The mater and pater can't wait to get *you* spliced, and at the same time *I'm* not allowed to even talk about a courtship. I met a fine girl tonight, simply splendid lass, name of Rita; and when I overheard you talking to her in the garden, and she said she was about to go to Chepstow to join a ship, I just thought, 'why not go along too, and get to know her better,' you know... Go home to the mater and pater when she leaves these shores and I've bade her farewell... Er, and all that... I wasn't thinking of going to sea with her..." He came to a faltering halt. "Fan?"

"Miles," Fanny said. "Are we talking about the same person? Dark hair and big hooped ear-rings with a pearl inside? Looks like a gypsy?"

"I should say so! Wild and care-free. That's the style, wouldn't you say, Fan? Suit you, too!"

"I dare say it would," his sister replied, crisply. "But I won't be copying her style, Miles, because that wasn't a girl, Miles. That was a boy in disguise, Miles."

"You don't say!" Miles did some thinking, while Nick listened in silence. Then – "Are you sure? The bloke with her said Rita is his cousin. From Italy, apparently. I don't think it's the same girl."

"Oh, yes, it is," Fanny said, rather more amicably, and she put her arm around her brother to explain. "Rigo was in disguise because he's one of the boys Papa is after, my dear little brother. The ones who all escaped yesterday morning."

"Oh, I say! No!"

"Oh, I say, yes," Fanny replied. "And we don't want to see him caught again, do we?"

"I should say not," Miles agreed. "Girl or boy, he was simply splendid... Well. No. But are you serious, Fan? Are you really going to run away to sea?"

"I don't know yet," Fanny said, thoughtfully. "I must try to disguise myself if I do. The trouble is, no-one who has ever met me would be fooled, not even for a minute. And with my looks, I'd be marked out and remembered by everybody wherever I go. My family would soon catch up and overtake me." She sighed. "Whatever my attire, Miles, all people will ever see of me will be my fatness, my flat face, and my squint. I suppose I had a vague idea that if I stayed away overnight in a boy's company, Papa would be forced to stump up a big fat dowry to make someone – anyone – marry me to keep my reputation intact. Stupid, wasn't it? No amount of money will ever get a man to accept a poor pathetic thing like me."

She kept her arm around her brother companionably, and they dozed in the back together while the cart rolled on.

Eventually, Miles asked, "I say, driver, where are we?"

Nick rallied his thoughts, which had drifted off along avenues of their own. "Er, we're on the turnpike road to Trellech, and we should be meeting – er – some other people…" His voice trailed off.

This was going to be bad. First Fanny, and then Miles had popped themselves into the melting pot, right in the middle where the water was hottest, and now Nick didn't know what to do. He had no Rigo in the back, as he had expected, and he was separated from Aaron and the rest of the music troupe. He had no-one to advise him what to do. Not only did he need to keep Miles and Fanny from getting wind of the reasons why he and that troupe were out and about together that night *at all*, but by tomorrow morning – no, it was today now – the whole of the Squire's household was going to be out in force, making an intensive search for a missing son and daughter: all Nick had was a couple of hours' head start on the dogs. He was in way over his head, with no-one to tell him what to do next. The burning of those two pieces of gold under his foot now took on a completely different quality, and Nick began to feel scared. What a way to spend Christmas Day! Ale, fire and privy dwindled, receded, and finally disappeared from his plans altogether in a hurried puff of sooty mental smoke. With all his promising visions dashed, Nick decided after some further consideration that his only option was to continue his present course, and once in Trellech, to await developments and possibly a Christmas cup to keep out the winter chills. But Fanny had other ideas.

"All right, we're on the Trellech road," she said. "But where are we going?"

"Trellech."

"Yes, I know that much, stupid. But where to after that?"

Nick wasn't bright enough to be more helpful, and he was way behind Fanny when it came to intellectual considerations, so his answer was predictable enough. "Umm, not sure," he said, as though Trellech was where his thinking processes ended: which, as of fifteen minutes ago, they very probably did.

"Right," Fanny said, "I'll tell you what. Instead of going to Trellech and stopping, we'll go straight through, and keep on going until we get to Chepstow. How's that?"

"What for?" asked Miles.

"Think about it, brother," she said comfortably, snuggling down next to him to keep warm. "Wherever Rigo is, he's on his way to his ship. And that ship is where? Why, Chepstow, of course! That's where he's headed, so that's where we'll go, too. We both want to see him again, don't we?"

"Well, you do, Fan, that's for sure; but I'm not so keen now I know he's a boy. There could be some other interesting fillies in Cheppie though, now I come to think of it, some that might be worth the candle. I don't mind going along for the ride and looking at them, if it will make you happy. Act as chaperone, and all that."

"Oh, for heaven's sake, how many more times do I have to tell you I don't *want* a chaperone," Fanny scolded, exasperated. "It's the last thing I want, don't you see? I *want* my reputation to be ruined. Then Papa will have to set me up with someone to save me from disgrace. I just hope it's someone passable, that's all." She began to chew her lower lip. "I don't expect anyone too gorgeous, naturally. I must keep my expectations reasonable. Someone not too bad-tempered would be nice – and not too drunk, of course. And who smells nice. With clean teeth."

"And hair," Miles added.

"Yes, clean hair. No lice."

"I hate having lice," Miles said, dreamily.

Nick surreptitiously scratched at a flea under his felt hat and made a resolution to get a haircut at the earliest opportunity, so he could comb out his own infestation. He couldn't afford a wig, he would just have to wait for his hair to grow back again. But at least it would be clear of vermin when it did.

"Old?" Miles was asking his sister, meanwhile.

"Oh, I don't mind too much," she was answering. "Though I would prefer someone nearer my own age, of course." She heaved a big sigh. "I just want someone who won't sneer at me for what I look like. I don't mind if he has no money – and cleverness and rank don't really matter to me. What do *you* think, Miles?"

"I think you'll have to take whoever you can get, Fan."

"And you, driver?" Fan asked. "What do you think? What is your name, by the way? I can't keep calling you driver, if you're taking us all the way to Chepstow, can I?"

"I'm Nick," said Nick, blushing in the darkness at being asked his name.

"Nick who?"

"Nick… er, Waggoner," he answered.

"Oh, and you're a waggoner by trade, as well. That's an odd coincidence," Fanny observed, idly, twiddling her hair as she talked.

"Not really," Nick said, deciding he may as well tell all. "My other name is Fludde, but I don't like using it."

Miles shifted around so he could see Nick better and engage in a proper conversation. "Why not?" he asked. "What's wrong with it?"

"It's my mother's name, not my father's," Nick said. "Think about it. I used to get ragged when I was a kid something cruel."

"What do you mean? That it's stupid name for a mother?"

"Oh, for goodness' sake, Miles, you are so slow," Fanny snapped, exasperated again. "Nick's father and mother were never married. Get it?"

"Oh. Right. I get it," Miles said, slowly. "But – I don't think it's *that* important. Is it? For people like him, I mean. Us, yes. But…"

"It matters to other people when they find out," Nick said, with rare bitterness.

It was Fanny's turn to adjust her position so she could see him. "Couldn't your mother at least have told people that your father was *dead* when you were a child?" she asked, with some disfavour. "We've had enough wars. She could have claimed he'd been killed in one of them, instead of just brazening it out and letting everyone think what they pleased. Urgh. That's a bit disgusting of her."

"No, it isn't," Nick replied.

"I think it is," Fanny persisted.

"Why is it?" Nick asked. "I was fed, I was looked after. She's been a good mother to me. How do you know that what she did was any different from what you're doing now? You don't know yet how today may finish up."

"Oh well, I suppose if you put it like that, there's not a lot wrong with it," Fanny said, settling back in her place again. "But if that was so, how did people know you didn't have a father? Did she tell them?"

"No. With a name like Fludde, she didn't have to. Nobody was likely to forget about her. When she left her farm, everybody round these parts knew that it wasn't to get married. People have long memories in the country. Ask anyone about the Fluddes of Chepstow, and they'll say what you just did – 'Euch,' because Connie Fludde had a boy out of wedlock and brought him up on her own. It's not so bad now, I'm just Nick; or Nick the waggoner. I

227

have my own identity. But when I was a nipper, people would say 'Yuck. He's a Fludde: that dirty, base-born brat of Connie's. Stay away from him, he'll be rough.' If she'd gone away to have me and given me away without saying anything to anyone, she could have started afresh somewhere, and still been called respectable. As it is, she kept her own name, and even her own family gave up on her. I'd rather go by some other name than be judged by mine unfairly. Waggoner's a good one, it'll do."

Nick plucked up a piece of straw and began chewing on it. Fanny and Miles didn't say anything. They were both lost in contemplation of his words.

Miles was the first one to break the silence. "I don't think Fanny said 'Urgh' because she thinks you're rough," he said. "I don't know why anyone would say you're rough, because you're not; not in that way. She was just saying it because it sounds as if your mother didn't care what anybody thought of her."

"Don't say any more, Miles," Fanny said. "I'm thinking."

Nick was thinking, too.

Chapter Twenty-One

Back at the Squire's house, the troupe had packed up their gear, and were now ready to leave. But there were a couple of problems. First, there was no sign of Ronald, and nobody knew if he needed a lift with Able as far as Hewelsfield; and second – and more importantly – they couldn't find Rigo. Where on earth could he have got to? No-one knew.

"It's all your fault, Aaron," Able complained. "You should have kept him in your sights. He must have got fed up of waiting for us and gone for a walk."

Aaron was crouched on a mounting-step in the stable yard with his head between his knees. He lifted his head at his father's reproach with a quiet groan. "A walk?" he said, as if he couldn't believe his ears, "Rigo?"

"Yes, a walk. You'd better go after him, tell him it's time to go."

"Dad! I'm not going out into the countryside in the dark, looking for someone who might not even be there. If he's not at the privies, then he must have hitched a lift with someone else." Aaron's head sank down against his arm with another groan.

"Oh, he might have, I suppose. The Dowager Duchess of Sandbrook was here, he might have gone with her."

The other musicians all shook their heads, and Aaron was inclined to agree. Practiced as Rigo might be at inveigling his way smoothly into strange ladies' good books, his luck would hardly extend to gaining an invitation to share a refined elderly female aristocrat's carriage dressed as a gypsy and smoking a clay pipe emitting noxious, intoxicating fumes.

"Do you think he took a cart and went off on his own?" Able asked; but when Aaron thought about it, he just couldn't see Rigo doing that, either.

Tom, as far as he knew, had gone on ahead in the Colonel's cart with Rowles, still dressed in his musician's clothes. Maybe Rigo was with him. He said as much after he had instituted a quick search to placate his father, and to satisfy himself, once it was obvious that Rigo wasn't in the house and gardens any more.

It was only when the Colonel joined them, loudly asking if anyone had seen his son, that they realised matters were worse than they had anticipated.

"No," Aaron said. "We haven't seen him, not for hours. Didn't he go home with Rowles?"

"Rowles? No, no. Rowles is still here. I've told him to sleep in the stables and take the rest of the day off. He can return to us tomorrow morning, after he has breakfasted and been to church."

Aaron looked suddenly worried. Tom as well? What was going on? "Maybe he went on ahead," he suggested hopefully, and the Colonel nodded.

"I had already thought of that," he said, assertively. "He must have taken the cart. Young scamp. He had no business. Could have caused me considerable inconvenience. As it is… Well, what are we all waiting for?"

"Two other people not here, Colonel," Able said. "Ron Baker, and the young Brazilian. We don't know where they are."

"Oh, really? Well, I think I may be able to shed some light on the whereabouts of Ronald… Been undertaking some work of a kind for me. Not back yet. Well now, look here. I'll wait about a bit, get Ronald sorted out when he does show up, and see if I can get the young foreign lad taken to wherever he needs to be at the same time. Shouldn't be too difficult. You fellows get off now and leave things to me."

It was a solution that at least allowed the rest of them to leave and get home. They thanked him, climbed into their two carts, and had scarcely clattered off over the paving stones out into the drive, when the Squire came out and joined the Colonel. There were a few moments of strained silence. Then the Squire very pointedly asked what he could do for him. The Colonel was the last guest remaining. It was obviously time to go.

He took the hint, and mounted his horse, which had been standing, still saddled and bridled after his recent journey, for the last half-hour.

"Er, if Ronald Baker or a young foreigner should happen to turn up before morning, send them on to me in Trellech would you, Strangley?" the Colonel asked, as he gathered up the reins.

"Of course, of course," Squire Speybury promised, relieved at being presented with a quick and amicable means of parting with his irritating, but highly honoured guest. "I'll be happy to, old boy." He patted the Colonel's horse to get it moving and waved him off. Taking his leave of the Squire in return, the Colonel followed Able's cart down the driveway.

Able was going home via the Wye Bridge out of Monmouth, and the Colonel decided that if he could catch the musicians up, he could go their way until they parted company at Bigsweir Bridge. He then intended to continue down the Wye valley as far as Llandogo – even though Rigo was unlikely to have got so far in the time – in case there were signs somewhere along the way that the boy had been taken again. Somebody might still be out and about on the road to tell him, if that were so. If everything turned out to be quiet, he would then heel back home to Trellech through Cuckoo Wood. The Colonel had no concerns for Ronald. He knew he could take care of himself.

He caught up with Able before he was through Monmouth, and they spent the time between there and Redbrook discussing their options, and between Redbrook and Bigsweir agreeing, before they went their separate ways, that Able should return home to Hewelsfield via Saint Briavels and do his own checking at the prison there, and then meet up with the Colonel later, at about mid-afternoon, in Tintern, by which time Able would be on his way to do the entertainment for the evening ball in Chepstow. Brockweir wouldn't be suitable as a meeting-place; it was too small a settlement and would get them noticed. The Bell and Candle was a better venue for a casual encounter on Christmas Day.

Chapter Twenty-Two

Rigo awoke very gradually in the still of the night. He lay where he was and listened awhile to the rhythmic grinding of wheels rolling on each side of him, and the steady beat of hooves clopping on an uneven road underneath him, then he adjusted his position. For some unfathomable reason, he had a feeling of vague disquiet that wouldn't go away. After a minute or two, he quietly raised his head out of the straw. He wanted to see who was driving. One careful look was all he needed to discern that he was still alone in the back of the cart, and that he didn't know who the driver was. He ducked back down again and began to think hard. Was everything all right? Or had something gone wrong somewhere? He had no idea what could have happened. Maybe they had just decided to change the driver and hadn't had chance to let him know. He didn't mind that so much, but he did wish they had still let him travel with Tom. He pushed his head up through the straw again to take another look, to make sure of his senses, and was just about to dive back down again when the driver started talking.

"How now, my fine young cock pheasant. Plucked and dressed to pass for a hen bird, and out on your lonesome? That makes a man take notice. And tucked up under my straw? That makes a man think. Didn't the King's men beat the countryside up an' down in these parts for a day, tryin' to flush out a covey of miscreants who've gone a-roaming without leave? That makes a man wonder. And who might want to creep on by 'em at the back of me, I wonder? That makes a man ask."

He was a very tall, very skinny, etiolated sort of fellow, with arms and legs as thin and long as a grasshopper beneath his thick blanket and tattered heavy frieze coat. From out of the darkness an odour rose that was almost as distinctive as his visible profile. It was the tart, dry, slightly sour smell acquired by those habitual travellers who live exclusively in the fresh air: a smell of sun-drenched sweat washed clean in icy brooks, and of rough and ready clothing worn and weathered and seldom changed, with just a hint of mildew. In the darkness, Rigo could not discern the man's features, which lay under the eaves of a shapeless slouch hat adorned with a sprig of holly. But despite the concealment of his face, Rigo knew at once who he must be: there was only one man in the whole kingdom who could be described in such a way, and he was Tony Lightfoot, the itinerant pedlar. But why was he driving this cart? Had he come from the Squire's?

Rigo deliberated quietly for a moment or two, then, as Tony's voice sounded sufficiently engaging to be called friendly, he decided to ask some questions of his own.

"S-S-Sir," he began, "c-c-can I ask you where we're going...?" But he was cut off by an explosive bark of laughter that echoed scarily through the cold night air, eddying into out the emptiness of the heathlands beyond the road.

"Sir? *Sir!*" Tony repeated, and laughed again. "Ah, but this is an experience to be told over," he exclaimed delightedly, slapping the skinny thigh protruding out of his coat. "Indeed, my young cocks-comb, if I *was* a 'sir,' I'd be in a fine carriage an' pair this very minute, bein' driven to my stately home at a spankin' pace by my own coachman. Now there's a satisfyin' thought for a poor man to ponder over! Stuff me wi' sage an' sausages, an' serve me up for a goose if I don't speak true! Though this much must be said, that drivin' along wi' you is a great contentment compared to my daily mode of travel, which is by the use of my own sad legs."

"Are you taking me to-to-to Chippistow?" Rigo asked, determined to get his first important point confirmed before trying to establish anything else. He could not make sense of Tony's rambling manner of talking, and hadn't registered a single thing of what had just been said.

"So, it's an owl you are; an' not a pheasant after all, if you want to travel by night all the way Chepstow – an' in such good, chillin' weather, to boot. That makes a man think hard. For here we are all on a Christmas morning, wi' nought but the prospect of a hearty breakfast an' a long easement by a warm fireside on our minds, an' we're asked to keep on goin' past our destination. That would make it a long, rough road; aye, and a hard one. It makes a man scratch his head, an' engage in a deal of puzzlement; for what purpose might a body have in requestin' such a dagglin' alternative to the promise of a mug of strong ale beside a snug an' cheerful fire?"

Rigo considered the question. He also gave some careful thought on how best to give an answer. This man was unknown to him. Nobody had made mention of him as a driver for his journey. Had the man just agreed that they were on their way to Chepstow? Or had he not? Rigo couldn't altogether make his style of speech out. And if he had said they were going there, were they really? Tony might be taking him somewhere completely different. He might even be going to turn him in! There might be a reward for the return of the missing prisoners! That was not a nice thought. It made Rigo shiver momentarily. He didn't want to be returned to that awful gaol, nor to any other. Not ever. But there was a quality to Tony's easy insouciance that made Rigo think it was unlikely the man was planning anything underhand; moreover, there was no aura of slyness or cunning about him, and Rigo was more than familiar with such subtleties, and such men, where they existed. Yet there was an indefinable strangeness about him. He was unsettling. For a start, he almost seemed to have known all along that Rigo would be hiding in the back of his cart; and Rigo had an uncomfortable feeling that Tony might also have an inkling of where Rigo was headed, and why. And from the observations he made, as he smoked his clay pipe and talked while the old horse clopped quietly along the rough road, Tony Lightfoot also seemed to have some sort of insight into the recent smuggling operation, and the arrests. Could he be involved in some way, or was this man simply a passing interested onlooker who just happened to see more penetratingly than most?

Rigo came to a decision; and spoke up again. "M-M-Mis-s-ster Tony," he said; then he stopped short and watched in silence as Tony complacently smoothed each eyebrow in turn with a middle finger and straightened out his ragged neckerchief as though it was a cravat, in gentlemanly acknowledgement of the title Rigo had just apportioned him. Rigo knew he had got it wrong again, but since Tony didn't comment on it, neither did Rigo, and the moment was allowed to pass. "Tony," he went on, deciding at last that this was how best to address a fellow like him, "I h-h-have to get to Chippistow tonight; so, I will have to leave you." He dropped his voice. "I have to m-meet someone before I leave England, Sir. Someone very important. My ship sails on the morning of Saint Steven's Day with the tide, so I haven't got much time. If you could just set me down and t-t-tell me which way to go, I will walk now. Thank you very much for the lift you have given me."

"Ah! Now that's a piece of information to shed another light over things, my young flittermouse," Tony said softly, bending his head so his mouth was close enough for Rigo to catch what he was saying. "And though a common man might not have the temerity do so, a 'sir' *may* ask just who this gentleman is that is so despert important to get to. He ain't your own captain, I'll be bound."

"N-N-No, Sir, not my own Captain, but another. I want to see Captain Henry Morgan, Sir. I want to join his crew and leave my own ship."

"Ah! Do you indeed? An' what makes you think such a fearsome man is hereabouts at this gentle an' convivial season o' the year?"

"Sir, I heard he is home visiting his dear old m-m-mother for Ch-Ch-Christmas. Somebody said so in a tavern in Rio, near where I live. So, I have come to find him."

"By all the salt in the vast seas and oceans, what a journey you have made just to see one man!" Tony exclaimed, startled at this information. "But you must know that you can't just walk up to a devilish man like Henry Morgan and start parleyin' with him, however far you have travelled. You'd burn to a crisp in the flames that lap around that man's heart. If a man really wants to join his crew – an' a bad an' wicked body o' men they be – then he must approach things sneaky-like, and creep up cautious."

"Cr-r-reep up on him? What, at night do you mean? Behind him, on the road?"

"Nay, nay, lad. I mean you would have to make your approach to him slow an' guarded, rememberin' that a dog like him has teeth and ain't afeerd to use 'em. Make a friend of one of his crew maybe, the one that's least likely to cut your throat. Talk at a distance in the taverns; gain one friendship gradual-like, an' then work on another, an' let yourself grow onward towards the Captain day by day like a beanstalk climbin' over a hedge."

"B-But that will take too long."

"Too long? Why! – how long did you think you had to get yourself engaged, you young rascal? Did you think a man like Henry Morgan would just take one look at you an' clasp you to his buzzim on the spot?"

"W-W-Why not? He can see all he needs to. I can tell him the rest later, if he wants to know more."

Tony gave another great barking shout of laughter. "And what is the rest, you young scallywag? Tell me first, afore you tell him."

"Sir, I am R-R-Rodrigo de Abílio, and I am f-f-from Brazil. Captain Henry Morgan is a very f-f-famous pirate in my country, and I want to join a gr- a gr- a great man."

"Is that it?"

"Y-Yes. That's enough. What more does he need to know?"

"And what about the time it will take to gain his good opinion?"

"I don't c-c-care about his opinion. Or what he thinks of me. Just so long as he hires me."

They had made their way about four miles further along the road while they were thus conversing, as near as Rigo could judge, when Tony pulled up without warning at a stone cottage built close by the road-side. Rigo tried to examine his surroundings, but he had no way of telling what road they were on, or where they were. All he could see were some shadowy houses and gated hedges indicating gardens just discernible as darker bulky forms under the dim starlight. He started asking questions in a loud whisper, but Tony, who appeared to be waiting for somebody or something, shushed him, saying they were at a friend's house, and that Rigo must be patient for a few minutes.

After lingering a while longer, Tony seemed to come to a decision. He looked hard all about him just the once, then stepped easily out of the cart, the ground being only a short step away for his long, lanky legs, and, leaving the reins tied to the shaft, strode up to the cottage in a few giant, swaying steps, setting the full skirts of his coat into a haphazard fluttering swirl about his ankles by his method of walking. He knocked softly at the door, listening intently with his ear pressed against wooden panels, and after a short lapse of time he was swiftly admitted, ducking his head under the lintel to get inside.

There followed a long silence. Rigo stayed in the cart, shivering uncontrollably. He was so hungry he could have eaten anything, but there was nothing in the back with him except straw. All was very cold, and all was very still.

Suddenly, an upstairs window in the cottage was thrown wide open, and an elderly woman's face appeared in the frame. Her features were difficult to distinguish, but Rigo could see greying hair set in white curl papers, and a frilled white nightcoif shining milkily in the darkness in much the same eerie fashion that a granny's nightcap flower in a hedgerow will, during the height of summer. In the darkness, she looked very like a quivering ghost. No sooner had the numinous comparison formed in Rigo's mind than it was dispelled by an inarticulate exclamation from the woman as she looked up, down, and roundabout before starting some hysterical questioning of the world in general.

"Aargh! What's happenin'?" she called from her eyrie, speaking with a strong Welsh accent. "I mean to say; will somebody tell me what's happenin'?"

Her eye fell on Rigo, who had not had the presence of mind to duck down in the cart. He was still staring at her, startled almost out of his wits by the noise she was creating.

"Eh! Who are you?" she shrieked. "What are you doin' over by there? What's goin' on? Maldwyn! Maldwyn! There's somebody out h'yur! Are we goin' to be murdered in our beds? Maldwyn! Where are you? What's happenin' out h'yur? Come out! Come out now!"

The cottage door was yanked open so hard it was a wonder it didn't come off its hinges; and an elderly man of small stature came leaping out into the garden like a demented marionette puppet, dressed only in his nightcap and a nightgown that barely fell below his knees, his hair sticking out madly in all directions in a wild, sleep-tousled disarray. Capering barefoot part-way down the garden path just far enough that he could see the upstairs window, he began berating the woman distractedly, dancing about on the pebble-stones and shaking his fist in a frenzy of irritation, hopping up and down continuously as he tried to keep his feet from freezing.

"What in God's name do you think you are doing, Angahrad-Elunid-Alis? Be quiet, will you? Be *quiet!*" The man's rasping voice carried almost as far into the night as his wife's hysterical demands for information. "Get back inside, woman! You'll rouse the whole neighbourhood!"

"Is that you, Maldwyn?" the woman demanded querulously, peering into the garden where the man stood. "I can't see you properly."

"Of course, it's bloody me. You can hear me, can't you?"

"Ah, but I can't see you properly, Mal. That's what I mean to say. You should show yourself. I can't see you properly."

"Well you know my bloody voice, don't you?"

"Ah, but I wasn't thinkin' about that. I was too busy worryin'."

"If you kept that bloody window shut and minded your own business, you wouldn't *have* to worry. Get back inside. Are you mental, woman?"

"Ah, but what I'm tryin' to tell you is, there's somebody out h'yur."

"No there isn't. And keep your voice down." He issued several menacing imprecations, lowering his own voice now to a penetrating whisper; but he also looked about him, despite his assertions.

Angharad-Elunid-Alis took absolutely no notice of her husband's anger. "I know what I saw, Mal," she persisted. "And I saw somebody."

"Well, where's this bloody person supposed to be, then?" Maldwyn gingerly tiptoed a bit further down the path so he could see for himself. "I'll make you bloody pay for this if I go looking and find there's nobody there. Getting me out in all this cold for nothing. You've got too much imagination, that's your trouble, Angharad-Elunid."

"He's out on the road Maldwyn, over by there, look. An' he's in our cart, with our horse!"

Maldwyn suddenly spotted Rigo's startled face, transfixed, round-eyed and wondering, staring at him through the open gloom. The colourful scarf and dangling, glinting ear-rings made a madly exotic display of his head, which was rising above the side of the cart like some head-hunter's unholy trophy. Maldwyn backed away several paces in alarm.

"Good God alive, man, who are you?" he exploded in challenge, just as soon as he had recovered himself. He put his fists up into a fighting stance and started to leap about again, full of a small man's aggression.

Very much taken aback by such open animosity from such an elderly couple, Rigo didn't immediately know what to say. Before he could think of an answer, Angharad-Elunid-Alis took over.

"Ah! There you are, see? I *told* you." The words floated out, triumphant, into the night air. "I was right, wasn't I? There *was* somebody there. Well, who is he? What I mean to say is, who is he? An' why has he got our horse an' cart?"

"How the hell do I know, woman? It's just some damned foreigner." Maldwyn began to edge bad–temperedly back towards the cottage, still swearing under his breath. Rigo he ignored completely. "Get back inside and close the window before you wake the dead. I'll put the horse and cart away."

The cottage door closed behind him, and the upper window was precipitately slammed shut. A heated discussion within the cottage followed, the bulk of which was audible through the cottage wall, with Angharad-Elunid-Alis's half of the conversation progressing steadily downstairs as she continued to harry her husband with demands for information.

While the occupants were still bickering, Tony Lightfoot came loping quietly down the garden path, his extensive legs well splayed out at the knees, and his long arms poised, hanging outstretched in the air to keep his balance on the icy stones. He was come to fetch Rigo inside with a few quiet words of invitation. Rigo was not averse to going with him, despite the many misgivings he was entertaining about the likely nature of his reception by the old couple. He was chilled to the bone, and crystals of rime were starting to form on the ringlets of his hair.

The room inside the cottage was nicely warm. The remains of a good fire lay glowing in the grate, and someone had added a fresh log to build it up and get it going again. Several candles were lit, each wavering in succession in the slight wind which blew under the door. Tony stopped the draught with an elaborately home-embroidered draught excluder and joined Rigo, shivering slightly as another draught unexpectedly eddied down the chimney. The place was neat, and very clean. It was a nice room to be in, and most welcome after several hours of jolting and bone-shaking in a hard, unyielding wooden cart.

Rigo gratefully took a seat on a settle close by the fire and breathed in the faint smell of linseed oil and turpentine polish rising from the warm wooden furniture. He arranged a cushion under himself and leaned into the fireplace to warm his frozen hands while he looked about him. He was impressed by the simple finery of the room. The couple living here clearly loved their home. What immediately drew his attention was Maldwyn's collection of books, housed in three bookcases up against the wall. All the books were identically leather-bound and matched, and all were in marvellous condition, despite their obvious age and considerable usage. One of the books lay open, cradled in a carved brass book lectern set on a dark oak table in the middle of the room. From the well-polished lectern, Rigo's eyes travelled to the gleaming and winking set of brass fire irons, and a copper kettle tucked into an inglenook beside the fireplace, where the logs of wood for the fire were also neatly stacked. He approved of what he saw. Everything combined to give an impression of order and homeliness. Whatever her other deficiencies might be, Angharad-Elunid-Alis was a very good housekeeper.

She and her husband had been out of the room for some while, getting dressed and stabling the horse and cart. Now they were on their way back in, Maldwyn first, with his wife following at his heels. The two of them were still exchanging voluble and contradictory opinions about the horse, the cart, the visitors, and everything else.

Rigo could now see the manner of woman Angharad-Elunid-Alis was, and she clearly presented herself well. She was of middle height and build, with greying red hair, a little taller than her husband, but nicely formed, and still very attractive to look at, thanks to a refusal to accept old age with anything like grace and dignity. She kept her hair neat, though dressed in a style better befitting a much younger woman, but it suited her nonetheless. Her gown was of fine quality, chosen to bring out all that was best in her slightly faded appearance. The only thing she couldn't disguise was the open resentfulness of her manner. She was carrying a laden wooden tray, and this she plonked on top of several papers spilling across the table, talking non-stop over her husband as she commenced the placing out of some comestibles.

"What do you think you are doing now, you maniac?" Maldwyn shrieked, clenching his fists and springing into an impromptu jig of savage vexation. "You can't set your things out on top of those, they're important! Give them to me this minute!" He snatched the papers out from under the tray and clutched them to his chest, breathing hard. "Stay there while I move these first," he commanded, holding the papers close. He moved rapidly across to a bureau that Rigo hadn't noticed before, set in one of the darker corners of the room. The handwritten trophies were swiftly bundled out of sight in there, and Maldwyn rushed back to the table to rescue the book off the lectern. "You think nothing of my books and writings! You're completely mad! As well as a Philistine!" He grabbed the volume, glaring at his wife, and returned it to its place on the shelf alongside its fellows, stroking it carefully back into alignment and soothing his ruffled feelings at the same time.

"Well, what am I to do, then? Where am I to put these things?" Angharad-Elunid-Alis asked of no-one in particular, doubtless wishing to avoid further abuse from her husband and so refraining from putting another question to him directly, but unable to resist asking anyway. "I mean to say, I didn't put anything down near that book, and I got nowhere else to put these things."

"What are you on about? You can empty your tray onto that side table there." Maldwyn gestured peremptorily to a long, low table standing over by the wall. He was still upset.

"Well, what's the good of that?" she demanded, still seeking clarification. "Our guests can't reach that table from where they'm sittin'. I mean to say, Maldwyn, they need to be able to reach the food from where they'm sittin', after all."

"Well, move the bloody table then, woman!"

"Oh, ah. I could do, I suppose. I never thought of that."

Maldwyn snatched up two mugs of cottage ale from the tray while she still stood puzzling, and handed them over to Tony and Rigo without her even noticing. Then he grabbed the tray out of her hands and waited impatiently while she very uncertainly dragged the table across the flagstones until it stood in front of Tony and Rigo.

"This table will be awful low for them to sit at, Mal."

Her husband did not respond. Still unsure, she took the tray from him and began to lay everything out in front of their guests. It was only two treen platters and a couple of two-pronged forks, a loaf of new bread and a slab of Caerphilly cheese, but she fussed over these few things as if she was doing the place settings for a formal banquet. Eventually she seemed satisfied and stepped back to invite the men to begin eating while she uncovered a jar of pickles. Then her nervous fluttering began all over again. The smell of vinegar was overwhelming when the top came off.

"This is a new jar of onions," she said, examining them anxiously. "We 'aven't tried them yet. Oh, I do 'ope they are all right, they smell awful strong."

"They'll be all right, Angharad-Elunid," said Maldwyn curtly. "Take yourself off, now."

"Ah, but what I mean to say is they smell awful strong. Do they smell all right to you? Only I couldn't get the onions I wanted this year, these are from Jilly, and hers aren't nowhere near as good as Joe Phillips's, but he was took bad, an' he didn't grow as many as he usually does, so he had none spare to give me this time, an'…"

"Look, we're not here to talk about bloody onions. Clear off, and don't come back until I call you."

"But aren't you goin' to tell me who these people are?"

"You know who Tony is. Go on."

Angharad-Elunid-Alis reluctantly prepared to withdraw. Her eyes remained fixed on Rigo. He saw her looking and decided to try his charm offensive. Swallowing an onion whole straight off his fork, he stood up.

"Hey. Miss Ann Harry, m-m-my name is…" he began, but Tony took his arm and dragged him back down.

"Not now, you young rooster," Tony hissed in Rigo's ear. "You're still in disguise, remember?"

"B-B-But I think she knows I'm a man," Rigo whispered from the side of his mouth, pretending to look for another onion to spear from the pickle jar.

"Pop my eyes out wi' a corkscrew!" Tony expostulated in a frantic undertone. "She won't have reasoned that far! She probably just hasn't noticed what you're wearing yet. Do you really want to say things that will make you have to start explaining yourself to this lady?"

"Can't I even t-t-tell her where I come from?"

"Not if you know what's good for you," Tony whispered again. "You'd be about as welcome as a maggot in that pickle jar. These people don't like foreigners."

So Rigo smiled his disarming smile at Angharad-Elunid-Alis instead, and waved his onion across the room at her, saying out loud, "Hey! I just w-w-would like to say thank you for the food, Miss Ann Harry. It is d-d-delicious. I know I eat too much, you could almost say I am a little bit fat, maybe." He smiled the deprecating smile that always came at this point and patted himself. "B-B-But I am very hungry, and I eat for my Mama, who worries about me when I am far away from home…"

"I don't know about *that*, my boy," Angharad-Elunid said tartly, eyeing him with undisguised disfavour and sniffing loudly. The sentimental reference to his mother was entirely lost on her. She had only attended to the first bit. She looked meaningfully at the ample stomach straining hard against his bodice and skirt. "I don't know about a *little bit* fat. You look more than a little bit fat to me. I mean to say. You could do with some salads if you ask me. Ah. What I mean to say is I don't know about *that*!"

Rigo sat stricken, his forkful of food frozen in mid-air, his noisy mastication of a pickled onion momentarily arrested. He was beginning to wilt under the pressure of these personal insults, having only ever experienced motherly concern on the subject of his eating before. He looked around, hoping for some guidance on how he should respond, but Tony was leaning uneasily up against him full of apprehension, pretending to reach for his stoup of ale, while Maldwyn stirred the fire vigorously with one hand, and gestured imperiously for him to be quiet using the other, the hand Angharad-Elunid-Alis could not see.

"Keep your tongue behind your teeth now, lad, and say no more," Tony whispered, raising a covert acknowledging eyebrow to Maldwyn at the same time.

Rigo smiled uncertainly in response. Angharad-Elunid saw him, and misinterpreting his smile as mere complacency, carried on with mounting disapproval.

"By your talk, you'm from over England way," she announced, accusingly. Maldwyn swung round from his exertions with the fire, seriously alarmed, and began pressing her to leave. She backed towards the door, still talking. "Ah. You'm not from round these parts, that I do know. I don't know who you are, but I can tell by your accent you'm not from round h'yur."

Maldwyn hustled her out, almost pushing her through the door, and her disembodied voice continued from the small passageway.

"Ah, but what I mean is, you should be goin' 'ome to your mam if you'm missin' her cooking that much. It's all that *eatin'* that's makin' you fat, my boy – ah! An' more than a little bit. If you ask me!"

Maldwyn ordered her back into her kitchen to make up some brandy and hot water and told her to be sure she put plenty of sugar and lemon in it. Then he shut the communicating door fast, checked it, and came swiftly back to Rigo and Tony, pulling up a nearby footstool ready to begin conversing. He was at once focussed and astute, abandoning the fitful agitation and contemptuous abuse that had marked his earlier dealings that night.

"You almost gave the game away back there, boy," he began, quietly, peering at Rigo narrowly over the top of his pince-nez glasses. "As a matter of fact, you've slipped up several times since you've been here."

"Ah," Tony agreed companionably, giving a slow smile and displaying several gaps amongst his black and broken teeth. "Easy to catch as a young partridge wi' a few grains o' good steeped barley, that's you, my lad, an' no mistake. Fill me wi' fine feathers an' sit on me if I don't speak true!"

"I?" Rigo enquired, with polite interest, having already recommenced his steady munching. "How?" Despite Angharad-Elunid's open disapproval of his rather lavish embonpoint, he had no conscience about eating more, and no intentions of depriving himself, since opportunity had obligingly presented him with such a pleasing meal.

Maldwyn eyed him evenly. "Tell me," he said. "Are you aware of just how much danger you are in at this moment?"

Rigo looked round the room, puzzled. "Am I? D-D-Danger of what?"

Maldwyn continued his look, and his eyes glittered behind his glasses. "Now listen to me, boy. If my wife can spot that you're some sort of interloper in less than quarter of an hour, there's not much hope of you getting away with whatever it is you're doing for very much longer, with or without Tony to help you. Who are you? And what are you doing on the road at this time of night? Tell me all."

"Sir, I am R-R-Rodrigo de Abílio f-f-from Brazil," Rigo said, standing up with a great scraping of wood and a clattering of metal as he nudged the table and knocked his fork off it. "A-A-And I took a ship bound for England to find C-C-Captain Henry Morgan, so I can join his crew. I was arrested last night for sm-m-muggling." He sat down again. That was enough information, he thought, as he retrieved his fork to finish off the cheese.

Maldwyn watched him for a moment; then he turned to Tony. "And what do you know about all this?" he asked.

Tony smiled his cracked-teapot smile again. "Don't you worry, my old confederate, nobody else has dropped any clangers." He leaned over to pass a small package over to Maldwyn, then eased himself back on the settle and spread his legs right across the rag hearth-rug as he watched Rigo re-assemble his eating implements. "This lad's the only one. He finished up in the back of your cart, though I don't know how; but I knew who he was straight away. He's the one who asked to be in on the dealings last night, the one they decided to let in. I had my suspicions about that at first, but on a better acquaintance with the lad, I think I can assure you he only did it to be fitty-like. I was told he has a good enough brain in his head, but it behoves me to say that the only use I'd put to the one *I've* seen would be to boil it up with a sprig or two o' parsley; for he'd be more than happy to sit and chew on it served up wi' a dollop of good bread sauce than use it for chewin' things over with."

"Never mind all that, man," Maldwyn said, opening the package. "How did he come to be here?"

Three letters lay revealed in front of him, one on top of the other. Maldwyn broke the seals so he could scan the contents of each while he was talking.

Rigo was still eating, oblivious to Tony's remarks, but he noticed the letters with interest. "A-Are they the letters Mister Baker was talking about?" he asked, conversationally, pointing at them with his knife. "I guess you can read, Mister Mould-win, huh? You m-must be very clever to be so educated, huh?" Both men ignored his question, so after a moment he tried again. "I think the King's m-m-men might be l-looking for those letters. The m-man carrying them was in the cart wi-wi-i-ith my friends when they were being taken to Saint Bubbles."

Neither man answered.

Maldwyn continued to scan the letters. At one place, an exclamation broke from his lips. For the rest, he read silently. Then when he had finished, he spoke. "It's as bad as I feared," he said quietly. "We need to act on this."

"How soon?"

"As soon as we can."

"Do these letters give us enough to go on?"

Maldwyn shook his head decisively. "No. Even so, we can't stand by and do nothing at our end. We must operate on guess-work and our good senses, based on what they are telling me. I will write answers to all three before you leave." He looked over his pince-nez at Rigo once more. "Can we trust you to keep quiet about all these?" He lifted the letters to indicate his meaning.

Rigo nodded in his turn. "You can trust me, M-Mister Mould-win," he assured him. "I won't say a word to anybody. A-A-And I'll be leaving tomorrow, anyway."

"Ah, yes. We have still to come to that." He returned his attention to Tony. "So, getting back to my original question: how has this boy come to be here?"

Tony shifted his position on the settle to get more comfortable. "This here lad and six men got overtook down at the river, because the look-outs didn't see the soldiers a-comin'. But 'twasn't from carelessness that it happened, the King's men had a tip-off. A full platoon was waitin' up the road with the revenue men. Could have been a whole lot worse, hang me for a jay if it couldn't. A couple of this lad's pals got snared up and took away at the same time, but that's all. They don't know anything."

"You're absolutely sure nothing has been compromised?"

"Certain sure. Nothing."

"Then what is this boy doing here?"

"Colonel sprung him out of gaol this afternoon."

"He did *what?* Sprang him? What the hell for? The old fool will bring the authorities down on everybody's necks before he's done. Has a search begun for this boy yet?"

"Don't think so. Brand Abbott was paid to slip in and be his substitute. I don't reckon they'll twig what's happened until the Assizes; and by then it'll be too late, they'll have to let Brand go. The rest of 'em will stand trial, I'm sorry to say. They'll be on their way to Oxford by tomorrow mornin'.'"

"Damn it. That's six men lost. Was any contraband seized?"

"Not much. Last few casks by the river waitin' to be took up."

"Well, that's something to be thankful for. They won't hang for a cask or two, I hope and trust. Can we get to them before the trial?"

Tony shook his ragged head. "No chance." He made a rueful face. "I wish we could."

"Ah well. The transporting will have to be dealt with as and when it arises. You know who you need to talk to about that." He regarded Tony with a gimlet eye, and Tony nodded in return. There was another, longer pause. Then, "When do you think you'll see him?"

"Soon enough." Tony inclined his head towards Rigo, who was staring into the fire half asleep. It was an indication not to say more. "Our men were lucky," Tony added, almost immediately, in continuance of his earlier discourse. "They nearly all got away through the tunnels. Most were already out the other end before the soldiers pitched up. But one of the lads taken in the round-up was the Colonel's son. He just happened to be out in the street at the same time. That's why the old boy went to the gaol; he wanted to get his son out before they realised who they'd got, or the family will be ruined. But it turned out the only one being held in Monmouth was this one here. The other two were on their way to Saint Briavels when they got free in the Forest."

"So, there's a hue-and-cry out there for them now?"

"Yup. Nobody will be able to carry anything that way for a while."

"And where are the Colonel's son and his friend now? Did they make it back to their homes?"

"Tom did; he's still there. The other lad is Aaron Arundel; he's gone back to the Forest with his old man. They're going to claim mistaken identity if they get stopped by soldiers, but he was only on a loitering charge anyway, same as Tom. Nothing to worry about."

He stopped talking as a knock sounded on the door and Angharad-Elunid-Alis came in, bearing three rummers of brandy and hot water. She set them down, and Maldwyn permitted her to clear away the tray and empty plates. There was no food left, Rigo had eaten it all. He watched her sheepishly as she came and went, bracing himself in case she started making comments about him again, but she didn't. She just carried on endlessly about their wants, and fretted about the quality of what she had been able to provide, until she left the room for the final time. Once she was gone, Maldwyn started discussing the best way of getting Rigo back to his ship.

"With all the fuss Angharad-Elunid has made from our bedroom window, people will come calling as soon as day breaks, wanting to know what went on here in the night," he said. "I'll do what I can to spin them a yarn, but I can't keep Angharad-Elunid quiet indefinitely. It won't take her long to put in her two penn'orth, and when she does the game will be up, so you haven't much time. Before the morning is out, everyone in these parts will be watching out for you, and they'll all be talking about you, no matter what I attempt as a cover for you from my end."

Another pause ensued, during which Tony reached up and filled his clay pipe with a bit of dried leaf from a tobacco jar on the chimney piece over the fire. He lit it using a glowing wood chip from the fire while Maldwyn watched him, his mind engaged.

"I think it's best if you go as far as your – how shall I term it? – your place of residence on Tintern ridge – and then go no further until the morning church services have finished," Maldwyn continued. "Stay off the beaten tracks to get there. You can't alter any aspect of your travelling from there on, which is a nuisance because you haven't got time on your side, but it will look too strange and unnatural to be out on the roads early on Christmas Day morning in the company of a stranger. People will remember it afterwards. Ideally, you need to get to wherever you are going, and get this boy under cover at the earliest opportunity. Where are you proposing to take him, once you do get to Chepstow, by the way?" He peered at Tony through his pince-nez glasses narrowly.

"Well now, I think the usual old hideaway is the best place to put him," Tony said, blandly. "Keep him dug in there like an old maldie-warp, soft-sorted an' close, till the very last minute. Then we'll take him down to his ship just before it sets sail. Bury me for an acorn if that ain't the best idea."

"When are you to set sail, boy?" Maldwyn enquired.

"Ser-Ser-Saint Steven's Day," Rigo answered. "If we have a f-f-fair wind, I think it will be with the morning tide."

"Hmm, Boxing Day," Maldwyn said, thoughtfully. "That's a fairish time for you to be trying to stay out of sight. Let's just talk ourselves through this. First, you two have got to get to Chepstow together on foot. Now I'm starting to wonder if that's altogether wise. At the very least you'll have to wear different clothes. You don't want to draw people's attention as you go, not when there's already interest gathering behind you."

Tony smiled his slow smile. "Ah, but therein lies a problem, my friend, as you already know, for I am ever the same. Like a cricket on the heath, nothin' about me changes, or can be changed, till I shed me next skin." Tony held out the skirts of his ragged old coat for inspection. "Before that, the maids must take me as I am, be they tart, town trollop or country wench; for I carry but one set of raiment, come fair weather or foul, and that's these poor rags I wear on my back now."

"I wasn't referring to you, I realise you will draw no particular attention by yourself. It will be the presence of a travelling companion that attracts it. But I can assure you that the only way Rigo will pass into the town unremarked, if not unnoticed, will be by presenting him as a boy again. You must pretend he's somebody who has joined you along the way. People know you have no living relatives, if you walk into Chepstow with a girl of any age or description it will set the entire town buzzing. Chepstow doesn't need any more tavern whores, the ones already there will stone him out of town the minute they see him, and we can't risk him being stripped for a tar-and-feathering."

Rigo roused himself at this unpleasant possibility and bridled up with indignation and alarm. "Stripped?" he asked, "wh-wh-why should I b-b-be stripped? Why would anyone th-think I'm a whore? I just passed for somebody's cousin tonight." He turned to Tony. "Didn't I? Squire Spray Berry's son asked to be intr-r-roduced to me, so I must look *okeh*."

Tony smiled his cracked smile again, and slowly shook his head.

"No? W-Well, what kind of a woman would the Squire's son want to meet, then?"

Tony smiled again and leaned back against the settle. "Sister, daughter or cousin, you're still trigged out like a camp follower, my plump pigeon," he remarked, with wry amusement. "If young Speybury *was* after ye, 'twas not to be his bride; for bride you never were, nor ever will be; an' if not a bride, then what other kind of woman can ye be, an' her not an honest spinster back home in her house?"

Rigo had no answer to make, being mystified all over again by Tony's mode of expression and philosophical bent. He absently re-filled his own pipe when Tony took down the tobacco jar again and attempted to quietly decipher Tony's last question whilst he lit it, ruminating at the same time on the implications of Maldwyn's concerns.

"You th-th-think I look ugly as a woman," he announced at last, having reached the end of his cogitations. "That is w-w-what you are saying. But I don't understand why that should m-m-make me a whore or a camp follower instead of a bride, it doesn't make sense. Why should a whore be any uglier than a br-br-r-ride? She's still being used the same way. Not all brides are beautiful. The men in my country don't choose their women like this."

Maldwyn looked up, absently. "Mmm? What's that?" he asked.

"Who said anything about ugliness, my raven-haired temptress?" Tony ventured, ignoring Maldwyn with easy good nature. "You mistook my meaning. It wasn't your looks I was thinking of, which are as beguiling as any I've laid eyes on, girl or boy, cram me wi' caterpillars if they ain't; it's more what you was born *with* that a woman *wasn't*, if you follow me; and if you got rid of *that,* though the very thought of it gives me morbid chills, you still couldn't get to a woman's estate, not if you was to be sprinkled wi' seekins an' set down in a hare-um full o' silks for a sultan's *conkibinn,* you couldn't."

But Rigo was still flummoxed about Tony's meaning. It was all getting beyond him. He mused for a bit longer, then gave up, and listened while Maldwyn took up the reins of the conversation.

"You will move fastest if you travel by night," Maldwyn was saying. "Unless you prefer to walk in casually the way you normally do on your usual route through Saint Arvans and call in at the country houses as you go."

"Shoot me for a squirrel, but I don't think I would dare," Tony said, displaying some genuine alarm on his normally placid features. "They'll have heard about the escapes in the Forest all over these parts. A strange boy straggling along with the local pedlar, however devilishly we present him, will stand out like fine feathers on a tinker's slut. I think I'll do as you suggest, friend, and get us both over to my shack well before morning. We'll lay up there quiet-like until tonight, an' then travel on."

After some more murmured discussion with Tony about other matters, Maldwyn went up the stairs to find some clothes for Rigo to change into before they left. Angharad-Elunid-Alis had returned to her bed, and the cottage was now quiet. He returned soon afterwards with some fine worsted stockings and black buckle shoes, which he put on the floor in front of the settle, and next unfolded pair of patched grey flannel britches and a matching old-fashioned doublet that had once gone together as a suit. The outfit was completed by a clean, but darned white linen shirt. He shook the items out and presented them all to Rigo, who was nodding off in the warmth of the fire now that his stomach was full.

"I didn't bring you the best of what we have put by," Maldwyn said, "but then you don't want to be out with Tony looking like a popinjay. These clothes are warm and practical. You could pass yourself off as my relative, if anyone asks who you are. Say you are Maldwyn Parry's cousin from over the water, but don't say which water. They can assume whatever they want, that way. And tell them, if they ask where you are going, that you are on your way to the Fox Hole in Chepstow. It is where some real relatives of mine live."

Rigo looked up at this, suddenly alert, as Maldwyn handed him over the lavender-impregnated garments one by one.

"Th-These are all very nice, thank you," he said simply, squeezing himself out of the colourful skirt and bodice with relief and leaving bits of fruit and fern scattered across Angharad-Elunid-Alis's nice clean hearthrug, and then scratching himself all over before attempting to confine himself with clothes of any kind once more.

"I'm glad you think so," Maldwyn said quietly. "These things once belonged to my only son." He looked away and said no more.

Rigo regarded him with sympathy, then looked across at Tony for elucidation.

Tony took his pipe out of his mouth, and said succinctly, "Died."

"I'm s-sorry to hear of that," Rigo said. After a slight hesitation, he asked, "It w-wasn't anything catching, was it?"

"No, nothing like that. It was an accident, something that couldn't be helped. But you can see how it left my wife. She was never a strong woman, and she's not been the same since."

Rigo started putting the clothes on, dragging the britches up first. "Sir do y-y-you have any daughters?" he asked, as he was fastening them.

"No, just two grandchildren: a girl and a boy. We'll see them again tomorrow, with my son's wife."

"I think I know your grandchildren," Rigo said. "I think I m-met them in the town. They said they live in a place called Fox Hole. This place is on the river bank near the water, right? And they are A-Adela and Andrew, right?"

"Yes, it is; and yes, they are," Maldwyn said.

"And you m-m-made their coracle for them, I think. Right?"

"My son did," Maldwyn answered, with a long sigh. "He made it a long time ago, before he was drowned. If I had known then what his end would be, I would never have encouraged him, or them, to go out on the water."

"Don't w-w-worry yourself about them, Mister Maldwin," Rigo advised, bracingly. "Th-Th-They are both very good with boats, and have good sense in the water, like ducks. I am a sailor; I have seen how m-m-many people, both foolish and wise, act around water. I know what I am talking about. They will not drown."

"We none of us know that for certain, boy, we can't read our own stars, but I thank you for your assurances all the same. And I appreciate the sentiments you express. When they visit, I shall let them know I saw you before they leave. That will be in the New Year, so you should be well gone by then. And if you ever return here in the years to come, after the fuss has died down and this has all been forgotten about, you will be most welcome to visit us here, with or without my grandchildren present."

"Now there's a handsome gesture," Tony observed, spitting into the fire and then relighting his pipe. "You're one of the privileged few, my lad, make no mistake. Old Maldwyn Parry here ain't a man to suffer fools, an' he ain't a man to make an offer like that every day of the week, Lord knows. An' most especial to foreigners like you."

"S-S-Seriously?"

"Seriously, lad. Catch me for a down o' thistle an' make a pixie's bedspread out o' me if it ain't so."

"S-S-Seriously?"

"Aye, lad. Catch me twice, an' you can add a fairy pillow, an' all!"

Chapter Twenty-Three

The long walk to Tony's shack was undertaken with all the precautions possible. They travelled through rough woodland for most of the way, even though it was still dark, because neither of them felt safe out in the open.

"It's not just King's men or soldiers we have to keep our eyes peeled for, lad," Tony whispered, as they set out. "There's plenty of gamekeepers in this neck o' the woods, an' all."

For the first mile, they progressed in silence. But Rigo grew tired of the darkness and wanted to raise his spirits, so he walked beside Tony for a while instead of behind him, and began to ask a few questions.

"M-M-Mister Tony, how do you know Mister Mould-win?" he began, when he judged a suitable moment for conversation had arisen, adding, just in case his first question was too vague, "is he in charge of you in some way?" Rigo didn't think the old man could have anything material to do with Tony's way of earning a living, but it might serve as a starting point for a discussion to pass the time. He was right.

"Not in charge of me, lad," Tony answered, his mind already casting about for a fitting description of the man they had lately left, "for Mal is not a man to concern hisself with anyone, really. He's a man for whom the good Lord made reckonin' an easy affair, havin' made him a thinkin' man as well as an eddicated one. I should have thought you'd have worked that much out yourself. He has a wonderful brain, see. It works like a water mill set beside a river, easin' round day an' night, workin' continual wi' the flow o' reasonin'. His larnin' comes from deep pools of knowledge, an' after he has dipped into them hisself, he passes on what he has taken up to any who may ask; though there's few enough of those. I admire that kind o' brain, for my thoughts be stored in my head like ripe cherry pips, which pops out at me as I comes across 'em, one by one. Nothin' flows in me, you understand. I has to go lookin' for my intellectual notions, an' bite round them to get at 'em."

"I-I-I saw all his books. He's very clever, isn't he?"

"Maldwyn? As I live an' breathe, that man could have been a great scholard if only the good Lord had extended his blessings and give him a birth in a great house, so he could have been born wi' money and influence behind him. But bein' born instead to a poor tin miner in the Forest, an' havin' three brothers an' two sisters as come after him, he only got enough eddication to larn his letters, an' so became a tutor in Tredegar House, instructin' the Morgan family. It was the Morgan family what give him that vallyable collection of beautiful books back there in his house, when he took his retirement; an' a rare an' wonderful collection it is, an' all. Not that he would ever sell any of 'em. They're as precious as children to him, each one a treasure. An' he needs 'em, too, for there's few an' meagre other diversions for him, now. You see how he lives his life, lad. He spends his days in his home, growin' ever more bitter in his heart from the unvaryin' dullness o' country life and the slow-wittedness of his everyday company. There's times I think the man is in a state of near-madness."

"Oh." Rigo thought deeply. "And how d-d-did you meet him? Excuse me for saying it, but I wo-o-ouldn't expect you and him to cross paths. If you don't mind me saying so."

"Ah! I larned bits off him when I was a lad. In those days I would gangle round from farm to farm, an' great house to great house, a-beggin' aid for my poor limbs; for bein' long-legged an' coltish-lookin', my looks made good people think I might grow up straight wi' some proper moulding, same as a hive of bees wi' a wild honeycomb placed right in May. He took me under his wing when evenings was drawin' in, an' tried his best to teach me what he could. But there's little went in I fear, for I be like a tom-tit, perky enough about solvin' problems where my daily livin's consarned, but flighty an' giddy an' easy diverted once livin' is satisfied, d'you see. An' Mister Maldwyn was ever a sore hard teacher who won't suffer fools."

They stopped talking once the terrain became harder. Their breath was needed for climbing through fallen tree branches and over trunks and rocks and boulders, and for breaking through swathes of dodder, and the rest of the trek Rigo thought the most awful of his life. It haunted his memory for many a night afterwards. He had no idea what part of Monmouthshire he was in, but Tom could have told him. They were in the heart of Itton Woods, and their way was now mostly through narrow lanes and gullies, all deeply mired, with miles of slippery fallen leaves and tangles of briars to negotiate in between. Even the ordinary wooded areas were tough going, thickly packed with hazel and rowan undergrowth, forcing them to beat a way forward in the direction Tony said they had to go once they breasted the ridge, which was up over some steeply graded bracken-crusted hills and across a boggy dale full of sedge.

They saw no-one. The frozen tracks and byways were devoid of all life. Even the animals were in their shelters. All they heard was one robin, and that was because it started up in alarm when they disturbed it. It went flitting through the stark bushes and away beyond their sight, chirruping a challenge, and then was heard no more.

The silence became oppressive. The first part of their journey had been through long tracts of decaying deciduous woodland, where Tony had been able to pick a handful of withered hips to put in his pocket and chew on, and pull a spray of woody nightshade berries to pin onto his coat-front; but as the nature of the woods gradually changed it became patchy pine forest, with trees on the rough slopes trailing long, soft boughs that drooped down to touch unwary necks as if they were dead men's fingers. Nothing grew under the trees here. It was all dead. Even the sounds of dripping water everywhere around made Rigo think dismally of corpses and drops of blood. He shivered and looked around half-fearfully. In the occasional patches of open land between the pressing trees, every rock now seemed to be hiding something terrible behind it, and he was sure the huge tussocks of rough grass and scrambling sprays of ivy were shielding malevolent hobgoblins and sprites. Every sough of wind now became a ghostly whisper, every movement in the trees something coming to get him. Now and again, a stifled wicked laugh seemed to bubble up from somewhere behind him. Ordinarily Rigo was in no way superstitious, but the very nature of the area they had to pass through gave him morbid chills.

He was no happier when they arrived at the tumbledown shack. It was an hour or more later, and still not yet dawn when Tony checked his long, slow stride and finally pulled off the track.

"Here we are," he said, sitting down on a huge felled tree trunk lying half-buried in thick grass and emptying his leaking boots of water and leaf litter. They had stopped somewhere close to the edge of a dense bulk of resinous pines. Rigo sat next to him and peered into the thick woodland around, full of apprehension when he saw how closely the undergrowth grew into the pathway they had just come in by. It was all tangled twigs and matted, withered foliage, and it scrambled across as far as the trunks at the forest edge, blocking all escape routes. There was only one way in or out, and that was by the way they had just come. He tried to locate the shack, hoping he would feel more optimistic once he had pinpointed his place of refuge for the day, but it seemed impossible to spot. There was no under-lighting beneath the trees, and no new moon up above yet, and the last of the starlight was fast fading from the night sky.

After several sweeps of the surrounding forest, Rigo's eye fell on two tar barrels and a pile of old timbers discarded close to where they were sitting. They were hard to visualise, partly because of the poor light, and partly because they were inside a small mixed thicket of silver birch and hazel. Rigo leaned forward and peered harder.

Was he seeing right? *Was* this a shelter of some description? It was so hard to tell, but if it was, it was the most ramshackle affair Rigo had ever seen; far worse than Christina's warehouse, and that was saying something. Even the squalid huts of the shanty villages around Rio de Janeiro were better constructed. Prolific trails of ivy and old man's beard tumbled in wild disarray between pliable coppiced tree trunks over what might have been a pitched roof. Underneath, a second inspection showed the rough assembly to be held up with patches of some sort of slapped-together daub. Handfuls of moss and dried grasses protruded in tufts from the gaps between the timbers, helping it to blend into its background, with the added concealment of the pine trees on one side, and a ditch choked with tall rushes and wild celery on the other. Rigo's heart sank. So, this was it. This was what Tony called home. And he was going to have to spend the entire day here.

He said nothing, but got up and followed Tony inside the wood-pile, entering through a broken wattle door held more-or-less upright by withy-bark straps tied up as hinges. Rigo sat in the darkness dispiritedly and waited while Tony took a flint to light up an old bulls-horn farm lamp hanging from a bough supporting some sort of low canvas ceiling. Once the lamp was aglow, Rigo could see with some surprise that he was in a small room, and that it was quite snug and comfortably arranged in there. Daub covered the walls completely on the inside, so no wind came in, and there were plenty of rushes over the beaten earth floor. The seat he had been ushered onto was a simple but well-constructed long bench fashioned out of wood, covered with rugs and blankets, which must have doubled as a bed. Rigo began to brighten. As long as he didn't have to sleep in the place, he felt he could while away the next few hours with much less inconvenience and discomfort that he had at first supposed.

He wrapped one of the rugs around himself for warmth, and then assisted Tony in pulling some firewood out of a box so they could get a good fire going in the small firepit set just outside the door. Life always looked more hopeful when there was a fire. Once Tony had a decent blaze going, he asked Rigo to fetch water, and bring an armful more kindling so it could be put to dry ready for burning later. He pointed the way with a long bony finger.

"I'll take it kind if you would fill this here kettle on my behalf, lad," he said. "For you be blessed an' kitted out wi' a grouse's good strong stumps, which have proved better 'n my long stork's legs for tackling the forest floors this day. An' when ye get back, you and I shall sit here an' share a few rummers of Schiedam to keep out the winter cold. We can spin a few yarns an' share a few long songs together once we're nice an' mellow, for there's nothing like a song to fill a man's lungs an' swell out his heart. It works like a bellows to glede up a proper good feelin' inside, for every poor, sad fellow needs a lift to his encouragement when his spirits are saggin' worse than his belly."

It made a pleasant little walk for Rigo. A few beams of early morning sun lit the way here and there as he followed a path strewn with needles and pine cones down to a bare-banked rill tumbling tumultuously along a rocky, stony course scoured clean of any weeds or fishes. Before he collected his water, he stood for a moment, looking downward through the black spiky trees at the almost sheer drop to the River Wye, snaking its shiny way through the valley floor hundreds of feet below him. All was lush green pasture down there along the banks of the river, all dotted with sheep and cows and cottages, and there was smoke rising from the chimneys of the village. The good folk living there were rising to greet the Christmas morning, and soon the church bells would be ringing. Rigo heaved a sigh as he thought of his father, who would also be in church today.

Mentally sending his father a salutation, he knelt and filled the kettle. He left it by the rill and wandered further down the hillside, collecting such small branches as were lying loose on the woodland floor that were not too wet to take with him. As he ambled about, he noted in passing a tiny church, almost like a hermit's cell, built among the trees a short distance along the ridge. It stood cold and silent, bearing an air of long-standing neglect, with no signs that it was ever in use, as it must once have been. Grass and weeds grew in tufts on the window ledge and across the door sill, and there was an emptiness emanating from there that had nothing whatever to do with a lack of worshippers. He could never have said why, but the longer he hung about nearby, the more the place gave him the shudders. He turned his back on the strange little edifice and moved away from the sight of it, and as soon as his arms were full, went thankfully back the way he had come to collect the kettle and return to the shack.

He pushed at the latticed door with his backside to open it, and placed his wood next to the box of dry timber before going outside to join Tony, and set the kettle into the glowing embers of the fire. The wood had been burning nicely for a good half hour.

Tony was back on his tree trunk, sitting with his legs stretched out into the long grass, silently smoking his pipe with his greatcoat wrapped tightly around him, his travelling blanket thrown across his shoulders over the top. Rigo took a place beside him and became watchful, wondering if this was a man he could safely befriend. Once more, he registered the smell on the skin and raiment of his companion. Rigo, who was used to being among men constantly scoured clean by salt water spray, still wasn't sure whether he liked it. He had never come across it before. He sat back and quietly studied other aspects of his new companion that were fast becoming visible by the light of the growing day. The man's height really was extraordinary. Being too tall and lanky for ordinary clothes to fit, Tony had extended the length of his overcoat in almost every direction to make it cover him, using parts from a second coat of thick twill of a slightly different colour to accomplish the task. The full, thick skirts lapping around his lower legs, reaching as far down as his ankles, were presumably his means of keeping them warm at nights when he slept under hedges or in caves and shelters on the hillsides. Homespun britches had been similarly extended, and the rest of his legs he covered with thick, hand-knitted woollen stockings, very much darned with sheep's wool and nettle fibres like all the rest of his clothes, all parts of which were so travel-stained that the original colours were now almost unidentifiable. His boots had once been well-made, but they were now so old, with the seams along the uppers repaired so many times, that there were places where there was no more leather left. In these parts the boots hung open, gaping where they were downtrodden along the sides because of his peculiar manner of walking.

While Rigo watched, Tony reached up and removed the holly sprig from his wrecked old hat and added it to his nightshade buttonhole. Then he placed a black and white feather where the holly had been.

"She'll be along here presently," he remarked, noting Rigo's interest as he crammed the feather into position by feel, using fingers that worked like slender, articulated icicles.

"Who will?" Rigo asked, wondering what kind of woman in the whole, wide, wide world could possibly be willing to come calling on a man who lived the way Tony did.

"Missus Mag," Tony announced. "I'm surprised she hasn't been here already. She usually calls in to see me first thing."

The water in the kettle was now ready. Tony half-filled a large pewter tankard with jenever taken from a dark blue bottle at his side, and added a good measure of hot water, settling the kettle back beside the fire to keep its contents warm. Then he chipped two large lumps of sugar off a chunk housed in a small wooden box kept next to the bottle, and stirred the resulting concoction with a twig picked out of the grass and wiped clean on his backside. At last, he offered it to Rigo.

"Drink your fill, lad," he said affably, holding out the tankard. "You'll need to keep your spirits up to suffer a full day hereabouts, I'm thinking."

"Th-Th-Thank you," Rigo said, accepting the tankard. He took several long pulls at the drink, and almost at once he could feel himself lighting up inside as the fiery beverage took its effect. He handed the tankard back to Tony, who emptied it at a draught, smacked his lips, pronounced it excellent, and announced that he thought it would be a good idea if they shared another. Rigo agreed, and began to relax under the combined effects of the spirits and Tony's beguiling companionship.

The daylight was strengthening. Tony seemed to be waiting for something, gauging the air. Just as he shrugged and said he thought she wouldn't be coming now, a large black and white bird flew down, making a bouncy landing on one of the hazel branches and giving a harsh rattling cry of greeting as it arrived.

"Ah, there you are. Good morning, Your Honour," Tony said to the bird. "I was just startin' to wonder where you had got to. Wait a bit, I'll bring your breakfast now."

"W-What bird is that?" Rigo demanded, alarmed. "It's really big. Is it dangerous?"

"That there is a magpie. You should always salute a magpie when you see one. Don't be afraid, it won't hurt you."

"I d-don't think I like it," Rigo said, eyeing the bird warily. "It r-r-reminds me of the bird they call the *albatroz* we see out at sea. I forget what it is called in English. We don't hurt them, but I still don't like them. They look too big. I think they could peck a man's eyes out."

"We call it an albatross in English, my timorous Tom Tiddler, and you don't need to fear them, either."

Tony had gone inside the shack while he was talking, and after a bit of rummaging he returned holding a cut morsel of some sort of meat. He held it out to the bird, which was bobbing up and down impatiently waiting for its titbit. Just as the bird flew off with its grisly prize, a second similar, but slightly smaller bird of the same variety arrived.

"Here she is," Tony said, gratified. "Missus Mag. I thought she would be round here somewhere. You didn't forget about me after all, did you, old girl? Here's yours, my darlin'." He gave the second bird a piece of meat, which she took in her beak before she flew away.

Rigo had watched the whole encounter with rising disquiet. These gruesome birds seemed somehow to contribute a sinister bent to Tony's manner of living.

"They are better seen in pairs, magpies," Tony observed conversationally, disregarding Rigo's perturbations. "One for sorrow, two for joy. We want good omens for today, young sorcerer."

Rigo said nothing. He had gone back to his drinking. And thinking.

Sometime later, Rigo began to talk. He had finally reached that level of confidentiality that a few good strong drinks will impart to a man, and his curiosity regarding Tony had in no way diminished.

"You know, I s-s-saw you come on board our ship two nights ago," he confided. "I-I-It was just before midnight. And I know you do it often because the s-sailors talk about you. Why do-o-o you climb over deck rails in secret the way you do, instead of coming up the ladder like everybody else? It makes all the seamen nervous about you."

"Ah!" Tony said, laying aside his battered hat to reveal straggly long trails of unwashed dark hair, "but you see, I ain't no seafarin' man like the rest o' ye. An' if a landlubber like me who wears leaky old boots is seen walking grandly up an' down gangplanks like he's a sea lord, tongues will soon be set to workin', which ain't a desirable thing; for where one tongue leads you can be sure a dozen more will follow. As for makin' men nervous, why bless you – everybody starts up like a hare in front of a hound the first time they sees me, mostly on account o' these strange an' peculiar limbs, d'ye see. An' what seems unnatural at the start don't always become more accountable on a better acquaintance; not when it jars on the senses continual, like – which is why I keeps myself to myself, out o' the way an' on one side of the ordin'ry common folk, who are ever fearful of what don't meet their expectations. It's an agreeable arrangement, an' one as I hope gives mutual satisfaction, for it lets the good people sleep easy in their beds at nights, while I lives out my life up here in peace, walkin' the sheep-trails and drovers roads over the hills and mountains of Monmouthshire, an' explorin' the glades and dells o' the Forest of Dean. 'Tis a simple an' pleasin' experience to be exchangin' tokens for gossip, or a basket o' herbs for a meal and a dry bed – an' I ain't averse to acceptin' a bit o' new cloth to contribute to the repairin' of my few clothes as a trade for my treatments in them what's ailin'. It's all as good as pennies an' ha'pennies, which are ever in short supply. I call no man friend except one; though I have friends enough to satisfy any man, squash me for a fly if I don't, for if my own kind fail me, why, the dumb beasts an' birds in field and forest are ever my abidin' companions, though they have no words to speak in tongues to me. I understand their wants, an' they mine, which is a proper salve to a man's heart. The folks all take me for a Jack o' Lantern when I roam the hills and moors, and they shrink from me as they would from Herne the Hunter, or the Green Man o' the Woods when they sees me under the trees. And maybe they're not far wrong in their reckoning, for I knows the tree ogham, an' do speak with the trees in shouts and in whispers, an' listen in good earnest to their creaking replies. For if they give me leave to use their livin' wood for my divinations, I must give 'em their due in return. I hold their sacred sticks even now, bundled up safe inside a cotton shroud made by a livin' witch for her own burial."

Rigo was listening to all this in rapt attention. This time, he had understood every word, and he was growing ever more intrigued despite himself. He waited a while before he asked his next question, allowing Tony time to drink some more jenever and mellow for a little longer before he risked any further enquiry.

"Are you ju-u-ust a pedlar, Sir? Er, Tony, I mean? A-A-As well as a sort of magician? You said just now you're not a sailor; but I think you know Captain Morgan. And I th-think Mister Mould-win does, too. He was talking about him when he was asking you about the men that were taken, am I right? A-A-And you know Captain Rothman, my own captain, don't you?"

Tony winked at Rigo over the top of the tankard but made no reply.

Rigo responded by saying, uncertainly, "Sir, have you ever been a pirate?"

Tony threw back his head and gave vent to a barking volley of mirth at the idea. "Bless you, you young cut-throat, you're thinkin' that pirating is all about gold, and jewels, and high-born ladies for the takin' in kidnap an' ransoming of, ain't you?"

"Well, d-d-doesn't everybody?"

"More 'n likely, young Sindybad, more 'n likely. Was that the sort of pirate you took me for? And is that what you're after too? It must surely be; for what young man don't want vast riches, an' a wild old time, an' high seas full of adventure? But there's other kinds of excitement to fill your life with, lad, as I larned back when I was little more 'n an ankle-biter. Snare an' jug me for a hare, if I don't speak true! It was my early experiences what larned me my real callin', if you can call it that, for the far hills and mountains an' the depths of the woodlands are my vast oceans and high seas. I roam far an' wide, flittin' here an' there by day an' by night an' through the long twilight hours, movin' past the eternal sleepers in the churchyards like one o' their own restless spirits, else gliding over the hills like a wanderin' phantom. I sees a good many people in a good many diff'rent places, wi' no mortal man darin' to question me about the whys or wherefores o' my bein' there, which is much the same way of livin' as a pirate, if you take my meanin'."

"So, your r-real calling isn't charms and tokens?"

"Ah! Charms an' tokens work a treat, lad. Don't ever deny 'em. With their use, I can cure the chin-cough, an' the quinsy, an' clear up warts in childer. I can treat the ague, an' Saint Anthony's fire, an' ease the bindin' pains of strangury an' bone shave. I can restore farmers stricken with a Tic Dolly Row as easy as I can temper childbed fever and make salves for the sloes in their wives. I knows how to keep meal-worms an' weevils out of flour, cockspurs out of corn, and maggots out o' cheeses. I can ward off the ringworm an' milk fever in cattle, an' cure distemper in dogs."

"M-M-My, th-that sounds very i-i-impressive, Mister Tony. So, why do you go around the ships at night, then, if you are so good, and have so many cures?"

"Oh, you might say ships is a part o' the gen'ral draft of my other occipations. But never say no more than that. I comes an' I goes, which gives me even more reason to move round places at nights when all is hushed an' quiet about me."

Tony's long, dark hair had fallen forward in a momentary gust of wind to partially cover his lean lineaments, and through the stray strands his cool grey eyes raked Rigo for a moment before looking away. It was a keen, incisive look, capable of drawing in vast amounts of information whilst giving away absolutely nothing. Rigo became uncomfortably aware that there were hidden depths to Tony that were simply not apparent in the ordinary course of events, and which most probably never came to the notice of ordinary people at all. Combined with his last words, it gave an impression that felt once more somehow sinister. Tony's feral look took on a new, almost predatory aspect. Rigo couldn't help calling to mind the giant Amazonian spiders of his own country: motionless, patient, silent, deadly; and he had a sudden vivid recollection of that slithering vision, two nights ago, that had been his very first glimpse of this man. He began to shift about uneasily. He now had an inkling he knew why sailors talked in low voices about Tony, and why they spoke about him in the way that they did; and some very unpleasant memories and disturbing feelings began to bubble up under the influence of the drink inside him.

"You know, S-S-Sir, if you don't mind, I d-d-don't think I want to wait around here all day. I don't want to travel through these woods at night, it's too scary. Can we st-start walking to Chippistow now, please? All this talk of f-forests and ghosts is making me feel nervous. And there was some sort of o-o-old church along the path down there that just gave me the c-cr-r-reeps." Rigo indicated where he had seen the neglected old building. "I still have the same feeling from it, even from where I'm sitting here beside you. I just don't feel comfortable right now."

"Ah! So, you've heard tales of the devil-worshipping that goes on in these parts, have you? You shouldn't believe everything you hear, lad."

"N-N-No, Sir, it's nothing like that. I just don't feel good."

Tony eyed Rigo reflectively. "I wonder why you should say that," he said, at last. "That little old church-cell stands sad an' empty. It likely ain't been used since Anglo-Saxon times."

"I can t-t-tell it isn't used by Christian people, but I think someone has been there. I had a feeling something had been going on around there when I was picking up the sticks. I think we ought to move on."

"Well, we could do, I suppose. But, you know, I would never leave you to deal with anything here all on your own, as if you was no more 'n a trembling young leveret. An' it will be a very long wait for you when we get to Chepstow, if we leave now. You'll be restin' by yourself, shut up in a priest's hole, which is where I have it in mind to put you. That may be just as frightenin' for you as stayin' here. Are you sure you want to go now? There'll be no turnin' back, once we start."

"I'm sure."

"Then stamp out the fire, lad, an' we'll head off. We can talk a bit more as we go, instead of stayin' here to eat, for chewin' the fat is as good a way o' dining as any I've heard of, when there's no true meat to be had. As for drink, why, we've as good a fuel in our innards from our Schiedam as if we had been wined an' dined by

Lord Dictus of Carrow. Though 'tween you an' me, it had been my intention to stay an' stew us a rabbit."

"Sir, e-e-even a rabbit won't get me to stay here. I'm sorry. It's not because of your house."

"No worries, my timid young huntsman, I understand your meanin', never fear. You're as nervous at thoughts of the devil as a parson's maid is at mention o' clergymen. That's no bad thing. Now, as we go, you must talk of the outlandish, far-away places you've been to; for whatever voyages you've took, I can see you've been on some good, pleasant pasture between times along the way. An' when you've done that, you shall tell all about your own good self, an' your own folk in your own country, for I dearly love to hear about another's family, havin' no kith or kin myself. So, come, my young shipmate, for shipmate I shall call ye, even though we be but a motley crew, a-meetin' an' a-partin' all in one night an' a day. Tell me all."

He struck a path along the ridge, cutting two walking sticks from a pollarded ash as they walked, and gave one to Rigo after he had whittled the twigs off and trimmed it to size; and with their use, they descended the steep and difficult paths that led down to the road below, gaining at last the main road that ran through Tintern to Chepstow. Rigo's heart was lightening with every step – not simply because they were leaving behind the oppressively dreary place where Tony chose to live, but because each step took him nearer to his heart's desire, and every mile brought him closer to achieving his dream. He cheerfully gave Tony all the information he could think of concerning life in Brazil as they went along, and so with Tony's slow and careful gait, and Rigo's unhurried one, their journey progressed with a gentle swing as the toll of church bells to mark the end of the Christmas Day morning service fell far behind them.

Chapter Twenty-Four

That same morning at the Fox Hole, Isla and Adela were sitting at the table in the kitchen, worrying. Ronald was not back, and they had heard no news of him since he had left the previous morning.

"Well, I wish a Merry Christmas to one and all this day," Isla said to her mother and daughter, "but how I wish Dad was here. Something must have happened." She crossed the kitchen to the window for the fiftieth time and scanned the river up and down, but there was nothing and nobody on it at all during those early hours of morning river mists and first awakenings. "Where can he be?" she wondered. "This isn't like him."

"I can go into Chepstow before church and see what I can find out, if you like, Mother," Adela offered. "I needn't be gone long, and I can pick up some Cornish vegetables as I make my way round. They'll have them out on the wharf by now."

Julia pursed her lips from her place before the fire. "I think it might be prudent to ask a few probing questions of Maldwyn Parry, myself," she said, giving the porridge a final stir, and then rising to her feet to set the cauldron on the table. "Now *there's* a man who knows a lot more than he says, if ever there was one."

Adela sat and thought while she ate her breakfast. "I'm sorry, Nana, but I'm afraid I can't go as far as Devauden to see Grandpa Parry for you," she said, when she had finished both her porridge and her deliberations. "It's too far to walk, and it will be icy in Itton Woods, even if I could get there. I'll have to walk over the bridge into town as it is, because Grandad took the coracle. I could see quite clearly from my bedroom window when I got up that it was gone. Ted's rowing boat is back in its place, but the coracle isn't on either side. He must have gone up to the town as he said he would, then taken it and gone on somewhere else."

"Well, wherever he is, it won't be Itton Woods," Isla said, as Julia pursed her lips again. "We can rule that out. No-one goes in there unless they must, apart from Tony Lightfoot. Even the King's men looking for contraband won't go in at night. Dad would never do anything that might involve an overnight stop there, short or long; he would stay at the Parry's, and then move on the next day."

"My point exactly," Julia said. "But wherever he stopped, he should have been back by now. Something is clearly wrong, and I don't think we should be expecting Adela to find out what it is. This calls for the weight and measure of some adults; and since the man of the house is absent, we shall just have to see what the women can do. If you don't mind, Adela, I think I will take a walk with you up as far as the church today. If we go before the service starts, I can catch a few people as they walk down, and see what they might have heard overnight. I could do with stretching my legs anyway, it's going to be a fine morning. I'll just get my cloak and walking stick, then I'll be ready."

Christina and Andrew were awoken and fed with a hasty bowl of porridge. They were both greatly excited because it was Christmas Day, and there would be carol singing, and dancing, and roast chestnuts to eat after dinner. Christina was especially excited at the prospect of having dinner at Martha's house with her family.

Leaving Isla to undertake the day's domestic duties with the help of Andrew, Adela and Julia set off with Christina, taking the lane that joined the road coming in from Tidenham. They had to walk slowly, because Christina's muscles were still stiff and sore from her wrestle with the rowing boat, but despite having painful limbs and an aching back, Christina's spirits were undaunted. Warmly and comfortably dressed in Adela's old clothes, she was back to her former optimistic, and slightly insubordinate self, eagerly taking small detours off the path into the undergrowth, ignoring Julia's remonstrations about the dirt and the cold, lingering to watch Tansy and Queen Elizabeth exploring the hedgerows for mice, and chattering happily and excitedly about the possibilities for the day as she unwittingly impeded their progression into town.

After the church service Adela and Julia led the way to the Hillenjaar's lodging house, while Christina capered happily behind. She had fidgeted without stopping all through the litany, unable to contain her joyfulness at the prospect of a whole day with her mother and brother in a place of safety, warmth and good cheer. The Hillenjaar's door stood propped ajar. Rapping with the door-knocker as they went in, Adela led Christina and Julia carefully down the wooden spiral staircase to join the family in the basement kitchen.

Poppea and Anthony were already comfortably settled in by the fire, eating toasted bread with butter and honey for their breakfast, having been collected and brought up by Kitty earlier. The lodgers had been in, and had all left for the day: some to the churches, others to the public houses or to friends and relatives, leaving piled-up plates and a detritus of scattered crumbs behind them. Moonlight, having entertained the lodgers all through breakfast, was now standing on the table in the litter of food debris, picking sesame seeds out of discarded bits of toast. Christina ran across to her mother and hugged her tight before hugging Anthony, who accepted her exuberance briefly and then shrugged her off so he could concentrate on his toast. Christina picked up a slice herself, even though it was not long since she had had her porridge, and stroked Moonlight while she ate until he too grew tired of her attentions, and flew up to the warmth of the mantelpiece, where he perched and dozed out of the children's reach for the rest of the day.

Adela put a bottle of her mother's lung remedy on the Welsh dresser for Poppea to take later, and Martha and Julia exchanged greetings while Martha made up beakers of brandy and hot water to drink a toast to Christmas Day. When she had done, the women joined her at the table for an exchange of information and news.

Martha was distraught when she heard that Christina had been out in a boat during the night-time, and devastated when she heard the reason why. "Tom and Aaron taken?" she exclaimed. "Oh no! Tell me it isn't true!"

Kitty broke down and cried. "He never told me was going to do something like that," she sobbed. "I would have begged him not to go if I'd have known. I don't want him to be hurt. Tom never causes trouble. This won't make any difference, will it? I can still see him, can't I, Mother?"

"I don't know," Martha said, looking worried. "Oh dear, I do hope this is nothing more than a misunderstanding. His situation with Mister Noble is a very important one, and his father is a man of considerable standing. I do hope Tom has sense enough not to do anything disreputable." She lapsed into an uneasy silence.

"He didn't do anything wrong," Christina said defensively, breaking in on it. "I saw it all. He didn't do anything. Nor did Aaron. They just happened to be a few streets away, that was why they were taken."

"But what were they doing there at that time of night?"

No-one had an answer, and Kitty continued to sob quietly.

"I wonder if these arrests have anything to do with those prisoners who escaped into the Forest," Martha presently mused.

This roused Julia from her own ruminations, and she looked sharply across at Martha. "What's this?" she asked, with quickening interest.

"Oh, some of the lodgers were saying this morning that there was a breakout last night, and that some prisoners got away. I don't have any details, and to be honest, I didn't pay attention when they were talking about it, because at the time I didn't think it was of any real moment. They were just passing remarks about it at breakfast. It could just be coincidence."

"I hope it's not!" Kitty exclaimed. "I hope it was my Tom, and that he's got clean away."

"Oh, Kitty!" her mother remonstrated. "Do keep a level head about this. We don't know anything yet. We must find out more before we give way. Dry your eyes, dearest, do."

Kitty dabbed at her eyes with a dainty handkerchief and blew her nose prettily into it afterwards.

Christina had remained where she was with Anthony, exchanging a few words with Poppea from time to time, until something was said that made her turn to Martha again.

"Nick's back in Chepstow today," she announced. "I've just remembered, because Ma is talking about the boy with a long stick, who has the cart pulled by a cow. She must have seen him from the warehouse when he was in the harbour. We can go and see him. He might have news."

"How so, dear?"

"Well, I just thought if he's Tom's friend..."

"Oh, I see. Well, it's always possible, I suppose. We'll think about it later." Martha went over to the fire to start heating the water for the Christmas pudding. "Dinner comes first, whatever has happened. We can't be of use to anyone with empty stomachs."

Julia agreed, but she added: "I still might be able to pick up a few snippets of information to be going on with, if I go out and see who's around now."

And while Adela and Kitty took up knives and prepared some green vegetables for the Christmas dinner, Julia draped her shawl several times about her, and took a short walk through Beaufort Square to pass the time of day with anyone she knew who might be out and about early.

An hour or so later, she came back with an announcement.

"Well," she said, unfastening her shawl, "I found a few things out. First of all, Aaron Arundel and Tom Meadows *were* arrested and detained in the early hours of yesterday morning with those smugglers, but they are not being held in Chepstow. One and all, they've been carted off somewhere else. I also found out that Aaron was supposed to have been playing with his father last night at

Squire Speybury's, so if his father still attended that dance he *might* have seen Nick, if he went through Monmouth early enough. He would surely have heard the news about Aaron's arrest and called in at the gaol on his way to see if he is there. Poor Able. He is such a bag of nerves, he hasn't the enterprise to organise any effective assistance for his son, wherever he is. And Nick, nice boy though he is, doesn't have much in the way of ready wit, so he would be of no help, either. I'm assuming this, because I now believe my husband must have called on Able yesterday. It seems that when Ronald left us, he went to the Town Gate first and had a chat with old Jimmy, who says he saw him go off towards the Castle barracks afterwards and hasn't seen him since. Or at least, he thinks it was the Castle barracks, because Ronald was so interested in the latest smugglings. Jimmy rather thought he might be going to see what he could find out about the arrests. That makes sense to me, because it would explain why Ronald went back for the coracle. Something he heard from the garrison must have prompted him to make an urgent call somewhere else. My guess is that it was somewhere upriver that would take too long to get to by road. It can't be anywhere in the Forest because Ronald knows all the shortcuts over land through there; but if he combined a trip to Able and then the Colonel's house, then that would certainly explain why a river run was prudent. And if he thought it was important to see them at the earliest opportunity, perhaps he thought it was equally important to stay on afterwards, as well."

"Yes, I agree with you so far," Martha said. "But where does it leave us?"

"Well, I've given you all I know now, the rest is just supposition. What we really need is more information. I was thinking about possible sources as I came back. There's a ball at the Assembly Rooms tonight, so if Able is playing, he will be along early this evening. We can go up there and ask him what he knows, if Nick doesn't prove helpful." She stopped for a moment, then carried on bravely. "I have to be practical about this. Ronald has stayed out overnight, so if he's not at home when we get back it will be no good expecting him before dark. And if he does come back under cover of darkness, I'll know there has been some dirty work going on. I can't help worrying slightly. I feel sure there's a story waiting to be told over this, and it probably concerns young Aaron. Possibly Tom as well; but the Colonel has enough influence to get his son out of trouble without resorting to anything... shall we say... shady. Aaron is not so fortune, so goodness knows what will be attempted on his behalf. As for Rigo – sadly, I fear you girls won't be seeing him again. He has no-one to help him out, so he and the others involved in the smuggling are sure to stand trial." She sighed. "Such a pity! I hate to see young lives wasted."

Kitty interjected suddenly. "Perhaps some of them will need hiding," she suggested, brightening up rapidly as she thought of it. "You never know. If any of them have escaped..." She lapsed into dreamy tearfulness and sighed. "He might have broken free to see me one last time," she murmured, and shook her head regretfully.

"Kitty!"

Julia was more pragmatic. "There *is* something in what Kitty says, Martha," she said. "Some of these prisoners could be our men. I'm of the opinion that one of us should wait somewhere near the Town Gate to intercept anyone we know, so we can quiz them quietly and see what they can tell us. We can regroup later in the day to exchange our information, perhaps late this afternoon. Adela, we had better go home now. We have delivered Christina safely back to her mother, and now we really should attend to our own end of the business, at least for this morning. I think I want to get a safe room made up ready. I really have no idea where Ronald went after he left Chepstow, but if I am wrong in my supposition that he went to see Able and the Colonel, and if he *did* go into the Forest instead, then he may have had more to do with that breakout than I would like. The timing of it seems a tad too coordinated to be entirely coincidental."

"Don't worry about getting anyone over the river to your place," Kitty said, sounding ever more cheerful. "It could prove too dangerous. If we do find any of our men, they can come here and be safe, can't they, Mother?"

Martha made a sign for her to be quiet. Then she quietly and unobtrusively followed Julia and Adela up the stairs to see them out.

"I would prefer that we don't say too much in front of Christina," she said in a low voice, when they had reached the main doorway. "We cannot presume that family to be trustworthy; they don't have their wits about them. I intend to tell Kitty the same."

Julia nodded in agreement. "You're right, of course," she said. "I'm sorry, I didn't think of it. I don't have any doubts Christina's good intentions, or her merits, but she's still a little child. She can't possibly be expected to remember the gravity of our concerns, let alone share them."

"Exactly," Martha said, and she looked slightly worried. "That child notices a great deal too much for my liking, and sees and hears far more than she should. She's too easily overlooked, and there, to my mind, lies our present danger. No-one pays her any real attention, so she could easily become privy to something that could put everyone's safety in jeopardy without us ever realising it. I just can't be sure she won't say the wrong thing at the wrong time in front of one of my guests. Strictly between ourselves, though, we do have a little hideaway downstairs. That's what Kitty was referring to."

"You have? Where is it?" Adela cast her mind over the entire room, wondering what wall it could possibly be behind. Unless it was out in the tiny garden.

"I shan't tell you; then you can't slip up yourself," Martha replied. "But just know that we have one, and that your grandfather can make use of it, if there's nowhere else he can get to that's safe. I suppose things could fall out the way Kitty suggests; the town is full of soldiers, and more came in at dawn today. Perhaps their arrival relates to the escaped men, perhaps not, but we would do well to bear it in mind. The Forest will be crawling with soldiers for the next few days if they have been called in to intensify a search, so it won't be safe on the roads anywhere in the Forest for anyone wanting to steer clear of the law, no matter what the reason. If Mister Baker is still out there and in any kind of trouble, and if he does turn up on this side of the river, it might be better to keep him here, especially if he is with these men on the run. We will do the same for Tom and anybody else we know and love."

"Thank you for that information," Julia said. "We also have a little hideaway, and we will do likewise ourselves. I won't say more, but it is useful, I think, if we both know of each other's strengths, as well as our weaknesses. Your weakness lies among your many guests; mine in our visibility from across the river. And now good day. Thank you for all you have contributed so far."

Julia continued her train of thought as she and Adela walked down to the harbour.

"We will prepare the cellar room for an extra person to stay, Adela," Julia said. "There should be room for two people, if we move the other things that have been tossed in there as far up as we can."

They walked over the Wye Bridge back to Fox Hole with a basket of winter kale and a celery bought at the quayside, and, once divested of their outer garments and settled in front of the fire, Julia told Isla of the morning's discoveries, and the talk gradually moved on to the care of anyone needing to hide out in the middle of winter. Andrew sat beside the cats and watched over the cooking of the chicken, while Adela kept a wether eye on the Christmas pudding and a bucket of mussels, and everyone shared their ideas and opinions until they sat down together and ate their family Christmas dinner.

That same afternoon, they all went into the garden and entered the chicken run. Andrew got the chickens shut up inside the hen-house to clear the run, after which the women scraped aside the litter with shovels so they could lift a wooden trapdoor set in the ground in the middle of it. The trapdoor opened straight into an underground storage room dug right underneath the hen-house. No-one could ever have guessed it was there, there was no sign of it whatsoever when the chickens were out. Laid on its floor at the bottom were two large wooden pulling blocks taken off some unknown ship, stacked one above the other and lashed together, serving as improvised steps to break the fall. They made a descent into the room wobbly and hazardous, but they were better than nothing for those who didn't have a long enough reach to hold onto the edge and drop down.

Everyone lent a hand to help move the casks. They were all full, of varying sizes, stacked between two large crates and a chest, and hidden beneath several hessian sacks filled with domestic paraphernalia. The bigger items were pushed and rolled up against the damp end wall, and everything else piled on top, to clear a space in the middle of the floor where there was less seepage and moisture. They managed to create enough room for two wooden pallets to be set down over the stone flags, and these, covered by a canvas and a few small rugs would, they thought, be enough to keep one or two people clear of the floor so they could stay dry for a few hours. The underground safe room would only be brought into use if a house-to-house search was being made, and someone had to remain completely hidden for a length of time. Otherwise, any fugitive would simply be kept out of sight inside the cottage and remain with the family. This wasn't hard to do; the house was so overgrown a man could move about in relative freedom, providing he didn't leave the garden. It was just, as Julia had already indicated, if anyone was watching from across the river that they could be undone, particularly in winter, when the trees and bushes were bare of leaves. The only other slight risk was that of some person coming by in the lane. That last wasn't likely, since the lane didn't lead anywhere, and there were no other dwellings beyond their own, but even so, it could happen. It wouldn't even have to be somebody they knew. Since Ronald was the only man in the family, any reports that a man was at Fox Hole would be enough to bring the soldiers knocking. But the family were well used to being careful: Ronald had several other reasons for being shy of the law – reasons that were never talked about, but which were well understood by the whole family.

They left the cellar and covered the trapdoor well, leaving the hens shut up for the night. Back inside the house, they looked out several rag rugs and feather pillows from the chests in the loft above Adela's bedroom, and brought them down to air by the fire ready to bring into service, should they be required.

The clock on the wall struck four, and dusk advanced...

Chapter Twenty-Five

Christina, ever helpful, inspired by Julia's investigations and moved by Kitty's distress, and utterly thrilled by the prospect of more danger now she was safely out of it and well supported, left the lodging house after eating her Christmas dinner and spent the entire afternoon sitting in the Wig and Mitre. She watched closely every cart, rider, and gaggle of people who came down the road to the Town Gate, keenly examining faces through the distorted glass of the window she was at, hoping to see Nick, or someone else she could recognise. She was thrown out twice, after customers spotted her curled up behind the curtain and complained to the tapster, and at last, tired of trying to sit quietly for so long indoors, she took a walk up and down the Saint Arvans road, pulling Adela's old shawl close about her, trying to get used to the feel of Andrew's outgrown boots on her feet.

The afternoon was well advanced, and the wind was picking up, and she was starting to feel very cold by the time she spotted Nick's cart approaching with his ox in the shafts and his two dogs at the wheels. He had a young man and woman with him, neither of whom Christina knew. Whoever they were, they seemed to be enjoying the trip immensely, sitting behind him on top of a bed of straw, talking freely and laughing together. Christina ran frenziedly up the road to meet the cart, excitedly calling out his name as she ran. Nick put his finger to his lips to hush her when she drew near, but she was too elated at seeing him to pay any attention. As soon as she reached the waggon, she started to jump up and down beside the wheel, skipping along in step with the ox and showing him her new boots, talking wildly, and asking him a dozen different questions. She mentioned nothing compromising, but her manner was so unguarded it was enough to make Nick's blood run cold. Fortunately, none of her spirited chatterings were noted by his passengers, whose intent, from the moment they spotted her, was to dismiss her from their presence.

"Just what do you think you are you doing coming up to our cart, you vexatious little creature?" Fanny exploded, leaning over the side so she could see her better. "Get away from here at once!"

"No!"

"How dare you say that! I'll come down and knock your head off your shoulders, you beastly little imp!"

"This isn't your cart, it belongs to Nick," the beastly little imp exclaimed, in no way intimidated. "So I've as much right to be beside it as you have to ride in it."

This information took Fanny very much by surprise. She turned to Nick, and asked in an undertone, "Is she right? Is this cart really yours?"

Nick nodded.

Temporarily shelving her curiosity about how a working boy like Nick could have gained ownership of something of such substantial value, Fanny returned her attention to Christina. "Well, watch your tongue then, you ugly little thing," she ordered, imperiously. "I've no mind to take back-chat from a saucy hobgoblin like you. And get down at once. You're not riding up here with us!"

"Look at who's talking," Christina rejoined contemptuously, reaching up to take the hand Nick had offered to help pull her up. "If I *am* ugly, you're no prettier – and I'm not riding with you anyway, I'm riding with Nick. He's my friend. If you don't like it, you can always walk."

Fanny drew back in outrage and surprise. She was not used to having anyone answer her back, and for the moment she could think of nothing else to say. So she turned on her brother instead. "What are you smirking at?" she snapped.

Miles was lying back in the straw, quietly laughing at Christina's impudence and his sister's inept efforts to maintain the upper hand.

"I'm not smirking, I'm laughing," he answered, simply. "I can't help myself. Sorry, Fan, but I do believe you may have met your match in that tiny lump of bone and gristle sitting up front there." He turned over so he could face Christina, still grinning. "Good day to you, Monster," he said. "You're a dirty little thing, but I expect you could be turned into something tidy enough, if you would submit to a bath. I think I'd like to have you back at our house for a maid."

"You'll do no such thing!" Fanny said furiously, thumping him hard on the back. "I refuse to even consider having a brat like that under our roof. I shall have hysterics if you so much as mention it again. She's completely ruining my adventure. I was really starting to enjoy myself until she came along."

She turned and glared at Christina, who, heedless of Fanny, was absorbing the views from the waggon. Christina had only ever had the pleasure of a ride once before, when her family had gone from Wells to Bristol, and she soaked up this repeat of the rare pleasure, gaping avidly at the last remnants of wooded countryside before they came right up to Chepstow wall and the Town Gate, where the torches were being lit to compensate for the fading light.

Miles started laughing again. "You've got to admit it, Fan, you're outfoxed by that brat whether you like it, or not." He turned back to Christina. "Now listen to me, you vicious little marmoset. I'm Master Speybury, and this is my sister Miss Speybury, so you had better stop cheeking us, or it will be the worse for you."

"Who are you to be upbraiding anyone for cheek?" demanded Christina hotly, prepared, as always, to be confrontational. "I don't know what a marmyzett is, but I expect it's something else insulting. You two should take a good look at yourselves before you berate the people around you for not measuring up. And what's more, I don't believe you are who you say you are. If you were, you wouldn't be riding in this old cart with the likes of us. You'd be in the Squire's carriage."

"Ah!" The remark struck home. Miles drew back somewhat ruefully, taking the great nudge he received in the foreribs from Fanny at the same moment with unusually good grace. "Yes. I think you may have a good point there." He turned over again and conversed in an undertone with his sister. "Do you still want to be *incognito*?" he asked her.

Fanny nodded vigorously. "Yes, I do," she said. "I want to get down to the port and see Rigo before he goes, now we've got this far. How about you?"

Miles considered. "Well, I don't want to be in disguise, but I would like to see him again."

"You do know they won't let us go anywhere near such a place as the docks if they see us, don't you?" Fanny said. "They'll scoop us up and hold onto us until Papa and Mamma arrive. I don't fancy having to face either of them when other people are looking on and listening."

"Oh flip. I hadn't thought about that," Miles said, seriously alarmed. "And there's a big ball tonight in the Assembly Rooms. That means there'll be tons of Grandees strutting about who know us because of Papa. We'll never get past them."

"We will if we duck back down under the straw," Fanny said, hastily pushing him down and retreating out of sight herself just as the waggon joined the queue of vehicles waiting to go in through the Town Gate. "Once we're through Beaufort Square, we can slip out and hide. I'll think of what to do next once we've got that far."

Nick, who had looked back over his shoulder at Fanny and Miles just the once to check what they were doing, and realising that they were safely hidden, told Christina to leave all the talking to him, and moved the cart forward to greet the gatekeeper.

"Now den, young Nick," the gatekeeper said with a strong foreign accent, coming up and slapping the side of the waggon, "what are you doing out at dis time of der day? Brinking some straw in, eh?"

"That's right, Bikk. Time to get a new roof up," Nick said carelessly, flicking his whip idly over the ox's shoulders.

"Are you only yust come beck from that trip you took to Monmouth then, lad?"

"Yes. The Squire kept me up there," Nick said, preparing to move off. He knew the mention of a county official should be enough to stop any further questioning, but he added, for good measure, "This is some of his straw."

"Ah, you are a gut lad, I see, and gut to your mudder to take care of her in her old age." The gatekeeper was full of kindly sentiment. "Tell me, you haven't seen any young boys, or young men hid out anywhere by der sides of der roads while you voss on your way here, did you?"

Nick shook his head. "Why, what's up, Bikk?" he asked.

"Oh, dair is a notiss about it in the Town Square. Some boys are in trupple for escaping on der way to the lock-up in Shent Brivvels," Bikk said, casually. "Dat iss all." He slapped the side of the waggon again and walked away to meet the next people waiting to enter the town.

Nick rolled the cart slowly into Beaufort Square. The front of the Corn Exchange was busy with the preparations for the evening's event. Barrels were being rolled up ramps into the building, trays of food carried in under snowy-white linen cloths, with armfuls of fresh decorative greenery and bolts of colourful cloth following. All was hustle and bustle, and, as the Town Square was also full of people who were still out and about enjoying the air, the crowding was quite intense. Soon everything would be swept aside and tidied, and the Square emptied of its wandering masses to make way for the splendid carriages and chaises that would shortly be rolling up and disgorging their contents of superbly-dressed local elite. This was to be no Squire's country dance. It was a formal ball, with only high-ranking dignitaries and landed gentry invited to attend the brightly-lit Assembly Rooms. From somewhere inside the building, distant strains of courtly music were already spilling out into the street from a practicing musician.

Nick couldn't read, so he paid little attention to the large proclamation pinned up on the wall of the Corn Exchange; but Miles, who attended the Haberdashers' Boys' School in Monmouth, got him to pull up beside it briefly so he could scan it. It was printed a flyer, stating that:

> *whereas Two Yonge Men formerly known in this Towne*
> *as AaronneArundell of Hyewelsfyelde and*
> *Thos. Bradleye Meddowes of Trellick,*
> *beyinge wanted on charges of loytering with intente,*
> *in relation to a Smuggelling charge layed aggenfte the*
> *Common Sea Man*
> *known onlye as Rigo, a reward of £5 is herebye offered*
> *for Information leading to theyre Apprehenshonne and*
> *Arrefte.*
> *Additionalie, Breache of the King's and Juftice's Peace*
> *and Efcape from Cuftodie*
> *have been laytlie added to the Severalle Charges.*

In smaller letters underneath, the flyer it also stated that:

> *whereas Seven other Prisonners, by name*
> *Donald and Desmonde Connaught,*
> *Terence Conningsbye, Francis Musgrave, Dickon Halte,*
> *Claude Hope and Sammuel Maltbye*
> *on Charges of Drunke and Diforderlye Conducte,*
> *have also had Breache of the King's and Juftice's Peace*
> *and Efcape from Cuftodie added to theyre Charge;*
> *they are now beying sought in good earneft*
> *within the Forreste of Deane.*

Any perfonne who has knowledge of these Men's
Deedes or Whereabouts should report
to the Conftable or the Sheriff of Monmouthshire's
Offices.

Nick patiently inched his ox through all the lingering onlookers of various sorts, listening in silent despair as Miles read out the awful words on the notice. He tried not to show emotion at what he was being quoted, but it was dreadfully hard not to panic. Just how far away was he from Bikk's 'trupple' himself? If he had to go to gaol, his mother would be left destitute. He knew he would have no chance of paying his way out, even if he sold his cart. You had to come from the right sort of family, like Aaron; or better still, like Tom, to think about even trying. And what could he do for his friends if they were taken in? Nick noted unhappily that Christina was raptly paying attention to the words Miles was reading out. All he could hope was that she didn't understand too much and wouldn't remember it afterwards if she did. And he hoped against hope that Fanny and Miles wouldn't spill any beans to their parents and family associates about this cart-riding episode, after it was all over. He would really be in the soup if they ever did. Privately vowing to stick strictly to waggoning in future, once he was through dealing with this escapade, Nick passed through more pressing throngs, this time of riding horses being saddled outside the stables, with hunting dogs of various breeds milling round, as preparations were made for journeys back to homes in the country. They were mixed with servants and attendants trying to arrange lifts back to their places of work after a welcome long day off, and it took Nick a good half an hour to get to the bottom end of the Square so he could pass into Roper Street and drive straight down to his own house.

Christina got out of the cart at that point, and Nick assumed she was going to find her family down in the warehouse. Nobody would be about much in that part of the town at this time of day, so she should be safe to go alone, and he proposed dropping Fanny and Miles off at the Cocklehouse himself, just as soon as he could. It might be several hours yet before Rigo turned up, and if the brother and sister had to wait, it would have to be somewhere decent until it was dark enough for them to move around outside without being picked out in a crowd. Nick knew well enough that his own house would never be acceptable as a refuge. Moreover, he was chary of what his mother's comments might be, should he usher in two members of the higher echelons of society and introduce them as acquaintances. Nick's mother was too much ostracised by the rest of Chepstow's poor to have the chance of talking out of turn, but she could and would call to mind both Fanny and Miles if anybody came enquiring after their whereabouts, and he didn't want to get his mother into any kind of trouble. It was bad enough that he had allowed them to carry on riding with him after he had found them in his waggon. The Cocklehouse, by contrast, would be full of drunkards at this time of day, with none of the customers likely to show more than a passing interest in two well-dressed young gentry among them, or to remember them afterwards if they did.

Chapter Twenty-Six

After getting down from Nick's waggon, Christina crossed Beaufort Square to Bridge Street and made her way down to Martha's house. As she approached the door she cast a last glance down the hill, and spotted the colourful costumes of a musical troupe at the bottom end of the street coming from the direction of the Wye Bridge. They were in two carts, making their way carefully towards the town.

She recognised Aaron among them by his sauntering walk, but that was all. She had never seen any of the other musicians before.

"Oh!" she thought. "So that's Aaron's music group, is it? I suppose they must be having a dance at the Pig and Parsley tonight."

So, it was true he had been let out, then. Or escaped – she didn't know which. He didn't see her, and neither did any of the others. None of the musicians were looking up or looking ahead. Her eyes drifted closer to home, and the next person she saw, and who didn't see her, was Tony Lightfoot. She didn't know who he was, either, but like everyone else she noticed him because of his extended stature and spidery walk. He slipped between two buildings and moved rapidly down the hill below her. There was something else about him that arrested her attention. It was a certain subtle air of intent. Christina had seen too many subversive activities during the days and nights she had spent around Bristol, Gloucester and Chepstow docks to be unaware of what constituted the clandestine, she could pick it out in an instant. This daddy-long-legs had a job in mind. Changing her own objective, Christina carried on past Martha's house and followed the long-legged man downhill as he made his way, now slowly and carefully in the open streets, now fast and flitting in the shadows and darker places, over the uneven cobblestones all the way down to the docks. Somehow, she wasn't surprised when he walked rapidly along the wharf and accosted a boatman who had just offloaded several baskets of shellfish. Instead of poling his way upstream to moor, the boatman rowed the longshanks out to one of the buoys in the deeper water, where the ship she recognised as Rigo's was at anchor. Christina saw the exchange of some coins, and the fisherman went on his way whilst the longshanks mounted the ladder fixed at the starboard quarter. She then lost sight of him aboard Rigo's ship.

She sat back on her heels and deliberated. Rigo's ship. Was this man anything to do with Rigo? He had boarded that same ship two nights ago. She knew, because she had seen him. She was equally sure he was something to do with all the smuggling because she so often saw him sneaking around the town and harbour after dark. She wanted to find out as much as she could in favour of her three new friends, because they were facing so much trouble, and now had to try and avoid being re-arrested, if she had heard and understood Miles aright. Everything was against them, if every entry and exit in and out of town was under surveillance. This tall man might be a friend, or he might be a foe. Or he might be just someone following his own intent: at present she couldn't tell, she would have to observe him for longer to decide. Accordingly, she made up her mind to come back later and watch to see if he left the ship, and if he did, to follow him again. She was certain she would have a better idea of his leanings once she saw where he went next. But first, she had to get to the Hillenjaar's house to give Martha her news about Tom and Aaron in the notice, and briefly to see her own family, before she came out again.

She made a hobbling run along the wharf and up the hill, and knocked at the door when she arrived at the lodging house, because the door was shut tight once more. Kitty answered, and Christina followed her down into the kitchen, the boy factotum having been given Christmas Day off. Poppea and Anthony were still sitting at their ease by the fire, but now Martha had joined them with a Bible, which she was reading aloud.

"Oh, Missus Hillenjaar, I've just seen Nick!" Christina exclaimed, interrupting the reading without a second thought. "There were two people with him in his cart when I saw him, a young gentleman and a young lady, and they said they're looking for Rigo before he sails, so he must have escaped! They said their name is Speybury, but I don't understand why they would be looking for Rigo, if they're the Squire's family. Do you think they were lying? I do. The young gentleman read out a notice that's been pinned up in the Square. It says they want to arrest Aaron and Tom for escaping. There's reward for them, but I don't think they're giving one for Rigo or any of the others."

"What? Escaped? That's wonderful! But – oh, no!" gasped Kitty, rising in delight and then turning a-flutter with fright and despair. "Mother what can we do? This is terrible!"

Before Martha could answer, Christina added, "Nick saw Aaron and Tom at the ball last night, and he thinks they would have gone home afterwards and stayed there. But I just saw Aaron with some musicians coming over the bridge, so he must have come to do a dance at the Pig and Parsley."

"Mercy! I hope you are wrong about seeing Aaron," Martha cried, jumping up. "Kitty, run out and see if you can stop those musicians. Bring Aaron back here, if you can. He can't know yet that he is wanted, and neither can his father if he's brought his son out with that musical troupe. They're playing at a ball, tonight, Christina, not a drinking house. He'll be seen for sure in a place like that – all the higher political men will be there. He won't escape their notice. Oh dear."

Kitty was already flying up the stairs, and seconds later the door slammed shut as she left the house, making Moonlight flutter round the room in a panic.

"Oh, and I nearly forgot," Christina went on, picking up Moonlight to calm him down, "Adela's grandfather went to Mister Able's house, and then he went somewhere else when they got to the Squire's, so he's all right. And – ooh! Is there some cake? Am I allowed to have some?" Christina peered hopefully across the abandoned kitchen table to where the Christmas cake stood in isolated splendour, her moment of triumph overtaken by the anticipation of more food.

"Yes, I'll give you some cake, but you must sit down quietly and eat it properly."

Christina did as she was bidden. Martha carved several slices of the rich fruit cake covered with marzipan and royal icing and handed the plates to Christina and her mother, together with glasses of mulled wine, while they all waited for Kitty to come back. Anthony shared Christina's cake, and Moonlight remained on the table, where he picked at some cake crumbs.

Suddenly there was a loud bang as the door upstairs was thrown back on its hinges, and a clatter of boots followed as several people came running down the stairs at top speed. Martha stood frozen, her knife in mid-air, and Moonlight fluttered to his refuge on the mantelpiece, squawking. A moment later, Kitty came bounding in ahead of Aaron and Able.

"I got to them just as they were starting to unload the carts, Mother," Kitty said, breathlessly.

"Goodness, I hope you didn't draw too much attention to yourselves," Martha said, running across the room to the large bread oven. "Do I need to hide anyone right away? Were you followed?"

She opened the bread oven to reveal a small bricked passageway inside that fell away into darkness. Just at that moment, there was some further loud banging from upstairs. Someone was hammering at the door with their fists, and shouting, too.

"Oh, my goodness, it sounds as if you were! Quick! Inside!"

Poppea and Anthony had hastily moved away from their places by the fire when the commotion started, flustered and alarmed by the general air of panic. They backed away from Martha, giving her more room as she displayed the bread oven to the two strange men she was assisting to scramble inside. Then mother and son clutched each other in uncomprehending terror as the men disappeared behind the wall close to where they had just been sitting.

"This tunnel leads down to the river bank," Martha was saying. "But there's a wider bit just beyond the back of the fireplace where you can sit and hide. You can hear what goes on inside this room from that part. Stay there for now, unless you hear me say different. We can pass you food, but it's pitch black in there, so don't move on unless you hear someone open the oven door. If it's me or Kitty, we'll say so. Meanwhile, stay under cover."

"Oh, thank you ma'am," Able said, as Martha started to close the oven door. "Oh, what a business! My nerves are all in pieces!"

Kitty, meanwhile, had gone upstairs as slowly as she could to give her mother time, and was now returning with two soldiers behind her.

"Mother, these men want to see you," Kitty announced, waving the soldiers into the room.

Martha straightened up from her seat by the fire, and gravely greeted the men. "Good evening," she said. "It's going to be a cold night. Can I offer you some cake and wine?"

"Now then, none of that," one of the soldiers said roughly. "I'll come straight to the point, mu'm. We've followed this girl down here with two men, and we've been given notice that one of those men is wanted. So, come now! Hand 'em over! Where are they?"

Martha looked at Kitty accusingly. "What have you been up to now, my girl?" She compressed her lips and set her arms akimbo. "You're never far from mischief, I do declare! Oh, if you only knew, Officer, how hard it is for a mother who's a widow to keep track of a wayward daughter."

"Oh, I see. I'm sorry to hear of that, mu'm," the soldier said, softening slightly. He rounded on Kitty severely. "You should be a good girl, and not give your poor mother more worries with your goings-on. Now come on, I haven't got all night. Where've you put those men? We know they came in this house, because we saw them follow you."

Kitty dimpled at the soldiers. "I'm so sorry to put you to so much trouble, Officer," she said, demurely, smiling her prettiest smile at them. "I can't help it, you know. Men like that just *will* keep coming after me. I'm sure I don't know why." She sighed, and flicked her long, curly black hair back over her shoulder. "I can't seem to stop it happening. It's such a nuisance."

The soldiers considered the idea. "You mean they didn't come in here with you?" the second soldier asked, looking puzzled.

"Oh, no, Officer. I came in alone, didn't I, Mother? I expect they followed me to find out where I lived and then hustled a bit at our door, and went on down the street. You must have lost sight of them in the crowds. Everyone is going home now, aren't they? It makes a lot of confusion."

The soldier's look of perplexity deepened. "I swear they come in this door after you," he said, but he no longer sounded certain. "Maybe they followed you in without you knowing and went straight out through a window at the back."

"Do you mind if we search the house, mu'm?" interjected the first soldier. "These men could be desperate, and they may not have left your house yet. I don't want to leave a good lady like yourself exposed to their menaces. Men like these can be really fearsome, if they're cornered, you know."

"Is that so? Then yes, if you would be so kind. It would make me feel so much safer. Come and check the upstairs rooms first," Martha said, leading the two men out. "I have lodgers, and they are all away at present…"

The voices faded as the soldiers clumped up the stairs behind Martha, leaving Christina still sitting at the table, watching everything round-eyed. Poppea and Anthony were still standing exactly where they had been moved to, their eyes rigidly fixed in combined fascination on the oven door, now shut fast and bolted. It was amazing the soldiers hadn't spotted them and followed their eyes in the same direction.

297

Kitty went swiftly across to Poppea and Anthony and quietly manhandled them back onto their settle. They were still focussed on the oven door, so Kitty gave them more cake as a means of distracting them, talking loudly about the men upstairs the whole time, so that Able and Aaron could hear exactly what was going on.

Christina spoke in a loud whisper. "Shall I sneak up and find out what's happening?" She pointed up at the ceiling, which was shaking slightly as tramping footsteps passed overhead.

"Not now," said Kitty. "When they leave here, go after them then, and see what they do and who they talk to. We need to keep up with the authorities if we can."

There came the sound of more clumping boots, and the opening of the front door. Kitty ran up the stairs to join her mother on the doorstep. The soldiers were just taking their leave of Martha.

"Well, good day to you, mu'm," the first soldier was saying, speaking amicably now. "Let us know if you hear anything. A word at the barracks, and we'll be up here in no time. You can't be too careful."

"I do so agree with you, Officer," Martha said, shaking her head.

The soldiers stepped over the threshold and looked back. "Oh, and just for you to know," the first one said, deferentially, "if you do send word, mu'm, I'm not actually an officer, just ordinary rank and file, you know. Bodkin's the name, if you'd like my personal attention."

"Thank you so much for your kindness, Officer," Martha murmured as she started to close the door. "You seem born to be in command to me."

"Oh, now mu'm," the soldier said, trying in vain to look modest. Then his eye fell on Kitty. "And no more trouble from you, my girl. You take care of your good mother from now on. D'you hear me?"

Kitty cast her long-lashed eyes downwards. "I promise, Officer," she said. "And if those awful men call here, I'll be sure to let you know."

"Or if you see them in the street," the soldier said, stepping away from the house at last. "There is a reward, you know. Mu'm," He saluted Martha respectfully, and left.

Martha shut the door on them and heaved a sigh of relief. "Thank goodness," she said, leaning her back against the panels. Then she rallied herself. "Come on," she said. "Let's go down and get Able out and send him back up to the Assembly Rooms. Aaron will have to stay with us here. But what we can do about Anthony and Poppea's eyes, I really don't know!"

Chapter Twenty-Seven

Tom had spent the day at his father's house. It had been quiet, with a visit to the church in Monmouth for the early morning Mass, followed by a dinner with his father in the draughty dining room at the Manor afterwards, while Elsie and Rowles ate separately in the kitchen. After the meal, his father had gone out with his dogs to see Able at the Bell and Candle, and Tom had been left alone.

There had been a time when all the liturgies had been held in the Manor itself, out in the main hall, back in the days when the Colonel had had a full staff of servants and labourers, and a stipend attached to the local clergy, but those days were long gone. It was a pity, Tom reflected. Christmas was just about the only time he ever did think of past glories and days gone by, though when he did it was only ever to idly dream of what it would be like if all the cheerful activity and good-natured bustle, and the familiar greetings that had once hallmarked the Advent season on his father's estate should ever be reinstated. He didn't miss money or an affluent way of living, but he did miss company.

The winter afternoon was drawing to its misty close. Tom had been wandering rather disconsolately around all the rooms on the lower floors of the Manor trying in vain to find something to do. He had finished up in the parlour standing at the French windows, looking at the garden with its untidy lawn as the sun slowly set over the boulder-strewn ridges of scrubby heathland that stretched away for so many miles beyond his father's neglected estate. He had been about to withdraw from the room when he had spied a pile of clothes placed neatly on a chair by the door. They were all blue sea-cloth, with a colourful bandanna folded on the top. Rigo! Rigo's clothes! Leftover relics of Rigo's bold enterprise, set aside for Rigo's disguise, after Rigo's escape from custody, prior to Rigo's unwilling sojourn behind a tapestry curtain, followed by Rigo's... what? What had come next? What had happened to him? Where *had* he got to, in the end? What had been the culmination of his escapades? Rigo had been on Tom's mind intermittently all day, ever since arriving back home in Trellech after failing to overtake him on the road as expected. He had stabled the horse and put the cart in its shed unhappily, and assumed that Rigo must have taken another route back to Chepstow. But it was such an unsatisfactory conclusion to have to make: such a poor ending to the tale. He would so have liked to have been certain of the outcome of Rigo's adventure, to have sent him safely on his way, to have been able to say farewell properly.

He stared at the clothes thoughtfully. The more he thought about it, the more surprised he was that Rigo had not called back in for them. After all the excitement, he must have forgotten. But if so, he must still be in his woman's garb somewhere. That would never do! He wouldn't be able to take his place back on board the *Senhora* unless he was able to find himself a change of clothes in Chepstow. He couldn't turn up as he was, it would draw down too many questions about where he had been, and what he had been up to; and besides, it was bad luck to have a woman on board. Or did that superstition not apply to men dressed as women? Tom had no idea; but he did know Rigo would have trouble on Christmas Day finding another outfit to wear. Nick wouldn't have anything, and there would be nobody else around he could ask. And besides, Rigo had no money for purchases. Plus, he was sure to miss his bandanna, if he didn't get it back. Such a nice one, too. He might not be able to pick up another one like it. Tom stared at the clothes, already knowing what he was going to do.

"I must be careful about this. I've already broken the law twice," he murmured to himself. "If I go ahead, I'll certainly be compounding what's already being held against me before the day is done. That's going to get me a weighty sentence if I am picked up again. Dare I carry on?"

He considered his father, who had so willingly played his part in getting his son out of the trouble he was already in, at no inconsiderable risk to himself. But it was no good. Tom's vitals were now gnawing at him, eating him up inside, telling him to go after Rigo. He had to, he simply must. It was the only right thing to do. Tom heaved a sigh. The words 'hang', 'sheep', and 'lamb' drifted through his mind as he swiftly gathered the clothes into a bundle and stepped out into the hall, calling out to Elsie as he went that he didn't want any tea, and wouldn't be in for supper.

Elsie came into the hall at a run just in time to see Tom grab his travelling cloak and take up the clothes bundle before he marched out through the door

"Are you going somewhere, young Master?" she enquired, taken aback, hurrying across the hall after him. "Don't go. It's getting dark out there. What shall I tell the Colonel?"

Tom turned. "I have to take these to my friend," he answered, indicating the bundle. "I don't think he can get back on board his ship without them. Just tell my father that, will you? He'll understand."

With a distinct feeling that serial crisis management was going to be taking over the rest of his life if he was making a wrong decision, Tom stepped out of the house into the gathering darkness. He had begun the walk to the back of the house to saddle Timothy before remembering that Timothy must still be in Chepstow, since no-one had yet gone there to fetch him. He stood still for a moment and thought. There were no other horses to be had. Rowles had gone on the plough-horse to visit his family, and the Colonel had stated his intention of staying on to share a glass or two of Canary with his neighbour after returning the horse he had been lent yesterday. There was only one thing for it. Tom changed direction and set out down the driveway on foot. He simply *had* to get to Chepstow now, and if that meant a journey on Shanks's pony all the way, then so be it. It was time to get old Timothy back. He knew his father was returning the horse to his neighbour that day because he couldn't keep an extra horse on as well as paying for Tim's stabling, Tom was aware of his father's straightened circumstances. And he knew Nick was no better off – Timothy was probably well on his way through another of Nick's roofs by now. He had an obligation to his friend, as well as his father. So first, he must get Rigo re-attired in his sailor's rig and see him off: that would be one good deed; then he would retrieve Timothy and ride him home, and that would be the second. He trudged along steadily, pacing down the uneven road. Tom fully intended to be on that quayside well before high tide the next morning.

He perused these, and other thoughts, until he ambled through Devauden village about four miles into his journey. The evening was now well advanced and the village quite dark, with the prospect of a deeper, more sinister darkness to follow, since he proposed taking the way through Itton Woods. This next part of the walk was not a charming prospect, and Tom was trying hard not to think too much about it. The village green coincided with a crossroads, where one of the three roads ahead led the way he intended to travel. It was a good place to take a short rest, and Tom did so, leaning gratefully up against a milestone sunk into the earth at the roadside.

He had only been there a short while when he heard two voices coming from a little way off. After a few minutes more, he decided he had better follow the voices to their source to find out what was wrong, because a rising pitch of the exchanges indicated a full-blown argument was already under way. The added neighing and stomping of a frantic horse further suggested a situation very close to crisis.

He crossed the road and entered a short driveway beside one of the larger cottages, and then stopped to weigh things up. In front of him an elderly little man was coming out of a small stable pulling at a most unwilling horse, and as Tom silently watched, he made a futile attempt, using threats and imprecations, to get the beast to go back into the shafts of a cart. At his first glance, Tom could see that the cart was slewed at an awkward angle, probably dragged out of alignment by previous efforts, and that it was now serving only to increase the man's difficulties; but either the man was too obstinate, or else he hadn't thought to straighten the cart back up again. Tensions were clearly mounting. Man and horse were being needled by an elderly woman whose unwarranted advice and useless instruction ran contrary to everything the man was trying to get the animal to do; all of which explained the racket that had initially attracted Tom's attention, but what he couldn't understand was why the rest of the village hadn't turned out at the sound of it as well. They would have been perfectly justified in doing so; it was amazing what bedlam two old people could create from just an exchange of recriminations. Even now the man seemed determined to coerce the horse into submitting to his wishes, and even now the horse seemed equally determined to refuse, and all the time a constant stream of flapping advice and criticism fuelled the struggle. All efforts by all parties were proving to be in vain, and there was the imminent danger of some awful accident.

The man was beginning to wax furious, not just with the horse, but with the woman as well; and Tom couldn't help feeling a certain sympathy for the old fellow. The woman simply wouldn't pipe down and let him get on with things. Not that she was listening to anything he said; both horse and woman were just going their own way. Tom took a decision and stepped forward just as the horse began to rear. More strident complaints followed, and the poor horse stood trembling, waiting for the next round of rebukes with its nostrils flared, breathing heavily, tugging hard to free itself from the bridle.

"Good evening sir; madam," Tom said, doffing his hat with a flourish that allowed the feather to feature prominently, "I couldn't help overhearing your difficulties as I was walking by. Perhaps you will permit me to assist you. I have some knowledge of horses."

"Well, I don't know about that, my boy," the woman said rudely, looking Tom up and down and ignoring the feather completely. "I mean to say, I don't know much about *that*. Who's to say you know any more about horses 'n what we do? Who are you, anyway? Who asked you to come interferin'?"

"Please allow me to introduce myself," Tom said, inwardly seething as he re-settled his hat. "I am Thomas Meadows Esquire of Trellech, Colonel Meadows' son. Did you want the horse between the shafts of this cart? I'll do it for you directly, then I can take my leave and let you good people carry on."

Tom strode up and spent a few moments calming the poor beast down. It was still inclined to snort and bridle, and at first, he wondered if the animal was a bit wild. Then he realised the horse was simply trying to shake off the little man, who was still hanging on with grim determination to the other side of the harness, almost lifted off his feet as he dragged at the animal's head.

"Sir, you can let go of your side now. I have the beast quite safe." Tom found it very hard not to get caught up in the anger himself at witnessing the couple's cruel ignorance. The creature was well fed and well looked after, there was nothing wrong with their husbandry, but their management of the poor thing was just awful and quite likely soon to turn a good horse, vicious.

"Ah," said the woman. "Well, I hope you know what you'm doin' if you'm goin' to come h'yur stickin' your oar in like this. I mean to say, we'd ha' done it ourselves already if Mal hadn't barged the horse up against the end of that shaft first time round."

"I didn't barge it, woman."

"Yes, you did, Mal. You barged it up against the shaft, an' then it tried to escape."

"Well, if you hadn't been out here under my feet, meddling and muddling things up, I might have…"

"I'm helpin' you, not meddlin, Maldwyn," the woman said, drawing herself up. "But you'm not listenin' to me."

"You were distracting me. You're always distracting me, woman. You should leave me alone to get the blasted job done, not hold me up."

"Well, if you'd only do what Joe Phillips says…"

"I'm not interested in Joe Phillips. I'm only interested in what I'm doing here in this yard."

"He said if you'd only get someone in to do the drivin', but the man he had in mind is sick now."

"I don't care if he's died. I've still got to get this horse into this bloody cart."

"So, you'm Colonel Meadows' boy, are you?" the woman asked, abruptly transferring her attention from Maldwyn to Tom, and ignoring her husband's last remarks entirely. "Well, you've turned out well, I must say. I knew your mam when she was alive. I liked her, she was a nice lady. What are you doin' down h'yur on a Christmas night? You should be at home with your dad."

"I know," Tom agreed, deferentially. "I didn't expect to be out, but I have something important to do in Chepstow tonight, so I'm on my way there now and coming back tomorrow. With any luck, I might get a lift," he added, hoping one of them would pick up on the hint. He had been gently coaxing the horse into position in the shafts of the cart while he had been talking. "Shall I lead him out to the road for you?" he finished politely as he fastened the animal in.

"Ah," the woman assented. "If Mister Parry h'yur does it, he'll probably take all night. That's if the whole cart don't finish up in the garden hedge, bag an' baggage." She began laughing, some of her fussy nervousness ebbing away now the harnessing had been successfully accomplished.

Once the horse and cart were pointed in the right direction out on the road, Mister Parry got in and picked up the reins. He was still impatient and heavy–handed, and Tom winced to see him hauling at the horse's mouth with such testiness before he had even set off, but at least the old man's general mood had lifted somewhat.

306

"Where are you heading, Mister Parry?" Tom asked, since the cart was facing the same way he was going. "Perhaps we can keep each other company for a while."

"I can take you to Chepstow if you want, boy," Maldwyn said peremptorily, "but I have to make a quick call on the way."

"Fine. I'll be glad to join you," Tom said, springing up beside him. "Shall I take the reins for you, sir?"

"No. I don't need someone still wet behind the ears telling me how to do my job," Maldwyn said, brushing Tom off irritably. "I know what I'm doing."

"Ah, well, you be careful now, Maldwyn," his wife shrilled up from the road, standing somewhere below him. "Don't forget the brake this time when you'm goin' down the hills."

"I know about the bloody brake, woman."

"Ah, but you forgot it last time Mal, an' Joe Phillips had to get the cart out of the bed of that stream for us that same afternoon, an'…"

"That wasn't because of the brake, Angharad-Elunid. That was because of a slippery road."

"That's not what Joe Phillips said. Joe said…"

"Look, he doesn't know. He wasn't there. He's not a bloody clairvoyant, and he's not my teacher. Now go inside, before you catch your death of cold. I'll be back in a few hours."

He instructed the horse to 'get going' and left Angharad-Elunid standing at the roadside, where she watched until the cart turned right at the village green to take the Shirenewton road before disappearing out of sight.

"Oh! Um, are you going far along this road, sir?" Tom asked, surprised. "Only I wasn't intending to come this way, and it *is* the longer way to Chepstow. I am very keen to get to where I'm going as soon as possible."

"Don't worry about Chepstow," Maldwyn said, shortly. "I'll get you there, I know what I'm doing. If you give me a hand, we'll be even quicker."

"What are we going to do, Mister Parry?" The horse began to speed up to a quick trot, apparently willing to oblige now it knew what it was supposed to be doing. "Where will you be going?"

"I have some things in the cart that need dropping off."

"Oh, right. In Shirenewton, is it? Well…"

"Blackrock."

"Black… *Blackrock?*" Tom tried hard not to squeak. "That's a long trip, sir. Perhaps it would be better if you just let me get out after all. If you drop me off here, I'll…"

"Don't fuss, boy," Maldwyn grated warningly, glaring at him. "I hate fuss. Sit still and be quiet. I'll get you there soon enough, don't worry."

Mister Parry's idea about small detours wasn't the only thing that was alarming Tom. His idea of a quick trip was disturbing, as well. They had been picking up speed with desperate haste as they went along, until the horse was puffing and snorting and cantering down the road at a frantic pace, passing through some very dark, extremely narrow country lanes at an impossible speed. High banks enclosed the route they were following, so if they should meet anything coming from the other direction there would be no room to swerve and no time to brake, for it was far too dark to look ahead or see round any bends. Indeed, at the speed they were doing it was hard even to see where the bends were. Maldwyn simply swung into them at the very last moment as the cart raced along, lurching up against the hedges before restoring the balance and rushing on.

"Er… could we slow down a bit, do you think, sir?" Tom asked desperately, after they had gone around two corners in this fashion. He was hanging on to his hat with one hand to stop it blowing off and gripping the side of the cart tightly with the other. "We are going rather too fast, I think."

"Rubbish," Maldwyn snorted, glowering at Tom instead of minding the road ahead. "We're doing fine. What's the matter with you, boy?"

"Sir, I am a bit concerned about your speed. Sir, I really do think… Mister Parry, please! Slow down! There's another blind bend ahead somewhere round here. What if there's something coming the other way?"

"There won't *be* anything coming the other way," Maldwyn snapped with ill-founded confidence, rattling the cart on madly with neither care nor thought.

Tom never knew afterwards if that clear road was due to sheer good luck, or if it was that no-one would dare defy Maldwyn Parry's assertions and be out on a country road at the same time as him. Perhaps his mad progressions always kept everybody off the roads. All Tom did know was that he was never *ever* going to go down any of those lanes again himself, ever. By day or by night. Just in case.

At last, about an hour and a half later, they came up to the end of the rough lane that led to Blackrock. It petered out at the edge of the sea-shore, right at the place where the shoreline had been banked up with a six-foot-high ridge of earth all along its length after the floods of 1607.

"That's it, boy, we're here," Maldwyn announced, cantering right up to the end before lurching to a precipitous and grinding halt.

"Thank God for that," Tom groaned, and fell sideways out of the cart.

Ignoring Tom's distress completely, Maldwyn jumped down and went around to the back. He began unfastening the tail-gate, apparently listening at the same time. There was a slight scuffling noise, and a head appeared over the top of the earthwork.

"Psst! Is that you?" someone asked, peering down.

"I'm the man you want," Maldwyn answered, leaving his cart to walk up and join him. "How many of you are there?"

"Three. How many have you got?"

"Sixty here, and another two hundred and fifty put by." Maldwyn beckoned the Someone to follow him back to the cart.

Two more heads appeared and followed the first over the earthwork and down onto the track. None of them had noticed

Tom's inert form lying in the dirt, where he was limply recovering, but luckily they all took a route round the cart that went the far side from him. Amid some muffled conversations, several huge armfuls of sheep's wool fleeces were removed from the back of the cart and carried up over the earthwork the way they had come. Shortly afterwards, the three men and Maldwyn walked a little way up the track, reappearing a short time later bearing more armfuls of fleece.

In less than an hour, everything had been dealt with. Maldwyn climbed with the men to the top of the earth ridge one more time and disappeared down the other side, then after another thirty minutes or so he came back and took the reins so he could walk the horse up to a nearby pond and let it take a drink after its protracted race to the shore. The pond was small and icy, with sludgy edges, and it smelt horribly of stagnation, but the horse didn't seem to mind. It had been quietly grabbing mouthfuls of frosty grass during the stealthy operations, its earlier terrors apparently forgotten.

When the horse had drunk its fill, Maldwyn climbed up into the cart and clicked the reins much more gently now his anger and agitation had abated. Quite possibly he was tired now, too. Tom certainly was. He climbed listlessly up beside Maldwyn and grabbed at his hat again as they took off, but he didn't need to. The horse had run itself out of puff, and the most it could manage now was a fast trot, a speed Tom was much happier to travel at, though Maldwyn still drove with a fine disregard for road safety.

"I'll drop you off at the Pwll-Meyric turn-off," Maldwyn said an hour later, as they were going through Pwll-Meyric village. "You won't mind walking that last bit, will you, boy?"

"Not a bit," Tom replied, with total sincerity.

He jumped out of the cart, and gave his thanks to Maldwyn, who turned left and shot off towards Itton Woods through the back roads. That ride had been quite the most hair-raising experience Tom had ever had, and he was never going to accept a lift from anyone ever again. Never.

Chapter Twenty-Eight

Nick pulled up outside his own house, and said quietly, "All right, Miss. Do you want to get out here?"

First Fanny, then Miles emerged from the straw, and began brushing themselves down.

"Is it safe around here?" Fanny enquired, trying to tidy her hair once again with her fingers and looking all around. She had never been to the poor part of Chepstow before, and she was sure there must be gangs of cut-purses, if not cut-throats, hanging about in the vicinity.

Miles stepped out of the cart first, and she allowed him to hand her down.

"By the way, Nick, I need a change of clothes," she said lightly, once she was standing in the street, speaking as if the matter was a mere trifle. "I want to go down to the harbour, and I can't go there dressed like this." She indicated her expensive ball gown and extended the gesture to include Miles' satin weskit and britches and his velvet jacket. "As you can see, we are slightly overdressed for a night's outing of this kind."

"Not if you go and sit in a corner at the Cocklehouse, you're not," Nick said, as he started to lead the ox into the stable yard. "They get all sorts down there. I can give you a blanket to put over your dress if you want to blend into the background a bit more, but that's all. I'm very sorry Miss Fanny," he added, "but I have no clothes other than these I stand up in, and I can't get you any from anywhere else."

"Don't you even have another smock?" Fanny asked, scandalised. "What do you do when you wash those?"

"I don't wash them," Nick said, simply. "Perhaps you would like to come inside my house and share a mug of ale instead? You won't have to change at all, then."

"Er, no thank you. I don't think we'd better..." Miles began, scarcely able to conceal his horror at the impoverished surroundings, but his thoughtlessness was fortunately overridden by Fanny saying they must press on and get something to cover themselves with, or they would never get to see Rigo.

"Rigo is why we're here, after all," she said. "You'd better give me *your* clothes instead Nick, so we can get on."

Nick's horror rivalled Miles'. "You want the things I'm wearing? I can't do that!" he gasped. "Miss, please! Think of your modesty! ...And mine!" he added, as that last thought suddenly occurred to him.

"Oh nonsense, of course you can," Fanny insisted. "You can wear my dress instead. Rigo didn't mind looking like a girl, and it won't be for long."

"Oh, I say, Fan," her brother remonstrated. "I say. I don't think you should, you know."

"Shut up," Fanny snapped. "I'll wear Nick's clothes and you can throw his smock over the top of what you're wearing. Then we'll go. The sooner we see Rigo, the sooner you can come back."

"Just me?"

"We. Or still... I don't know..."

"Oh, I say!"

Five minutes later, two boys of different heights made their way through the last reaches of Roper Street, heading for the harbour. One of them was stumbling over a smock almost as long as a dressing-gown, the other was in a rather odorous brown corduroy jacket and britches, both a size too small, and a pair of seven-league boots. Back at Nick's house a tall girl with straggly shoulder length dark-blonde hair, wearing a voluminous limp rose damask gown and baggy satin slippers, sat down unhappily beside the ox, which was now quietly eating at its stall. Once ensconced there, she took out a pipe and lit it while she awaited developments. She didn't dare be seen doing anything else.

Able staggered across Martha's kitchen floor after being hauled bodily out of the bread oven. He seemed to have no strength or willpower left to wriggle out on his own, but that didn't stop him from babbling wildly as he was being released.

"Oh, my goodness," he wailed, wringing his hands as soon as someone let them go, "this is turning into a terrible evening, and the ball hasn't even started yet. I'll have to get up there straight away. They'll have had to start without me, as it is. Thank you very much Missus Hillenjaar for helping us out like this. I don't know how I'll ever repay you. If I can ever be of service, please let me know. I'll do anything. Anything. It's my boy here who we must keep in safety. He's been a completely innocent bystander, I can assure you, but what do the authorities care? It's worse than a bad dream. I'll have to do the dance on my own now, but I'll manage it with a bit of luck. I don't mind. I'd rather give a bad performance and know Aaron is all right than risk him being out there, even if we put him at the back of the stage. What Phyllis will say to this, I don't know. She still knows nothing about any of it. I thought we could keep it from her, since it seemed to have turned out all right." He suddenly remembered Aaron, still stuck in the secret passageway, and peered back inside to address him. "I'll be back after the ball finishes, son, don't worry, I shan't leave you for long. Then we'll have to work something out. Perhaps you'll have to get a berth on a ship and go abroad for a while. I'll see what can be done. I wish Ronald was here. He has a good brain for these matters, but I haven't seen him since yesterday evening. Oh dear, oh dear."

Aaron came slowly out of the oven and shut it. Then he sat himself on a stool close by, where he remained quietly keeping one watchful eye on the stairwell, just in case. Able left the room, still wringing his hands and lamenting. Kitty saw him up to the door, and met Adela on the doorstep coming in. After checking the street up and down, Able left and Adela followed Kitty downstairs.

"Good evening, Missus Hillenjaar," Adela said. "I hope you don't mind another visit from me. Mother asked me to come out again to see if I can find out where my Grandad is. We still haven't heard anything about him."

"Have you not?" Martha was momentarily quite shocked. "I do hope he is all right. I don't like the way events are turning out, I must say. But we can't change them, so we must adapt to them instead, and unfortunate though the circumstances may be, your arrival here at this moment is fortuitous, because I want to send you two girls out. I've been baking this afternoon, and made some marzipan sweetmeats. Here they are, look, I'm going to put them in a basket for one of you to sell tonight in the taverns. You must have something which will serve as an excuse to get you into town at night without comment and allow you to check the drinking places without being remarked on. I had thought you would just be looking after Tom's interests, but now it looks as if you will have to extend your enquiries to include Mister Baker as well. So, which one of you wants to do it?"

"Me, of course," Kitty said, carelessly. "Adela is too young. The men won't get talking to her the way they would with me."

"Yes, well, you just mind how much talking you do yourself, my girl," Martha said, with some asperity. "Don't wag your own tongue, and make sure you don't lead any men on. With your looks and pert manners, there are many who will take your ways as a clear invitation unless you are more careful in the future than you are at present."

"Oh, Mother," Kitty scolded, "you are such a nag. I'll be fine. I know what I'm doing, I can handle them all, don't worry. You saw how I was with the soldiers."

"It's exactly because of what I saw that I *do* worry," Martha said, firmly.

"But I was only doing the same as you were, Mother," Kitty protested.

"I did as much as was necessary to win them over and that was all," her mother said, "whereas you play fast-and-loose for sport. It's thankful I'll be when you are safely wed my girl and become your husband's responsibility. Glad indeed. Now. If I get Kitty to go off with the sweetmeats round the rough-houses, I can get Adela into the Wig and Mitre under some other pretext, so she can watch from their window for anyone coming into town who knows Tom. We simply must get a message to him so he knows he's still wanted, before he tries to come in himself. Any ideas?"

They all thought deeply.

"What about me?" Christina asked, after a few minutes of penetrating silence. "I want to be useful, too." She had returned from following the two soldiers to report that they had gone straight back to their quarters in the Castle.

Martha studied her intently for a few moments. Poppea and Anthony were sitting beside the fire, half asleep. They had taken no notice of what was going on around them since they had been replaced on the settle.

"I could do it much more easily than Adela," Christina urged, seeing Martha's deliberations and wondering fearfully if they were veering against her. "I'll stay safe, I promise. I did it this afternoon with no trouble. I'll just take my tapers with me this time, in case I get spotted."

Martha studied Christina some more. Her earlier concerns about Christina's reliability were proving unfounded, she decided, having now spent a day in close association with the child. Christina might be very young, but she was exceedingly bright and capable, and was already demonstrating great loyalty. Martha had heard so much over Christmas dinner about Christina's life and her terrible brush with death on the river that even now the thought of what that child had endured brought tears to her eyes. As for the mother and brother, they both had full stomachs and a place by the fire, so their

315

interests were satisfied. They would be happy and content if nothing disturbed them again. The poor things were quite safe. Martha made up her mind.

"All right," she said. "I think you may be right in what you say. If I allow you to sit in the Wig and Mitre, it will free Adela up to walk about town and eavesdrop on street chatter. If there is nothing to be heard that way because it's too quiet, she can go down and cover the Tidenham road, in case any of the men we want come in from the Forest. My only worry is that anyone coming in from *anywhere* will be so well hidden that they'll get past us, but it's a risk we'll have to take. Doubtless, the accomplices of these escaped prisoners have made plans of their own that are already being implemented. Ours must just run alongside theirs, and hope that no one of us scuppers the others. So, we keep Aaron hidden here, listen for news of Mister Baker, look out for men fleeing from the peacekeepers, assume that Rigo is somewhere not too far away ready to board his ship, and that Tom is safe in his own home and will remain there once we get a warning to him. That's it, girls. We've finished our deliberations. Good luck with you, all three, and let's hope we can discover these lads and help bring them to safety before the law catches up with them!"

Chapter Twenty-Nine

"What shall we do when we get to the ships, Fan?" Miles and his sister were entering the lower docks near the rope-maker's yard. "Do you know which one is Rigo's?"

"Oh, drat." Fanny stopped short for a moment. "No, I don't. That could prove a bit awkward. I don't want to ask around too much; too many questions about Rigo could draw unwarranted attention to us. Hmm." She began to walk on again, looking about her and thinking hard.

A distant rhythmic splashing of oars out in the river attracted her notice, and she walked up to the very edge of the quayside to scan the dark waters, which were just past a high tide.

"There's someone out there in a rowing boat," she whispered, as Miles came up alongside her and peered too. "It's heading for the steps by the fish market. Let's walk on up and wait for it to come in. I think I can risk asking the person in it if they know how to find Rigo, since there's no-one else around."

They almost ran along the wharf to reach the steps. By the time they arrived there, a small cockle-boat containing half a dozen wide, full baskets was just coming in. It was being rowed by a young man, with a much older man sitting in the bow accompanying him, whose voice drifted across as he talked continuously and determinedly.

"Not too fast comin' in now, slow down a bit," the old man was instructing, "draw her in here, just over here, look, that's right; an' then get them baskets up onto the quayside for me. Do 'em one at a time, an' mind you don't tip 'em over. You'll have to come back to move 'em across to the fish-stalls when you've put the boat away for me." He rubbed at his legs in satisfaction as the young man shipped the oars and prepared to jump out to make the boat fast.

"Now fix the rope at that bollard there for me, yes, yes, that one there. No, not like that, boy, slip a loop over. Yes, that's right, that's more like it, an' make sure you put two proper hitches in it this time like I showed you. We don't want it comin' undone again like the last one you did, do we? Now then. When you take the boat on up the river, go up to where the old jetty is, you can't miss it, it's the one right at the end of the wharf, right at the very end – and moor somewhere this side of it. See you clear the water out the bottom before you leave her. I don't want to come down and find her half flooded next time I want to take her out. Right, I'm off home now. See you finish up properly, an' don't you worry about me. I'll be all right, I can get home from here without trouble. You can be off about your business an' find your own ship just as soon as you've got them baskets shifted. I shan't need you after that."

The old man got slowly and carefully out of the cockle boat and followed the young man up the steps to the quayside, giving a few quiet groans as he got his stiff legs moving.

At this point Fanny barged confidently forward between the two men, completely disrupting their disembarking.

"Excuse me," she interrupted, without any consideration whatsoever, "but could you tell me where a sailor called Rigo might be found?"

"Eh?" said the old man, putting his hand behind his ear. "What's that you say? Here, Tom. What's this lad askin' of me?"

The young man took no notice of either of them. He heaved a basketful of cockles along the boat, lifted it out, and began humping it up the steps without answering.

"Here," the old man repeated, suddenly plucking at Fanny and forgetting about her question, "give my lad a hand, will you? And you, boy, you as well." He indicated Miles. "Come on. Step up, lad, step up. Give an old man some assistance. It's cold, an' it's Christmas, an' I want to get back to me own fireside before me bones is too froze."

Most unwillingly, Fanny and Miles took the basket from the young man, and between them dragged it across the quayside to some rather smelly wooden trestle tables used for cleaning and gutting the fish in the catches that were destined for the markets further inland. By the time Fanny and Miles got back to the old man, another basket was ready for them to drag across. He watched them move everything to and fro in silence until the last basket was stacked against the others at the nearest fish stall.

"Thank ye all kindly," he finished, pleased that the job had been done to his satisfaction. "You can all go home once the boat's put away." He hobbled off along the wharf in the direction of the town without a backward glance. The young boatman watched him go, then prepared to cast off again.

"Quick, Miles, get in the boat with him," Fanny suddenly hissed. "We'll be able to see the ships better from the river." And she gave her brother a great push that nearly shot him over the edge of the wharf into the water.

"I say, Fan," he protested, as he stumbled down the steps. "Have a care, do. You can see I keep tripping over this smock thing."

Fanny took no notice in her haste to shift him out of the way so she could accost the boy before he moved off. "I say," she hailed the boy, running past Miles down the steps to detain the boat with her hand, "I say, you couldn't give us a lift, could you?"

"Well, I suppose I don't mind," the boy said, grudgingly. "Just as long as you don't give me any hassle. I've absolutely had enough for one night."

"Hang on a minute, I think I know you," Miles exclaimed, peering at the boy as his sister scrambled clumsily over the gunwale to get in. "Yes, yes, I do. You're the chappie who was with Rigo at our house last night, aren't you?" He leapt in after Fanny, almost upsetting the boat.

"That's right," said the boy sarcastically. "Just empty us all into the river to round the evening off, why don't you?" He began to pull away from the wharf as Miles teetered unsteadily into place beside his sister at the stern end.

"You're supposed to be with those musicians, aren't you?" Miles persisted, studying him closely.

"And what if I am?" Tom had already realised who Miles was. He had no idea about Fanny. He had never met her before.

"By all that's wonderful," Miles exclaimed, excitedly. "Fan, this chap knows Rigo. I was with them both last night!"

"Good," Fanny said, peering over the side into the dark swirling water. "You can take us to him, then. We're here to see Rigo before he leaves. And be careful what you're doing, Boy. This boat seems very rocky."

"Oh, not you as well," Tom groaned, dispiritedly. "I've had an absolute gizzardful of hearing all the ways in which I fail to measure up. It would seem there are so many." He spoke from a rank bitterness of heart. "For a start, I'm living down a situation I can't possibly talk about with my father and hoping my mother won't turn in her grave too many times over a son who just wanted to keep a friendly eye out for someone he had just met. On top of that, I've been arrested and shackled up with a cartload of farting drunks simply for being in the wrong place at the wrong time, and put on a charge for daring to raise a light-hearted question over the ethics of a member of the judiciary who I know for a fact has some highly debatable practices of his own; all of which has resulted in me being jettisoned into an unwanted – and unwarranted – outlaw's existence in a hide-out in the freezing countryside in the depths of winter with some distressingly insalubrious fellow-detainees of unspeakably disgusting personal habits, in order to effect a decidedly illegal escape which now makes me complicit in a load of other illicit dealings I daren't even begin to mention. I have yet to explain the whole episode to my mentor, a most respected representative of the legal establishment I have unwittingly fallen foul of, who will doubtless demand when he hears of it to know why I agreed to dress in an embarrassing court jester's suit sporting bits of old rabbit fluff and jingle bells to pose alongside a supposed band bawdie who is actually a bloke in drag, thus exposing myself to the risk of ridicule from the public-at-large at a time when I am accepting his personal tutelage as part of my initiation into his esteemed and august profession. I've had disgusting fish pushed in front of me and been expected to salivate over it when all I really want to do is throw up over it. I have been called on..."

"Yes, I do know what you mean about that fish," Miles murmured.

"...to improvise in front of a doughty, intimidating middle-aged lady about a supposed relative who it turned out I couldn't vouch for and who I've since allowed to get lost. I've had my arse kicked for trying to mediate in a bun-fight between two voluble and rude old people who tell me I know nothing about horses, or an appropriate speed for driving a horse and cart. And now it would seem I can't pick cockles, pack baskets, row a boat, or tie ropes to save my life. I really do think this Christmas has offered me all I can take of exposure to my own shortcomings and miserable limitations, so please excuse my pathetic lack of interest in any further chances of self-improvement."

"Have you really been doing all that since I last saw you?" Miles asked, with genuine interest. "You've been busy, haven't you?"

"For the last two days," Tom said, "I've been trying to make myself useful to friends and family in a manner appropriate to the spirit of the festive season and look where it's got me. And I just bet there's someone else in the offing right now, lined up and waiting for their chance to criticise and browbeat me for letting you two to sit in my boat. I'd get you to do some rowing and start making things up to myself, since I don't feel like doing anyone any more favours, but I dread to think where I'll end up next if I do."

"I almost didn't recognise you at first," Miles said, oblivious to Tom's profound distress. "I didn't know you were a sailor."

"I'm not."

"But you're…"

"These are not my clothes. They're Rigo's. I was returning them so he can get back on board his ship. But I didn't know how to get into town without being recognised. I was afraid I might be re-arrested if I tried. I obviously couldn't go through the gates, and I'm not limber enough to get over the wall, so I decided I had better go down to the shore and wait for a crab fisherman, or something. And I put these things on so they would assume I'm a seaman going back to my ship after a night out drinking. It seemed a good way of getting to the harbour, and from there into the town, without question. What I didn't expect was that it would involve a monumental cockle-picking expedition first. I won't be trying anything like that again in a hurry, I can tell you. I can't wait to get out of these clothes. I simply stink of seaweed. Why anyone would want to be a fisherman or a sailor beats me. I'm never going to eat fish from Chepstow again. Or Cannop Ponds."

"Hmm. Pity about you not wanting to take to sea, in a way. That bandanna does suit you," Fanny said, eyeing him critically. "So, you're one of the other young men Papa is after, are you? Rigo did say there were two others. Did you know there's a notice put up in the Town Square about you?"

"Oh, good grief, there's not, is there?"

"Yes, there is. We saw it. At least I think it's you. Are you Tom Meadows? You do look familiar, but I haven't seen you close to since your mamma died. Is it you? Well then yes, it names you; and Aaron Arundel is on it, and Rigo. And seven others. What are you going to do?"

Tom sank his head down momentarily before taking up the rowing again. "I've no idea," he said. "All this fuss, and it all started because we were out in the street late at night. I can hardly believe such a run of bad luck. My father thought we would be able to claim the whole thing was a case of mistaken identity, because we got away. Now, it seems escaping has just made things worse."

"It certainly has. I don't think even your father can get you out of this. Sir Fusby will be swinging his axe when he comes back, he's bound to be. He'll take something like this personally, and he's never disposed to give people second chances. I think he'll be sending you to the Assizes. You're looking at a good long spell in prison, Tom."

"You could always come with us instead," Miles suggested, encouragingly.

"Could I? Why, where are you going?"

"Rigo's ship. Fan wants to run away to sea. I'm just going to see Rigo."

"No thank you," Tom said, lugubriously. "I can't run away to sea without saying goodbye to my father and… someone else." His thoughts turned wistfully to Kitty. He wouldn't have the chance to walk out with her, after all. The very thought of it made him want to cry.

"You can still say goodbye to Rigo, though, can't you?"

"That's true." He carried on rowing for a while. "I need to give him these clothes back. I don't think he'll be on his ship, because he'll still be dressed as a gypsy woman. I don't think he would dare present himself looking like that, in case of bad luck. – Huh. He should try having some of mine. – But anyway, I'll still take you to his ship first, before I go looking for him on shore, and you can see if he's there. We haven't got far to go now."

"Well, here we are," he said, a short time later. "This is Rigo's ship. The *Senhora da Luz*. Did you want to board her? I don't think there's anybody awake up there. I can't hear anybody about."

They had reached a creaking vessel moored to a buoy about half-way along the bend in the river. Tom had been rowing mid-river to avoid obstacles like anchor chains, and they were now at the ship's stern, well away from the wharf.

Miles looked over at the shore longingly. "Are you positive about this, Fan?" he asked, his voice subdued. "You'll get into a fearful row when father finds out."

"Hmm, I don't know now," Fanny said. "Look, I'll tell you what. Let's go up and see if Rigo's there. If he's not, we'll come back down again and go with Tom to put this old dosser's boat away, and then help him with his search. At least that way we'll have been on a ship."

"Good idea," Miles said, relieved. "Wait a bit, I'll come up with you."

With much ado, and as much expostulating, Fanny and Miles climbed the ladder up the side of the ship and disappeared over the deck-rail at the top. Tom remained in the boat below, wondering if he should be joining them. Maybe he should present himself and ask if they had any places for a common seaman. It was either that or go into hiding until his father could arrange some sort of amnesty with the judiciary after the dust had settled, perhaps by-passing Sir Fusby altogether, if such a thing was possible. His father might have to invoke some aid from Westminster to do that. It was going to get very complicated. What a way to end an evening's adventure, when it had all been done for a bit of excitement! He infinitely preferred the predictability of a tame and uneventful existence after all. And what of Aaron? Aaron had probably come out with the rest of the musicians, blissfully unaware that he was on a wanted notice, and had gone into the Assembly Rooms and been arrested on sight! That swung the balance. Tom couldn't possibly take to sea without knowing what had happened to his best friend. He would *have* to return to shore. Yes, that was it, go back to shore, go into hiding, get word to Kitty – no, no. No. He had to get word to Kitty first, *then* go into hiding, once she knew where he was and could come and visit him. Tom's doldrums began to lift as he considered the prospect. Things mightn't be so bad after all, if he could still see her... Perhaps it would turn out even better than walking out together. Seeing each other in some secret hide-out, sitting aside, talking quietly with each other... Tom's thoughts were still agreeably engaged when he heard a disturbance above him heralding the return of Fanny and Miles.

"He'll be back before dawn!" Fanny whispered triumphantly, as she thumped down into the boat from the bottom rung of the ladder, rocking it dangerously. "I've just seen somebody, and they told me he'll be back before high tide in the morning, because that's when they'll be sailing! Do you want to leave Rigo's clothes with us? We're going back up because the man said Rigo isn't in town. He thinks he'll have gone to the Cow and Bucket to see some captain or other about something to do with Mexico. I don't exactly know what it was."

"Drat," Tom breathed. "I might not get to see him at all, then. I can't hang around. The longer I'm out, the more likely I am to get lifted. The trail will be hot for a good while, if there's a wanted notice up in the Square to remind people of who I am. All right, if you're going back up, I'll give you Rigo's clothes, and then I'll put Ted's boat back and get myself out of sight few a few days. Or weeks. Tell Rigo when you see him that I sent him my best, will you?"

Fanny climbed back up the ladder. Miles waited in the boat while Tom changed back into his own clothes and set his hat firmly on his head. The fine feather was looking decidedly bedraggled, but Tom gave it a tweak and put it in at a new angle and rolled Rigo's clothes into a bundle and handed them over to Miles.

"Wait a bit, Tom, and I'll bring you the carter's things down," Miles whispered. "We borrowed them off him. You know the chap I mean. Nick the waggoner."

"How do you and Miss Fanny know Nick?" Tom asked, mystified.

"We came down with him. Long story, ask Nick," Miles said, and clambered up the ladder after Fanny. Within a few minutes he was on his way back down again; and there was a sudden flump as an armful of ripe-smelling garments were flung the last few feet into

Tom's boat. "Good luck," Miles called in hushed tones from his station part-way down the ladder. He had decided not to risk coming all the way down hampered by Nick's stuff, and was conducting the conversation under one of his arms whilst clinging tightly to the ladder. "We might see you again tomorrow, we might not. If we do decide to stow away and have an adventure, can you let our parents know we are all right? I don't think Fan will leave this ship now she's on it, she really does want to be with Rigo. And I don't know yet whether I should stay with her, even though she insists she doesn't need a chaperone. Or at least, she doesn't want me as one."

"You should stay with her, whatever she wants," Tom said firmly. "You'd feel really bad if you went home and she set sail, and you never saw her again."

"If I never saw Fan again, I'd know she was with some sailor chappie," Miles said, with cheerful certainty. And he retraced his steps back up the ladder.

"Hey ho," thought Tom. "The to-do list is growing. Here we go: moor Ted Johnson's boat, then get Nick's clothes back to him. Phew! They really do smell of animals. I must get him to wash them. Maybe I'll get him a suit out of father's old chest when I put Rigo's gypsy outfit back. Then I must ask Nick to fetch Kitty as soon as it's light, so I can tell her what's going on. I just hope Aaron is all right. Maybe I'll ask Nick to find him for me, too."

He carried on rowing upriver.

Ted cursed and scratched his head in angry vexation when he passed the jetty later that same evening. He was on his way to the Cocklehouse for a pint, keeping a lookout for his boat as he came by, but he had failed to spot it anywhere in the parts he had expected to find it. His annoyance was compounded when he did eventually see where it had been left. Contrary to his instructions, that young Tom Fool had put the damn thing fifty yards *up* from where he usually kept it, not down, as he had asked; and what was more, he had left it in an almost inaccessible place where it was a mighty

326

long scramble along the river's edge, well beyond the end of the jetty, to get to it. Ted reluctantly made the difficult and demanding excursion to retrieve it, climbing unsteadily over rocks and brambles and picking his way round thorn bushes, getting scratched and then filthy as he tip-toed through a final squelchy reed bed to reach it, promising himself as he dragged it back that he would tell that boy exactly what he thought of his ideas and methods of mooring boats when next he saw him.

Tom, meanwhile, could he have seen Ted's outrage and inconvenience, would have considered his one and only act of petty revenge against a self-absorbed and unpitying world to have been very – *very* – sweet.

Chapter Thirty

Christina went out with Adela and Kitty, but she didn't go straight to the Wig and Mitre. She went back down to the port instead, and took up a position beside a stanchion with a big coil of thick rope alongside it that concealed her. She had been away from her lookout post for nearly two hours. She did hope she hadn't missed her man.

It was about twenty minutes later that the daddy-long-legs re-emerged from his place of conference and took the ladder down the side in four long steps. This time, he stepped into the ship's own blunt-ended boat and was rowed across to the wharf by one of its own seamen. From there, he clambered back up the stone steps almost without any word of thanks or farewell to the sailor who had brought him, and began to wend his way back up to the town. Christina considered the two men's parting as she quietly and surreptitiously followed. It could be that these men scarcely knew each other, or it could be that it was an everyday matter the daddy-long-legs had been out on and that this boat ride was routine and of no consequence; but there again they could be so familiar with each other, with such a strength of camaraderie, that partings didn't have to have any kind of formality between them. Whatever the circumstances, be he friend, or foe, or go-between, all Christina could tell for sure was that as a subversive he was very, very well practiced.

Far from clarifying things once the long man arrived at the Town Square, the mystery only deepened for Christina. He stopped and spoke with the same man who had been carrying dead rabbits in the market the day before, only today he didn't have the rabbits; then he slipped into Doctor Dranks' shop for several minutes before disappearing out of the Town Gate.

Christina sought out Adela, who was patrolling the Square on her own while she waited for Kitty to come out of the Broken Drum. Despite Martha's carefully calculated strategy, Kitty and Adela had decided to go around the town together. Adela felt she was just as likely to get into conversation with people outside an inn while Kitty was inside, as she was walking up and down on her own in the Square. Besides, the Square was filling up extremely rapidly with all the carriages arriving for the grand ball, and everyone associated with the big event was much too busy to stand around gossiping with an ordinary girl.

Kitty left the Broken Drum moments later and came over. "No news in there," she said briskly. "It's full of drunken soldiers. But I did sell some sweetmeats."

Adela told her what Christina had just seen.

"Oh, yes, I know that man. And I know what you mean about him." Kitty slowly fell into step beside them, and they made their way up to the Wig and Mitre. "He's an odd sort of fellow in all respects, I think. I'm not sure whether I like him. I think I'm scared of him. You never see him in company like other people, and he hardly ever talks, and nobody really knows anything much about him. And whenever I *have* noticed him, he always seems to be skulking in the shadows with the likes of Doctor Dranks or sneaking off round corners in different parts of the town. He doesn't look so peculiar when he's out in the countryside loping over hedges and ditches, but here in the town he seems a sort of lurking presence, doesn't he? And now you tell me he's been on a ship. That's very strange. What was he doing? He's no sailor. I think I'm going to start asking a few questions about him, as well as about those arrests. It seems the more we ask, the more there is waiting to be found out. It's most puzzling. I had always assumed Tony Lightfoot to be a travelling man who was lonesome because he's mysterious and outlandish; but maybe not. I think I'd like to know a bit more about him, now we've found out this much."

Adela and Kitty left Christina in the Wig and Mitre once Kitty had finished making more fruitless enquiries there, and together they walked down towards the Cocklehouse.

"This one will be more difficult," Kitty said to Adela. "Anyone asking questions of any description down in the Cocklehouse gets chalked up and earmarked. Even I will have to be careful."

As they walked past Nick's house, their attention was caught by the sound of someone quietly hailing them from the region of the cowshed outhouse.

"Udda!" the voice cried, from somewhere within the gloomy interior.

"What was that? Did somebody just call me?" Adela asked of Kitty. "Were they calling 'Adela'?"

"I think they were," said Kitty. "Who can it be?"

Both girls stopped and peered into the yard.

"That's Nick, I do believe," Adela suddenly said. "Nick! Are you in there? Is that you?"

"Yed," said the voice. "Cad you help me?"

"I don't know. What do you want, Nick? Shall we come in?"

"Yed."

Kitty moved the gate aside as quietly as she could, and went into the ox's yard with Adela at her heels. They found a very woebegone Nick sitting in the back of his waggon in the straw, his dishevelled hair sticking out in all directions, with some sort of rose-coloured finery looking suspiciously like an evening dress that had seen better days draped about his body. He sounded as if he was getting a severe head cold.

"Nick! Whatever are you doing...?" Adela began, but Nick had stopped her.

"Before you say anyding else," he said, "led me dell you der is a perfegly good eggsplanadon for all dis. Cad you ged me anodder sed of clodes, plead. Preferably sub very warb wods. Ad brig dem

330

as sood as bossible if you can banage id, plead. Dank you very butch."

"I think *I'd* better do it," Kitty said, handing her basket over to Adela. "That'll be quickest. I'll go back home and get an old suit of father's. Will that be all right for you, Nick?"

Nick nodded. "Anyding," he said, miserably.

Inside the Assembly Rooms, the music for the ball was going much better than Able could have dared to hope. After the initial consternation among the other musicians about Aaron's unexpected and imminent danger, and the panic-stricken message Kitty had brought up to them as a solution, the rest of the troupe had rallied round to fill in the gap made when Aaron left, and had hastily put their heads together and quietly rearranged their groupings to make sure the absence of one of the troupe would not be noticed. So far, it was working well. Able was almost ready to start relaxing again, with only the problem of Aaron's getaway left to consider, when he spotted Colonel Meadows across the ballroom. And he was heading their way. Able's heart plummeted like a shot partridge. Then it rebounded and started a wild hammering inside his chest. He was performing on his lute at the time, and he twanged several discordant phrases from the jolt it gave him. Lyndon! What on earth was he doing out and about again? He was on his own, so he must have left Tom at home. Able kept a smile fixed on his face and picked up from where he had left off, accompanying Sam Chantry who was leading the saltarello they were halfway through, while he tried to puzzle things out. He almost buckled at the knees as it suddenly occurred to him that it was quite likely the Colonel had decided to take Able to one side and give him the news about Aaron being on a wanted poster. If so, Able was going to have to stifle him. The fact that they were in full view of the public would never occur to Colonel Meadows: to the Colonel, what he couldn't hear didn't exist. Able could feel his nerves starting to unravel. Aaron's mother still didn't know anything at all about her son's desperate situation, and now, after all this time, Able was going to have trouble explaining any of it to her, particularly those parts which featured him, Aaron's father. He listened nervously as Sam beside him finished their saltarello with a recorder solo. After a round of applause, the usual kind of chatter took over among the dancers still on the floor, and Able's worst fears were realised. The Colonel was within a few feet of the stage, and his voice was penetrating the extraneous noise and conversation as he made his way with numerous unwanted interruptions to the raised platform.

"…Just ridden into town and heard about the dance. As I was coming through the Town Gate!… Spur of the moment decision to join the company – wonderful! Ha! Amazing coincidence! – nothing else to do for the moment…"

Able didn't believe a word of it. He carried on watching, anxiously waiting for mention of Aaron or Tom. At that point, the Colonel's eye fell on him and the other musicians, and he made his boisterous way over to join them.

Chapter Thirty-One

Rigo had been settled into an old priest's hole at the back of the snug in the Pig and Parsley. It was a favourite hiding place for men on the run and was as good a place as any for long-term concealments, because it was so easy to pass food and water to anyone inside. It had been used many times for many men in flight, and was not the safest place Tony could have chosen because its existence was well known in wider circles, but it was the closest place to the docks and a quick getaway by sea.

Rigo was still determined to go and meet Captain Henry Morgan. He and Tony had sat together for an hour when they first arrived in Chepstow and had shared a simple meal, but at Rigo's first mention of it Tony had insisted such a venture was way too dangerous.

Time went by. Tony came and went a few times, and they did more talking, and matters were turned over while they waited for the night to pass; their conversation moved back to piracy, but to Rigo's consternation and dismay, Tony continued to refuse to take him to meet Captain Morgan. When pressed to give a reason why, he would only repeat that it was too risky to meet Captain Morgan on the terms Rigo proposed; that Rigo had no idea what he was putting his neck into; that the Captain and all of his crew were exceedingly dangerous men.

"You would have to be brash, as well as bold, my fearless young ruffian, to set a course along such lines, for some leys are bad, an' hard to draw off from, once a man starts treadin' them. They will lead a man to his doom, of that there's no doubting. Mebbe Captain Morgan *will* be found outside Chepstow town wall on the Pwll-Meyric road tonight as he by-passes the town, but if he comes 'twill be very late afore he ventures there. An' if he calls in at the Cow and Bucket at all, 'twill be to pay his respects to the ale served in there, which he claims is the best in all Monmouthshire – an' who dare gainsay him on that, or any other matter? – an' not to pay court to aspirin' sailormen. An' he will have a terrible covey of cut-throats, robbers, an' murderin' villains about him. You would need someone very sure and very true alongside o' you to keep you from losin' your heart in the face o' such terrors. You will be lost afore you take two steps towards the man you are seekin' if you set this course."

"Oh." Rigo was crestfallen. "Sir, do you kn-kn-know of anybody who would do that for me, if you won't? I don't have any money, you see. That's why I want to be a pirate. I want to be rich."

"Rich? By all the thieves in Dodmore Wood bottom, what use to be after such wealth, you young scoundrel, when naught but a long stretch of rope dangles at the other end of it? What are such riches, but somethin' to feast your mind upon? They won't buy you a long life, nor a good one. Riches are the dew-drops on a cobweb in a soft green bramble bush at dawn, lad. Or a shrivelled leaf a-twirlin' in the cuttin' winter wind that brings you so gladsome to your own hearth an' fireside. Real riches last but an instant, and the treasury lies in your memory of 'em. Reach out to touch 'em, they are gone. Count the moments, they are gone. Come by that way again, they are gone. Man's riches are best seen from a distance, my young magpie; for like the glitterin' sunset lightin' up the vault o' heaven above us all an' blessin' the bountiful fields wi' a benediction of glorious fire, the glister goes when you walk up close. Stay where you are known best, an' be safe, lad. Gather your wealth from nature, an' forget about full pockets, for they drag a man down an' slow his progress, stud me wi' diaments an' call me a Markiss if I don't speak true."

"I-I-I can't do what you say, Sir. Let me go there by myself if you won't take me. I'll risk the other men."

But Tony gave his slow smile and said that with the place of venue being outside the town gates, it was impossible even without the risk of personal attack. "You'd find yourself locked out of town until dawn, my young renegade, unless you knocked up the gatekeeper to get back in. Do that an' you'll be snared like a rabbit, seein' as you have somethin' memorable about your features. An' if you was to bide awhile an' wait for the gates to be unlocked at dawn, you would miss your ship for certain sure, for if the wind should be favourable, she would've gone on ahead of you long afore."

A short while after this, Tony left Rigo again, saying that he was going to play the part of water-boatman instead of spider for a change, as there was somebody he had to see before dawn. He slipped out of the priest's hole door and went through the snug, leaving by way of the back door of the tavern.

Rigo gave it half an hour, and then slipped out himself. Outside, he found the night was well advanced, with the sounds of elegant revelry still filtering out through the open doors of the Assembly Rooms in the Corn Exchange. Nobody noticed him as he passed by. He walked unobtrusively up through the more shadowy parts of the Square until he got to the Town Gate, where he boldly asked a soldier which way to take to find the Cow and Bucket. Part of him wanted to challenge the notion that anybody in authority could easily recognise him, and instantly remember who he was. The soldier simply pointed the tavern out to him through the partially open gate, and Rigo was satisfied. As for the tavern, it was on a corner of the road leading straight out of town, part-way up another steep hill. It didn't look too far.

It was getting very late, but there were still enough people straggling through the streets for Rigo to saunter out of the Town Gate unnoticed. He did it by joining a motley crew of inebriated sailors who came tottering along together in a crowd demanding to be allowed out of town to continue their revelry, and the size of the group allowed him to pass through the gate unidentified and unimpeded. A couple of the sailors knew him by sight, and they welcomed him with intoxicated affection, putting their arms round him and bawling out a discordant version of an indecent song as they dragged him past the buildings outlying the town wall. His breath fogged the night air and he panted hard with the effort of keeping up, but he just about managed as they all staggered up the short hill to the turn in the road. There the lights were ablaze and the festivities clearly visible through the massive gaps round the edges of its heavy double doors, the roar from the carousing commoners inside indicating an evening in full swing, set to keep going until morning.

The sailors pulled open both doors at once and walked boldly in, moving as a body straight up to the rough bar, elbowing their way through thickly packed bodies and yelling out greetings and salutations to all and sundry. After some initial surly replies, and a few snarled imprecations and pushes that threatened further violence for several tense minutes but didn't progress to anything, they were finally allowed to pass by, and were from then on ignored and absorbed, since they were already drunk enough to filter in and blend with their new-found fellows. They melted into the crowded men standing about or sitting in front of the bar on tables and benches, and disappeared from Rigo's view.

The rest of the room was full of rowdy groups of ruffianly men sprawling on odd benches and leaning up against the long bar and stone walls or crouching on the beaten earth floor where there was no room to sit. The noise of the combined shouting, singing, game-playing and arguing was deafening. A cock-fight was in progress inside a dense mass of men in the centre of the room, with a huge amount of shouting from its participants. Rigo took no notice, but looked all round, having deftly extricated himself from his companions while they were still making their entrance so he could remain by the door. He knew what he wanted, and he had no time to waste getting embroiled in futile drinking or betting.

Having failed to spot anyone he could immediately identify as the man he wanted to meet, he deliberated for a moment. Nobody in the vicinity held a knife in their hand or looked more murderous than his neighbours, and nobody was in the process of being killed, so Rigo decided to risk asking a small sortie of ill-clad men immediately in front of him if they knew where he could find Captain Henry Morgan. One closest to him wordlessly pointed over to a huge man sitting amid the largest group of people at the largest table beyond the cock-fight, dressed in an enormous jerkin of the colour popularly known as Dead Spaniard. The big man's great head was thrown back as he gave way to an immoderate burst of laughter, displaying a mouth full of strong white teeth, and he tossed his wild mane of jet-black hair over his shoulders and set his massive beard waggling over the heads of smaller men as he made those gathered around him into butts for his heavy chaffing and sporting. He made a daunting image, but Rigo was in no way deterred. He edged his way past the cock-fight, working steadily through the people thronging the space between him and the loud man, until he eventually stood before him.

There was something about the combination of guileless confidence and irrepressible egotism in the young man who had just barged up to his table that made the huge man stop his boisterous conversation and acknowledge Rigo's initial greeting with a grudging good humour.

"Ah, an' a good evenin' to you, too, son. May you have many more on 'em. Somethin' I can do fer ye?" Despite his geniality the man's manner was abrupt, and his face remained shrouded in equal measures of doubt and suspicion as he looked Rigo over.

"Y-Y-Yes, sir. If you are C-C-Captain Henry Morgan, that is," Rigo said.

A sudden hush fell over the men at the table. There was a pause. Then, like ripples on an ebb tide, all conversation died away, from near too far, until the whole room lay deadly silent. Even the gaming with the roosters stopped. Everyone had frozen at the unknown young man's thrown gauntlet, unwittingly presented by his question. The men who faced Rigo dropped their eyes imperceptibly. They knew what would follow a challenge like that, and they were full of fear of what they were about to witness.

"Now who might you be, my young stripling, to be askin' after a man like him?" the great man demanded slowly and menacingly, as the terrified silence deepened.

"Sir, I-I-I am Rodrigo de Abílio, and I am f-from Brazil," Rigo said, making a sweeping bow and taking no notice whatsoever of the deathly hush that was rapidly engulfing him. "I have a stout heart and strong arm, and I am here to offer both in your service, Captain." He made another low bow.

"Is that so?" the man said thoughtfully, looking steadily at him, stroking his curly black beard and nodding his great shaggy head. "And what might a young shaver like you be wantin' wi' the likes o' the man you take me to be?"

"S-S-Sir, I heard you are a g-g-great man, and I w-w-want to join your crew," Rigo said, as one of the unseen cockerels suddenly gave vent to some hysterical babbling that sounded ominously like unrestrained laughter.

"Ah ha!" the great man said, reflectively and dangerously. The cockerel precipitously hushed its noise. "You're a very discernin' young man, I see. But what makes you think I might be the great man you're seekin'? – though it's pleased I am that you should think of such a simple soul as me in such a complimentary way, I'm bound to say, an' I thank ye kindly for it."

"W-W-Well, Sir, I heard you w-would be calling at the Cow and Bucket on your way to visit your dear, s-s-sick old mother, so I came to find you."

The man immediately threw back his head and bellowed out more explosive laughter. "Ah, yes! My poor, dear, sick old mother! I mustn't forget her, now must I lads? It bein' Christmas, an' all."

A few of the men closest to him managed to raise a few titters, but they all dried up the instant he started speaking again.

"And who was it p'inted me out as the man you wanted when you walked in here, my lad?"

"That m-m-man over there, by the door."

Rigo turned around to specify who he meant; but there was a sudden scraping of wood on flagstones, and half a dozen stools were upturned and abandoned as the group of men in front of the door leapt out of their seats and vanished into the night. Stark, cold air came eddying in through the empty doorway, and somebody quickly pulled the door shut, looking furtively over his shoulder across the room to check he was doing the right thing.

Henry Morgan had sprung to his feet with an oath. Standing at his full height he looked frighteningly aggressive, but he made no comment as the door was closed. He snapped his fingers and made a gesture to two savage-looking men sitting close by, both of whom got up without a word and went out after the ones who had bolted. People in their path cowered down with looks of undisguised fright, but Rigo, being well used to Man-of-Wrath, was undismayed by this display of swelling rage and dreadful retribution. What would come, would come.

He stood silent while the Captain sat down again, and then waited while a small, bald man with deep slash scars across his face tugged at the Captain's shirt sleeve and began whispering agitatedly into the Captain's ear.

Captain Morgan frowned and seemed to consider the small man's words. Then he nodded and dismissed him and returned his attention to Rigo.

"Well now. Havin' dispatched a party to search for the few men who so kindly p'inted me out to ye – just to invite 'em to come back into the warm, you understand, so as not break up the party

339

too early – let's come to the next question, which is who told ye the Captin ye sought was to be found in this place on this particilar night?"

"S-S-Sir, it was a man in Rio. I d-don't know who he was, I never saw him before. But I believed him, and I came here, because I wanted to meet you, Sir. Sir, I am really very h-happy now. I-I-I have been searching for you f-f-for two years."

"Ah, you and a good many others, I dare say. So, Rodrigo de Abílio from Brazil, you say you want to join me, do you?" He motioned for more drink to be brought to his table, and for Rigo to sit down. It was an unconscious acknowledgement of Rigo's successful identification of him.

Rigo nodded and took his seat, too full of admiration for his hero, now he had finally met him, to say another word.

A curvy, slatternly girl with her bodice half-undone slammed a jug of ale down on the table and then retreated, laughing, when the Captain gave her bottom a playful slap in passing. Around them, the tavern gradually started breathing again and re-erupted into a score of tumultuous conversations. The cock-fight, however, was dismantled, and its organisers crept away.

"Now p'raps you'll kindly explain why a young whippersnapper like you would want to try joinin' the likes o' me an' come disturbin' the peace in this here hospitable tavern," Captain Morgan suggested with equally hospitable menace, as he poured out a good measure of the ale. "Come now. Give me your reasons."

Rigo said, "B-B-because of my f-father, Sir. He is also a g-great man, a-a-and he says he is like you."

"Is that a fact, now?" The Captain stared hard at Rigo, growing ever more thoughtful. "D'you know, my young blade, I do b'lieve I've heard your name afore... Amelia... It has a strangely familiar ring to it. In fact, now I come to think on it, I have a feelin' I might know who your father is. He wouldn't go by the name of Amelia Sowerarse or some-such heathenish name, would he? Ran a tavern

340

in Cartagena for a black-hearted dog called Emmanuel Soto a good few years ago? That wouldn't be him, would it, lad?"

Rigo looked uncertain. "S-S-Sir, my f-father's name *is* Abílio Soarez. But he was never in New Granada. He lived in *México*. He s-s-saved a little girl from a dangerous bull in the bull-ring there, and he was richly rewarded for his bravery."

"Ah! Did he now? Interesting. See, the man I knew of fought a bull, but this man, he did it for a bet. A Brazilian Portugee he wor, an' *he* was livin' along o' Mexico at the time. Man I knew give up the tavern an' took to piratin', he did; an' last I heard he had got hisself a mort o' gold to put in his purse."

Rigo's perplexity increased. "Sir, when m-m-my father fought with the b-b-bull in *México* he became very famous, a-a-as well as very rich. Perhaps that's why you have heard of him. He lives in the town of his birth in Brazil now, and his r-r-reputation has travelled far and wide."

Captain Morgan's gaze remained fixed on Rigo, and his expression assumed a deeper quality. "Indeed? Yes, that could be it, my lad. Yes, that could explain a lot. Maybe… So, saved a little girl, your father, did he? Now that's strange. Seems as if he *might* be the same man as I knew of, but we mustn't make assumptions. See, the Amelia I come up agen wor not so much famous as *infamous* now, all up an' down the coast of the Americas. An' when he fought a bull, it *was* fer a gel, but it warn't exactly fer the *savin'* of her, if you understand me. See, this gel warn't little, she was… well… An' that bull warn't exactly… Still, we may not be talkin' o' the same man, it could all be a different story an' another shipful o' characters fer her crew. An' even if I'm right, I expect it was all long before yer mother's time."

"S-S-Sir," said Rigo, unhappily, "I d-d-don't think it can have been my father who you met. He has told me of his life in *México*, and he lived quietly on *el rancho* until he met my mother."

"Yes. Yes. O' course he did. An' a chaste and honest man he will have bin, you can be sure. And just who *is* your mother? Who *did* the old devil marry in the end?"

"Sir, my m-mother was a Yucatec Indian, but she died of *xekik* fever after I was born."

"Ah, a *mestiço* are ye?"

"Y-Yes."

"I thought so. Hmm. An' the gel's name?"

"Well, Sir. My mother's n-n-name was Xuxa. But it…"

"Aaah! Now that *is* a source o' grief to me. I'm sorry to hear of her untimely death, lad, for 'tis a sad business to have no mother livin'. You'd ha' bin proud to have knowed her, she was a comely lass. An' hard it musta bin fer yer father, for I make no doubt he kept himself to himself after she was gone."

"Sir, my f-father took another wife after he came back to Brazil."

"Did he, now? Well, well." The Captain smiled into his beard, and quietly shook his head to himself. "An' a sore trial in times o' trouble she must be, lad," he philosophised. "Fer I've a notion that a man loves but once in his life, if he ever loves at all, an' I make no doubt yer father buried his 'eart along o' yer mother in her grave under them old cactus plants out in the desert in Mexico." The Captain fell silent and seemed lost in reflection for a few minutes. Then he held out his hand to Rigo, and said, "Join us lad, an' welcome; for now, I've met wi' ye, I've a mind to call in on yer father an' see how the old villain's doin'. 'Tis a good long while since I've bin down to the Rio Grande. I should like to meet up wi' him agen, an' swap a few yarns under a sweet-smellin' jacaranda tree along the way; fer he was ever a man to spin a good yarn, yer father was."

Rigo grasped the proffered hand in complete bewilderment, and said, "Sir, my father l-l-lives in São Paulo; he has never been to the Rio Grande. But I will be v-very proud to introduce you to him on your way there."

"Be at the *Kilkenny* before high tide in a couple of hours, lad, an' we'll set sail to join my own good ship, the *Satisfaction*. She's waitin' for us somewhere 'tween here an' Land's End – away from pryin' eyes, you understand – an' once we're aboard her we'll set sail fer the Spanish Main an' get all them Spanish spoils gathered up into one grand vessel." He raised his voice and roared over the crowd to the whole company. "Here's a glassful o' good luck to the *Satisfaction*, boys, an' long may she live up to her good name."

The rafters were almost lifted by the resounding cheer that went up. The air was still ringing as the small man ran up and whispered frantically into the Captain's ear and was waved off again. A short time after that, Rigo was finally permitted to leave.

He went off in high spirits, smiling and frowning by turns as he mulled the meeting over in his mind. Leaving the shouts and laughter in the tavern behind him, he made his way jauntily down the road and headed back towards the town.

He had to wait for his moment to slip through the Town Gate again, which wasn't until the carriages came out of town after the ball had finished; but he managed to sneak through, having paid no heed to the cold and discomfort he had endured in the meantime. He didn't care about anything any more. He was a pirate at last, which was what he had always wanted to be, and he was jubilant.

Chapter Thirty-Two

It was Squire Higgins of Pwll-Meyric who drew Colonel Meadow's attention to the notice pinned on the wall outside the Corn Exchange. He had seen it on his way in, and, full of merriment, he took the Colonel aside to slap him on the back heartily and ask what the devil his son had been up to. The Squire's gleeful enjoyment of the situation was largely due to the fact that, had not Squire Speybury been acting as the absent Sir Fusby's satrap, the embarrassment and disgrace of this farrago would now be resting with Squire Higgins himself, and the notice posted up on his own orders. Such a narrow squeak could not be allowed to pass unremarked, and the full force of his happy relief fell right on the Colonel with that back-slap. Colonel Meadows had absolutely no idea what the Squire meant, and so he was directed outside to see for himself.

Since he had come down to Chepstow with the sole intention of instituting another search for Tom, having returned home to find only Elsie relaying Tom's message, the Colonel's feelings when he marched outside the Corn Exchange were a mixture of puzzlement and disbelief. Tom hadn't been away long enough to get into any more trouble, had he? His horror when he read the words in the wanted poster was staggering. Realising that nothing could now be glossed over or laid to rest, and that he would not be taking his son home at all for the foreseeable future, he tottered back inside the Corn Exchange to find himself a drink. His interest did not extend to Aaron. Or Rigo. He felt he had discharged his duty on all counts where they were concerned.

Even after some deep thought over a glass of neat brandy which he drank by himself in a darkened corner, all he was able to conjecture was that Tom, having come to Chepstow to return Rigo his clothes, must have then gone into hiding somewhere, having read that poster himself and realised his predicament. He must still be in or near Chepstow, since the Colonel hadn't met him making his return to Trellech anywhere along the road. Feeling an anxiety coupled with a sense of desolation he couldn't fight off, he listened absently to the sounds of music and dance coming from the room beyond, and before long he was theorising that perhaps, with a ball in progress, Tom might have hidden with the music troupe again in much the same manner as before, since it had worked well as a stratagem on the previous night. That idea perked him up considerably, and he decided to return to the Assembly Rooms and surreptitiously see if Tom was tucked away in there.

No sooner said to himself than done, and since the Colonel's speculations placed Tom somewhere safely behind the stage at the far end of the room, the Colonel sought to keep the general populus well away from the whole area as soon he was back in the ballroom. He walked here and strode there, pacing the public venues and directing the other citizens with troubled thoughts that made his attempts at conversation officious, and his voice much too loud. Able listened unhappily to snatches of his bellowing pleasantries for almost half hour, growing ever more uneasy. By the time the Colonel was making his way close enough to approach the musicians, he was in an agony of apprehension.

"Ah! Missus Bullimore!" he could hear the Colonel saying, "Fine evening, madam, fine evening. Yes, yes, no don't go that way, my dear, go back. Back! Yes, that's right, you can admire the proportions of the room so much better that way... Hilloo! Someone calling me? Ah! Didn't see you, Mister Davis. How's that son of yours doing? Heard the young blighter has got the pox. Bit of a surprise. Didn't know... What, *small* pox? Not...? Well, yes, I suppose it is a bit dreadful, but still – better than the other, eh? ...Good evening, Miss Dumpling – *Rampling!* Ha, ha! Rampling, of course, of course, how silly of me. So sorry, thinking of something else… All these girls… Lady Fragnett! Goodness me, ma'am, you've changed! Been ill? I would hardly have recognised you. Let me see, now, when was the last time we met? Must be seven, eight years… No, wait, wait, wait, it's longer. Are you *sure* you feel well? There's something different about you. Perhaps it's your hair. Your servant, ma'am… Good grief, did you see that, Davis? Did you notice? Lady Fragnett. Looked awful, don't you think?… Good evening again, Squire, yes, and to you, too, Lord Dictus. You know Mister Davis here, I take it? We're just going to get a drink from… Come along, everyone, come with me, attend to what I say – oh very well then, drat it, we'll go this way... Yes, sirs, yes, I know. Yes, I do believe my boy would have liked to attend here, not that the young fool's much of a dancer. No, no, he's not been taken off. Not a word of truth in it… Well if you did, it must have been some other young idiot that was picked up. What's that? No, I didn't know his notary was here tonight. Dash it, that's inconvenient. Where is the fellow? Well, let's hope he stays there. …Hmm? No, I don't know where my boy is. Haven't seen him for days. Days and days. Won't be hiding anywhere among his friends, that's for certain. Wouldn't be here at all. Ha, ha! And he certainly won't know who the musicians are either. None of them known personally to him, or me either. Absolute… er…"

In desperation, Able swung out a passing manservant whose hands were full of vol-au-vents. The tray flew from the man's hands with a tremendous crash, and the poor servant, taken completely by surprise, sprang away with an oath. Able went after him and took another swipe.

"Here, gerroff," the servant shouted, pushing Able away. "Wotcha doin'? You drunk or summing? Gerroff, I say."

The music ground to an inharmonious halt, the dancers stopped dancing. Everybody stared at the source of the disturbance.

"Idiot," Able bawled at the man. "What did you do that for?" He took another swing at him, and the other musicians leapt off the stage to try and stop him. Several gentlemen from the floor gladly stepped forward to intervene, being utterly bored with the dancing, and filled with delight at the prospect of a decent diversion from the vitiating ennui of another round of humdrum Christmas socialising, and a real brawl began.

Adela was by the outer doors, standing with a huddle of people who were watching the dance from the side-lines. She had given up patrolling the streets some time ago, drawn by the warm air billowing out of the open doors of the Corn Exchange, and she observed the Colonel with mounting apprehension as he stamped about, barking out conversational solecisms that only brought him under intensifying scrutiny. But that was nothing compared to her horror as she watched Able knock a tray of canapés flying, then wade into the dancing couples and punch one of the pirouetting dancers, and so begin a fight. Adela could hardly believe it. The ball ground to an immediate halt as formal dance sets disseminated into marauding packs of pugilists, and pandemonium ensued. The rest of the musicians, having failed to prevent a drama, hastily packed up their instruments and made their way as best they could to the doorway and freedom, ducking under blows and flying objects that were being spasmodically hurled about the ballroom by gleeful husbands and brothers who were temporarily let loose to do as they pleased, and were making the most of it.

"This way, come on," Adela mouthed, beckoning them on frantically, trying to get the musicians together outside and out of trouble as fast as possible. That was about as much as she could do. She had no idea where to take them from there, and in the distance they could hear the rattle of swords and irregular tramp of running feet indicating that there were soldiers fast approaching, having been summoned from their battery inside the Castle.

The musicians were still hovering, uncertain what to do next, when there was an unexpected whisper at their side from deep in the shadows. It was Christina, who had been standing observing them for several minutes, having lately left her post in the Wig and Mitre to come across the Square and see what Adela was doing.

"What's a little girl like you doing out at this time of night?" Able began, but she shushed him at once.

"Be quiet, we haven't time for explanations," she urged. "Come over here with me." And she drew back and allowed them to join her, melting out of sight of the main street. "Listen," she continued, speaking under her breath as the soldiers rushed straight on past to enter the Corn Exchange at a run. "I think I know a secret way down to the harbour through a tunnel near here. It might not be a very good way, nor very safe, but it's the only one I know that we can get to, that might take you all away from this horrible place."

"Oh, thank goodness," Adela said, relieved. "Bless you, Christina. Saving us all again!"

Christina rounded on the musicians, who remained huddled together, shivering in their decorative outfits, up against the darkest part of the rear of the Corn Exchange. "How can you be such idiots?" she scolded, quietly. "Don't you know how close you were to being cornered and rounded up in there? Why did you start that fight?"

The musicians murmured some protests, shouldering their instruments and jerking their thumbs meaningfully towards Able, who sought miserably to explain.

"I know, I know," he said. "It was stupid. Spur of the moment thing. Done to shut Colonel Meadows up." He sighed. "I can tell you one thing. After doing it the same way three times now, I'm getting the idea that there are better methods of problem-solving." Able looked sorrowfully at Christina. "So, you're that little girl that Ronald said nearly drowned, are you? Well, you may only be a little tiny thing, but you've a lot of spirit, I must say. We'd better get out of here," he added hurriedly, as more soldiers came into the Square at a run. "Come on, Chrissie, show us where we need to go."

Without another word, they followed the little form gliding along in front of them through the shadows at the side of the street.

She went up the hill as far as Doctor Dranks' shop, where she stopped to check that they were all keeping up with her.

"We're going in here," she breathed. "Keep quiet, and don't make a sound. We need to all go in together as soon as I open the door."

"In here? What for? I don't think I want to…"

"Ssh! Just do as she says and follow her, will you?"

"Just a minute, there's somebody missing. We can't go on yet, we haven't got Phil with us!"

"Phil? Where is he? Anybody know?"

"He was at the far end of the foyer, last I saw. He must still be there."

"Sure he isn't behind us? Should one of us go back and see?"

"I bet the silly bugger decided to stop and pack his harp up. You know what he's like about that harp."

"I'll do it," Adela whispered. "You go on with Christina. I'll look for Phil, I need to find Kitty now, anyway. I'll tell him to take the cart and wait for you all down at the Bridge. Good luck!" She slid away along the street, keeping to the shadows.

Once she was out of sight, the musicians followed Christina in single file through the door, which was unlocked, and across the shop floor, moving as quietly as they could. They ducked one after the other under the counter, still clutching their instruments. Christina led the way along the wall behind, slipping past a wide-open door leading out to the back, where Doctor Dranks could be heard talking to someone in his old man's rasping voice. They ran on tip-toe to a much smaller door set up in the wall at the far end of the counter above a couple of high-rising stone steps.

"Quick! Undo this!" Christina hissed, swiftly moving aside some herb jars to clear a bit more space for the door to open. Sam Chantry, who was next in line, reached up and undid a small finger-latch set close to head height in the door. "Last one through will have to pull the door shut behind us," Christina whispered over her good shoulder, as she led the way up, over the steps and into the inky blackness beyond.

"Where are we going?" Able asked nervously, peering in and blocking the doorway, despite their desperate hurry.

"Cellar," Christina called back. "Come on now. We've no time to lose."

"It's a bit dark in there," Able persisted. "Can't we use a light or something?" He looked about him. "Are there any candles out there?" He indicated the empty shop, but it was all too dark to make out where the candles might be, though they could all smell the clean, purifying scent of beeswax rising from somewhere nearby.

"Get moving, Able," Sam urged, giving his fellow musician a bit of a push. "Come on, we need to get out of here."

Suddenly, out at the back, Doctor Dranks' voice stopped talking. Everything was now silent. Alarmed, and with one more push, Able was at last persuaded to get going and he followed Christina into the dark, feeling his way along the wall, making his way down some uneven stone steps at a distressingly slow pace for the others piling up behind him, until the steps came to an end in a room that felt and smelled like a cellar. Christina had already gone ahead, and she was just in the act of lighting one of her tapers to aid their descent when they all came tumbling down the last few steps together. By the aid of her smoky little light, they had just about been able to see where to put their feet, and now they could see just as well where they had ended up.

It was a small room, damp, with mildew on the walls, but it was surprisingly warm in there after the cold outside. A few kegs of brandy and a chest redolent of something spicy stood half-covered by a tarpaulin thrown over a wooden pallet in one corner, and a shelf full of apples filled one wall. The rest of the room was filled with the sort of bric-a-brac any house will accumulate, and it was possible to pick a way through to reach the other side of the cellar, albeit with some difficulty.

"Don't make any noise," Christina said quietly, as she chose a pathway through all the bits and pieces, making her progress with ease. The others came after her with considerably more effort, as they had to lift their musical instruments to keep them clear of the items in storage. Able several times got himself speared in the leg by various protruding items, and once he almost tipped over a pile of boxes. The contents clanked ominously as they teetered, but Sam, who was right behind him, grabbed hold of the pile and steadied it, once Able was past, until everything settled back into place. Then they all stopped. On the wall in front of them, a few feet off the floor, was a wooden hatch extending up as far as the ceiling. It was also latched shut and Christina was pointing up to it.

"Undo the bolt, please," she whispered. "We can't hang around in here, it isn't safe. We must go on. This hatch opens into a tunnel."

"How do you know?" Able asked, amazed, as he reached over her and slid back the ring-latch. The door swung open to reveal a wide, low, brick-clad tunnel yawning ahead of them, beginning at about waist height and sloping downwards into nothingness beyond the reach of the light from Christina's flickering taper. "I don't like the look of it. It looks dark in there." He stared in, wretched.

"I'll go in first," Christina offered, boldly. "I've got the light." She lit a second taper off the first, and handed it to Sam, together with a spare for him to carry. "Mine's about to finish, so you'll need to light us along the next bit. The thing is, I don't know where this passage leads to."

"What?" Able squawked, as Christina clambered onto a wooden box and pulled herself up into the tunnel entrance, where she remained on her hands and knees, the remains of her taper still in her hand. "Oh, my God," he went on, miserably. "I don't think I want to do this."

"Go on, Able," Sam said, pushing him into the tunnel head-first after Christina. "We may as well see where we end up."

"End up? Entombed is where we'll end up!"

"Rubbish. If we meet a roof fall or a dead end, we can make our way back. Go on, get moving. We've got to get out of here, Able. Don't forget there are soldiers up there behind us. We'll be trapped if we stay here."

Able reluctantly agreed and had almost stepped into the void when he thought of something else. "What if this hatch is bolted against us when we come back?" he demanded.

Sam sighed. "Then we'll look for another exit," he said, impatient now. "Come on, Able. You know as well as I do that these cliffs are riddled with tunnels. We're bound to come out somewhere, we just don't know where. That's all the kid is saying. Now for the last time, will you get going and stop being such an old woman?"

Without another word, Able followed Christina. He carried nothing with him, his lute had been left on the stage when he started the fight. But behind him, Sam had his tin whistle and two recorders tucked into the doublet of his costume, and he was followed by Alan Fielding holding up a very cumbersome bodhran and tambourine like a couple of platters, the one inside the other. Allen Priest's set of deflated bagpipes made a flickering shadow on the wall eerily reminiscent of a dead cat in the wavering taper light, while Paul Heath brought up the rear bearing a reassuringly normal case containing his fiddle.

They began to shuffle along, crouched in single file, slithering in places where the floor was running wet, and whenever the slope downwards was particularly steep. Christina was on all fours, the rest of them were sliding along mostly semi-prone, using knees, elbows and bottoms to protect themselves and their instruments. They were talking quietly to each other to pass the time, wanting to divert their attention away from the claustrophobia they had all felt as soon as Paul had quietly pulled the hatch into place behind them. Their world was now restricted and cramped to a place of confinement, definable only by the limited extent of a wavering, uncertain taper light, hollow subterranean drippings, and the far-off squeak of rats. One and all, they knew how terrifying it was going to be if that light, by some unlucky slip, or drop of falling water, should suddenly go out. They all carried flints, but even so, no-one wanted to entertain the idea that they could be stranded underground in impenetrable darkness. One and all, they wanted to get this tunnel escape done as fast as they could and get to the other end. At least if they kept going, they went downwards and forwards. It was easier somehow, than thinking of going upwards and back...

"I found this tunnel when I came in to Doctor Dranks yesterday with my brother," Christina informed them all casually, seemingly less affected by the conditions than the men. "I was sent to buy some lungwort so Isla Parry could make up another bottle of physick for Mother. But there was no-one there to serve me when we arrived, and no-one heard us come in. Doctor Dranks was out at the back, the same as tonight, and the cellar door was open into the shop. Anthony had Moonlight, and Moonlight got startled by some of the dried herb bunches in the rafters when they rustled in the breeze, and she flew off his shoulder straight into the cellar. So, Anthony went after Moonlight, and I went after Anthony. We got to the bottom, and while Anthony was busy catching Moonlight, I saw this tunnel. There's another one like it in the Wig and Mitre, but I don't think I could have got you in there without being seen. That's why I brought you to this one."

"The Wig and Mitre?"

"Surely not."

"You're joking!"

"No, I'm not. I could see what was going on out at the back while I was sitting there today. I've been up there for hours, so I've had plenty of time to work things out."

"And just how *do* you work things out?"

"You don't miss much, do you?"

"You can tell it's more than an ordinary cellar, there's too much activity going up and down for the men just to be bringing barrels of beer out. And two men came up who hadn't gone down from the tap-room, so they must have the same arrangement as here. When I came down to the cellar here with Anthony, the hatch we just came through was standing open and those casks we saw back there had been dumped on the floor beside it, so I knew where it must lead. We were lucky there was nobody still down here at the time. They must have been in just moments before."

"You were lucky not to get caught. Darned lucky, both of you. How did you get out?"

"We went straight back upstairs, and because we're both little, we were able to duck down and sneak quietly along behind the counter. We hid where some other customers were standing. They had just come in to buy something, and none of them noticed us. We crouched under the counter beside them, behind a sack of cloves. Gosh, they were smelly. I almost had a sneezing fit." Christina flapped her hands as she recalled the spicy smell, wafting the imaginary fumes away. "Doctor Dranks came rushing in, all of a bother, to see to his customers, and he didn't notice us, either. We left after everybody else did, so nobody was any the wiser and nobody knows we found this place out."

"You're a smart girl, Christina," Paul said, from his place at the very back; and the flickering semi-darkness hid Christina's blush of pleasure.

When Sam's second taper ran out Christina lit another, her last, and they all hoped it would be enough to lighten the way to the very end of their subterranean journey. Hands, knees and backsides were not an ideal way to progress at the best of times, and the tunnel was rough and often broken in parts, but Able was now quiet and reasonably calm so they took their time at the hazardous bits, making careful and cautious headway where they had to go more slowly. They had all night to get to where they were going, as long as the too-fat taper lasted.

Chapter Thirty-Three

Tom was on the wharf approaching Slushy Lane when he saw Kitty ahead of him. She hadn't seen him; she had just come out of the Cocklehouse carrying her basket. He hastily smoothed down his hair and checked his feather, then tip-toed up behind her and tapped her on the shoulder. She jumped, very much startled.

"Oh! – Oh, it's you, Tom! Oh, Tom, dearest Tom, where have you been? Where did you spring from?"

"Pleased to see me?" Tom asked, smugly, drawing her arm into his. "Where are you going? To your mother's?"

"Oh, yes I'm pleased to see you," Kitty said. "Pleased, and *so* relieved. I've been so worried, we all have. But no, dearest, I'm not going to my mother just yet. I've been seeing first what I could find out about you all round about the town and now I've just come from Nick."

"Nick? Why?"

"Well, I've just given one of my father's suits to him."

"What? What for?" Tom fought off a feeling of indignation. Fancy getting Kitty to go outside on a cold winter's night like this! And taking personal items from her, too!

"He was in some sort of fancy dress. No, listen, Tom. We went past his house and he was sitting in his cow shed wearing something most unsuitably thin that doesn't belong to him – no, listen, please – and he's got a most frightful head cold from it – I don't know, I don't know why, Tom. Oh, do please be kind about him. He could hardly talk when we found him."

"Who's we?"

"Me, and Adela. We were out trying to find news of you. And Aaron, and Rigo."

"Hmm." Tom was still mildly indignant. "Well, I think I ought to go and see Nick. Give him a piece of my mind for putting you to all this trouble."

"I don't think you had better, my dear. And since you mention trouble, perhaps you will permit me to give you the teensiest hint that you *are* putting your own loved ones through quite a bit of it yourself. I can see, of course that it's not your fault, any of this, but do you know that your name is up on a wanted poster in the Square?"

"I do now," Tom said, ruefully. "I don't know what I'm going to do about it, either. I'm glad I've bumped into you, Kitty. I was just on my way up to your house to try and find you. I'm going to have to go into hiding."

"Hiding? Oh, my love! For how long?"

"That's just it. I don't know yet. I can't leave the country, not straight away. I had to see you first, and then find Aaron and warn him, and see my own father to say goodbye first."

"Oh, Tom, how very sweet you are! I knew you would do things honourably. But Aaron already knows, dearest. I ran up and warned him, so now he's in our bolt hole."

"What bolt hole?"

"We have a secret place in our house for people to stay in."

"What! And Aaron is in it?"

"Yes."

"Where?"

"Behind the kitchen wall."

Tom simmered down with some difficulty. "Hmm. Yes, well, that's all right, I suppose. Any chance I can stay there too?"

"I don't think I dare take you up that way. There are a lot of soldiers about. I just heard a unit of them running up Steep Street, that's why I wasn't walking that way. A tunnel does run from our bolt hole to somewhere down near the river, but I don't know where it comes out. I've never been down it. It might even have fallen in, I don't know, and since I'm supposed to be meeting Adela now, I think we would be safer to ask her to take you away at once and look after you."

"Adela? Look after me? How?"

"Well, her family have a hidden room as well. They told us about it today. If you're just across the river, I'll come over and visit you whenever I can. That will be all right, won't it?"

"Dear Kitty!" Tom embraced her fondly. "You don't know how happy that thought makes me. But I think you should get Aaron out of your house as soon as possible. I don't like to think of him being there, so close to you – er, that is you and your mother, of course. It's putting you – and your mother, naturally – er, both of you, at risk."

"Oh, but his father is coming to collect him after the ball. And I expect Mother will say it's all right for you to move over to us once the town is a bit quieter. We don't want Adela's family to put themselves at risk for us, either. Do we, dearest?"

"That's right, we don't. No. Most definitely not. The sooner I get to your house, the better."

"Oh, Tom!"

"Kitty!"

Outside the Assembly Rooms, Phil sat in a corner of the entrance hall with his head in his hands, wondering what on earth he was going to report to Phyllis when he took home the lutes without Able and Aaron, and presented her with all the other spare musical instruments and paraphernalia packed up in an otherwise empty cart. Inside, the Colonel was stamping about again, muttering to himself. He had lost his hat, and his waistcoat had several buttons missing. Squire Higgins, who had hosted the ball, was sporting a shiny black eye, a sprained thumb, and an unrestrained smile of satisfaction at an evening well spent. He had set his female staff and four menservants to undertake the general clearing up, the ball being now effectively finished, whilst the remaining servants were still clearing up the mess left by the vol-au-vents and pasties upset from their trays, all of which had either been flung across the room, or else trodden on.

Tony Lightfoot saw a group of military men toiling up the hill ahead of him, joining those still milling about in the Square, just as he was loping up the hill himself towards the Pig and Parsley. The shutters were being put up at the windows of the tavern when he arrived, so he dived into the priest's hole to find Rigo, but he found to his surprise that Rigo wasn't there. He decided to go on to Beaufort Square instead of waiting, and see what had been going on up there. He had an inkling that Rigo might have gone out during his absence, and got himself into more trouble.

Outside the Assembly Rooms he found a spare maidservant and took her to one side, putting some gentle questions to her, curious as to what manner of incident could have brought so many soldiers out. While he was listening to her account, Phil came to put his harp into the cart with the last of the instruments, and he told Tony the rest. Tony stood back and listened in silence. He had no idea what to do about Rigo now. This business with the musicians sounded equally dangerous and urgent. In any case, even if he found Rigo, he couldn't take him to his ship, not now, not yet, not with this increased military presence. The lad was more likely to be recognised and arrested. Nor could he take him back to the Pig and Parsley. It was now closed until morning, unless he risked knocking them up and waking the whole neighbourhood. Wherever he might be, Rigo was better left for the time being. Phil, who was starting to suffer under this unaccustomed strain, worriedly asked Tony what he thought he should do about locating the rest of his band.

"Leave that to me, my old heart-string plucker," Tony said. "They'll be at the bottom end of town if they're anywhere. They won't have stayed up here, that's certain. I'll go down Roper Street way, you go down Steep Street, and we'll meet beside the Wye Bridge; see if we can seek 'em out together."

Just at that moment Kitty stepped up, having walked up the hill from the end of the wharf where she had lately left Tom. She overheard Tony's last words to Phil.

"Oh! Are you… are you going to help us?" she asked timidly in a quiet undertone, her musical voice faltering slightly in her nervousness. "Is that why you are here? Oh! I do hope so. I don't know if we can manage this all on our own. We need somebody kind on our side, somebody who will… Somebody who is… Somebody who can *help*. It's all so hard, and so – well, so *scary*."

Tony looked down at her from his toppling height and smiled his slow smile. "You could say that's why I'm here, my pretty little lamb," he answered, equally quietly. "You could say helpin' people out o' difficulty is my line o' business; which *may* be why you've seen me lurkin' around the town from time to time, on diff'rent occasions, already."

He stepped aside as men bearing bolts of decorative cloth and limp boughs of dying evergreen emerged from the Assembly Rooms, carrying their burdens between them to a line of waiting domestics' carts. Kitty stepped neatly after Tony, feeling wretchedly self-conscious at the words he had used. It could just be coincidental, but she had the uncomfortable feeling that Tony must have been somewhere closer than she had thought earlier that evening when she had been talking to Adela, and that he had overheard her thoughtless comments. And yet here he was, apparently still willing to back them up and assist them in their time of trial, no matter what.

"I could do with a nice, kind man to help me find a safe place for someone," she said with brimming eyes, not quite liking to ask a direct favour of someone she had just lately been so unguarded about, and feeling she should be much more circumspect about what she said this time around. It was important not to give away information, in case it should turn out later that she was wrong to be changing her mind and placing her trust in him. She was looking up at Tony through her dark eyelashes even so, despite harbouring a last few tearful doubts. She was sure that this time she was right. She usually was, she could usually tell, once she got up close to a man – and he *did* look kind, on closer observation, in a strange, unconventional, peculiar sort of way. He should only need a bit more winning over, if there was still any lingering uncertainty about his motives.

"Ah, you have him put by, do you? That's to the good." The words flowed quietly out from the shadows under the pedlar's hat while Kitty was still thinking him over. "Where is he, my pretty song-bird? Where've you got him hid? Speak up, an' trust me, for we have precious little time. The King's men will be out again wi' more soldiers before long, seekin' to flush out what miscreants have got away already. Your boy will get caught in the same net as he did before if we don't move soon."

"Oh heck, that's right. I forgot about Tom," Phil Goode interjected, giving Kitty away completely without realising it. "And what did you do with Aaron?"

"Aaron is all right," Kitty said, keeping what she could under wraps. "He's safe. I think you had better come with me, and we'll talk at our house. It isn't safe out here."

"No time! Alas, no time," Tony answered, before Phil could say anything. "We must delay the pleasure o' makin' your better acquaintance, my lovely. Leave the decision-makin' to me now. Tony's used to keepin' his head square on his shoulders in a crisis. You go straight to Aaron, be as quick as you can, an' get him for us. Hold him at your house, just inside the door, an' Phil here will come by in his cart an' put him in it. Your part after that will be to run on an' get your own good man out of his place o' concealment so we can put him in as well. Have you seen the musicians?"

Kitty shook her head, and he made an exclamation of vexation.

"Agh! Then I must go ahead myself an' see if I can locate them; for on top o' them, there's another lad has slipped away who I could do wi' findin'. This is getting' to be a rare covey o' birds for keepin' safe in one basket." He turned to Phil. "Delay for five minutes, then follow in the direction this lass takes, and bring the cart with you. Go slow, an' be prepared to pull up when you see her again."

Kitty paused just long enough to hear what he said before she sped away, and then Tony left too, taking long strides towards Roper Street and the docks. Phil made a pretence of checking the horse's bridle for as long as he could, then he led the horse out of the Square, his heart in his mouth in case the soldiers decided to apprehend him. They obviously didn't know it was Able's cart yet, but they could find that out at any minute.

Chapter Thirty-Four

The night was now almost fled, though everywhere was still dark. The tide was coming up to the full. More than one ship was astir, getting ready to put to sea. Tony was strolling back and forth at the bottom end of Bridge Street when Aaron emerged from a small indent halfway up the rocky cliff face some way up the river. Soldiers were still at large, spasmodically appearing in groups of four and six, though none of them seemed to be aware that the Castle Dell was a place that could prove to be of interest: they were still patrolling the quayside and lower quarters of the town. Fortunately, no custodians of the law had been along to the furthermost end of the wharf in the last hour, and the search at the top end of town had been largely abandoned.

"Tony," Aaron said, slipping out from between the crags and bushes and approaching him, "listen, mate. Are there any sailors around, or rowing boats that could take me aboard a ship?"

"Now where might you be wantin' to voyage to, my bold young venturer? Does your dad know you're wantin' to leave these shores?"

"No, but I'll get word to him as soon as I can. P'raps you'll tell him for me, will you? I can't go into hiding, it's terrible. Dark and lonely and miserable. And spooky and scary. And cold. I had to go down that hole tonight, and man it was bad. I'd rather take my chances on the high seas with Rigo. Matter of fact, I've got his little bird with me. I thought I'd bring it and give it back to him. We'll be all right, won't we? You can get me to the *Senhora da Luz,* can't you?"

"Ah, I can, lad. But are you certain sure you really want to go?"

He paused, but Aaron made no sign.

"We have to get movin' right away if you mean it, or you'll miss her."

Still no sign from Aaron.

"I shall have to shelve some other despert urgent obligations to take you there, lad. Are you sure you won't wait for your father? I'm waitin' for him an' the rest of the musicians to make an appearance somewhere hereabouts. They'll be here soon."

At last Aaron spoke. He looked down at his feet, shuffled them a bit, and said, "Look, I know it's bad of me Tony, but I just can't do that. He'll want to take me home, I know he will. And after a couple of hours in that dungeon behind Martha's mantelpiece, I know I can't do it." He heaved a short sigh. "And there's something else, to be honest. I overheard Tom while I was hiding out at those cliffs back there. He was talking to Kitty. He's going to stay here. And if his dad can work out an amnesty, I might not even have him for company. I want to go with Rigo. That's what's best. And I need to go before Dad comes. Please. Help me keep my freedom, man."

Tony took Aaron by the arm and began leading him down the river bank. "It shall be as you wish, my lad. I think I understand what's goin' on. Step over to this boat an' I'll get you to the *Senhora*, for I bargained you boys a couple o' places on her a long time earlier." They climbed into the boat and Tony cast off, catching the tide at once, and the boat moved straight out into the middle of the flowing water. "Only thing is, lad, Rigo won't be with you. Whatever you do, you'll be doin' it alone. Rigo's got hisself a place wi' Captain Morgan, after all."

"Oh, great!" Aaron's dismay was almost palpable. "I was with Tom and Tom has turned back, and now I want Rigo and he's taken another ship. I can't sign up on my own, Tony. I can't, man. I need my friends. I can't face a man like Man-of-Wrath all by myself, I've already heard about him. He doesn't give a damn about anything, does he? And he's as mad as a snake, isn't he? You have to look out, if he is your captain. I think I'd rather face Henry Morgan. At least then I'll be with Rigo."

"But I've got you a place wi' Man-of-Wrath as a common seaman," Tony urged Aaron, with simple concern. "If you don't choose to go to sea, that would be one thing; but if you take another ship instead of his now, he'll give you the cat over a cannon if he ever catches you. Tie me up for a rat-catcher's dog if he won't."

"Listen, he won't catch me, or ever see me," Aaron said, desperate to reassure him. "By tomorrow he'll have forgotten my name. Men like that don't remember come-day go-day chancers like me."

"Well, you might have a point, my tremblin' young aspen. But if you really have decided to flee wi' some other vessel, make sure you don't fall foul o' this man in the next few weeks, or even months. You'll be sailin' along the same waters as him all the way to Jamaykey, and Man-of-Wrath has a hefty memory and an even heftier hand, smoke me for a kipper if he don't. So stay out of his way for as long as you would under English law if you want this matter to stay settled all to your likin'."

Tony had been rowing to the buoys while they were talking. He hesitated at the *Senhora da Luz,* then pulled hard at his larboard oar, and took the boat over to the other side of the buoys to draw up alongside the *Kilkenny.*

"Ahoy, there, shipmates," Tony called up aloft. A round head bound up in a knotted scarf appeared over the deck rail almost at once, peering down at them.

"Who goes there?" shouted the head, squinting into the gloom, then added, with a note of agreeable surprise, "Well I'll swim sideways to the South Seas! Tony, as I live and breathe! I'd ask ye to step up and share a pint wi' me, but we're about to set sail, as you must see. What is it you want, you grisly old buzzard? We've not much time, so make it quick. Anchor's coming up behind me."

The noise of the anchor chain could clearly be heard clattering onto the deck on the other side of the ship with a low sea shanty being sung to accompany it, and as it slowly lifted from the riverbed, the ship swivelled round on her last remaining anchor to settle into the tide.

"Well met, Rennie, my old cut-throat. Listen, I have a boon to ask of you." Tony looked over his shoulder to make sure they were not about to be overheard, then he said in a carrying whisper, "Ask the Captain to take on one more seaman, would you? I wouldn't request it, but the law is after him, and he's a friend of the young Americee aboard who's already found a bit o' favour wi' him."

"Ah, I knows which one you mean. Very fetchin' lad. Better bring this 'un up an' put beside him, then. Cap'n likes to inspect his meat afore he eats it. Throw us your rope."

Tony did as he was bid, and the sailor caught the rope and made the small boat fast to the deck rail beside the ladder. Aaron led the way up, feeling more nervous and queasy than he had ever done in his life. He was wondering where his father was, and he wasn't at all sure he liked being referred to as 'meat'. Tony followed with waving arms and legs like a gigantic ghostly crab.

It was edgy. Captain Henry Morgan was up on the quarter deck assessing the wind, which was still fresh and salty and blowing in off the Channel. He had only to wait for it to change quarter, for the tide was quickening around the bows below. It was very evident that their departure was imminent, and that the Captain was unlikely to be impressed with an unwarranted interruption at such a critical stage of decision-making.

"Cap'n," Rennie said carelessly, nevertheless. "Here's another young stowaway desirous of makin' your acquaintance. Friend of the *mestiço* with the tiddly blue parrot, an' pleased to meet ye." Rennie pushed Aaron forward and stepped back himself, then sped away to his duties, leaving Tony and Aaron with the Captain. Aaron began to tremble at the knees and was suddenly afraid he might pee in his britches. For the first time in his life he felt a lot of sympathy for his father.

The Captain gave an order to the Boatswain, then turned to look at Aaron, who was still dressed up in his jaunty musician's costume of gold-trimmed blue and scarlet. He stared goggle-eyed at the rabbit fur and bells, and at Moonlight, who was crowning it all on top of Aaron's one shoulder.

"That's no seaman's kit that I ever saw before," Captain Morgan said, at last. "You look like a fairy, lad, and you'll be treated like one if you don't get out o' them togs pronto. Go below and ask Loomis to look you out some proper sea-farer's riggin', and welcome aboard. Loomis will show you yer duties fer the first day or two. They'll be simple enough. If yer a friend o' young Amelia, you'll do fer me. I'll go light on both o' yer till we get to the high seas, providin' ye do all that's asked of ye. And you, my old and everlastin' acquaintance," he said, turning to Tony and embracing him heartily, "unless you want to find yerself some sea-legs to better the ones you was born with, you'd better skedaddle afore we cast off, an' wait for yer pals to come back to shore in a year or two."

"I will do that," Tony replied, composedly. "An' thank you kindly for taking on the lad. He was missing his pal already, d'you see?"

"Ah, I bet he was," the Captain said, taking up his telescope and shoving it under his arm. "Missing him as much as he misses them soldiers what's swarming all over the town a-lookin' to take him in, I make no doubt. But even so, the heart is a curious and consuming organ, is it not, my daggly old ugly-bug? For where it loves it loves, an' where it hates, it hates. An' if a friend should miss another friend full sore, then who am I to keep the two of 'em apart? 'Twould be a cruel man that did so. Us old uns have tougher gristle inside of us. We bear the loss o' partin' more noble, don't you agree?"

Tony smiled his cracked-tooth smile, saluted the captain without comment, and took his leave. He was almost back at the ladder when an inconspicuous figure came pattering over the main deck, hissing desperately at him.

"Hst! Tony! Tony! Wait! I forgot to ask you. Will you give my best to Dad?" It was Aaron, weak with fright, coming forward to catch hold of his sleeve, clinging to him in desperation.

"Don't you worry about him, my wriggly young elver," Tony said, soothingly, patting the young man's arm. "I'll go back now, see if I can find him, an' let him know where you are. It might be that he's safe to go home; but since he's been fighting again, if they do put up any charges, I shall do my best to get him off these shores to somewhere safe, the same as you. Whatever happens, I'll send you word by another ship bound for the Indies so you know where he is, an' when you can come back."

"Promise?"

"Ah, I do indeed, lad. I promise. Cut my guts up for chitlins if I don't. I promise you'll hear from me about your father, and I promise you'll hear when you can safely come home. Give it a year or two, an' by then, if your luck holds, you'll have made your fortunes. Add my heart an' liver, too, if you don't."

"I hope so," Aaron said bleakly, all his insouciance gone. He seemed very forlorn. "When you see Tom again..." his voice trailed away, and he turned his head. Then he turned back again. "...Tell him 'the best man won'."

"Ah, I will lad. And now I must away. Time is ever shorter, and I've still got to find your father. Go on, now. Loomis is beckoning you on, look; your duties take over from here. Get off, and make a brave beginning for your mother's sake, if not your own."

Aaron nodded and thanked him, then sped back to where Edgar Loomis, the Boatswain, was standing waiting for him.

Tony slithered down the ladder to his boat, and rowed away as fast as he could, out of the wake of the ships already leaving the port and setting their mainsails.

Chapter Thirty-Five

The tunnel from the cellar room in Doctor Dranks' house came out at the base of the cliffs below the Castle at a point just above the high-water mark of the river. Its entrance lay under a lip in the rocks, and it was from here that the dishevelled musicians emerged, one by one, just moments after Phil had rolled up in his cart. He had pulled over to the side of the road near the Bridge so he could wait for Tony, since he wasn't expecting to see anybody else so soon, and Able, who had gone ahead of the other musicians to scout, thinking they would have to try and make their way back up to the Square, spotted him with infinite relief and gave a low whistle which brought Phil up at a run.

"Thank God you're down here already. Bring the cart over," Able said in a low voice which was breaking with emotion. He was crouching among the twiggy bushes where the wharf ended, soaking wet and very uncomfortable. "We don't want to be seen on the street in these outfits, they're way too noticeable."

Phil nodded. "Stay where you are, and call the others. I'll bring the cart up and put you all inside just here. Don't come out, there are still soldiers everywhere. They could turn up at any second. I'll be right back."

By the time Phil had got the cart to the wharf end and turned it around, five musicians were assembled inside the bushes, clearly visible in their bright garments, looking like a bouquet of gaudy pheasants roosting among the branches there. Christina, kneeling beside them, was much less noticeable. She remained where she was while the men were being stowed away safely inside the cart, and they would have driven off and forgotten her completely if Phil hadn't been joined by a long-legged passenger just as he was seating himself up at the front. Tony stepped onto the cart as easily as if he was lifting a leg to step over a stone on the ground.

"Pick that little girl up and give her to me, then keep goin' till you get to the Bridge," Tony whispered. "There's a squad or more of soldiers just up the road, startin' a search of this whole area street by street. If we get stopped, I'll distract 'em while you get your men down on the river bank out o' sight. Have you found 'em all?"

Phil, who had collected Christina while Tony was talking, silently pushed her between Tony's angular knees and took up the reins, clicking the horse into a trot before he nodded in reply. "They're all here," he answered, *sotto voce.*

"What about Rigo?" Christina asked, in a penetrating whisper.

"We don't have him my little wren, though I do know where he is," Tony murmured. "An' he's secure. I wouldn't want to be standin' in his shoes, to be sure, but he has cast his die, and now he must accept whatever turn of fortune waits on the result, as must his venturesome friend. Now keep still an' quiet, for I must have a parley with our musical companions afore we part company. Much depends on what we say, an' we have despert little time." He half-turned so he could be heard by the men in the back. "Can you old warblers hear me in there?"

There was a chorus of acknowledgement. And a muffled complaint from Able that someone had their boot in his ear.

"Then listen all, an' listen well, and be crafty about the path you choose to take, for this ain't a time to show misplaced loyalty. I have some news that don't augur well for any of you. Aaron's offences you already know about. But now Able will be charged as well, if he's taken."

"Oh, no," Able cried, from underneath the tarpaulin. "What with?"

"Damage to public property, public affray, an' disorderly conduct. I heard talk as well of threatenin' behaviour. These are serious charges. You will serve a long time in gaol for them, longer than your son. If you go back home wi' these friends o' yours, you

369

can try an' hide out, but if you do that an' someone gives you up later it will be the worse for everybody who has tried to assist you, includin' these men here." There arose a chorus of murmuring alarm. "Now my suggestion is this. I already set up a couple of places on the *Senhora*, thinkin' they would be needed for Aaron an' Tom." (The murmuring chorus was over-ridden by a strangled cry from Able, which Tony ignored.) "Neither o' those lads will now be takin' 'em, so there's a berth can be handed over to you." (There was another strangled cry.) "Things is lookin' a bit uncertain, because there's so little time now until the ship sets sail; but if I can get you on board you only need go as far as France. Go there, wait while the dust settles, an' then you can negotiate a truce with the powers-that-be so you can come back in a few months. If things don't work out for Tom, he'll be there along o' you in the next day or two, an' you'll have all the company you need, for his sittyation is ever the same as Aaron's."

The audible dismay from Able subsided, and Sam's voice could be heard speaking over him.

"Do it, Able," he said. "You've got to tell your wife what's happened if you go home. You'd be better off letting the others give her the bad news, and then letting the dust settle with her as well. It can't be any worse in France than it would be for you to hide out in the Forest. And you must think about the rest of us. We've already done as much as we safely can."

Able's voice agreed with him, steeped in misery. A few seconds later there was a ruffling of the tarpaulin and Able climbed out. "Can I take my lute with me?" he asked mournfully. "I shall need to pass the time somehow."

"O' course you can," Tony said, stepping easily out of the cart and lifting Christina down, just as Able retrieved his favourite instrument before replacing the tarp. "Stay here wi' me now an' say your farewells, for you an' me go by water to the ship. 'Taint safe to walk the road. Hey, wait a minute, wait a minute." He suddenly reverted to hissing again. "There's somebody a-comin'. I can hear 'em. No, don't get back inside the cart." He grabbed Able by the scruff of his neck and pushed him down the bank. "We might not have chance to get you back again afore the tide. Get down there an' get in the nearest boat – Phil, you get goin'. Move, now! Move!" He pushed at the cart to start the horse up, and it departed at a smart trot, going out onto the bridge and taking the road to the Forest of Dean, leaving Able well down on the river bank below.

When she reached home and found Aaron was no longer behind the bread oven, Kitty wanted to go after him by way of the cart with Phil, assuming he had already made his way down to the river via the tunnel. She wanted to say goodbye to him and wish him good luck, but she was stopped by her mother who insisted on her remaining at home.

"You can safely leave all the rest of this to the men," Martha said, with a resolution that brooked no argument, as they sent Phil onwards alone.

They sat together for a while, waiting up for Christina, until Martha eventually gave up and went to bed with a declaration that Christina would have to learn some civilised behaviour if she was to be permitted to remain with them. Kitty was left sitting resentfully by the fire next to Poppea and Anthony, who were both sound asleep on shake-downs placed on the hearthrug. She watched them for several precious moments after her mother had gone before boldly deciding to flout her instructions and go out without her mother's knowledge. Not only did she not know for sure where Tom now was – and she desperately wanted to see him and bring him back – she also wanted to locate Christina. A child like her should not be out so late on a winter's night. Kitty looked at the bread oven. It would be quieter to go that way than to try and undo the front door. It would avoid waking her mother, and it would avoid the soldiers, too. She could still hear the occasional tramp of feet up and down the street outside. They were searching the town thoroughly and well for the increasing number of prisoners who were proving too fleet-footed for the authorities to hang on to.

Chapter Thirty-Six

Able found himself limping badly when he tried to walk. He had several bruises to the muscle of one thigh from his haphazard encounters with abandoned furniture across Doctor Dranks' cellar, a sore backside and heels from the tunnels, and a strained knee on the same bruised leg from his unceremonious slither down the river bank, so he stumbled markedly as he made his way to the water's edge, but at least he was back on his feet and still free. He wasn't even aware of his injuries from the fight any more. He was feeling quite elated.

"I can get in by myself all right," he said, eagerly putting one foot into the boat, though he winced to do so. "We'll catch up with Aaron and Tom now, it won't take me a minute to get in, if you just hold her steady for me. Was it you who took them to their ship? I'm glad they didn't need those berths, that was a stroke of luck for me, wasn't it? I'd have had to stow away, otherwise. Ha! I'll soon find them out. They'll have a shock when they see I'm coming too, I'll laugh my head off when I see their faces." All the time he was climbing clumsily into the boat, he was talking with nervous animation.

While he was waiting for him, Tony turned and quietly praised Christina for getting the musicians through the tunnels unscathed; and she smiled happily through her shivers as she crouched to keep warm among the sedges at the bottom of the river bank beside him.

"I did help, didn't I?" she exclaimed proudly. "I found Able and the others and got them here safe." She sounded delighted, and it seemed that her shaking was as much from excitement as it was from cold. But Tony was concerned to note a feverish element to the glisten in her wide eyes, and he made a mental note that the child should be given a hedgerow simple for her tiny lungs before morning. If she took a cold now it would go to her chest for sure, and he had enough honesty within himself to admit that his own charms and tokens were more for warding off evils than anything else. "Can I stay here and see you off?" she asked brightly, and Tony nodded. He gave her his travelling blanket to put round her, because her little form felt frozen now she was inactive, though the chilliness didn't seem to be penetrating as far as her spirits.

He was in the boat and just about to cast off when he heard a soft voice calling out from the shadows at the lane end. It was Kitty. She was searching through the Castle Dell, calling out for Tom, asking him to show himself to her. Tony hastily retied the painter and leapt up the bank to intercept her and shush her cries.

"Oh, Mister Lightfoot," she tearfully exclaimed, "where is Tom, if he isn't with you? He was supposed to wait down here, exactly in those bushes where I put him, but now he's gone. Wherever can he be? Do you suppose he has been taken again?"

"Hush, my pretty fairy," Tony said, brushing aside her tears and putting his arm about her shoulders to comfort her. "I've seen and heard nothin' to give cause for anxiety on that account. If he ain't where you left him, maybe he's gone on ahead. Where did you intend hidin' him?"

"In Adela's house. I didn't think Aaron would leave us so soon. But oh! Of course! Tom's probably gone on with her already. Let me look." And she sped off to the end of the jetty, returning just as quickly to confirm Tony's guesswork. "It's all right Tony, he must be all right, the coracle is in the grass on the other side of the river." Her pretty face was alight with thankfulness.

"Well now, there you are, my little linnet; if the coracle has gone, he must be safe. We must hope so, anyway, for now I must away with this good man an' get him safe aboard his ship. If Tom should show up from somewhere diff'rent before the ship sets sail, I'll willingly make a separate journey for him and get him aboard as well; for I am ever at the disposal of a fair an' sweet young maiden. An' if we find him after the ship has departed, why, there are plenty of places I know of where we can put him, out in the heaths and mountains. We can keep him safe for as long as needs be, never you fear. Tony will take care of your man for you."

Kitty dimpled at him and then smiled, her eyes dewy with unshed tears. "I had better go back," she said, in a voice so soft it was little more than a whisper. "If you find him, tell him… Well, you know, I'm sure."

"I do." Tony spoke with genuine feeling. He turned and stepped back down the bank to get in the boat again, this time casting off immediately and pulling away from the shore. Kitty walked along the wharf to keep up, her musical voice following them over the water.

"Tell him that I beg he will face the law and go back to his father rather than leave me behind and live far away from me over the sundering seas."

Tony gave her a wave of acknowledgement which Able seconded, and the boat swept on out of her sight. Then Kitty reluctantly turned and began to walk back to her family house. She no longer cared if her mother saw or heard her.

Tony sat in silence, rowing hard for a second time, his legs and body crumpled over the thwarts, his arms bent up to fit around the oars he was wielding with weary finesse. A sudden shout came from the shore behind, and they turned to see two soldiers running along the wharf to where Christina still stood, alone on the river bank, gazing wistfully out after them.

"There's no going back now my friend," Tony observed, nodding towards the soldiers, who had pulled up beside Christina and were shouting and calling after them, their words indistinguishable over the wind now driving straight across the water.

"No! Phew! You just got me off in the nick of time." Able wiped his forehead with his sleeve. "I'll get changed out of this rig-out as soon as we get to the ship," he declared, plucking at his costume, "and then when I get hold of Aaron, we'll start tackling the business of sailing. We'll soon get the hang of it, don't worry. Turning into a bit of a boy's adventure, this, isn't it? Which one of these ships is he on, then? Is he all right with Tom? I hope they're behaving themselves, for once."

He had changed his sitting position slightly so he could see better where they were headed, staring ahead hopefully. Tony turned as well, looking over his shoulder at the ships still moored along the buoys. The *Kilkenny* was not one of them. There she was in the distance, out in the middle of the estuary, her sails up, her sailors scattered across the rigging like small pixies as she billowed off towards the Bristol Channel. One more turn in the river and she would be out of sight. Tony turned back to face Able and gave an inward sigh.

"I b'lieve he will be safe where he is, but I doubt if he'll be wi' Tom for some time to come," Tony answered. "I think I have some bad news for you, my nervous old fugitive. The vessel you wanted is the one flitterin' off like a chaffinch over a hedge there, out in the water."

"What?" Able almost screamed. "Aaron is on that boat? Out there? Without me? But what am I going to do?" He began to fidget as if he wanted to get out, and if he could have run after the *Kilkenny*, Tony was sure he most certainly would have.

"You'll have to do the next best thing, and join a ship what's goin' after her," Tony said. "Aaron was supposed to join the *Senhora da Luz*. He declined to honour his obligation with the noble vessel because his legal friend who was a-goin' to accompany him was too love-lorn to go, an' has gone into hidin' instead, remainin' alongside his ladye-love to await the settlin' o' the laws o' justice he was so quick at larnin'. But you'll do just as well in his stead, fry me for a herring if you won't. Your lad was no more 'n a name to them aboard the *Senhora*, and one man is very like another when you're atop the riggin' in a boilin' sea, an' the rain beatin' down on your face, an' the crew three men down. They'll be glad enough to see you aboard her, shell me for a prawn if they won't."

Able was still watching the disappearing *Kilkenny,* his face utterly woebegone. "Is the next ship going to go soon?" he asked, his voice choking with emotion. He began inspecting his nails again, but they were all bitten down to the quick, so he began chewing at a finger instead.

"Just as soon as you come aboard, is my guess," Tony calmly replied, pulling the boat round with one oar, and making it fast to the ladder at the starboard quarter of the *Senhora da Luz.* It was a slightly longer ladder than the *Kilkenny's* and reached right into the water when it was let down. "Come up behind me, my old jitterbug, and I'll make you known to the Captain."

"Who is he?" Able demanded, clambering noisily up behind and missing his footing several times. "I don't like this ladder. Oo-er! Nearly fell just then." He stopped and looked back. "Oh no! It's a long way down to that water. I think I've changed my mind, Tony. Come on, I don't think I want to do this. Let's go back."

"Too late, my fickle friend," Tony said, reaching the top and climbing onto the deck with ease. He offered Able his hand and helped him over the deck rail. "Welcome aboard the *Senhora da Luz,*" he said, firmly. "Two hundred and fifty tons, out of Rio de Janeiro, now leaving Chepstow fully rigged, fully loaded and almost fully manned. Captain: Earl Rothman of the West Indies, also known as 'Man-of-Wrath...'"

"Man-of-Wrath Rothman?" Able squeaked, so fearful suddenly that he could hardly articulate the name, "I think I've heard of him. In fact, I'm sure I have. Isn't he the one who doesn't give a damn? And is as mad as a snake? Who they say is a hard man, and never far from trouble? Oh, my God, I think I've got a congestion of my heart." He clutched at his chest and began to shake his head. "I've definitely changed my mind, Tony. I can't do this. My leg is troubling me, I'm wet from those tunnels, and I just want to go home. I'm not really cut out for this sea-faring business. I need to lie down and recover. Oh, help. I think I'd rather face Captain Morgan."

"Funny. I seem to have heard those words spoke afore," Tony said, reflectively. "An' yet I've got you a place as a common seaman wi' Man-of-Wrath, it's all fixed an' settled, an' if you don't stay now, he'll have your guts for garters if he ever catches you. He'll already be after your son for not joinin' his crew. You must stay on board. Call it time served as is obligatory for the amelioratin' of his wrath. He don't carry a name like that for nothing."

A man was approaching, and Tony went over to meet him. He looked so savage, Able was sure this man must be his Nemesis. He was about to come face-to-face with Captain Earl Rothman. He sank to his knees.

"Avast, shipmate," the rough-looking man said, hauling Able up onto his feet again. "Stand up and look ship-shape. This is a poor start, if yer sea-legs is so soft they'm like a jellyfish's already. We ain't even movin' yet." He gave a coarse laugh. "Stalls is my name, first name Sobriety. An' you'll be answerin' to me for the voyage, because I'm the Bo'sun, which means I'm in charge of you. See? Any questions afore we go? For the wind is up and pullin' and the Captain won't hold up for anyone. Lightfoot, cast off and pull away, shipmate. Ye've no time left."

Tony gave a salute and disappeared over the deck rail again, leaving Able a quivering wreck.

"I think I'll just go with Tony..." he began, but Sobriety, who had been looking him over, interrupted him.

"You'm older than I expected, but you'll do, once we get that riggin' took off you an' some proper shrouds put on. I hear you've no experience, but that's no hardship. You'll soon learn the ropes. Are you Aaron, or Tom?"

"Neither. They couldn't make it, apparently. I'm Able."

"Right, Able, get below, an' ask the ship's cook to get you into your weatherproofs. Then come back up, we'll be needin' you straight away."

"Cook?" faltered Able. "Er, weatherproofs?"

He was looking around, his fingers in his mouth, wondering where to go. Boatswain Stalls pointed to a small door under the quarter deck, and Able tottered off, staggering as the ship began to move in the water. They were under way. The voyage had begun.

Tony had cleared the ship's bows and, tired and weary now, was making one more foray for the shore. The wind, which was picking up, was now blowing nor'westerly from the mountains inland of him, and hampering his efforts. By the time he got to the quayside, there were stiff little waves developing on the water, indicating a storm in the offing. He moored downstream from where he had taken the boat, because he simply didn't have the strength left to take it any further. The owner would have to collect it himself.

Ted didn't have occasion to go down to his boat until after the thaw set in; but when he did, he was mystified all over again. This time, it had moved two hundred yards.

Christina was still waiting where Tony had left her, and now her shivers were unmissable, and undeniable.

"Come on, my brave lass," Tony said, putting his arm around her. "It's time to get you home an' set beside a roarin' good fire. Puff me up a chimbley wi' the woodsmoke if I don't speak true. Tell me where you live, and I'll take you there."

They moved away from the water's edge, and began the long walk up the hill to Martha's just as the church of Saint Mary began to toll for the morning service.

"It's Boxing Day today," Christina observed, her teeth chattering slightly. "If I go around the houses when the service is done and wish them well, I might get given a few pennies."

"Ah you might," Tony agreed. "But I believe you've done enough for a day or two, my little snowdrop. You've bin up all night, an' you ain't no heavy horse made for hard work. Time for you to sit back and let some o' the others take a turn. People will give you aid without you havin' to ask, now they are gettin' to know who you are. Always better to stick wi' the folk you know for favours, where you can."

"Really?"

"Really, really. Give me thirty shillin's an' call me Judith if I don't speak true."

"Do you think Moonlight will be happy now he's back with Rigo?" Christina presently enquired, her breathing, like Tony's, gradually becoming more laboured as they walked uphill.

"Aye, I do. Rare an' fine as a throstle in its nest, she'll be," he said, comfortingly.

"Do birds miss people?"

"I don't know," Tony said, honestly. "Maybe they do, maybe they don't. But I don't see why they shouldn't, them bein' God's creatures, an' knowin' day from night, an' pleasant from dour the same as us."

"Do you think she'll miss me?"

"Why, if she doesn't, she's an ill-sorted bunch o' feathers, an' not a proper bird at all," Tony declared. "An' if you're missin' her, I'll get you a little bird of your own to take care of. How would that be?"

"Another parrot?"

"Well, maybe not a parrot. But I can find you another talkin' bird, if that's what you want."

"What will it be?"

"Jackdaw," Tony said promptly. "But not till the spring an' I can get you a young 'un. They talk beautiful."

"Do they sit on your shoulder?"

"They do," he gravely replied. "I had one when I was a nipper. Lived to be twelve-year-old it did, and as perky – and as pesky – as could be."

"What was he called?"

"Many things by many people, accordin' to his misdemeanours. But his name was Fidel."

"Fidel?"

"Ah. It means 'faithful' in Spanish – and French, and maybe in a mort of other foreign languages, ones as I don't understand a word of, not bein' an eddicayted man, like people in them beautiful, far-off cities where the universities is."

"Was he faithful?"

"Who, Fidel? Very."

Christina was quiet for a while. She was getting so short of breath that Tony picked her up and carried her under his greatcoat, slowing his pace right down to do the walking for the two of them. She made no protest at being carried; she quite liked the undulating rhythm of his walk. Soon, she began again. "Do you think we'll ever see Rigo and Moonlight again?"

"I do."

"And Able and Aaron?"

"Of course, my precious. They'll be back. Where else would they all go to, when there's stout friends like you an' me a-waitin' for 'em back on their own doorstep ready to give 'em a 'huzza', an' a welcome home? They'll be back before you know it, full of outlandish talk and wild ways to amaze an' charm us all. An' if good fortune goes with us, you'll still see Tom in the meantime. I should like to meet up with him, an' get to know him proper. Ah. Here we are, look. Here's your door. I know it now, an' sha'n't forget it when I come by again."

"You'll come and see me again?"

"Indeed I will, my little catkin, an' right soon. Meantime, there's much for me to be gettin' on with, an' I must leave you for a few days."

"I'll miss you. What will happen next?"

"How about findin' that family o' yours after a day or two, when you're fully rested? Will that do for a start?"

Christina nodded thoughtfully and Tony knocked at the door. A few stray snowflakes drifted past his face as he waited for Kitty to open it.

"Good morning to you, my pretty," he said, when she appeared after a few minutes. "This is a special delivery for you." He lifted Christina over the doorstep. "I must hand over the care o' this little mossel o' humanity to you an' your good mother for now. She's well wore out, an' would benefit wonderful if you could give her a physick in case her lungs do swell. Thank ye both most kindly for doin' it." He touched his damp and glistening battered slouch hat in a gesture of farewell and stepped back from the doorway. Then he looked up at the sky and breathed in deeply. "Morning's almost on us," he observed. "And the snow ain't far behind it. I can't stop, my lambs, I must be off. The skies is thickenin', an' the hills is callin', an' if I don't get a move on an' start walkin' them I shan't have the pleasure of comin' back again to sing an' make merry with you all; an' that would never do, for Christmas is fleetin' by an' we' ain't had the chance of celebratin' it yet. So, fare ye well. I shall be back before the snowdrifts dwindle an' the ditches fill, to share a stoup o' hot negus with you."

"Promise?"

"Ah, I promise, my little tree-pipit. Smother me wi' spiders if I don't speak true!"